First Baptist Church
1616 Pacific Ave.
Everett, Wa 98201

DATE DUE

AF
PET

#1

Peterson, Tracie
A Daughter's Inheritance

GAYLORD M2G

Books by Tracie Peterson & Judith Miller

BELLS OF LOWELL
Daughter of the Loom ✢ *A Fragile Design*
These Tangled Threads

LIGHTS OF LOWELL
A Tapestry of Hope ✢ *A Love Woven True*
The Pattern of Her Heart

THE BROADMOOR LEGACY
A Daughter's Inheritance

www.traciepeterson.com

www.judithmccoymiller.com

0108

THE BROADMOOR
LEGACY · BOOK ONE

A DAUGHTER'S INHERITANCE

TRACIE PETERSON
AND
JUDITH MILLER

First Baptist Church
1616 Pacific Ave.
Everett, Wa 98201

BETHANY HOUSE PUBLISHERS
Minneapolis, Minnesota

A Daughter's Inheritance
Copyright © 2008
Tracie Peterson and Judith Miller

Cover design by John Hamilton Design
Cover photography of 1000 Islands: Reprinted with permission from Ian Coristine's book *1000 Islands*, his fourth book of photography of the region.
www.1000islandsphotoart.com

Published by Bethany House Publishers
11400 Hampshire Avenue South
Bloomington, Minnesota 55438

Bethany House Publishers is a division of
Baker Pubishing Group, Grand Rapids, Michigan.

Printed in the United States of America

Library of Congress Cataloging-in-Publication Data

Peterson, Tracie.
    A daughter's inheritance / Tracie Peterson and Judith Miller.
       p.   cm. — (The Broadmoor legacy ; bk. 1)
    ISBN 978-0-7642-0471-5 (alk. paper) — ISBN 978-0-7642-0364-0 (pbk.) —
ISBN 978-0-7642-0487-6 (large-print pbk.) 1. Inheritance and succession—Fiction.
2. Cousins—Fiction. 3. Thousand Islands (N.Y. and Ont.)—Fiction. 4. United
States—History—1865–1898—Fiction. I. Miller, Judith, 1944–   II. Title.

    PS3566.E7717D384   2008
    813'.54—dc22

                                              2007034145

Dedication

In memory of
Edward and Louise Hughes,
the aunt and uncle who
made my summer vacations
a special time and created
fond memories.

—Judith Miller

TRACIE PETERSON is the author of over seventy novels, both historical and contemporary. Her avid research resonates in her stories, as seen in her bestselling HEIRS OF MONTANA and ALASKAN QUEST series. Tracie and her family make their home in Montana.

JUDITH MILLER is an award-winning author whose avid research and love for history are reflected in her novels, many of which have appeared on the CBA bestseller lists. Judy and her husband make their home in Topeka, Kansas.

Broadmoor Family Tree

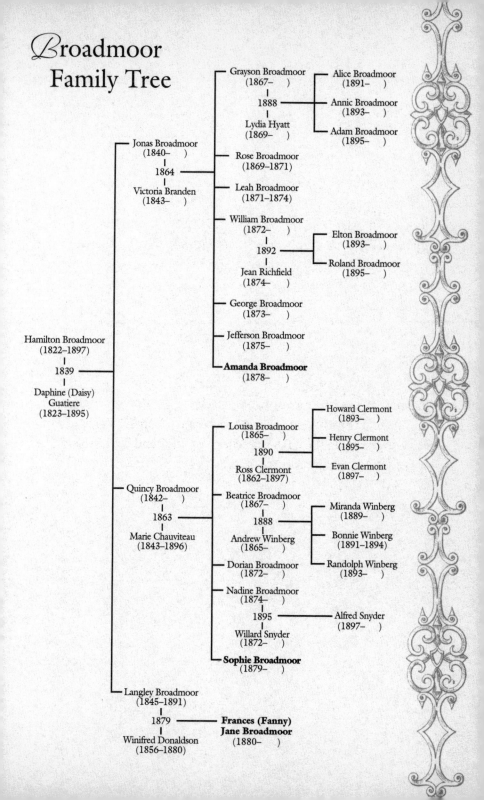

Hamilton Broadmoor
(1822–1897)
|
1839
|
Daphine (Daisy)
Guatiere
(1823–1895)

Jonas Broadmoor
(1840–   )
|
1864
|
Victoria Branden
(1843–   )

Grayson Broadmoor
(1867–   )
|
1888
|
Lydia Hyatt
(1869–   )

Alice Broadmoor
(1891–   )

Annie Broadmoor
(1893–   )

Adam Broadmoor
(1895–   )

Rose Broadmoor
(1869–1871)

Leah Broadmoor
(1871–1874)

William Broadmoor
(1872–   )
|
1892
|
Jean Richfield
(1874–   )

Elton Broadmoor
(1893–   )

Roland Broadmoor
(1895–   )

George Broadmoor
(1873–   )

Jefferson Broadmoor
(1875–   )

Amanda Broadmoor
(1878–   )

Quincy Broadmoor
(1842–   )
|
1863
|
Marie Chauviteau
(1843–1896)

Louisa Broadmoor
(1865–   )
|
1890
|
Ross Clermont
(1862–1897)

Howard Clermont
(1893–   )

Henry Clermont
(1895–   )

Evan Clermont
(1897–   )

Beatrice Broadmoor
(1867–   )
|
1888
|
Andrew Winberg
(1865–   )

Miranda Winberg
(1889–   )

Bonnie Winberg
(1891–1894)

Randolph Winberg
(1893–   )

Dorian Broadmoor
(1872–   )

Nadine Broadmoor
(1874–   )
|
1895
|
Willard Snyder
(1872–   )

Alfred Snyder
(1897–   )

Sophie Broadmoor
(1879–   )

Langley Broadmoor
(1845–1891)
|
1879
|
Winifred Donaldson
(1856–1880)

**Frances (Fanny)
Jane Broadmoor**
(1880–   )

1

Sunday, August 2, 1891
Broadmoor Island, Thousand Islands

The warm summer air rang with laughter as eleven-year-old Fanny Broadmoor made her way up from the river's edge. The day had been perfect, and she couldn't help but be pleased.

Her companion gave a tug on her pigtail. "What are you giggling about now?" fifteen-year-old Michael Atwell asked. Michael lived year-round on the island with his parents, the primary caretakers for the Broadmoor family castle and island estate.

"Do I have to have a reason?" Fanny questioned. "I'm just happy. We caught a great many fish. Your mother will be pleased."

"I think your grandmother will be less excited to see you've spent a day in the sun. You've got at least a hundred more freckles."

9

Fanny touched her hand to her face and shrugged. "Papa says it goes with my red hair, and he thinks they are quite delightful."

Michael shifted the string of fish and waved them in the air. "I think these are far more delightful. When my mother gets through frying them up, you'll think so, too."

Fanny gave him an adoring smile. She practically worshiped the ground he walked on. He was dashing and adventurous and never failed to treat her kindly. Other servants passed her over as nothing more than a child, but not Michael. He was always good to listen to her and never too busy to stop and see to her needs.

"You're lagging," Michael said as they reached the back of the house. "It's probably due to all that giggling."

Fanny caught up and put aside the fishing poles she'd been carrying. "Grand-mère says that being of good cheer is the secret to a long life."

Michael opened the back door and grinned. "Then you ought to live to be a hundred."

"There you are," Mrs. Atwell said as they stepped into the kitchen. "I thought I'd have to send your father out to find you." She spied the string of fish. "I see 'twas a very productive day."

"The very best," Fanny agreed. "I caught the first fish, and then Michael caught the next two. After that I lost track."

Mrs. Atwell laughed. "Well, I can see I'll have my work cut out for me. Just put them over there in the sink." She motioned to her son. "I suppose you're both ready for a bit of refreshment."

"We are. We ate everything you sent in the basket, but now we're famished."

"I'm not surprised." Mrs. Atwell affectionately tousled her son's wavy brown hair. "I'll bring you refreshments on the porch, but first I need to fetch Fanny's father. I was just on my way when you arrived. Your grandmother wants to speak with him."

"I can get him," Fanny told her. "Where has he gone?"

"To your special place," Mrs. Atwell said with a sympathetic smile. "The place he always took your mother—and now you."

Fanny nodded with great enthusiasm. "I'll go. It's not so very far."

"I'll go with her," Michael said. "It's farther than a young lady should go by herself."

"The island is hardly that big," Fanny declared, "and I am eleven years old."

Michael laughed. "And very opinionated."

"All right, you two. Get on with you now. Miss Fanny, it would be the better part of wisdom to allow Michael to join you. Besides that, if I remember right, your father took a picnic basket with him. Michael can fetch that back for me."

Fanny didn't really mind Michael's company. She simply didn't want him to think of her as a helpless child who needed to be watched over.

They made their way across the well-kept lawn and headed for the northerly side of the island, where the trees thinned out and gave way to rocky outcroppings. Fanny knew where she would find her father. Langley Broadmoor had often regaled her with stories of how he'd courted her mother on this island—how they would love to steal quiet moments in a very secluded place during their whirlwind romance. Fanny loved coming here each year. The island caused her to feel a sense of her mother's presence just in knowing how much she had cherished this place.

The family always tried to spend some time on the island during the warm summer months. The Thousand Islands of the St. Lawrence River were popular gathering retreats for the very wealthy, and this popularity had only increased in the years since Grandfather had purchased the island. The opulent way of life had increased, as well. What had once been a modest summer retreat was now a palatial estate with a six-story castle that held over fifty rooms.

"I found some fossils over this way," Michael told her. "Maybe we can go hunt for more tomorrow."

"That would be grand," Fanny replied and then frowned. "Oh, but I cannot. Your father is taking us to some birthday party on one of the other islands. Amanda and Sophie insist I come."

"Your cousins can be rather bossy, but I'm sure a party will be far more fun than scouting about in the dirt with me."

Fanny thought to deny that idea but spied her father down the path a ways. He was leaning up against a tree, the basket beside him. Apparently he'd fallen asleep while watching the river.

"Papa!" Fanny hurried down the path, barely righting herself as she tripped on the loose rocks.

"Slow down, you goose!" Michael called from behind her. "You don't want to fall and tear your dress."

Fanny checked her step and slowed only marginally. "Papa, wake up. Grand-mère wishes to see you." She reached her father's side and knelt beside him. Reaching out, she gave him a shake, but he didn't open his eyes.

"Papa?"

She shook him again, and this time his body slumped away from her. His hand fell to the side, revealing a small framed photograph of her mother.

"Michael, something's wrong." She looked to where Michael had come to stop. "He's . . . he's sick. He's not waking up." Fanny shook him harder, but he only slumped closer to the ground. "Papa!"

In less than a second, Michael was at her side. "Mr. Broadmoor. Wake up, sir." He gently reached out to touch the man, then pulled away. "Fanny, I think you should go get my father. Maybe get your uncle Jonas, too."

"But why? What's wrong?"

"Just go now. Hurry."

Fanny straightened and, seeing the grave expression on Michael's face, did exactly as he told her. She fairly flew up the path, and despite knowing how much her grandmother would disapprove, she ran as fast as she could to get help.

The men were easy to find. Fanny let them know the situation in breathless gasps that left little doubt to the serious nature of the moment. The men headed out, demanding she stay behind, but Fanny wasn't about to be left out of the matter. She allowed them to leave without her then followed behind, ignoring her cousins as they bade her to come and play.

Something inside Fanny's chest felt tight. She couldn't help the sense of dread that washed over her. Papa was very sick, otherwise he would have awakened. What would happen now? Would they remain on the island while he recovered, or would they head back to Rochester early? Deep inside, a most terrible thought tried to force its way through the maze of fearful considerations. What if he wasn't sick? What if he had. . .

She couldn't even breathe the word. Fanny couldn't imagine life without her beloved father. She'd already endured the horrible loneliness of being without a mother. Her mother had died giving birth to Fanny, and all she had of her were a few trinkets.

Edging up quietly to where she'd left Michael with her father, Fanny watched the men as they dealt with the situation at hand.

"This is just great," her Uncle Jonas declared. "Langley always did have a flair for the dramatic."

"Jonas, that's uncalled for," Uncle Quincy countered. "You know he's been lost in grief ever since Winifred died."

"He was a weakling. He couldn't even end his life like a man. What reasonable man would take poison?"

Fanny shook her head and flew at them. "No! My papa isn't dead!" She pushed past Uncle Quincy and reached for her father. It was Michael, however, who stopped her. He pulled her away quickly.

"Get her out of here," Uncle Jonas growled. "Take her away at once, Michael."

Michael pulled Fanny along, but she fought him. "No! I want to be with my papa. He needs me."

"He's beyond need now, Fanny." Michael's soft, gentle words caused her to halt her fighting.

"But . . . he . . . he . . . cannot be . . . ." She looked back to where her uncles and Michael's father stood and then braved a glance down to her father's silent form. Tears poured and blinded her eyes as she looked up to Michael.

"Come on."

Fanny gripped Michael's hand tightly and closed her eyes as he led her up the path. Her father was dead. It seemed impossible—horribly wrong. How could it have happened? Uncle Jonas said it was poison. Her father had taken something to end his life.

"Why did he . . . do this?" Fanny barely whispered the words. "Was it my fault?"

Michael dropped to his knees and pulled Fanny against his shoulder. She sobbed quietly for several minutes, just standing there against him.

"This wasn't your fault," Michael finally said as she calmed. "Your father was just too sad. He couldn't bear the pain of being without your mother."

"But he had me," Fanny said, pulling away. "He had me, and now I have no one."

Michael reached up and gently brushed back her tears. He offered a hint of a smile. "You have me, Fanny. You'll always have me.

First Baptist Church
1616 Pacific Ave.
Everett, Wa 98201

2

"Fiddlesticks. Where are they?"

The heels of Frances Jane Broadmoor's shoes tapped a rhythmic click on the Italian marble tile as she paced the length of the entrance hall. Thus far, the technique had failed to control her impatience. At seventeen Fanny was usually not given to such displays, but this occasion merited her frustration.

"Amanda is never late. Sophie would be late to her own funeral, but not Amanda." She went to the window and pulled back the sheer fabric. One glance told her the same thing she'd known for over fifteen minutes. Her cousins had not yet arrived.

They hadn't seen each other since last Christmas, when Fanny was home from finishing school. Amanda had gone away shortly after that to take a grand tour of Europe, while Sophie remained at home. The separation had been absolute misery for the girls. They were closer than most sisters.

17

"Why must they torture me like this?" She dropped the sheer and began to pace again. Passing by her grandfather's study, she peered inside at the ornamental frame that held her grandmother's likeness. Grand-mère. Fanny smiled at the French word. Her grand-mère's aristocratic French ancestors would be appalled at the English use of Grandmother.

There were those who thought Fanny resembled her grand-mère, but the young woman couldn't see it for herself. Fanny had a ghastly collection of dark auburn curls, while Daphine Broadmoor had hair the color of ripe wheat. At least when she'd been younger. Even as an older woman with a snow white crown, her grandmother's beauty surpassed all rivals.

Fanny heard a noise from outside and rushed back to the window. Frowning, she let out a rather unladylike sigh. It was only Mr. Pritchard, the gardener. He offered a smile and waved. Earlier in the day they had worked the garden together, one of Fanny's greatest pleasures. She waved but then quickly walked away from the window.

Had she known both of her cousins would be late, she could have allowed herself additional time in the garden. Mr. Pritchard would have been pleased for another half hour of her help. Though the gardener could be cranky, Fanny had convinced herself years ago that the man enjoyed her assistance. Hamilton Broadmoor hadn't been quite so certain, but her grandfather's assessment hadn't quelled Fanny's desire to learn from Mr. Pritchard.

With no more than the fleeting thought of her grandfather, Fanny glanced up the mammoth stairway. Sunlight spilled from the circular skylight and cast dancing prisms across the palatial landing above the first flight of stairs. She should go upstairs and see if he was awake, but she'd ascended no more than a few steps when the front door burst open.

Amanda rushed inside, holding her straw hat with one hand while lifting her skirts with the other. "I am terribly sorry, Fanny. As usual, Sophie has made us late. Goodness, but what happened to your hair?"

Instinctively Fanny pressed a palm to her unruly curls. No matter how she brushed and pinned the tresses, they popped loose and circled her face like unfettered coils. "I'm afraid my pacing has undone my grooming." She tried to force the pins back into place while scanning the entryway for some sign of Sophie. Giving up on her hair, Fanny descended the steps and hurried to embrace Amanda.

"And where is Sophie? Still in the carriage?"

"Absolutely not! I finally departed without her. Next time she'll believe me when I say I'm not waiting any longer." Amanda pulled away, removed her hat, and twisted a blond tress around her finger to ensure proper placement.

Fanny smiled at the gesture. Amanda's hair was just like Grand-mère's—the same golden shade and never disheveled in the least. "Exactly where did you leave poor Sophie?"

"Poor *Sophie*? Don't you *dare* feel sorry for her. I arrived with the carriage at exactly one-thirty. The time we had both agreed upon, by the way. When she still hadn't gotten into the carriage by two o'clock, I warned her and then departed." Amanda frowned and shook her head. "Some fellow I've never seen before was sitting in the parlor visiting with her when I arrived. Even though he clearly knew of our plans, he made no move to leave. Certainly no gentleman, wouldn't you agree?"

"Well, I . . ."

"When I issued my ultimatum, he grinned and the two of them continued their private conversation. I decided I'd wait no longer. I knew you would be worried about us." Amanda's high cheekbones bore a distinct flush; her usually gentle brown eyes flashed with anger.

"'Tis true I wondered at the lateness of your arrival. In fact, I'd decided to go upstairs for a brief visit with Grandfather, though I wasn't certain he'd be awake." She lowered her voice. "The doctor gives him a great deal of medicine, and he sleeps almost constantly. Hazel and I take turns sitting with him."

Amanda bobbed her head. "Oh, how I've missed you. It seems we've been apart for years instead of months."

"I know. I was thinking the same thing." Fanny's voice was barely audible.

"Why are you whispering?"

Fanny shrugged. "Habit, I suppose. I've become accustomed to keeping my voice low when someone is sick. I guess it's silly."

The girls looped arms and walked into the parlor. "Not so silly. You've been around more sickness and death than most of us."

That fact was certainly true, although Fanny tried not to dwell on it. It just made her all the more lonely to think about what she'd lost in her young life. She couldn't remember her mother, but her father was a different story. Memories of their years together only served to make the loss seem new all over again. She had thought they'd been happy together—that they would always have each other to hold fast to. Remembering him dead only made her loneliness more acute.

After her father's funeral, Fanny hadn't had to make any adjustment to her living arrangements. At her grandmother's insistence, Fanny and her father had been living with Grand-mère and Grandfather at Broadmoor Mansion since the day after Winifred's death and Fanny's birth. But once her father had died, there had been subtle changes in her life. People talked about her father in hushed whispers. After all, it was quite unacceptable to take one's life. Fanny felt as though she'd been hidden away from society while the gossip died down. Still, she'd been fortunate, for her grandparents had easily slipped into the role of both legal and emotional guardians of their youngest granddaughter.

But now Grand-mère, too, was gone, and Grandfather seemed destined to follow. Fanny had suffered greatly when the older woman had taken ill and died two years ago. Her grandparents had insisted she remain at finishing school, and there had been no time for final good-byes with Grand-mère. A situation Fanny continued to regret. She'd had no control over that decision or anything else in her life, for that matter. With Grandfather hovering on the brink of death, she now feared losing him, as well. The two of them had become inordinately close throughout the years, but even more so since Grand-mère's death.

Amanda grasped Fanny's hand and pulled her toward the divan. "Now look what I've done with my dreary talk of illness and death. You've turned gloomy. I can see it in your eyes. Do promise you'll cheer up. I want to hear all about what's happened during your final session at Greatbriar. I know you must be delighted to have completed your education at that distant place. I do wish Grandfather would have permitted you to remain at home and attend finishing school here in Rochester."

Still clasping hands, the girls dropped onto the floral upholstered divan. Greatbriar Manor for Young Ladies of Exceptional Quality, located in Montreal, Canada, had been Grand-mère's choice. Her father had never acquiesced, but after his death, Grand-mère had insisted Fanny would love the school. She hadn't.

"He was following Grand-mère's instructions. She thought it best I finish my schooling at Greatbriar, but who knows what will happen now that I've completed my final year. Grand-mère said after my grand tour of Europe, I could consider attending Vassar." Fanny scooted into a corner of the divan. "From what you tell me about Sophie and this young man, it sounds as though she's adjusted."

Amanda cocked an eyebrow. "To her mother's death, you mean?"

Fanny nodded. It seemed all of their conversation this day would center upon the topic of death. "Yes. She appeared terribly downcast when I saw her during the Christmas holidays. She wouldn't even accept my invitation to come and spend time with Grandfather and me. I didn't take offense, of course. I knew she must be missing her mother terribly."

"You are a sweet girl, Fanny, but I don't believe Aunt Marie's death—"

Before Amanda could complete her response, footsteps clattered across the marble floor tiles. "Forevermore, where is everyone? Fanny? Amanda? Doesn't the butler answer the door anymore?"

Fanny jumped to her feet and hurried toward the parlor doorway. "We're in here, Sophie." She touched her index finger to her lips.

"Why am I supposed to be quiet? And where are the servants? No one answered the door when I arrived. Ever since grandfather has taken ill, the servants take advantage. As head housekeeper, you'd think Mrs. O'Malley would issue some reprimands."

"Grandfather is resting, and the servants are attending to their duties." Fanny frowned. "I didn't hear the doorbell."

The girls exchanged a brief embrace before Sophie shrugged and crossed the room. "You were very rude to my guest, Amanda. And I absolutely could not believe my eyes when I saw your carriage departing without me. I should think you'd have acquired better manners while traveling abroad these past six months."

Amanda squared her shoulders. "My manners have always been impeccable, Sophie. If either of us has disregarded proper etiquette, it is you. I arrived at the assigned time and gave you fair warning before I departed. You failed to heed my word."

Their long-awaited reunion was quickly turning into a disastrous affair. Fanny clapped her hands together. "I have a wonderful idea. Why don't we go out and visit in the garden? It will be just like old times, when we were little girls. Besides, I want both of you to see my lilacs."

"No need to go to the garden for that. I saw a vase of your lilacs sitting on the pier table in the front hall when I arrived. Do you like my new dress?" Sophie cast a glance at the billowing leg-of-mutton sleeves that made her waist appear even narrower than the fashionable handspan.

Fanny assessed Sophie's latest purchase and nodded. It certainly wasn't a dress she would have chosen for herself, but it suited her cousin. Intricate dark brown embroidery embellished the entire length of each sleeve and decorated the pale pink yoke before flowing downward into a simple gored skirt. The deep brown embroidered stitches were a near match to Sophie's coffee-colored tresses, and the pale pink shade of the gown emphasized her skin tone to perfection.

Amanda shifted forward and stood. "I think we should go outdoors and enjoy the garden." She ran a finger along the embroidered sleeve of Sophie's dress. "Only last week you were lamenting the fact that Uncle Quincy was pouring all of his funds into helping the homeless. It appears as if you've managed to redirect his thinking. I'm certain you paid a dear price for this dress."

"The price was fair," Sophie defended. "And after a bit of cajoling, Father agreed. How could he refuse? The dress had been custom made for me."

They all three understood that Quincy Broadmoor could have refused to pay for the gown. Likely he'd been overcome by the need to please his daughter, or Sophie had simply worn him down. Fanny suspected the latter was correct. When Sophie wanted something, she wasn't easily deterred. Fanny waved her cousins toward the entrance hall. "Come along. I promise the lilacs I want to show you are different from the ones you've already seen." She tilted her head. "They are like nothing you've ever before observed."

"If you had a hand in raising them, I'm certain they are absolutely gorgeous." Dimples creased Sophie's cheeks, and her brown eyes sparkled as she walked alongside Fanny through the conservatory and into the garden. "I used the services of the same dressmaker to design and sew my gown for the Summer's Eve Ball."

Amanda slowed her step. "Truly? Then you ought not complain in the least about Uncle Quincy being tightfisted with you."

"Easy enough for you to say, Amanda. Unlike Fanny and me, you have a mother who delights in shopping and purchasing the latest fashions for you. You live in elegance and beauty, while our home has been all but stripped of such amenities in order to finance Father's home for the friendless. He only lets us keep a housekeeper because I refuse to do the work and need someone to lace me up in the morning and help me dress."

"Perhaps it wouldn't hurt you to help him with his endeavors," Amanda countered. "At least your father cares about the impoverished."

"I'd rather he care about our place in society, like your father does. Besides, I don't see you down there volunteering your time."

Fanny could barely keep pace with the flying barbs. Where had all this animosity come from? The three of them had always been dear friends. Cousins who shared everything. Even their secrets—at least most of them. Now it seemed each comment was followed either by an angry rebuttal or injured feelings.

"Has your mother completed arrangements for the ball?" Fanny stepped between her cousins, hoping to ease the banter.

Before Amanda could respond, Sophie bent forward and peeked around Fanny. "Personally, I am surprised your mother is hosting the event this year, Amanda. There are other prominent families here in Rochester who could have stepped in to host the event for one year. Did she not consider Grandfather's medical condition?"

Amanda exhaled a loud sigh. "Grandfather specifically requested that the annual ball take place here in Rochester. And he even said he expects the family to depart for Broadmoor Island as scheduled."

"*What?* But that's impossible." Fanny yanked on Amanda's arm. "Grandfather can't possibly ride a train to Clayton and then take a boat out to the island. He's unable to even come downstairs to eat his meals."

"I don't think he was implying that he would join us, Fanny. Merely that he expected the family to maintain the annual tradition. He promised Grand-mère."

Fanny loosened her hold on Amanda's arm. "I'm eager to return to the island, but—"

Sophie held up a hand and interrupted her cousin. "As far as I know, you're the only one who wants to return."

"You enjoy our summers together at Broadmoor Island." Fanny looked back and forth, waiting for one of her cousins to agree. "You do, don't you?" The Broadmoor family had been summering on their private island located in the heart of the Thousand Islands in the St. Lawrence River for as long as Fanny could remember.

"Of course we do, dear girl," Amanda said. "Now, let's go and look at those lilacs you promised to show us."

But instead of her earlier excitement, Fanny's thoughts piled atop one another in a jumble of confusion. All these years she'd believed her cousins had enjoyed the endless summer hours whiled away on their grandparents' private island.

Her grandfather had purchased the island on a whim, an anniversary gift to Grand-mère, because the land was located in close proximity to Brockville, her Canadian home—or so he said. Grand-mère's version of the story differed. She said George Pullman had convinced Grandfather that the seaway islands and small communities of Clayton and Alexandria Bay were destined to become the summer playground of the wealthy, and Grandfather wanted a hand in the matter.

Fanny didn't know which story was correct, but time had proved Mr. Pullman's assessment correct. Each summer the number of vacationers flocking to the hotels and resorts that dotted the seaway increased in number. And each summer the excitement and merriment increased, also—at least that's what Fanny had thought until today.

The three cousins silently marched toward the far end of the garden. The profusion of pale purple, deep lavender, and milky white blooms swayed in the spring breeze and filled the air with their perfume. Unlike the sweet fragrance and silent beauty of the lilacs, their conversation had been a mishmash of fragmented comments and angry retorts. Before her cousins left this afternoon, Fanny hoped they would regain their former unity of spirit.

Moments after Amanda and Sophie had departed, Fanny raced upstairs. She slowed her pace in the upper hallway and tiptoed to the door of her grandfather's bedroom. Hazel sat near his bedside reading from the newspaper an update on the Cuban war. From what Fanny could hear, the paper reported that Spanish officers stated they were receiving a higher rate of pay than their counterparts in Spain and had declared their willingness to indefinitely remain and fight for Spain on Cuban soil. Silly men! Why would anyone want to go and fight in another country? For that matter, why would anyone want to participate in war at all? Thoughts of dying young men clouded her mind. She was pleased when Hazel folded the paper.

Fanny quietly approached and touched her grandfather's veined hand. "How are you feeling this afternoon?"

His color remained pale, but his eyes were clear. He motioned her toward the chair. "Sit and take Hazel's place. You can read to me."

Hazel handed Fanny the newspaper. "If you're going to be here for a while, I'll go up to the third floor and complete my chores."

"Yes, of course. Take all the time you need." Fanny glanced down the page, hoping to find something to read other than war reports.

"Well, are you going to read?"

Her grandfather had never been a patient man, and his illness hadn't changed that particular trait. "Let's see," she murmured. Tracing her forefinger down the page, Fanny scanned the report of a body being found in the river, the description of a steamer collision, the account of a bank president who had killed himself, and a tale of destruction due to an earthquake in Montana. Was there nothing cheery or uplifting in the news these days? She snapped the pages and refolded the paper.

With an air of authority, she placed the paper on the bedside table and folded her hands in her lap. "Let's visit instead."

Her grandfather cast a longing glance at the paper. He did enjoy his newspaper, but he didn't object. "What shall we talk about? The war in Cuba, perhaps?"

She giggled. "You can save that conversation for Uncle Jonas. Did Hazel tell you that Amanda and Sophie came to visit this afternoon?"

He nodded. "When I asked where you were, she mentioned your cousins were expected."

"If I had known you were awake, we would have all come upstairs for a few minutes."

Wisps of white hair circled his head like a lopsided halo. "I've been awake only a short time. You can tell me all about your visit with the girls. I'll see them the next time they come." A convulsive cough followed the rasping words.

Fanny jumped up and poured water from the cut-glass pitcher sitting on the table near his bedside. She offered the glass. He coughed again and then swallowed a gulp of the liquid. "Better?" She waited until he nodded and then returned the glass. Grandfather was adamant: they were not to make a fuss over his coughing spells. And though it was difficult, Fanny adhered to his wishes. "Let's see. Where shall I begin?"

He grinned at her and winked. "At the beginning."

She and Grandfather had exchanged those same words many times over the years. It had become their own private joke, and she was pleased he remembered. Scooting her chair closer to the side of his bed, she recounted the afternoon's events—at least a goodly portion of them. She didn't mention the barbs that had been exchanged early in the afternoon, for Grandfather didn't need to be bothered with their childish discord. He appeared pleased when Fanny mentioned Sophie's fine appearance and her beautiful gown. "She was absolutely radiant in her pink dress."

Hamilton patted his granddaughter's hand. "I'm pleased to hear Quincy purchased Sophie a new gown. I'd be happier if he'd devote a bit of time to her, though. From what I've been told, Quincy has been spending all of his time and money on the Home for the Friendless, which he's determined to make successful."

His response surprised Fanny. She considered her grandfather a generous man, someone who was willing to aid the less fortunate. Not with his time, of course, but certainly with his money. "You contribute to many charities, Grandfather."

"Of course I do. But Quincy isn't using wise judgment right now. He's allowing his emotions to rule his good sense. Marie kept Quincy on an even keel. Since her death, he seems intent upon forging ahead with these plans for the less fortunate."

"Perhaps it's his way of dealing with his grief. If my father had had such a project, he might still be with us." She frowned and looked away.

"You are right, of course. I'm sorry. I didn't mean to cause you distress."

"It's just that losing loved ones is so very hard."

"Your grandmother and I always tried to ease your pain."

Fanny nodded. "And you did. I could not have asked for a better home or more love. Still. . ." She let the words trail off.

"Still, it would have been better to have grown up with a mother and father at your side. I know that full well, Fanny dear. We never hoped to replace them in your life but rather to comfort you—ourselves, as well, for we had lost a son most dear."

"Of course. I sometimes forget that," Fanny admitted. She forced a smile. "I'm sure that Uncle Quincy will not succumb to sadness as did my father."

"He needs to think more objectively about the use of his time and energy. He needs to think about business and family." Grandfather turned loose of her hand and rubbed his cheek. "Why am I discussing this with you? Tell me more about your visit with Amanda and Sophie."

"Amanda said you insisted upon Aunt Victoria and Uncle Jonas hosting the annual Summer's Eve Ball and that you expect the family to depart in July for Broadmoor Island in spite of your illness." She leaned forward and pressed closer. "I won't leave you here alone, Grandfather. You know Grand-mère insisted I return to school when she was ill." Her forehead scrunched into a frown, and she wagged her finger. "As much as I love Broadmoor Island, I won't leave you."

Her grandfather brushed an auburn curl from her forehead and smiled. "Never fear. You won't be required to leave me behind, dear Fanny."

3

Saturday, June 12, 1897

The upstairs maid carried Fanny's silk taffeta gown into the bedroom and waited for Fanny's approval.

"Thank you, Hazel. The dress looks wonderful." Fanny beamed with pleasure. The color was perfect, the precise shade of the lilac blooms from the first bush she had planted many years ago with Mr. Pritchard's help—exactly two weeks after her father's death. At Grandfather's insistence, the dress had been fashioned by a local dressmaker for the Summer's Eve Ball. Outsized caps of lilac taffeta topped the full ruffled lace sleeves, and a thin ruffle edged the neckline. Crystal beads in an iris motif embellished the bodice and skirt. Had she designed the dress, she would have used a lilac motif instead.

Hazel fastened the gown and handed Fanny a pair of long white gloves. "You look lovely, miss. That shade is perfect with your hair."

Fanny bent forward and pecked Hazel on the cheek. "You're always so kind, Hazel. What would I do without you?" She took one final peek in mirror. "I'm going to go and tell Grandfather good-night before I depart."

Hazel fluffed the hemline of the skirt and gave an approving nod. "He said to waken him if he's asleep. He wants to see you in your dress."

Fanny hurried out the door and down the hallway. When she neared her grandfather's room, she slowed her step. After a gentle tap on the door, she entered. "Are you asleep?"

He opened his eyes and waved her forward. "Come. Stand by the window and let me see you."

Fanny followed his instruction and took her place in front of the window. He waved his forefinger in a circle, and she compliantly turned slowly for inspection.

"Lovely. Simply lovely."

"Thank you, Grandfather." She leaned down and kissed his pale weathered cheek. "I promise to tell you all the details tomorrow morning."

He nodded. "I love you very much, Fanny. Now off with you and have a wonderful time."

Fanny promised to enjoy herself, and she would make every attempt. But a formal dinner followed by dancing with the eligible bachelors of Rochester, New York, didn't rank high on her list of pleasant pastimes. She would much prefer dipping her toes off the dock at Broadmoor Island or stealing away for an afternoon of fishing with Michael Atwell. He knew the waters of the St. Lawrence Seaway and could navigate her grandfather's skiff into the finest fishing spots along the river. Grandfather enjoyed referring to the young man as his boatswain. Michael had been charged with maintaining the Broadmoor boats and equipment for the past five years—since the summer he had turned sixteen. Through the years, the size and number of Grandfather's boats had increased, and so had Michael's ability. Without Michael, life on Broadmoor Island wouldn't be nearly so pleasant. This year, however, Fanny doubted whether she'd be seeing Michael or fishing at Broadmoor Island.

She stepped into the carriage, sat down, and smoothed the folds of her skirt before resting her back against the leather-upholstered seat. It was strange the way things occurred. Her cousins would be delighted to forego the annual summer visit at the island. In fact, except for Fanny's youngest nieces and nephews, the entire family would prefer to remain in Rochester for the summer—or at least choose a hiatus away from one another along the New Jersey shore or touring abroad. There was little doubt that time on the island would be less stressful if the entire family weren't there at the same time. Though the house on Broadmoor Island far surpassed the Rochester mansion in size, there had been no structure created that would peacefully house all members of the Broadmoor family. The possibility remained an enigma, but that hadn't stopped Grand-mère from insisting upon the family coming together each summer for what she had called "reunion and refreshment." Other members of the family had created their own special names for the summer get-togethers, designations that weren't nearly as lovely as the one chosen by Grand-mère.

"I don't understand why they all hate each other and the island," Fanny murmured to herself. "They don't understand how blessed they are to have one another. I would love to have brothers and sisters. I would give anything to have my mother and father alive and well. How can they be so flippant about the blessing of family?"

She couldn't reason the matter in her mind. The extended Broadmoor family seemed worse than strangers. At least with strangers a modicum of manners remained in place. With family, however, the Broadmoors seemed to have a penchant for insult and upheaval. They were masters at taking offense for the silliest things. Fanny could recall a time when much of the family had been in a complete tizzy when Grand-mère had had the audacity to serve roasted lamb at the evening meal on what was clearly a beef day.

"They're all a bunch of ninnies," Fanny said, shaking her head. With the exception of Sophie and Amanda, she couldn't even pretend that any of them cared one whit for her.

Much too soon the carriage came to a halt in the driveway of Jonas and Victoria Broadmoor's impressive home and abruptly ended Fanny's musings. Soft music, played by string musicians, wafted on the warm evening breeze to greet the arriving guests—pleasant melodies that were intended to delight even the most severe critic. And there were many among the social set who would judge not only the music but every aspect of the party. Each one eager to discover any faux pas or indiscretion that would fuel local gossip.

Fanny would have preferred to enter by a rear door and mingle without fanfare, but her aunt would be scandalized by such an arrival. Aunt Victoria had obviously taken great pains to ensure an illustrious review in the society column of the newspaper. Her niece would be expected to enter through the front door and stand before the gathered assemblage for her introduction. How she longed for Grandfather's presence and his strong arm to lean upon at this moment. She didn't realize how much she had depended upon his support at these ghastly social affairs.

She followed the servant's instructions and stepped to the entrance of the oversized parlor. "Miss Frances Jane Broadmoor." His voice bellowed above the twittering guests, who momentarily ceased their chitchat and stared in her direction. With her chin lifted to what she hoped was the proper height, Fanny entered the parlor. She could only hope she wouldn't trip and embarrass herself. With a quick glance, she scanned the area for an out-of-the way spot where she could gain her bearings before commencing the required rigors of mingling with the other guests.

"*There* you are!" Amanda pulled her cousin into an embrace and then stepped back, her gaze traveling up and down the length of Fanny's gown. "Your dress is lovely. You didn't mention it when we were at the house." She touched Fanny's shoulder. "Turn around and permit me a view of the back."

Feeling somewhat foolish, Fanny completed a quick pirouette. Her appearance couldn't begin to compare to that of Amanda. Though the attention was offered in kindness, the close scrutiny only caused Fanny further discomfort. Although Hazel had maintained it would take an explosion for even one hair to escape the nest of curls she'd created atop Fanny's head, the hairpins had already begun to pop loose. The maid truly lacked a full understanding of Fanny's unmanageable tresses. She forced a curl back into place and glanced about the room. "I haven't seen Sophie. Has she arrived?"

Amanda nodded toward a far corner. "Over there, surrounded by that flock of young men. No matter where she leads, they follow."

Moments later the group of men separated and Sophie walked toward them. The scene was somewhat akin to the parting of the Red Sea, Fanny decided. Amanda beckoned to their cousin and she approached, her entourage following close on her heels. When she stopped in front of her cousins, the young men clustered into a tight knot directly behind her. It seemed that each one longed to escort the vivacious young woman to the supper table.

"All my friends are wondering who will sit next to me at dinner, but I've told them I had no say in the decision." She batted her lashes at the assembled group standing behind her.

Anticipation glazed their eyes as they awaited Sophie's further attention. Amanda pointed her fan toward the distant doorway and then looked at the huddled group of bedazzled followers. "You may inquire of my mother if you desire."

None of them moved. It appeared as if the young admirers feared leaving Sophie for even a minute. And Sophie seemed to enjoy the suffocating attention. Before Fanny could contemplate the situation further, one of the servants announced dinner.

Amanda looped arms with Fanny, and they followed Sophie's formally attired devotees toward the massive dining room located on the third floor. The rooms were used only for large parties, and the servants were aided by the dumbwaiters in the dining hall. Otherwise they'd not survive such ordeals. Amanda giggled when they neared the doorway.

"Each year the young men become increasingly smitten with our cousin."

"And with you, also. If you didn't shoo them away, you'd have a large assemblage following you," Fanny replied. While Sophie's vivacious personality attracted the men, it was Amanda's natural beauty that wooed them. Fanny decided it was Amanda's regal deportment that set her apart, along with her perfect blond hair and striking features.

They parted at the table in search of their place cards. This was yet another scheme Aunt Victoria utilized at her dinner parties. She insisted that her guests delight in the process of locating their assigned seats. "Utter chaos," Fanny muttered while she circled the table in search of her name.

"Over here, Fanny." Lydia Broadmoor, Grayson's wife, waved her forward. "You're on the other side of Grayson."

Although Aunt Victoria enjoyed the unconventional method of requiring her guests to search for their place cards, she continued to insist upon a traditional male-female seating arrangement. Accordingly, Fanny knew she would be flanked by men. Sitting next to Amanda's oldest brother wouldn't have been Fanny's first choice, but at least he was a relative. After rounding the table, she glanced at the place card to her left. Mr. Snodgrass. So she would have Amanda's older brother on one side and old Mr. Snodgrass, Uncle Jonas's favorite banker, on the other. This would be a long dinner!

She exchanged pleasantries with Grayson and Lydia and politely inquired after the health of their three children. Fanny hadn't seen any of them since Christmas. "Are the children looking forward to the summer on Broadmoor Island?"

Lydia silently waited for her husband's response. "They enjoy their time at the island, but our plans remain indefinite."

"How is that possible? Nothing has changed."

Grayson looked at her as though she'd lost her senses. "*Grandfather?* You do realize the gravity of his illness, do you not?"

"Yes, of course, but that changes nothing. He still expects—"

"It changes *everything*, dear Fanny. While the youngsters and one or two older members of the family enjoy summering on the island, the rest of us will be relieved and, dare I say, delighted to end that compulsory tradition."

Fanny's jaw went slack. How could they find anything objectionable with that lovely island? She felt as though she'd been jabbed in the stomach by a sharp elbow.

"Appears as though Victoria surrounded me with both beauty and youth this evening." Fanny turned to see Mr. Snodgrass smiling down at her. The lanky old man towered above her; he looked to be at least six feet tall. Beatrice, one of Sophie's older sisters, had been positioned on the other side of the banker. Though Fanny wouldn't have described Beatrice as either young or beautiful, she couldn't fault Mr. Snodgrass. Fanny didn't consider herself pretty, either—young, but certainly not pretty.

Fanny nodded and returned a smile. "Good evening, Mr. Snodgrass." She leaned forward. "How are you, Beatrice?" Most of the time, Beatrice seemed to be either in pain or sad. Fanny couldn't decide which it might be this evening. Even when Beatrice smiled, her lips drooped at the corners.

"I'm well, thank you, Fanny. When did you return to Rochester?"

"I've been home nearly two weeks now." She scoured her thoughts for some tidbit that might keep the conversation flowing. "How is Miranda?"

"Fine. She seems to think she's all grown up; she was insulted that she wasn't invited to the ball this evening." Beatrice forced her drooping lips upward. "I explained that eight-year-olds aren't considered adults, but she would hear none of that."

"I'm certain she's looking forward to spending July and August at the island."

"Island?" Mr. Snodgrass pointed a bony finger at Fanny. "You mark my words: this country will have men in Cuba before the end of the year. With the newspapers pushing for intervention, Congress will follow suit. We'll march onto that island, even if it's not the intelligent thing to do. And you can quote me on that!" Everyone at the table was now staring at them.

"We weren't discussing Cuba, Mr. Snodgrass," Fanny shouted. She disliked speaking so loudly, but she didn't want the old man to misinterpret anything else she said.

"Well, even if you weren't, you *should* be. This country is going to find itself in a real mess. Folks need to wake up before we're in the middle of someone else's war. I say, let those Spaniards and Cubans fight it out for themselves."

Aunt Victoria nudged Uncle Jonas into action.

"No talk of war or fighting at the dinner table, William. Victoria insists it ruins the digestion."

Wisps of white hair appeared to be waving at the guests as Mr. Snodgrass enthusiastically nodded. "The whole matter is more than I can digest, too, Jonas. That's why I say we need to stay out of it. What do you young fellows say? You don't want to see this country involved in war, do you? Why, you'd likely go over there and get yourselves killed."

Aunt Victoria visibly paled. From all appearances she was about to faint. Lydia signaled across the room, and one of the servants soon arrived with a cool cloth for Victoria. Mr. Snodgrass appeared not to notice, for he continued to solicit comments from several of the young men. If he received an answer that didn't suit, he immediately shouted an angry rebuttal and then turned to the next fellow.

Although a hint of color returned to Aunt Victoria's cheeks, her displeasure remained evident. Uncle Jonas tapped his water goblet with a spoon until the room turned silent. "My wife does not wish to hear any talk of fighting or war at the dinner table, William." He shouted loud enough that Fanny was certain anyone within a two-block radius could hear the admonition.

Mr. Snodgrass appeared unperturbed by the comeuppance. "Fine. We can discuss it over a glass of port and a good cigar later in the evening," he muttered.

Throughout the meal, which progressed at the usual snail's pace, Fanny did her best to talk with Grayson and Mr. Snodgrass. The extravagant floral centerpiece prohibited much visiting with guests seated across the table, though it mattered little. Fanny doubted she could interest them in discussing fishing at Broadmoor Island.

Several servants returned to the dining room and started to remove the dinner plates. When one of the servers approached Fanny, Mr. Snodgrass shook his head and turned a stern eye on Fanny. "You've eaten only a few bites of your food, young lady. Do you realize what food costs nowadays?" Before Fanny could respond, he cast a look of doom at the guests seated around him and proclaimed the country would be hard-pressed to recover from this latest depression. "I'm a banker, you know. I understand economics, and even though you all think this country is on the mend, we've a long way to go. Best think about that when you're agreeing to this war, too."

Thankfully, the servant ignored the conversation and removed Fanny's dinner plate while Mr. Snodgrass predicated the country would soon lapse into complete ruination.

Uncle Jonas cleared his throat. "William . . ."

Mr. Snodgrass waved at Jonas with a quivering hand mottled with liver spots. "I know, I know. No talk of war, no talk of financial ruin, no talk of anything other than the weather and the ladies' gowns." He dipped his head closer to Fanny. A strand of white hair dropped across his forehead. "Do none of you young ladies have interest in anything other than frippery?"

"William!" Uncle Jonas shook his head. Mr. Snodgrass failed to take into account that his whispers could be heard by everyone in attendance.

"Fine, Jonas!" Mr. Snodgrass turned toward Fanny and cocked an eyebrow. "Tell me, Miss Broadmoor, who fashions your gowns for you? And what color do you call that particular shade of purple? Did you bead the gown yourself?"

The old man's voice dripped with sarcasm, and several of the other men snickered until their wives disarmed them with icy stares. While one of the servants placed a dish of lemon ice in front of Fanny, she leaned close to Mr. Snodgrass. "The color of my gown is referred to as lilac, Mr. Snodgrass."

He grinned. "Makes sense. Same shade as Rochester's famous blooms, right?"

"Yes. My favorite flower, too."

"Well, I find lilacs quite lovely myself. What about you, Jonas? You prefer roses over lilacs?" The old man winked at Fanny.

Her uncle was clearly annoyed. "Neither. I prefer deep purple irises."

Mr. Snodgrass swiveled toward Fanny and arched his bushy brows. "Your uncle dislikes the color of your dress, Miss Broadmoor. This bit of news will likely render you unable to digest your supper. I'm certain you're wishing you had purchased a deeper shade of purple." Mr. Snodgrass tipped his head back and laughed. "Shall we discuss the beading on your gown, or perhaps I could ask Mrs. Winberg if she prefers lilac over purple."

Unless Uncle Jonas vehemently objected, Mr. Snodgrass's name would likely be permanently removed from Aunt Victoria's guest list. Perhaps he would depart early this evening, for he'd evidently not read his invitation. Dinner guests were expected to retire to the ballroom immediately after the evening meal. For this auspicious annual occasion, Aunt Victoria always invited fifty guests to partake of dinner prior to the dance. However, many more guests had been invited for the ball—a veritable array of New York society. Instead of enjoying a cigar and glass of port, Mr. Snodgrass would be expected to locate a dance partner. Fanny wondered if the man's legs would support him for an entire waltz.

She'd never been so pleased to conclude the evening repast.

Amanda stood on tiptoe and waved her fan in the air until she captured Fanny's attention. Weaving her way through the crowd would take a bit of effort on Fanny's part. Within moments, Amanda lost sight of her cousin amidst the throng of guests. She had hoped to visit with Fanny before the promenade, but it didn't appear that would occur.

The musicians had gathered in their appointed places. The grand promenade was a tradition that had begun years ago at the very first Summer's Eve Ball. At least that's what Amanda's mother insisted when anyone suggested eliminating the ritual.

Instead of Fanny, Sophie arrived at Amanda's side, her entourage in tow. "Is your mother angry that Father didn't make an appearance this evening? Or has she even missed him?"

"Of course she misses him, Sophie. We all miss him. Mother mentioned last week that he hadn't responded to his invitation." She shrugged. "You know Mother. She detests any breach of etiquette. Uncle Quincy will be in for one of her lectures the next time they see each other."

"He's so consumed with expanding his charity shelter that he thinks of nothing else." She jutted her chin in the air. "He doesn't consider that his own children consider themselves parentless."

Amanda offered her cousin a sympathetic smile. Sophie tended to exaggerate from time to time, but her cousin's feelings of abandonment were genuine. Ever since the death of Sophie's mother's last year, her father had been consumed by his work with the homeless. "Well, I doubt you can speak for your brother and sisters, Sophie."

Sophie shrugged. "I suppose you're right. They all have their own lives now. I'm the one who deserves at least a bit of my father's time and attention."

That much was certainly true. Sophie's eldest sister, Louisa Clermont, who had been widowed five months ago, lived in Cincinnati with her three children. Nadine, who had been the youngest sister until Sophie's birth, lived in Rochester with her husband, Willard Snyder. They had welcomed their first child, Alfred, only a few days ago, and no one had expected them to attend tonight's festivities. Nor did anyone expect Dorian, Sophie's only brother, to be in attendance. Dorian had departed Rochester three years ago to explore Canada. He'd written only once since he left, and none of them had the vaguest idea how to contact him. He didn't even know his mother had died a year ago. Of course Beatrice and her husband, Andrew Winberg, were in attendance this evening. Beatrice might not be enjoying herself tonight, but she would never breach social etiquette or disappoint her relatives—especially those of higher social standing. Beatrice had married a Winberg—a Rochester family but certainly not of the same social standing as that of the Broadmoors, not by any stretch of the imagination.

Not that Amanda cared a whit about making the "proper" marriage. Personally, she wasn't interested in marriage at all. At least not now. Jonas and Victoria Broadmoor desired proper marriages for all of their children, but they had conceded to the choices made by both of their sons. Grayson and William had each married a young lady of lower social standing. The Broadmoor social status had, of course, assured that their wives would be accepted into all of the proper circles. Neither Jefferson nor George, Amanda's two other brothers, had chosen a wife. They were no more interested in marriage than was their sister. Yet when the time came for Amanda to choose a husband, her parents would expect a wise choice. For when a daughter married beneath herself socially, remaining a member of the higher class wasn't guaranteed.

The musicians struck the first chords of the promenade march while Amanda's parents took their places at the far end of the ballroom, the guests' signal to find their partners and position themselves in line.

Sophie grasped the arm of one of her many admirers, leaving each of the others to locate an unescorted young lady. "Come on, Amanda. We need to get in line." Sophie glanced over her shoulder while her escort preened like a peacock.

Before one of Sophie's rejected suitors had an opportunity to ask Amanda, her brother Jefferson swooped her into his arms. "I've decided to escort my beautiful sister in the promenade," he said.

She grinned and grasped his arm, thankful he'd saved her from a member of Sophie's entourage. "All the unmarried young ladies will be wondering why you chose your sister instead of favoring one of them with your attention."

His boisterous laugh caused several couples to turn and stare at them. "I would tell them that I chose my sister because she is the most beautiful woman in the room."

"And would you also tell them that dancing with your sister prevents any expectations from your dance partner?" She leaned into his arm. "An invitation to escort one of those girls onto the dance floor is not tantamount to a marriage proposal, Jefferson."

"I'll favor several of them with my attention later in the evening. But you know how everyone watches to see the couples in the promenade. They all make assumptions. You know that is true, dear sister."

"Oh, dear me, I hope not." She stopped and clasped her hand to her bodice. "Do look at who is escorting Fanny. If people make assumptions, our Fanny is doomed."

Standing near the middle of the line, old Mr. Snodgrass was clinging to Fanny's arm.

Fanny turned away and hoped her cousins wouldn't notice she was now standing beside Mr. Snodgrass. If she had possessed more gumption, she would have loudly refused when he clasped her arm and insisted upon escorting her in the promenade. Instead, she'd mumbled a polite rebuff that he'd misinterpreted as an acceptance.

"Fanny! This is my first opportunity to visit with you this evening." Jefferson's eyes twinkled as he leaned down and kissed her cheek. "How are you, dear girl? And welcome to you, Mr. Snodgrass." Jefferson extended his hand to the older man. The hearty handshake was enough to cause Mr. Snodgrass to wobble even closer to Fanny's side.

She cringed and took a sideways step. She longed to wipe the grin from Jefferson's face. "I am fine. Thank you for your concern, Jefferson." She stabbed him with an icy glare. "I'm certain we'll have time for a chat later this evening."

"I'd be delighted, but I certainly don't want Mr. Snodgrass to think I'm attempting to steal his girl." Jefferson's lips curved into a devilish grin. "Are you planning to keep Fanny all to yourself this evening, Mr. Snodgrass? I've never been one to come between a happy couple."

Mr. Snodgrass scratched the white fluff of hair that barely covered his balding pate. "Couple? Oh, we're not married yet," he shouted.

Silence reigned. All eyes turned on Fanny. At least that's what she felt. There may have been one or two folks near the back of the room who weren't staring at her, but she couldn't imagine why not. Mr. Snodgrass had shouted his remark loudly enough for everyone in town to hear him. If she could have found a hole, she'd have crawled inside and pulled it in after her.

"Nor will we ever be—married, that is." Everyone continued to watch. Why had she bothered to justify the old man's remark with a response? Coupled with Mr. Snodgrass's statement, her response appeared to affirm they were romantically involved yet not planning to wed. Forevermore! How did she get herself into these situations? She should have screamed her refusal. Well, it was too late now.

The orchestra began to play the promenade music while Jefferson and Amanda retreated to the rear of the line. Fanny lifted her chin and continued to step forward, with Mr. Snodgrass resting heavily on her arm. Could the man even dance? she wondered.

Jefferson had thoroughly enjoyed her embarrassment. Well, turnabout was fair play. She'd have her chance to return the favor once they were at the island. Fanny grinned, relishing the thought. But her smile soon vanished. Instead of spending her summer at the island playing jokes on her cousin, she'd be caring for Grandfather in Rochester.

When the final chords of the promenade waltz finished, Fanny freed herself of Mr. Snodgrass. She helped him to a chair, fetched him a glass of punch, and promptly escaped to the other side of the room before he could shout a marriage proposal in her direction. Kindness was one thing, but dealing with Mr. Snodgrass for the remainder of the evening went above and beyond what she could endure. The waltz itself had been sufficient torment. Dancing with Mr. Snodgrass had been comparable to attempting a waltz with one of her young nephews, only worse. Much worse.

Fanny didn't need to concern herself with Mr. Snodgrass throughout the remainder of the evening. As soon as he'd consumed his liquid refreshment, he fell asleep in his chair. Once some of their guests began departing, Uncle Jonas called for the old man's carriage. After a final shouted warning about the war in Cuba and the state of the economy, Mr. Snodgrass bade the remaining guests farewell.

Jefferson stepped to Fanny's side. "I think you should have accompanied Mr. Snodgrass to his carriage, Cousin. He obviously is smitten with you."

Fanny jutted her chin. "I believe I'll ignore your silly remark."

"You're letting a good catch get away, dear Fanny. Mr. Snodgrass is quite wealthy. All the widowed dowagers would love to get their claws into him. Didn't you see the evil looks Widow Martin cast in your direction while you were dancing with him?" Jefferson folded his arms across his broad chest and grinned like a Cheshire cat.

Without further thought, Fanny stomped on his foot. He yelped and danced about, though Fanny knew she'd not hurt him in the least. He'd probably felt no more than a slight thump. Jefferson continued to hop about until his mother walked toward them with a solemn look on her face. Fanny wasn't certain whether she or Jefferson would be upbraided for their unseemly behavior.

"All of the family needs to go to the parlor immediately." That said, Jefferson's mother continued to seek out their other relatives.

Amanda grasped Fanny's hand. "What do you suppose this is all about?"

Jefferson fell in behind them. Soon Sophie caught up with the trio, clearly annoyed. "Why have we been summoned to the parlor?"

"None of us know," Fanny replied. "I doubt we'll be detained for long."

"I hope not. I promised John Milleson he could accompany me home."

Jefferson exhaled a low whistle. "Does your father know about John?"

"My father wouldn't care even if he did know, so you can't use that bit of information against me, Jefferson." She chucked him beneath the chin as though he were a little boy rather than a young man four years her senior.

Jonas Broadmoor stood in the center of the room, watching as each of the family members filed into the parlor. When they'd all assembled, he nodded for one of the servants to close the pocket doors. "I received word from one of the servants at Broadmoor mansion that my father died a short time ago."

Grandfather dead? It was Fanny's last thought before she fainted.

4

Friday, June 18, 1897

The day dawned bright and warm, a glorious summer day that Grandfather would have enjoyed. Fanny could easily picture him sitting on the balcony outside his bedroom on a day such as this. But Grandfather wouldn't be sitting on the balcony this day or any other. Instead, he would be buried in the huge family plot next to Grand-mère in Mount Hope Cemetery.

Relatives had been arriving at the mansion—crawling out of the woodwork, as Grandfather used to say. There had been no reason to inquire as to the length of their stay: the reading of the will would take place three days hence. None would depart until hearing the terms of Grandfather's will—not even the most distant relative. Once the mansion had been filled to capacity, additional relatives had been sent to Uncle Jonas's home and then to Uncle Quincy's. A rare few had opted to stay at a hotel once they reached Quincy's abode, for he had sold his mansion shortly after Aunt Marie's death and purchased a small house in a less affluent section of Rochester.

All of this had been done against Sophie's strenuous objections, but Uncle Quincy refused to hear her protests. Shortly thereafter he poured all the profits gained from the sale of the family home into his fledgling charity. While Grandfather and Jonas shook their heads and warned against such a disproportionate contribution, Uncle Quincy chided them for their selfish nature.

Fanny didn't know about Uncle Jonas, but she certainly didn't consider her Grandfather tightfisted. He regularly contributed to the church and charitable organizations. He'd even given a tidy sum to Uncle Quincy's Home for the Friendless. But after Quincy had gone off on a tangent, which was the term Grandfather used when he referred to her uncle's behavior, all gifts to the charity had ceased. Grandfather had thought it would bring Uncle Quincy to his senses, but it seemed to have had the opposite effect. Instead of kowtowing to his father, Quincy had disposed of his other assets and contributed much of the money to his charity. Only the small house remained. Until now. With Grandfather's death, both of her uncles would inherit a vast sum of money. At least that was the assumption of most family members. Still, the majority held out hope that they, too, would be remembered in the will.

Sophie, Amanda, and Fanny sat side by side at the funeral service. At first Aunt Victoria had opposed the arrangement, but when Uncle Quincy stated he had no objection, her aunt conceded. Sitting through the funeral service would be difficult enough for Fanny, but sitting by herself would prove unbearable. Her cousins would provide the added strength she needed to make it through this day.

Too soon Fanny's future would be decided by someone other than her grandfather—but by whom? If only she had reached her age of majority prior to his death. Then she wouldn't need to concern herself with worries over a guardian. She suspected Uncle Jonas would be appointed, but what if Grandfather had decided upon some lawyer or banker? Someone like Mr. Snodgrass? She shivered at the thought. Surely Grandfather wouldn't do such a thing.

A half hour before the service, the church had already filled to capacity. Fanny didn't realize her grandfather knew so many people. It appeared as if all of Rochester had turned out to honor him. Once the preacher began to speak, Fanny plugged her ears. Not in the literal sense, of course, but she quit listening. If she listened, she would cry, and she considered her grief a private matter.

"Fanny? Fanny, are you all right?" Amanda asked. She gave Fanny's shoulder a bit of a shake.

Fanny realized Amanda had been speaking to her. The funeral was over and people were already filing out. She straightened and squared her shoulders. "I'm fine. So sorry to give you worry."

Sophie and Amanda exchanged a look before each one took hold of Fanny. Fanny thought it strange that they should fuss over her so, but ever since she'd fainted the night of Grandfather's death, her cousins treated her as though she might break apart should any further bad news come her way.

"I thought it was a very nice service," Amanda began. She moved the trio out to follow the others.

"It was quite nice," Sophie agreed. "Grandfather would have loved the kind words said about his business capabilities and the importance of the Broadmoor family to the community."

Fanny nodded. She didn't have the heart to explain how she'd kept herself from hearing a single word of the eulogy. In her mind she remembered the last time she'd seen Grandfather alive. She was to have told him all about the party. But of course that would never happen now.

She couldn't help but wonder how this event would alter the family. Jonas would now be the head of the Broadmoor clan. As eldest brother he would no doubt be the one who would decide her fate. She supposed it didn't matter, but she'd never been all that close to the man. He had opposed the idea of her living with her grandparents, believing it would have been better for her to have been sent away to live with distant relatives who were closer to the ages of her deceased parents. Grandfather had refused the idea, however, and Fanny had blessed his name ever since.

But he's gone, she thought. *Who will protect me now? Who will encourage me and show me such tenderness?*

"Well, I hope this puts an end to our miserable summer routine," Beatrice said rather haughtily. "If I have to spend one more summer listening to Lydia criticize our family, I might very well take to violent behavior."

Louisa, Sophie's oldest sister, nodded. "I hate that woman. Just because she married into the Broadmoor family doesn't make her a true Broadmoor."

"I know. There is certainly no love lost between the cousins, as far as I'm concerned." She looked up, as if seeing Fanny and the girls for the first time. "Well, I suppose there are exceptions."

"I should say so," Amanda replied coolly. "It would probably behoove you to stick to talking about what you know, rather than speaking in generalities." She pushed Fanny away from the two women.

"You two are really quite the pair," Sophie threw out. "If you've no love for this family, then be gone and have nothing more to do with it, but leave the rest of us alone."

"No one cares about this family—at least not in the way Grand-mère had hoped," Louisa said.

Fanny stopped and turned to face Sophie's sisters. "Perhaps that is because no one tried to care. Everyone seems so caught up in their own troubles and issues, they've forgotten the blessing of family. You all have one another now, but I have no one."

"That isn't true, Fanny," Amanda said, hugging her close. "You will always have Sophie and me. We are your sisters in every way."

"Better sisters than my own are to me," Sophie said, coming to stand in support of Fanny. "Of that you can be sure."

Fanny was touched by her cousins' support. Their words reminded her of what Michael had told her so many years ago when her father had died. He'd remained a dear friend, and yet Fanny knew that their time was no doubt coming to an end. He was four years older and surely had begun looking for a wife. No woman in her right mind would understand her husband slipping off to go fishing with his employer's daughter.

Sometimes promises simply could not be kept forever. The thought saddened her more than she could express.

The three days after the funeral had been the longest of Fanny's life. She'd been surrounded by people, but except for the short periods of time when Sophie and Amanda had come by the mansion, she had felt completely alone. Soon it would all be over and the expectant relatives would return to their homes. She'd come to think of them as vultures, each one waiting to prey upon Grandfather's estate. Where had they been when he was alive? Most of them had been invisible, except on those occasions when they had wanted something.

The extended family was looked down upon by the immediate relatives, who knew they stood to gain much from Grandfather's passing. The three Broadmoor sons—Jonas, Quincy, and Langley—had always been the foundation for Hamilton Broadmoor's estate. That didn't keep second and third cousins from showing up to see how they might benefit, however.

Fanny had been appalled to actually find a collection of women she barely knew rummaging through the house, declaring which pieces they intended to ask for.

"I don't understand why we have to be here," Fanny said to her cousins. They sat on either side of her and waited, along with the rest of the family, for the reading of Grandfather's will.

"I don't, either," Amanda said, looking around. "I suppose it's some formality, but Father said that everyone was to be present."

"They just want to pick apart Grandfather's possessions and get what they can for themselves," Fanny said sadly. "They were never here for him or for anyone else. They hate one another and treat one another abominably. The only reason they came to the island each summer was to get what they could."

Sophie squeezed her hand. "Ignore them. They are undeserving of your concern. Grandfather was no fool."

"It's true," Amanda whispered. "He didn't brook nonsense, and there's nothing to suggest he will now."

"But he's dead. He has no say over anything anymore." Fanny fought back her tears. She couldn't help but wonder if this loss would signal the final demise of family as she knew it.

"If I know Grandfather," Sophie said, leaning close enough for them both to hear, "he will control this family long after he's in the ground. You mark my words."

"Is everyone present?" Mortimer Fillmore stood in the center of the library and looked around the room. Extra chairs had been carried into the room to provide seating for the family.

Uncle Jonas nodded. "I believe everyone was notified of the time and place for the reading. You may begin."

Fanny stared at the lawyer and decided he was probably close to the same age as old Mr. Snodgrass. She tentatively lifted her hand.

"This isn't a classroom, Fanny," Jonas said. "You need not raise your hand before speaking."

"Where is Grandfather's lawyer? Shouldn't he be reading the will?"

Mr. Fillmore's complexion paled. She hadn't meant to offend the man, but Mr. Rosenblume had been her grandfather's lawyer for many years. It seemed only proper that a member of the Rosenblume Law Office would be present today.

Her uncle frowned. "Since I am to be executor of the will, I have requested that my personal attorney handle the estate."

Fanny ignored the other relatives, who had by now begun to fidget in their chairs. "Did Grandfather inform you of your selection as executor before he died?"

"Yes, Fanny, he did. Now if you have no further questions, I believe the rest of us would like to proceed."

A hum of agreement filled the room. If she asked anything else, the shoestring relatives would likely toss her out on her ear. All eyes were fixed on the old lawyer. He walked to Grandfather's desk and sat down before he unsealed the thick, cream-colored envelope. He pressed the pages with his palm and faced the relatives one final time before he began. In a clear, crisp voice that belied his age, Mr. Fillmore first read a brief note to the family.

"I do not want or expect my family to mourn my death. I am at peace with my heavenly Father, and I do not desire any family members to drape their houses with black bunting and wreaths or to wear the mourning clothes dictated by society. Those we love should be honored and loved while alive. Few of you honored or loved me while I was alive, and I don't want the pretense of mourning now that I'm dead. You've all gathered to divide my money—not because you held me in high esteem; of that much I am certain. I have, however, placed a stipulation upon specific family members who will receive a portion of my estate. It is my specific direction—"

Mr. Fillmore coughed, cleared his throat, and poured a few inches of water from the glass pitcher. They waited with bated breath while he consumed the liquid.

"See, I told you. Grandfather was no fool," Sophie said, elbowing Fanny.

Fanny scooted forward on her chair, eager to hear her grandfather's stipulation. The money wasn't important. She expected her uncles to divide the lion's share of Grandfather's estate, while a few specific gifts would be distributed among close friends, loyal staff, and favorite charities.

"All of my family members who were expected to spend their summers on Broadmoor Island in the past shall continue to do so until the summer following Frances Jane Broadmoor's eighteenth birthday."

Angry stares were immediately directed at Fanny, and she slouched low in her chair.

Mr. Fillmore drummed his fingers across the wooden desk. "Please! If I may have your attention?" Thankfully, the relatives turned to face the lawyer.

"The usual exceptions will be allowed for illness, including childbirth. Once recovered, however, I will expect that person to rejoin the rest of the family. There is also the work provision for the men. They may come and go as needed but will spend at least a portion of the summer in residence on the Broadmoor Island. In their absence, their families will remain on the island."

The announcement was followed by several loud sighs. Uncle Jonas could be counted among those who thought the edict repugnant. "Let me see that." He walked around the desk and grabbed the letter from Mr. Fillmore's hand. "I should have known he'd find some way to torture us," he muttered, tossing the letter back across the desk.

Sophie giggled. "I told you Grandfather would continue to control this family."

"It is rather amusing," Amanda agreed, leaning across Fanny. "I've never seen my father turn that shade before. This most assuredly is a kick in the knickers for him."

Sophie's sister Beatrice waved her handkerchief toward Mr. Fillmore. "Does this mean that if we don't go to Broadmoor Island, we won't receive our inheritance?"

Amanda's eldest brother, Grayson, jumped up from his chair. "Exactly what makes you think *you're* going to receive an inheritance, Beatrice?"

"I'm merely inquiring how it's supposed to work, Grayson. You need not become defensive. I don't know any more about Grandfather's will than the rest of you do." She folded her arms across her chest and tightened her downcast lips into an angry frown.

"Beatrice plays the innocent, but I know from overhearing her that she's already making plans to add on to her house with her share of the inheritance," Sophie said, leaning closer to her cousins.

"But why should any of us expect that kind of thing?" Fanny whispered. "There are sons to receive their father's wealth. It seems pretentious that the grandchildren and distant relatives should expect something, as well."

"I think it's nonsense to have the island imposed upon us," someone behind Fanny muttered. Several other voices rose in agreement.

The reading wasn't going at all as Fanny had expected. The relatives continued to fire angry barbs while Mr. Fillmore rested his chin in his palm and stared across the desk. At this rate she wondered if they'd ever hear the remaining portions of Grandfather's will. Finally Uncle Jonas shouted above the din, and an uncomfortable silence fell across the room.

Mr. Fillmore picked up the letter. "If you'll remain silent, I'll continue." The last paragraph of Grandfather's letter explained that he intended for the family to continue the summer tradition of gathering at Broadmoor Island until Fanny's eighteenth birthday, where annual monetary distributions would be disbursed, a custom that had begun after Fanny's birth.

Grand-mère had wanted Fanny to spend time with her relatives each summer. In order to accomplish that feat, she convinced her husband to distribute an annual bonus from company profits each summer, but only to those who came to the island with their families. Fanny hadn't been privy to that bit of family information until two summers ago, when Jean, her cousin William's wife, had told her. In retrospect Fanny realized Jean had been angry and blamed Fanny that they must spend their summers on the island. Jean had wanted to go to the New Jersey coast with her own family, but William insisted she come to Broadmoor Island instead. She had been willing to forgo the bonus, but William wouldn't hear of it. Although Jean later apologized, Fanny remained uncomfortable in her presence, especially on Broadmoor Island.

Jonas gasped at Mr. Fillmore's revelation. "My father's *entire* estate will be divided into summer distributions? For how long?"

Mr. Fillmore shook his head. "Please, Jonas. If you would permit me to read the will, your questions will be answered."

The lawyer unfolded the document while Jonas dropped into a chair alongside the desk and waited. In a monotone voice, Mr. Fillmore read her grandfather's dying wishes. As Fanny anticipated, her grandfather had made a number of small bequests. Mr. Fillmore continued:

> "Other than the specific bequests, my entire estate shall be
> divided among my three sons, Jonas, Quincy, and Langley,
> as set forth below."

Mortimer continued to read the details necessary to obtain the distribution. Fanny could see that Uncle Jonas was not at all pleased. He had hoped, as had most, that the requirements would be abolished with the death of the family patriarch. And although seventy percent of the estate would be distributed as soon as possible to the beneficiaries, their remaining thirty percent would be received in yearly allotments—at Broadmoor Island—a plan they'd not anticipated. It appeared even Uncle Quincy wished it might have been otherwise.

When the chatter ceased, Mr. Fillmore read the next stipulation.

"My granddaughter Frances Jane Broadmoor shall be entitled to receive my son Langley Broadmoor's one-third share in its entirety."

"What?" Jonas jumped to his feet and sent his chair crashing to the floor. "Whatever was my father thinking? How could he possibly have done such a thing?" Fanny's uncle turned his full attention upon her. "She's not even an adult!" He directed his rage at Mr. Fillmore, but his anger was meant for Fanny. Anger that he'd be required to share his father's fortune—anger that she'd ever been born.

"There's more, Jonas. Please!" Mr. Fillmore pointed to the overturned chair.

"In the event my granddaughter Frances has not reached her age of majority at the time of my death, I hereby appoint my son Jonas Broadmoor to act as her guardian and trustee. Once Frances has reached her majority, she may elect to maintain Jonas as her advisor or select another person of her choosing."

Fanny gulped a deep breath. *Not Uncle Jonas.* She had figured as much but wished it could be otherwise. She knew Grandfather would choose his eldest son to handle any and all unpleasant details—herself included. Admittedly her uncle was a better choice than someone such as old Mr. Snodgrass, but Fanny would have preferred Uncle Quincy or even Grandfather's lawyer, Mr. Rosenblume. Uncle Jonas had never respected her father, especially not after he'd taken his own life. Fanny had heard more than one tirade about Langley Broadmoor's lack of spirit, strength, and admirable qualities. In fact, Jonas barely acknowledged Fanny in the aftermath of his brother's death. He'd wanted to send her away—remove her from sight. And now he would be in charge. He'd be a wretched substitute for her father and grandparents.

When Mr. Fillmore concluded, he carefully refolded the pages and looked up. He scanned the room. "Any questions?"

Shouted inquiries rang from every corner of the room and the many spaces in between. Mr. Fillmore waved the folded document overhead until the relatives quieted. "I'm unable to hear your questions with all of you talking at once. All necessary paper work will be filed with the court. I will contact you by letter, advising each beneficiary when you may expect payment. Unless you have questions beyond what I've told you, please feel free to depart."

Fanny turned to Amanda and then to Sophie. It suddenly began to dawn on her that they, too, might be offended at the provision Grandfather had made for her.

"I don't know what to say." She shook her head. "Please tell me that you don't hate me like the others do."

"Of course not, silly," Amanda declared.

"No. I was rather pleased. Now I have a wealthy cousin who will come of age in March and then treat us all to a very wonderful party."

"Sophie!" Amanda rebuked in a stilted tone. She glanced around her. "Don't speak in such a way here. Most of the family is fit to be tied. Your sister Beatrice looks as though she'd like to wring Fanny's neck."

Fanny met Beatrice's hateful stare and felt her strength wither. "Oh, I have a feeling Grandfather has managed to put me in a very difficult situation."

"Don't worry about Bea," Sophie said, offering her sister a smirk. "She complains the loudest, but she has no backbone. I can deal with her."

One by one family members got to their feet. The grumbling continued even as chairs scraped across the oak floors that surrounded the imported Turkish carpet her grandfather had always thought quite lovely. Fanny thought it rather ugly, but she'd never told him. And since it had been placed in Grandfather's library, she was certain Grand-mère also considered it unattractive. Otherwise she would have placed it in the center of the grand entry hall for visitors to admire. Today, however, the rug seemed different, not nearly as ugly as the character exhibited by the Broadmoor relatives.

While many of the family members scattered from the room, Uncle Jonas and Mr. Fillmore turned their backs. With their heads close together, they spoke in hushed tones.

"We might as well leave," Amanda said, getting to her feet.

"You two go ahead without me. I need to ask some questions," Fanny replied.

Amanda nodded. "Very well. We'll wait for you upstairs."

Fanny's mind whirled with the uncertainty of concerns that seemed to have no answers. The death of Grandfather had turned her entire world upside down. She wasn't even certain where she would live now. When the shuffles and murmurs ceased and the room was once again quiet, Uncle Jonas lifted his head.

His jowls sagged when he caught sight of her. "What is it you want, Fanny?"

"I have questions."

"*You?* Why, you're not even of legal age, Fanny. What questions could you possibly have that are important enough to detain Mr. Fillmore? I'm your guardian now, and I can see to any matter necessary."

Either her uncle's tone of voice or an interest in Fanny's questions brought several members of the immediate family scurrying back into the library like mice after a morsel of cheese. They folded their arms across their chests or sat on the edges of their chairs, their eyes shining with anticipation.

Fanny drew in a deep breath. "I'm wondering about my personal living arrangements. Not immediately, of course, for I realize the family will soon depart for the Thousand Islands. But afterward. With my schooling complete . . ."

"I don't know that I consider your schooling complete. There is college to consider. And I believe my father planned for you to begin your grand tour of Europe after summering at the islands. It is much too soon to make such determinations. Once decisions are completed regarding your future, you'll be advised."

An auburn curl escaped from her hairpins and curved alongside her cheek. "But I don't want to go on a grand tour. Grandfather said he would reconsider my wishes later this summer."

"She's an ungrateful orphan who doesn't deserve a third of the Broadmoor estate," Beatrice twittered.

Stunned, Fanny remained silent. Soon other family members added their angry opinions. To Fanny's amazement, most of them sided with Beatrice.

Fanny jumped to her feet and scanned the group, her gaze finally coming to rest upon Beatrice. "You act as though I've taken something that belonged to you, when in fact it belonged to none of us. Grandfather's wealth was his to distribute as he saw fit. I didn't ask to receive my father's share of the estate. And from what Mr. Fillmore has told us, there is ample money for distribution. I don't believe any family member is going to be forced into poverty. I don't see arguing over money as a way of honoring Grandfather."

Beatrice pinned her with an icy stare. "We could cease this squabbling, and you could honor Grandfather by giving up your inheritance, Fanny. I don't see why you think you should be entitled to an entire one-third of the estate."

Mr. Fillmore waved the bulky envelope containing her grandfather's will overhead. "People! There is no use arguing over distribution and who gets what. This will is valid, and its terms complete. If one of you attempts to have it set aside, I predict you will meet with utter and resounding failure." He peered over the glasses perched on the tip of his nose. "In addition, such legal action will delay any partial distributions of the estate—which is not something the majority of the beneficiaries will take lightly."

A clamor of voices echoed the lawyer's assessment while several family members glared at Fanny as though everything that had occurred were her fault. She startled when a hand touched her shoulder.

Her Aunt Victoria offered an encouraging smile. "You need to pack a few things, Fanny. You'll come home with us this evening."

"But I'll be fine here until we depart for the island. The servants will be here. There's truly no reason for me to—"

Uncle Jonas stepped to his wife's side, his brows knit together in an angry frown. "Must you argue about everything? This day has proved most stressful for the family, and you continue to add to the strife with your incessant questions and lack of cooperation."

"But I wasn't attempting to be obstinate. I merely thought it would be less disruptive if I remained here until we all depart for Broadmoor Island." Her shoulders slumped in defeat. "If you truly want me to pack and come to your house this evening, I'll go upstairs and put together the items I'll need for the night. I can return tomorrow and—"

"Please don't prattle on like a senile old woman, Fanny. Do as your aunt instructs." Her uncle turned on his heel and strode across the room toward Mr. Fillmore.

"Don't let him frighten you, dear. He's more bark than bite. What with the added responsibilities since your grandfather's death, he's become more abrupt." Her aunt grasped Fanny's elbow. "Do you need help?"

"Amanda and Sophie are waiting upstairs for me. They can assist me in packing."

Aunt Victoria nodded. "Try not to be too long. I'll send someone up to help you with your trunks."

Fanny made her way upstairs to the bedroom she had known for most of her life. It seemed strange to imagine that this house would no longer be her home. She entered the room to find Sophie and Amanda in a deep discussion.

"Oh good. You're here," Sophie said as she straightened.

"Not for long. Aunt Victoria has sent me up here to pack. Uncle Jonas insists that I come to live with them immediately."

"How grand," Amanda said. "You know we will have great fun. Just like at the island."

"But this is my home." Fanny sank to the bed. "Every memory I have is of this place."

"My comment was thoughtless," Amanda said in apology.

"But still, you don't want to just ramble around this big place alone," Sophie put in. "It might be very frightening—especially at night."

"I don't think I would ever be afraid here." Fanny looked around the room and felt tears come to her eyes once again. "Leaving here will be like leaving them all. Father. Grand-mère, and Grandfather. I don't know how I will bear it."

"We will bear it together," Amanda said softly. "Won't we, Sophie?"

"Absolutely. We've always been there for one another. Nothing is going to change now that you're far richer than the rest of us." She grinned.

"Sophie!"

Fanny actually smiled. "It's all right. I don't mind her teasing. It's the anger of the others that hurts me."

"Forget about them," Amanda said, getting to her feet. "Come on. Let's get you packed. There's nothing to be gained by standing here shedding tears. It won't change the fact that Grandfather is gone. We will all miss him, but perhaps none of us will miss him as much as you, dear Fanny."

Jonas leaned against his father's desk and waited until Victoria and his niece were well out of earshot. "We need to talk, Mortimer. My father's bequest to Fanny came as a shock."

The lawyer dropped into a chair opposite Jonas. "Obviously! Your behavior nearly set off a storm among the family. I must say I've never seen you lose control of your emotions at such a critical moment. You usually play your cards close to the vest, Jonas. Such restraint would have better served you today, also."

"I know. I know. But something must be done in regard to my father's bequest to Fanny. He blindsided me." Jonas attempted to hold his irritation in check.

Mortimer settled back in his chair. "How so?"

Several relatives gathered in the entrance hall, and Jonas couldn't be certain if they were bidding each other farewell or attempting to overhear his conversation with the lawyer. "Just one moment, Mortimer." He strode to the library door and waved to the gathered relatives before sliding the pocket door closed. He returned to his chair. "I'll be glad when they've all departed."

The lawyer retrieved his pocket watch and, after a glance, shoved it back into his vest. "You said your father had blind-sided you."

"Yes. He called me to his bedside last week and advised me that he'd made me executor of the will and Fanny's guardian and trustee until she reached her age of majority. Of course I agreed. The old man has been dying for years. I didn't count on him actually up and completing the process before Fanny's next birthday. I also didn't think to question how much of an inheritance he had left her. I assumed he would leave a small bequest—enough for her to make her grand tour and keep up appearances until she made a proper marriage. He certainly gave no indication she would receive a full third of his estate or that we'd be required to return to Broadmoor Island in order to receive final distribution. An abomination, as far as I'm concerned. The girl knows nothing about handling money. Is there no way my father's bequest can be set aside?"

"I'm afraid not, Jonas." Mr. Fillmore shook his head. "And have you considered the effect such behavior would cause throughout the community? You would appear an ogre who is attempting to take advantage of a poor defenseless young woman. There are other ways to overcome this bit of difficulty. We need only to plan a strategy and work within the purview of your father's will."

"What do you have in mind?"

"You know the girl much better than I. Does she trust you? Will she comply with your decisions? If not, we'll need to rely upon a more cunning method."

Jonas edged forward on his chair. "I have no doubt she'll be difficult. My father mentioned she'd likely object to the grand tour. Knowing Fanny, she'd much prefer to spend the remainder of her days living on Broadmoor Island. It's the place where she's most content—at least according to my father." Jonas tugged on his vest. "Unlike most young ladies, she's always enjoyed fishing and being outdoors. She knows every inch of Broadmoor Island like the back of her hand."

"If she goes on her grand tour, she'll be out of the way and you'll have full authority over her funds. We mustn't lose sight of the fact that an accounting to the court will be necessary. Good judgment in how we manage matters will be key." Mortimer massaged his forehead. "I believe you have several choices for your niece's future. With both of us considering all options, we'll arrive at the perfect solution. I'm confident of that."

For the first time since hearing the contents of his father's will, Jonas held out hope he could gain control of Fanny's bequest. Money that rightfully should be his! Money he needed to cover some rather bad investments. His irritation mounted at the remembrance that his father had given Fanny the same bequest that he, the eldest son of the family, had received. Never would he have believed his father would do such a thing. The girl obviously had a way about her if she'd enticed his father to leave her such an inheritance.

Then again, had he preceded his father in death, Jonas would have expected his father to divide his share of the estate among his family members. But this was different. His brother Langley hadn't been of much use during his lifetime, especially after his wife's death. And Jonas thought his parents had already done more than their share for Langley's daughter. They'd reared and educated Fanny since she was an infant, even though Langley had lived until Fanny turned eleven.

Langley was the one who had turned the girl's fancy toward the outdoors and encouraged her to try new things, even if they weren't considered completely appropriate for young ladies. Fanny had been threading worms onto fishing hooks from the age of five. When Jonas's wife had objected, Langley had simply brushed her comments aside. He professed a theory of permitting children the opportunity to explore the wonders of nature. Jonas considered his brother's theory no more than an excuse for lackadaisical child rearing. But then, Langley had remained apathetic about all important matters of life. He had cared little about money, power, or position; yet his daughter had received a full share in the estate. But not for long. Not if Jonas had his way in the matter.

Mortimer shoved the will inside his leather case. "Well, my friend, what do you think? Shall we banish the girl to Europe or to Broadmoor Island?"

"Let me think on it. Once we've transported the family to Broadmoor Island, I'll be better able to consider the best path to follow." Jonas leaned forward and rested his chin atop his tented fingers. "This situation seems entirely unfair. In all probability, Quincy will pour every cent of his inheritance into that charity of his. I don't know which problem is more irritating."

Mr. Fillmore raked his fingers through his thinning white hair. "I do understand your frustration, but I'm certain your father understood Quincy would donate his share toward the home. If he'd objected, your father could have easily placed conditions on the money or even written Quincy out of the will if he'd so desired. As Fanny's guardian and trustee of her estate, you'll have a much easier time if you concentrate on her and put aside any ill feelings toward Quincy. In fact, you might consider making him an ally."

5

Thus far, being at her aunt and uncle's home hadn't been nearly as uncomfortable as Fanny had anticipated. After Uncle Jonas's behavior during the reading of the will, she'd expected to be the object of his anger. Surprisingly, he'd proved most amiable during supper, even inquiring if she'd taken an interest in any young men. This was a topic that had made her the recipient of much teasing from both Jefferson and George throughout the remainder of the evening—at least until she and Amanda escaped upstairs.

The two girls curled into the comfortable chairs situated at the far end of Amanda's bedroom. Victoria Broadmoor had objected to the easy chairs, stating they were far too masculine for a young lady's sitting room. But Amanda had successfully argued that once upholstered in rose and beige silk damask, they would be perfect. Fanny was glad her cousin had won the argument, for the chairs were far more comfortable than the straight-back, open-arm chairs in her own rooms at Broadmoor Mansion.

"I'm pleased you agreed to come and stay with us until we leave for the island. I find it a great comfort. It's so terribly sad to lose the people we love," Amanda said with a sigh.

"I'm glad I didn't remain at the mansion, too. I know I would have been lonely." Fanny tucked her legs beneath her and rearranged her skirts. Aunt Victoria would certainly disapprove of the unladylike position. "I'm thankful your father was more pleasant at supper. He nearly frightened me to death when he knocked over his chair at the reading of the will this afternoon."

"His reaction *was* startling. I asked Mother about it, and she said he sometimes acts strange when he's caught off guard. She attributed his offensive behavior to grief over Grandfather's death and the unexpected contents of the will."

Fanny didn't argue. Perhaps Aunt Victoria was correct and her uncle was suffering from grief. If so, he'd quickly recovered, for he'd been all smiles at the supper table while quizzing her about any beaus and the possibility of her grand tour. Neither topic interested Fanny in the least. "I was pleased your father at least mentioned my love of Broadmoor Island. He didn't seem overly put off when I suggested remaining there year-round. Do you think he might agree?"

"Oh, Fanny, don't be silly. He didn't argue at the supper table, but I don't believe either of my parents would agree to such an arrangement. And why would you want to live on the island during the winter? There's nobody there except the help. What would you do with yourself once the cold weather set in?"

"The Atwells are there, and Michael would take me ice fishing. I could help him with the chores. I'm certain I could find plenty to keep me busy."

"You? Doing chores? Will you milk the cows or perhaps feed the chickens?" Amanda's lilting laughter filled the room.

Fanny folded her arms across her chest. "I can do those things. You forget I've spent much more time on the island than the rest of you. I could milk a cow years ago, and I learned to gather eggs without being pecked by the hens, too."

"Well, those are accomplishments all young ladies of society want to list among their credentials. *Really*, Fanny. I do understand that you're not interested in the social life of the family, but milking cows is carrying the matter too far."

"And what do you think you'll be required to do if you truly want to work with the less fortunate? Or have you changed your mind since traveling abroad?"

Amanda shook her head. Fanny was mystified when her cousin's blond tresses remained perfectly in place. Why wouldn't her hair cooperate like Amanda's?

"I haven't changed my mind in the least, but I don't consider charitable work on the same level as milking cows and feeding chickens." Amanda patted her head. "And why are you staring at my hair? Does it need to be brushed and refashioned?"

"Quite the contrary. There's not a strand out of place." Fanny cupped her chin in her hand. "Tell me what you've planned for your future. I'm interested to hear about the work you're thinking about."

"Nothing is laid out just yet. Mother has agreed she'll talk to some of her friends who are involved in several of her charitable causes. Of course everything will hinge on what Father says. He's permitted Mother to have her freedom working with her ladies' aid groups and the like, but now that I've returned from my grand tour, he seems determined I should wed." Amanda shivered. "And most of the men he's suggested are either simpletons or bores."

"Likely sons of his wealthy business associates," Fanny said. "Did you tell him of your dream to perform charitable work?"

"Yes, but he says there's plenty of time for that after I wed. He pointed to Mother as a prime example, saying she's been involved in more good works than most unmarried women."

"Have you ever considered the fact that your mother is more suited to Uncle Quincy than to your father?"

Amanda jolted upright in her chair. "*What?* No. I can't even imagine such a thing!"

"Well, it's true. They both believe in giving of their time and money to aid those less fortunate, while your father is interested only in his business success and accumulating a vast fortune. He disdains those of lesser social position and wealth. He never exhibited love for my father, and he holds Uncle Quincy in low esteem. I think the reason he permits your mother to perform her charity work is because he can take credit for her good works. His name is automatically attached to the many hours she devotes to working with the underprivileged."

Amanda frowned. "You make him sound simply dreadful. He can be caustic, but he is esteemed in the community. And he donates money to charity," she defended.

"I suppose I was a bit harsh, but I've given you points that could bolster your argument. Explain that your good works would bring additional prestige to the family name, but that prestige would go to your husband if you were to wed—along with a sizable dowry, I'd venture. If all else fails, you could insist you'd prefer college over wedding plans."

Amanda sighed. "I do wish Father would put forth as much effort finding wives for Jefferson and George. After all, they're older than I."

"But they act like young hooligans, what with their silly pranks and constant teasing. It seems they've become even more immature since they've been away at college. I would think your father would tire of their unruly behavior."

Amanda shrugged. "He hears little of their antics. He's gone most of the time, and Mother says she doesn't want to upset him with such trivial matters. She insists he has more important issues weighing on his mind."

"When Mrs. Donaldson discovers your brothers are the ones who have frightened her young sons by donning sheets and pretending to be ghosts, I doubt she'll consider their behavior trivial."

"Are you certain my brothers were involved?"

Fanny bobbed her head. "I heard them talking with some of their friends after the funeral service the other day. They're planning a return to the Donaldsons' tomorrow evening. All of them think it's great sport scaring those little fellows. I wish we could think of some way to turn the tables on them."

Amanda tapped her chin. "With a little thought, perhaps we can."

"Fanny! Wake up! I've come up with a plan." Sunlight poured through the east window of Amanda's second-floor bedroom.

Fanny rubbed her eyes and sat up on the edge of the bed. "Plan for what?"

"My brothers. How we can even the score for the Donaldson children." Amanda waved her forward. "Come and look."

Fanny shoved her feet into her slippers and padded to the window. She peered into the garden and then looked at her cousin. "What am I supposed to be looking at?"

"Do you see old Henry whitewashing that fence out near the far flower garden?"

Fanny nodded. She wished her cousin would come to the point. Her brain was still fuzzy from lack of sleep. They'd stayed up last night talking and giggling until the wee hours of the morning. Now Amanda wanted her to wake up and immediately solve some silly puzzle about one of the servants whitewashing the fence.

"I'm going to have Henry give me some of that whitewash. After my brothers sneak out of the house tonight, I'll convince Marvin to help us rig it up above the back door. When they return home, they won't need sheets to turn them into ghosts." Her eyes sparkled. "What do you think?"

The plan delighted Fanny, but she doubted whether Marvin, the butler, would be inclined to help them. The man was as rigid as the bristles on a brand-new scrub brush. "I like your plan, but what if Marvin won't help? We could be the ones who end up doused in whitewash."

"Don't fret. Marvin will help us. Now let's get dressed and go tell Henry to make certain he has plenty of that whitewash left over for us."

The entire day had been filled with the excitement evoked by a mixture of fear and anticipation. As Amanda had predicted, Marvin agreed to lend his help and meet them in the kitchen at exactly ten o'clock. Thankfully Aunt Victoria and Uncle Jonas had retired to their rooms earlier in the evening. Now that the designated hour had arrived, the girls silently picked their way down the back stairs. Fanny struggled to stifle the laughter bubbling deep in her throat. She clung to Amanda's hand until they finally reached the kitchen, where Marvin stood at the ready.

"Well, ladies, are you prepared for this bit of folly?" His shoulders were stretched into formal alignment as he addressed them. "Not rethinking your decision, are you?"

The girls shook their heads in unison. Amanda pointed to the bucket of whitewash. "My brothers deserve to receive their comeuppance. Frightening small children isn't humorous in the least. The next time they consider such a plan, I believe they'll remember what happened to them tonight."

Marvin nodded and pulled a ladder near the back door. "As you wish, Miss Amanda. Once I've secured the ropes and this board to the transom, you can hand me the bucket." The two girls craned their necks and watched as Marvin fitted a board between the knotted sling he'd created with the ropes and secured them above the doorway. He stepped down and tested the device several times before making his final ascent on the ladder. After retrieving the bucket from Amanda, he placed the pail of whitewash strategically atop the board.

After descending the ladder, he tipped his head back for one final look and then gave a firm nod. "I believe that will serve your purpose quite nicely, miss."

Amanda agreed. "Now all we must do is wait."

"Which is sometimes the most difficult thing of all," Marvin said. "If you'll excuse me, I believe I'll turn in for the night and permit you ladies to maintain your watch."

"Yes, of course," Amanda said. "And thank you for your help, Marvin. We couldn't have done it without you."

Marvin grinned. "Let's make that our little secret, shall we? I wouldn't want to incur the wrath of your father for aiding in this tomfoolery."

Amanda glanced at her cousin. "Our lips are sealed."

"Absolutely," Fanny agreed and touched her index finger to her lips.

After a final instruction that they should turn out the lights, Marvin retreated up the stairs, and the girls began their vigil in earnest. The minutes ticked by slowly as they listened for any unusual sounds near the back of the house.

"You don't think they'll return and use the front door of the house, do you? Or perhaps they've devised some way of crawling through an upstairs window and we'll end up sitting on these steps all night." Fanny grimaced. "The joke would surely be on us if that occurred."

Amanda shifted on the hard wooden step. "No. They'll come in this way. I'm certain of it."

Though she wished they could see a clock from their vantage point, Fanny was certain at least two hours had passed since Marvin's departure. Her backside ached, and she wanted to go up to bed. Her cousins were likely spending the night with some of their friends. Just as she opened her mouth to suggest they call off their prank, Amanda nudged her.

"Listen! I hear voices. It's them." Fanny clutched Amanda's hand in a death grip.

Amanda squeezed back until Fanny thought the bones in her hand would break. "That's my *father's* voice. He's with them." Amanda's gaze fastened on the door, her eyes now as big as saucers. "What are we going to do?"

"Maybe it's not—"

Amanda wagged her head. "It *is* him. I know my own father's voice. Do you think we have time to stop them?"

"Let's pray the boys walk in the door—"

Before she could complete the sentence, the back door opened. Just as Marvin had predicted, the whitewash descended like a milky shower from heaven. Only instead of dousing her cousins, Uncle Jonas was the surprised recipient.

He sputtered and gasped, his arms flailing while the whitewash poured over him.

The girls considered running up the stairs, but Jefferson had already spotted them. "Look what you've done, Amanda and Fanny," he chided in a loud voice. He stood behind his father, grinning like a silly schoolboy, obviously delighted by their plight.

Amanda jumped to her feet. "I'm so sorry, Father. It was a silly attempt to put Jefferson and George in their place. I thought you had retired for the night, and we heard the boys talk about frightening the Donaldson children, and . . ."

Her father yanked his spectacles from the bridge of his nose. "Do cease your prattling and fetch me a towel, Amanda."

Once he'd removed his jacket and wiped off a portion of the whitewash, Uncle Jonas pointed the girls to the table. "Sit down and explain." He turned toward his sons. "And you two sit down at that end of the table."

One look at Uncle Jonas was enough to deduce that if their scheme had gone according to plan, they would have achieved perfection. Fanny's older cousins would have turned into ghosts. Instead, her uncle was glowering at the two of them and awaiting a full explanation.

"I'll let you tell him," Fanny whispered to her cousin. After all, the plan *had* been Amanda's idea, and Uncle Jonas was unhappy enough with Fanny already.

All of them focused on Amanda while she explained how the entire scheme had been formulated in order to teach Jefferson and George a lesson and force them to quit harassing the young Donaldson boys. "How were we to know you would be with Jefferson and George? If only one of them had entered the door first."

"Well, they didn't. And what makes you think that you need to take charge of supervising your brothers and their behavior? I am well equipped to manage such matters without your intervention. Your brothers had already been strongly chastised before our return home."

"But how did you know what they were up to?"

"Mrs. Donaldson spoke to me before she departed the other day. She apprised me of your brothers' pranks, and I had gone to confront them in the midst of their frivolity this evening. All had been resolved, until this." Uncle Jonas gestured toward the dripping whitewash.

"What on earth is all the commotion down here? Oh, dear me, Jonas! You look like a ghost." Aunt Victoria clapped a hand to her mouth and shook her head. "What has happened to you? I thought you went out to put a stop to all these pranks, and now I find you've joined in. I never would have believed my husband—"

"Oh, forevermore, Victoria. I've been caught in a prank set up by your daughter and niece. I'll explain when we get upstairs. For now, I suggest we all get a few hours of sleep before the kitchen staff comes downstairs to prepare breakfast. I don't want them to find me sitting here with this painted face."

Aunt Victoria removed several dishcloths from one of the drawers and dampened them with water. "You children run along to bed. I'm going to help your father."

Amanda and Fanny didn't hesitate. They raced up the back stairs at breakneck speed, with Jefferson and George not far behind, both of the young men chuckling over the girls' blunder. When Amanda reached her bedroom door, she turned around and pointed her finger at her brothers. "Don't think you've had the last laugh. We have two months at the island, you know."

Jefferson chortled. "I believe these girls are throwing down the gauntlet and offering us a challenge, George." He offered a mock salute. "To an exciting and entertaining summer, dear ladies."

Fanny and Amanda watched them swagger down the hallway. This would, indeed, be a summer of challenges.

Fanny twirled in front of her cousin. "I think this dress will do just fine."

Amanda pointed to the pink sash that surrounded the waist of her own pastel foulard dress. "If you don't mind wearing last year's frock, who am I to object? Would you tie my sash?"

While Amanda watched in the mirror, Fanny tied the sash in a proper bow. "I don't see why a new frock is needed to attend church and the Independence Day festivities."

"I think the celebration is a perfect excuse for purchasing a new dress. You merely dislike going for fittings, so you're willing to wear your old dresses. Grand-mère would be most unhappy with you," Amanda said. "She didn't approve of appearing at a public function in the same gown."

"No one remembers what I wore last year. You wouldn't have known if I hadn't told you. I do wish your father would let us attend some of the other celebrations in town after the parade. I don't know why the family always insists upon immediately returning to East Avenue. I hear the celebration at Brown Square is great fun. Sophie said some of her friends are going there. She plans to sneak off and join them. I wish we could, too."

"We'd be found out for certain. Sophie doesn't have to worry about getting into trouble because Uncle Quincy seldom knows where she is. Sometimes I don't think he even cares. On the other hand, my mother and father won't let me out of their sight for a moment. There should be some sort of balance, don't you think?"

Fanny agreed. She would love just a taste of the freedom Sophie enjoyed. Not that she wanted to run amok and stay out late, but she would like to see some of the things Sophie had mentioned—like all of the girls removing their stockings and dipping their feet in the wading pool that Sophie referred to as the mud pit. Hearing the German musicians play their accordions and seeing them dressed in their lederhosen while celebrating the independence of the United States would be great fun. Sophie had enthusiastically told Fanny of the beer drinking, singing, and laughter that continued until well after midnight. Perhaps she and Amanda could steal away for just a little while during the early evening hours. Then again, she knew they wouldn't be brave enough to do anything so daring.

Aunt Victoria stood at the foot of the staircase, wearing a pale green corded silk dress with a square yoke of white chiffon. White ospreys and pale green ribbons adorned the fancy straw hat—a perfect match for her gown. "Come along, girls. We're going to be late for church. The carriage is waiting." She stopped midstep and inspected Fanny's dress. "Isn't that last year's frock? I thought you told me you had a dress for today's festivities."

Fanny shrugged. "It's perfectly fine. No one will know I wore it last year."

Her aunt frowned. "*I* knew. The dress is out of fashion. I don't want people thinking your Uncle Jonas isn't treating you well."

"If you hear any of the local gossips prattling, you may send them my way and I will set things aright."

Aunt Victoria tapped her index finger on her chin. "Amanda has another new gown. Perhaps we have time for you to change." She glanced at the grandfather clock.

"Mother! You can't give away my new gown." Amanda folded her arms across her chest. "Besides, it wouldn't fit. Fanny is shorter, and the dress would drag on the ground."

Her aunt waved them toward the door. "I suppose there's nothing to do then but hold our heads up and pretend that all is well."

"All *is* well, Aunt Victoria. We need not pretend," Fanny replied as she looped arms with her aunt and proceeded down the front steps. "Will Sophie and Uncle Quincy be meeting us?"

"I invited them, but Quincy didn't respond to my note. That man is in a world of his own. And who knows where Sophie will be. Certainly not her father. You girls keep an eye out for Sophie at church this morning. If you see her, tell her she's expected at the family festivities this evening. Uncle Jonas has arranged for a spectacular fireworks display."

"That's what he said last year," Amanda commented.

Her mother held her finger to her lips. "Shh. It wasn't your father's fault that the fireworks didn't arrive. There was some mistake in the order or some such thing, but he's told me the fireworks arrived last week, and he's arranged for them to be discharged once it turns dark. It's going to be great fun."

"They have fireworks and Japanese lanterns and music at Brown Square. And the children play in the wading pool, too," Fanny said.

Her aunt regarded her with a stern expression. "Very unsanitary, Fanny. And who's been telling you about the activities at Brown Square?"

"Some of the servants were discussing the festivities," Amanda replied.

"The servants need to cease their chattering and tend to their duties. They have more than enough to keep them busy, what with preparing food for the picnic and guests this evening."

"And packing our belongings to depart for the island. I can hardly wait. I do wish I could go with the servants on Tuesday." Fanny sighed.

Her uncle assisted the three women into the carriage. "I thought you ladies were never going to join me. At this rate we're going to be late for church, and you know how I dislike making an entrance. Where are Jefferson and George?"

"Don't fret, dear. They departed earlier and said they'd meet us at church."

"Likely story. Those boys are going to be the death of me."

While the coach traversed the short distance to the church, Uncle Jonas continued muttering to his wife about the behavior of his two youngest sons. If Jefferson and George weren't at church, there was little doubt they would incur their father's wrath.

Fanny thought that would be a delightful turn of events, considering the whitewash episode two weeks earlier.

"Uncle Jonas certainly seems pleased with himself," Fanny murmured as she scooted closer to Amanda on the garden settee.

A burst of silver shot up overhead and sprayed out against the black skies. The little children clapped and cheered while the adults oohed and ahhed. The fireworks had truly been amazing, and now as the evening's festivities were nearly over, Fanny was sorry for it all to end.

"Everything has gone off as scheduled," Amanda replied. He's always pleased when he has charge of everything." She leaned back and sighed. "It has been a very pleasant day, to be sure."

"I agree. I prefer celebrating the Fourth at the island, but this was quite grand," Fanny admitted. "I ate too much, however."

"It's hard not to when there are so many delightful delicacies to choose from."

"Especially the iced creams. Goodness, but I had to sample a bit of each one," Fanny said rather shamefully.

Amanda laughed. "As did I."

A yelp from Jefferson caused everyone to take note. One of the lit fireworks had fallen over, and when it erupted, it sent sparks into the few remaining fireworks near Jefferson's feet. It was only a moment before everything was firing off at once and flames were burning up the paper wrappings.

"Grab a bucket of water," Amanda ordered Fanny, "and follow me."

There were many well-placed buckets around the gathering, and everyone raced for them at once. They knew that keeping the fire under control was critical, and plenty of water had been made available for just such a purpose.

Jefferson grabbed a bucket offered by his mother and put out the bulk of the flames right away. George followed suit, dousing much of the remaining fire, while their father, too, cast a bucket of water.

Amanda came up behind Jefferson, who already had another bucket in hand. She motioned to Fanny and pointed at George. Grinning, she nodded and Fanny immediately figured out her game.

Without warning, the girls tossed the water, drenching George and Jefferson. The young men gave such loud cries of protest that Victoria immediately worried they were injured.

"Have you been burned?" she called out.

Jefferson turned to face his sister. Water dripped down the side of his face. "Not burned, but nearly drowned."

"I'm so sorry, brother dear. I was attempting to cast water onto the flames," Amanda said innocently.

"Yes, we were just trying to be helpful," Fanny agreed.

"Of course," George said, narrowing his eyes ever so slightly. "Just like we're going to be helpful in return."

"Boys, get inside and change those clothes before you catch your death," Victoria instructed. Fanny thought she detected a hint of a smile on her aunt's lips. "Girls, I suggest you avoid trying to help with the fire next time."

Amanda and Fanny grinned. "But of course, Mother," Amanda replied as she looped her arm with Fanny's. "At least until our aim improves."

"I'd say your aim was just fine," her mother said with a wink.

6

Monday, July 5, 1897
Broadmoor Island

Even though there were many duties that required Michael
Atwell's attention, the hours couldn't pass quickly enough for
him. He would work day and night to complete the necessary
tasks if it would hasten Fanny's arrival at the island. While most
of the island staff dreaded the return of the Broadmoor family,
Michael counted the minutes until their return—at least until
Fanny arrived. The influx of the family meant added work for
all of the staff, but Michael knew he would find ample time to
spend with Fanny.

From her early years, Fanny had been different from the rest
of the Broadmoor family. She hadn't cared that Michael was
the son of the hired help or that his status could never match
that of the Broadmoors. She had taken to Michael and then
to his parents, treating them as though they were family and
exhibiting a fondness for Frank and Maggie Atwell that amazed
Michael.

"There you are!" Michael's mother stood in the doorway of the kitchen. "There's no time for daydreaming. The family will be arriving this week and there's much to be done. Come in and help me rearrange some of this furniture." Michael strode toward her, his mass of wavy brown hair tucked beneath his cap. "And take off that cap when you cross the threshold, young man."

He grinned and doffed the flat-billed cap. "I'm twenty-one years old, Ma. I know to remove my hat when coming indoors."

"Then why is it I find you sitting at my table drinking coffee with your cap atop your head from time to time?" She didn't wait for his answer. He knew she didn't expect one. His mother was more concerned with all the work that must be accomplished in a short time.

Though Michael and his parents remained on the island year-round, the remaining servants who would care for the needs of the Broadmoor family would arrive either a day in advance or with the members of the family. The servants' quarters would easily accommodate the twenty staff members, but for Michael, the added staff created an air of discomfort. Even as a child, he'd considered the separate servants' quarters to be his home. And now that he was older and in charge of the Broadmoor vessels, he'd developed a sense of ownership over the boathouse, along with the skiffs, canoes, and steam launch housed within its confines.

The granite and wood-framed servants' quarters didn't begin to compare with the six-story, fifty-room stone castle where the family resided during their visits, but Michael possessed no feelings of ownership for the castle. Unlike the servants' quarters, he found Broadmoor Castle cold and uninviting—overindulgent, like most of those who would inhabit the rooms throughout the summer months. Like Mr. Broadmoor, the castle loomed large. A huge flag bearing the family coat of arms flew from the castle's turret and could be distinguished among the islands that had become known to tourists and locals alike as the Thousand Islands. In truth, the copious islands varied in size and shape and numbered far more than a thousand. So numerous were the land masses that began at the river's mouth and continued downriver for nearly fifty miles, even the locals couldn't always be counted upon to distinguish the international boundary line between New York State and Ontario, Canada.

While most of the servants, including his mother, spent long hours in the castle, the bulk of his father's time was committed to the grounds and the separate stone edifice that housed the coal-fired, steam-powered electric generator. An addition to Broadmoor Island that allowed for even greater elegance, the generator fully electrified both the castle and the servants' quarters, something not many in the islands could boast. But the permanent residents of the area hadn't failed to note that most were beginning to follow Mr. Broadmoor's lead to electrify. Likely anxious to keep both their image of wealth intact and their complaining wives happy, Michael suspected. It seemed it was either one or the other that caused these wealthy island owners to continue in their attempts to outdo their peers. If one purchased a larger launch or hired additional servants, others followed suit by the summer's end.

He'd found only Fanny to be different from the rest. Though she dressed in the same fine clothes and attended the required parties and social gatherings of the elite, she much preferred donning a pair of ill-fitting trousers, tucking her hair beneath an old cap, and fishing for hours in one of the boats. His blood raced as he contemplated seeing her once again.

"Michael!" His mother's voice echoed in the vast room. "Quit your daydreaming and help me move this divan. We don't have time to lollygag. There are supplies that need to be brought over from Clayton once we finish with this furniture."

Michael would be glad to escape the confines of the island and pick up supplies. Though he routinely visited Clayton, the flourishing village situated on the New York shoreline, he'd been relegated to the island for the past week, helping with the myriad preparations. The thought of taking the launch to Clayton was enough to keep him following his mother's directions at a steady pace for the remainder of the morning.

His mother surveyed the rooms and then returned to the entry hall. "We'll eat dinner, and then you can go over to Clayton. And don't plan on spending the afternoon visiting with the locals or the fishermen. I need those supplies back here so I can begin preparations."

Michael followed his mother out the front door of the castle. "If you would have sent me this morning, I'd already be back."

She shook her head. "And I'd still have all that furniture to uncover and move into place when you returned." She looped arms with her son and held his gaze with her hazel eyes. "I know you're anxious for Fanny's return, but you need to remember that she's all but a grown woman now. The two of you can't continue to go off by yourselves, fishing and reading books and the like. It's not proper. You didn't heed my counsel last summer, and I can already see the glimmer in your eyes every time her name is mentioned. She's not yours for the having, Michael. Those people are in a different class from us. You'll have no more than a broken heart when all is said and done."

His mother's words stung, and he turned away. "Fanny and I have been friends for years. She's not like the rest of them. You know that."

"She's a sweet, kind girl. I'll not disagree on that account, but she's still not available to the likes of a caretaker's son. I don't want any trouble."

Michael kicked a small rock. "There won't be any trouble, but I'll not agree to ignoring Fanny, either. She's a friend, and I look forward to seeing her again."

His mother sighed and waved him inside. He was thankful she didn't argue further. He didn't want a windy discussion to ensue, for it would delay his trip to Clayton.

Michael steered the steam launch into the bay and docked at the Fry Steam Launch Company pier. After securing the boat, he peeked inside, offered a quick hello to Bill Fry, and headed off toward Warnoll's Meat Market. He'd leave his list and come back to pick up the cuts his mother had ordered once he'd completed the remainder of the shopping. He nodded and spoke to several acquaintances as he made his way to the market.

"Morning, Albert," Michael said while he ambled toward the large counter. He shoved the list in Albert's direction.

Albert took the paper and glanced at the order. "Guess this means the Broadmoors are coming after all. Right?"

Michael frowned. "Why wouldn't they be coming?"

"With old Mr. Broadmoor dying, folks was speculating whether the family would return this summer. None of them seemed particularly fond of the island. We just thought maybe—"

"Wait! What did you say about Mr. Broadmoor?"

Mr. Warnoll arched his brows. "That he's dead?" He studied Michael for a moment. "You mean you folks didn't know?"

Michael shook his head. "When did this happen, and how come nobody let us know?" Word traveled quickly from island to island, and Michael didn't understand how this important bit of news could have bypassed them.

"Everyone figured the family had advised the staff. When we didn't see any of you in the village, we thought you might be observing your own period of mourning or some such thing. We didn't want to intrude."

Michael wasn't certain why Albert thought they'd be in mourning out on the island, but the fact that everyone else knew Mr. Broadmoor was dead and the servants on his island hadn't been advised was baffling. Why hadn't the family sent word? Since they hadn't contacted the island staff, did that mean they were coming as scheduled, or had they assumed word would somehow reach the island and the staff would realize they wouldn't arrive? Michael was nonplussed by the odd behavior.

"Do you still want me to fill the order, Michael?"

"I suppose so. I'll assume they're still coming since we haven't had any word advising us to the contrary. They'll expect the larder to be stocked if they arrive."

The man nodded. "And empty if they don't. I'll get busy on your order. Should have it ready for you in an hour."

"I'll be back then. I've got to fill an order at the general store and pick up some items at the drugstore." Michael pulled his folded cap from his back pocket and headed out the door. "And cut those chops nice and thick the way my ma likes them," he called over his shoulder.

Mr. Warnoll's hearty chuckle filled the room. "I'll see to it. I don't want your mother coming in here and giving me a lecture on how to cut a proper lamb chop."

Michael waved to Mr. Hungerford as he passed the plumbing and tinware store and offered greetings to several men visiting outside the Hub Café with Mr. Grapotte, the owner.

"My condolences to you folks. I'm sure things will be different now that Mr. Broadmoor's passed on." Mr. Grapotte stroked his whiskers and shook his head.

"I suppose they will," Michael replied. He didn't intend to tell others that today was the first he'd known of Mr. Broadmoor's death. He still didn't know exactly when his employer had died.

"Family still arriving?"

"Far as we know. Got to keep moving. I've got a list a mile long." He waved the piece of paper and hurried onward.

By the time he'd filled the lists and the launch had been loaded, Michael was exhausted. Not from the work itself but from fielding the many questions and comments from the village residents. He knew they meant well. The death of someone such as Mr. Broadmoor was no small thing in this village. He had been, after all, one of the wealthiest men in all of New York State and an elite member of the Thousand Islands community. Before making his final visit to Mr. Warnoll's, Michael stopped by the newspaper office and purchased a copy of *On the St. Lawrence,* the edition that had announced Mr. Broadmoor's death. Michael felt the need to have tangible proof before he carried such shocking news home to his parents.

He attempted to formulate some simple yet straightforward way to break the news to them as he crossed the water in the *Daisy-Bee,* the name Mr. Broadmoor had christened the launch—in memory of his wife, he'd announced after purchasing the boat last summer. Several of the family members had been offended, but Mr. Broadmoor had insisted his wife would have enjoyed the tribute. With great fanfare, he'd had the name painted in large gold and black letters across both sides of the hull and then commanded the presence of the entire family and staff when he broke a bottle of champagne across the boat's prow and formally christened his steamer the *DaisyBee*. Michael didn't care what Mr. Broadmoor named the boat as long as he was the one who would have the pleasure of guiding her over the waters of the St. Lawrence River. Against his better judgment, Michael had been forced on occasion to hand over the helm to some of the younger male members of the Broadmoor family, who then insisted upon showing their prowess to young female passengers on the boat. Infrequent as those instances had been, Michael always dreaded having Jefferson and George Broadmoor aboard—especially when they were imbibing.

He guided the steamer past Calumet Island, where Charles Emery's castlelike home, constructed of Potsdam sandstone, sat directly opposite the village of Clayton. Folks said Mr. Emery, one of the partners who had formed the American Tobacco Company, decided to build his new house on Calumet Island and provide a view for Clayton residents that would rival George Pullman's Castle Rest on Pullman Island. Some thought Mr. Emery had succeeded, for his was the first large castle-type home that ships would see as they headed downriver from Lake Ontario. Michael wasn't so sure a winner could be declared, for the castled structures hadn't yet ceased to rise out of the water. Inspired by Pullman, other giants of industry had purchased islands and established magnificent homes for themselves in what they now dubbed their summer playground. George Boldt of Waldorf-Astoria fame, Frederick Bourne, president of the Singer Sewing Machine Company, Andrew Schuler, owner of Schuler's Potato Chips, and many other wealthy capitalists now descended upon the Thousand Islands every summer. Life on these islands continued to change—a transformation in progress.

Once downriver, Michael turned toward Broadmoor Island, the island that had been his home since birth. He knew every inch of this two-mile-long island like the back of his hand. Since his early years, he'd explored the dog bone–shaped island with its sloping lawns that led to the docks and its craggy ten-foot-high seawall that protected Broadmoor Castle as it towered toward the heavens. Now he wondered if his days on this island were numbered. With Mr. Broadmoor's death, the family would possibly sell the island. Few of them enjoyed this magnificent treasure, and Michael knew wealthy men would be willing to pay a generous sum for the palatial summer home of Hamilton Broadmoor.

He docked the boat and glanced toward the house. His mother had been watching for him, for she was already picking her way down the path to the boathouse. Moving with haste, he lifted the bundles of food and dry goods onto the dock, where he would transfer them into a cart for transport to the residence. It would take several trips, but the cart would be easier than attempting to carry all of the items in cumbersome baskets.

"I was beginning to worry," his mother called out when she neared the boat.

He bit his tongue. No need to remind her how many items she'd requested or how long it took Mr. Warnoll to fill her massive order for roasts and chops.

"Did you pick up the mail?"

"I did, though that reminder wasn't on your list." He pecked her cheek with a fleeting kiss.

His mother extended her arm, and he handed her the bundle of mail. If she was looking for a letter from Broadmoor Mansion, she'd find nothing there. He'd already checked. She riffled through the mail while he loaded the cart, always careful to keep the newspaper hidden from view.

By the time he had unloaded the final cart of goods, his mother was already scurrying about the kitchen, arranging the new supplies in their proper locations and checking to make certain he'd purchased every item in the quantity requested.

"So far I haven't found any mistakes." She lifted her chin and gave him a smile.

Without fanfare he spread the paper across the table in front of his mother and pointed to the picture of Hamilton Broadmoor. She gasped and dropped into a nearby chair.

7

Tuesday, July 6, 1897

They didn't need to worry long. Early the next morning, Mr. Simmons from the telegraph office arrived by boat with a message that servants from the Rochester mansion would begin arriving that afternoon. Michael was instructed to meet the train and transport the servants and the family's trunks to the island. Unlike some of the summer residents, who transported their riding horses and milking cows to their homes each summer, the Broadmoors' two riding horses as well as the farm stock were kept at the island year-round, expediting the process of moving their goods to the island. With the arrival of the servants several days in advance, the family's clothing would be pressed and hung in their wardrobes, menus would be planned, and the individual needs and desires of each family member would be met prior to their coming.

Michael was waiting outside the Clayton station when the train from Rochester hissed and jolted to a stop. He would have no difficulty recognizing at least some of the Broadmoor staff. Each year several new servants arrived with those stalwart members of the staff who were expected to spend each summer at the island, regardless of their families back home. Michael's mother always looked forward to reuniting with some of them. No doubt his mother's favorite, Kate O'Malley, would be among those arriving. As head housekeeper at Broadmoor Mansion, Mrs. O'Malley's presence was expected. Maggie Atwell and Kate had become good friends over the years. Yet not good enough friends that Kate had written to inform them of Mr. Broadmoor's death, he thought while watching the housekeeper detrain.

He waved his cap and headed across the tracks. "Welcome, Mrs. O'Malley. The launch is in its usual place. I'll see to the baggage if you want to direct your staff."

"Good afternoon, Michael. It's good to see you." She waved the other members of the party together. "I trust your parents are well."

"We would have sent word if anything were amiss." He had hoped to gain a reaction, but Mrs. O'Malley merely offered a curt nod and led the group toward the launch. As expected, there were some new faces, but there were fewer servants this year. Was this decrease in staff an ominous sign? His mother had said they must maintain their faith, for their future was in God's hands. Michael knew that much was true. However, he feared their future also lay in the hands of the Broadmoor family, a family that wasn't fond of the Thousand Islands.

His mother stood on the dock awaiting their return. She waved and greeted the new arrivals with the same enthusiasm she offered to her own family.

The moment Kate stepped off the boat, the women hugged and exchanged pleasantries. Kate turned and beckoned a dark-haired, blue-eyed young woman forward. "This is my daughter

Theresa—the youngest. I was pleased to be able to have her come with us this year. Miss Victoria wanted her along—says Theresa is the best at styling hair and choosing gowns and the like." Kate tipped her head closer. "I didn't argue. Theresa is getting to an age where I don't like leaving her at the main house for the summer, if you know what I mean," Kate said with an exaggerated wink.

Michael pressed by the women with one of the trunks in his cart. He didn't care to hear any more of this discussion. He had started up the path when Theresa caught up with him.

"Can I help you with that heavy load?"

Michael shook his head and continued pushing. "No. It's easier for one person to push, but thanks. There might be some other items down there you could carry."

She ignored his suggestion and continued alongside him. "How long have you lived here, Michael?"

"All my life."

"How can you stand it? I mean growing up all alone on this island with no one to talk to or play with?"

Michael laughed. "I was never bored. Besides, I had two older brothers to keep me company while I was young. Now one of them lives in Canada and the other in Delaware. They were anxious to leave, but I love this island. I have no desire to live elsewhere."

Theresa's dark unbound tresses blew about her face, and she brushed the strands behind her ears. "Well, I suppose that's a good thing for the Broadmoors. They don't have to worry about finding a replacement for you."

Perhaps Theresa could answer some of his burning questions. He wondered if he should broach the topic of Mr. Broadmoor's death. "How long have you worked for the family, Theresa?"

She shrugged. "It seems like I've always worked for them in some capacity. Mother was working for Mr. Jonas and his wife when I was born. My father died when I was five years old. The Broadmoors didn't want to lose Mother, so they permitted her to move into the house and me along with her. As you heard, she was delighted when Miss Victoria listed me as one of the servants to come here this year." She lowered her voice. "I truly was surprised. I thought with Mr. Broadmoor's death they'd all be wearing their mourning clothes and not care about parties and the like."

Michael raised his brows. "And?"

"Mr. Broadmoor said in his will that he didn't want them mourning him." She stepped closer. "He said they hadn't cared about him while he was alive, so they didn't need to mourn his death."

"He said that?"

"Well, something along that line. The servants weren't invited into the library to hear the reading of the will and such. But Treadwell, he's the head butler at Broadmoor Mansion, was close enough to the doors to hear most everything that was said."

While Theresa held the door open, Michael hoisted the trunk and carried it inside. Theresa pointed to the trunk. "That one belongs to Miss Fanny. You can put it in whichever room is hers."

Throughout the remainder of the unloading, Theresa remained by Michael's side. She carried an occasional basket or pretended to help him with a trunk. It was a charade to avoid helping her mother in the kitchen, he decided. He didn't object, for Theresa seemed to enjoy talking more than most anything else. His simple questions were answered with lengthy, informative replies. Theresa was a virtual fount of details. He'd learned more about Mr. Broadmoor's death and the family's reaction to it in the past hour than the other servants would have divulged over the next two months.

"Since this is my first time on the island, why don't you take me for a tour, Michael? Once the family arrives, I doubt I'll have much free time for exploration."

Theresa's interest in the island pleased him, and he agreed to meet her once he'd completed his chores. When he returned to the house a short time later, she was waiting outside.

She formed her lips into a tiny moue. "I thought you'd forgotten me. It's been nearly an hour."

He laughed and shook his head. "I needed to complete my chores and secure the boat in the boathouse. But I have enough time that we should be able to walk a good portion of the island. Does your mother know you're going with me?"

"She's busy preparing menus with your mother. They won't miss us." She skipped ahead of him. "Tell me what it's like living here. I'm amazed that this house is even bigger than the mansion in Rochester."

"It was built that way because the entire family comes here every summer. Each family is accustomed to being in their own home, so Mr. Broadmoor wanted to be certain there would be adequate space when they gathered under one roof. That's what my mother told me when I was a little boy." He grinned. "I can't imagine they truly need all this space, but the men who build these houses aren't happy unless they are huge."

"Status. They all want to outdo one another," Theresa said. "They act the same way in Rochester. One after another, they build their enormous houses along East Avenue. Perhaps I would do the same if I possessed their wealth."

Michael led Theresa to an outcropping of rocks that overlooked the water and assisted her as she sat down. "Not me.

If I had enough money, I'd buy my own island." He pointed toward the diverse plots of land that dotted the river like a hodgepodge of stepping-stones. "I'd be happiest with even the smallest piece of land out there. No big house or steam launch needed. I'd settle for a tent and a canoe or skiff—at least until winter set in. Then I might build something a little more substantial."

Theresa laughed. "You must want more out of life than a small island and a tent."

"A woman to love me and children someday." At the mention of marriage and children, he pictured Fanny. She would make the perfect wife for him—if only . . .

Theresa tickled his ear with a wild violet. "And who might you be thinking of as a mother for those children you hope to have one day?" She tucked her knees beneath her chin and batted her lashes.

"That's not yet been decided. Most of the girls who live on the islands or in the villages can't wait to move to a large city, and the girls who come here to vacation are wealthy socialites. I may never find the perfect woman." He glanced toward the sun. "I need to get back. There will be things needing my attention with the family soon arriving."

Theresa took his outstretched hand and jumped up from the rock. With a sharp cry, she clenched his hand. Michael attempted to grab her other hand as she toppled to the ground. "I've twisted my ankle." She lifted the hem of her skirt.

The ankle hadn't yet begun to swell. Michael carefully removed her shoe and gently moved her foot until she yelped in pain. "I doubt it's broken, but I can't be certain. Let's see if you can sustain any weight on it." He complimented Theresa on her brave attempts, but from her anguished cries, he didn't think she could walk back to the house.

She tilted her head to the side and looked up at him. "Perhaps you could carry me—if I don't weigh too much."

Michael surveyed her form and laughed. "I doubt I'll have much trouble. You're no bigger than a minute. Since the terrain is rough, maybe it would be best if I carried you on my back. I won't be able to see as well with you in my arms."

She gave him a momentary pout, but then agreed. Though riding on his back would not prove the most ladylike position, Michael didn't want to chance a further injury. He was afraid Mrs. O'Malley wouldn't be pleased when her daughter returned with a swollen ankle. And if Theresa wasn't up and about by tomorrow, he imagined the Broadmoor women would be displeased, also.

Theresa's hands were clasped around his neck, and he could feel her breath on his ear as they continued toward the house. She was good company—not like Fanny but nice. "We'll need to get ice on your ankle."

"You're panting. I'm heavier than you thought, aren't I?" She giggled. "You can say so. I promise I won't be angry."

He shook his head and rounded the corner of the house. "I'd never admit—" At the sound of laughter and voices, he glanced up, straightened, and nearly dropped Theresa to the ground. "Fanny! When did all of you arrive? I mean, how did you get to the island?" The entire Broadmoor family stood in the path before him. One glance at the river and Michael knew they had ferried from Clayton on the *Little Mac*.

Theresa wiggled and then whispered in his ear. "You can put me down, Michael."

He lowered her onto the steps leading to the rear of the house while the family continued onward. "I thought you weren't to arrive until tomorrow. Mrs. O'Malley said . . ."

Jonas Broadmoor looked over the top of his glasses. "And I decided we would arrive today." He turned a cold stare on Theresa. "Don't the two of you have duties to perform? I'm not paying you to play about in the woods."

"Yes, sir. I mean, no, sir, we weren't playing about. Theresa fell, and . . ."

Mr. Broadmoor continued walking, obviously not interested in an explanation, but Michael didn't fail to see the look of betrayal in Fanny's eyes. He must talk to her. Goodness, but she was more beautiful than ever.

"Michael!"

His mother was calling from the kitchen, Theresa was injured, Mr. Broadmoor was angry, and he'd obviously caused Fanny pain. On his way up the steps he promised to return with ice for Theresa's ankle. So far it was a glorious beginning to the summer.

Mrs. O'Malley was down the steps in a flash, without the ice. Michael and his mother followed close behind.

"So you're already thinking to get out of some work, are you?" Mrs. O'Malley was standing on the step below her daughter. "Let me see that foot." She lifted Theresa's skirt, wiggled the ankle, and pointed a finger under the girl's nose. "Put your shoe on and get upstairs. There's nothing wrong with your foot."

Theresa didn't attempt to argue. She shoved her foot into the shoe, laced it up, and followed her mother up the stairs. With a grin and a shrug, she strode past Michael.

"There's no time for romancing Theresa O'Malley." His mother's brows knit together in a frown. "We've enough problems with the family arriving unexpectedly, Michael. You know better."

Without giving him an opportunity to explain, his mother marched back up the steps to begin meal preparations for the unexpected family members. He sat down on the steps and rested his head in his hands.

"I see you and Theresa have become fast friends."

He startled and lifted his head at the sound of Fanny's voice. "Fanny! I'm so glad you've come outdoors. Would you let me explain?"

"There's nothing to explain, Michael. Theresa injured herself and you were kind enough to assist her."

"Well, that's what I thought until Mrs. O'Malley chided Theresa and declared the injury a hoax. After watching her scurry up the stairs, I realized I'd been duped. I wanted to explain so you wouldn't think I'm courting her."

Fanny smiled. "I've known Theresa for many years. Further explanation isn't necessary. She's a nice girl who is anxious to wed and begin a life of her own."

Michael changed the subject. "I was sorry to hear about your grandfather. We didn't know he had died until I went into town yesterday to pick up supplies. One of the shop owners told me."

"Uncle Jonas didn't send word?"

"No, but that's not what's important now. How are you doing, Fanny? I can hardly believe my eyes. You're all grown up."

"For all the good it's done me," she declared. "My life seems to constantly be in the hands of others to order about."

He listened while she told him she'd been forced to move from the mansion and that her uncle Jonas had been appointed her guardian and the trustee of her estate. "He wants me to go on a grand tour of Europe, but I truly want to remain here—on the island."

"Would your uncle agree to such an arrangement?"

Fanny tucked a curl behind her ear. "Not without proper supervision. Even then, I'm not sure he'd agree. He's angry that I inherited my father's share of the estate, and I think he's determined to force me to bend to his will until I've reached my majority."

Michael rubbed his jaw. "It's lonely out here on the island once all the summer people return home."

"I know what it's like, Michael. Don't you recall the many summers when my grandparents and I would arrive well ahead of the family and remain at least a month after they'd all departed? I enjoy the solitude and beauty of these islands as much as you do."

He didn't dare tell her he remembered every minute of every day that she'd spent on this island with him. When they were young, he'd been like an older brother to her. Sitting under the trees with a picnic lunch and reading books together, teaching her how to thread a worm onto her fishing hook and then how to remove the fish, exploring the river in her grandfather's skiff and finding caves beneath the rock outcroppings—he remembered it all.

"Do you think your parents might agree to take on the responsibility of providing proper supervision?" she asked. "We could talk to them, and if they thought it was a feasible plan, perhaps they could help convince Uncle Jonas. After all, I'll be eighteen in March."

"We've nothing to lose by asking them, but I think we should wait a few days. Your family wasn't expected until tomorrow, and Mother won't want to think about anything except food preparations."

"Thank you, Michael." She glanced toward the house. "I better go back inside before I'm missed, but I'm looking forward to a picnic very soon."

He nodded his agreement and then watched her return to the house, his thoughts jumbled. Fanny was now an heiress with a vast amount of money. To some, that might be exciting news. To Michael, it meant only one thing: the chasm between them had grown even wider. Unless he could find some way to bridge that gulf, she would be lost to him forever.

8

Wednesday, July 7, 1897

Jonas sat beside Quincy in one of the outlook rooms in the castle turret. He'd been anxious to speak with his brother privately, but since his father's death, either they were surrounded by other members of the family or Quincy would sneak off and return to his Home for the Friendless, which remained a matter of contention between the brothers. But Jonas was determined to present a magnanimous spirit this day. He wanted his brother as an ally.

Jonas settled into one of the heavy leather chairs and puffed on his cigar. "It's only early July, and already this has proved to be a summer of difficulties. Let's hope our troubles will soon ease."

Quincy fixed his gaze on a freighter moving downriver. "I won't be able to spend much time on the island, Jonas. I know the provisions of Father's will require the men of the family to devote as much time as possible to the family during the

109

summer, but I'm sure you understand that if I'm to keep the shelter afloat, I must be absent a great deal during the week."

"Yes—Father's will left us all in a bit of a bind, didn't it?" He took a long draw on the cigar and blew a smoke ring into the air above his head. "I completely understand your need to oversee your work, Quincy. Just as I must oversee mine. For a man who made his own fortune, Father seemed to remember very little about how time-consuming it could be."

"I do hope Victoria is willing to supervise Sophie during my absence. My daughter can be a handful at times."

"I'm certain Victoria won't mind. The three girls will spend all of their time together anyway." Jonas flicked the ash from his cigar. "I've wanted to talk to you about other provisions in Father's will."

Quincy turned back toward the river. "The terms of his will were very precise. What is there to talk about?"

"Fanny's inheritance. Surely you don't think she's entitled to the same inheritance you and I will receive. It's not as though Langley ever contributed anything to the family."

"He was our *brother*, Jonas!"

"I don't deny that, but think about it—what did his life amount to? Langley was completely useless after Winifred's death. He may have talked about his journalism career, but he never put pen to paper, and you know it. And how many grown men do you know who would have moved back home with a child after the death of their wife?"

"Mother insisted. You know that. She wanted Fanny to have a woman's influence in her life. You can't fault Langley for giving in to her. To be honest, if Marie had died when our children were young, I might have done the same. It's been difficult enough raising Sophie for the past year by myself. And she was seventeen when Marie died." Quincy tented his fingers beneath his chin. "Left with an infant, I think I would have succumbed to Mother's wishes, also. Langley and I never were as strong as you. Perhaps it has something to do with your being the eldest son."

"Don't sell yourself short," Jonas said. "You were quite successful while working for the company. Father couldn't have run the milling business or his later investments without your astute business acumen. And if you'd give up that idea of spending all your time and money on your Home for the Friendless, I could terminate Henry Foster. He can't hold a candle to you when it comes to accounting and investments."

"I'm not interested in the business. I feel God's calling to do this work, and if you've brought me up here to convince me otherwise, you'll not succeed."

Jonas silently chided himself. He didn't want to put his brother on the defensive. He needed him as an ally if he was going to succeed in gaining Fanny's share of his father's estate. Though some of the other relatives agreed with him, it was Quincy who would prove most beneficial. With Quincy on his side, he could present a unified front to any dissenting family members and to the court, if necessary.

"I think we should contest Fanny's inheritance."

Quincy stood and walked to the window. "I don't think that's wise. Didn't you hear what Mr. Fillmore said? I don't want the funds tied up because we contest the will. I need cash to keep the shelter operational. Besides, Fanny is entitled to Langley's share. It's what our father wanted."

"And what if I could find some method other than contesting the will? Would you side with me then, dear brother?"

A wave of Quincy's dark brown hair streaked with strands of gray fell across his forehead. "I think she's entitled to her father's share. Unless you can show me a reason other than what you've spoken of this afternoon, I don't think I could agree. Of course, she's much too young to handle such a large sum, but Father placed you in charge of her funds. I trust you will handle her money with the same care with which you handle your own."

Jonas's lips curved in a slow smile. "You may rest assured."

"If there's nothing else, I believe I'll go downstairs. The architect delivered his most recent renderings for expansion of the shelter before we departed. I brought them along and want to examine them."

Jonas waved his cigar. "As you wish. I'm going to remain up here awhile longer." He didn't add that he needed to gather his thoughts and suffuse the anger that burned in his heart. Quincy's offhanded dismissal galled him. Now he'd be forced to develop another plan. And develop one he would. He had to. The investments he'd made earlier in the year had not played out well. Added to that, his own company was failing to make the same level of profits it had the year before. None of that by itself would have been damaging, but Jonas had spent large amounts of money on expanding his house and gardens, as well as purchasing a team of matched horses that had cost him a pretty penny. And the bills from Amanda's trip abroad had been far more extensive than he'd originally thought they'd be. He wasn't destitute, but his finances were greatly strained. Dangerously so.

One way or the other, he'd have Langley's share for himself, and Quincy need not think he'd share in it, either. He'd given Quincy his chance. At the very least, with a bit of finagling, he'd mange to skim and pilfer a goodly portion of her inheritance with no one becoming the wiser.

After stubbing out the cigar, Jonas pulled his chair near the window and stared down below. Amanda, Sophie, and Fanny were gathered together on the front lawn enjoying a game of croquet, while Jefferson and George, along with several of the younger children, shouted instructions from the sidelines. Fanny waved and Jonas watched as Michael Atwell approached from the far end of the lawn.

Fanny touched his arm and then perched on tiptoe to whisper into Michael's ear. The young man laughed and nodded while Amanda and Sophie continued knocking the croquet balls toward the metal hoops. Michael withdrew something from his pocket and then held out the object for Fanny to examine. Jonas leaned forward, his forehead touching the glass. What did Michael hold in his hand? Whatever it was, the object had captured Fanny's interest. It appeared the young man had a way with the girls—first Theresa and now Fanny. If the young boatswain continued his amorous behavior, one of the local girls would have him at the altar before long.

Jonas continued to stare at the young couple. He paced back and forth, his gaze flickering down toward the lawn each time he passed the windows until he recalled his conversation with Mortimer Fillmore. They had discussed the possibility of an arranged marriage for Fanny.

He stopped. Fanny had placed her croquet mallet in the stand and was strolling toward the boathouse with Michael. He'd have to find additional work to keep that young man busy! Fanny tucked her hand into the crook of Michael's arm. From all appearances, she was encouraging the young man's advances. Surely young Atwell didn't think he could woo one of the Broadmoor girls. Jonas would never permit such a liaison. If anyone thought Hamilton Broadmoor's granddaughter was being courted by the hired help, she'd be blacklisted from ever making a proper marriage.

Jonas massaged his forehead. An arranged marriage was exactly what he needed for Fanny. And it looked like he needed to move swiftly. He would begin to prepare a list of possibilities. With a word to his business associates, he could surely locate the names of a number of possible candidates with the proper lineage and little intelligence. That was precisely what he needed. Unless he could arrive at some other solution, he must find the perfect marriage partner for his niece.

"I missed you," Fanny told Michael as they walked along the island path to her special place. She had brought a bouquet of flowers to put there in memory of her father, just as she did every year.

"I missed you, too, although I have been quite busy. We built a new boathouse that kept us occupied."

"I saw it. I thought it looked grand." She gathered her skirt and climbed down the rocky trail to where she used to sit with her father.

The tree where she'd found him dead still stood as a reminder. Fanny could almost see him there. She bit her lip and forced back tears. How could it still hurt so much after all these years?

"I don't know if it's a good idea for you to keep coming back here," Michael said as he came alongside her. "It seems to only make you sad."

"It's not just sadness," Fanny told him. "It's the wondering about what might have been. I miss him so much. I miss my mother, too, but I suppose that seems silly."

"Never. Everyone longs for a mother's love."

His voice was soothing and very compassionate. Fanny couldn't help but look up into his eyes. No one in the world mattered more to her now. "I'm glad you understand."

"I do. I can still remember that day—finding Mr. Broadmoor here. It seems like just yesterday."

"I know," Fanny agreed. "I always wished Papa would have left me a letter or something to show that he was thinking of me—that he loved me."

"His actions showed that every day," Michael whispered.

"Every day but the last," she countered. "If he had loved me that day, he would never have left me."

Michael reached out and gently touched her shoulder. "He loved you that day, too, Fanny. His pain caused his actions, but it couldn't take away his love for you."

"I suppose you're right." She placed the flowers at the trunk of the tree and then straightened. "I'm so glad to be back here—on the island—with you."

He smiled and the look he gave her caused Fanny's heart to skip a beat. If possible, he was even more handsome than he'd been the year before.

"It always seems to take forever before the winter and spring pass and you return. I always fear this will be the year you won't come back."

Fanny laughed. "I'll always come back, Michael. This is my home. I love it here more than anywhere else on earth. I'll never leave it . . . or you . . . for good."

9

Later the same afternoon, the three girls sauntered across the lawn until they reached their favorite spot beneath one of the large fir trees that dotted the lower half of the grassy expanse. They carefully positioned their blankets to gain a view of the river—watching the water flow by was one of Fanny's favorite pastimes on warm afternoons such as this.

Sophie tucked her dress around her legs and leaned against the trunk of the ancient conifer while Amanda settled between her two younger cousins. Sophie had promised to give them a full account of the Independence Day party she had attended at Brown Square. Though Amanda and Fanny had been much too frightened to sneak off with Sophie that day, they both were eager to hear the details now.

Fanny brushed a persistent fly from the sleeve of her striped shirtwaist. "Well? Did you have as much fun as you expected?"

Sophie bobbed her head. "Of course. In fact, even more. I met two wonderful young men who were ever so sad to hear I would be leaving Rochester for the summer. They've promised to come calling the minute I return to town. Both of them were quite handsome, too." She giggled and tucked a curl behind her ear. "Promise you won't tell a soul, but I permitted one of them to remove my shoes so I could get my feet wet."

Amanda gasped and clutched her bodice. "Please tell me that's *all* you let him remove."

"If you're worried about my stockings, fear not, Amanda. I would have preferred to remove them, but it didn't seem prudent at the time. Instead, I waded in with them on. The men thought me a good sport." Sophie leaned forward and sighed. "They were both so attentive all evening. I think they were competing to see which one would have the privilege of escorting me home. The boys offered to buy me some of the German beer that was for sale in the park, but I told them I didn't like the taste. Do you know what Wilhelm did then?"

Amanda quirked her brows. "I can only imagine."

"He went and got me a large cup of fruit punch." Sophie glanced over her shoulder. "And then he removed a silver flask from inside his jacket and poured some whiskey into the punch. It was wonderful."

Amanda's eyes grew wide. "That's disgraceful, Sophie. Those boys were likely hoping to get you drunk in order to take advantage of you." She grasped Sophie's hand. "Please tell me that didn't occur."

Sophie laughed. "You need not worry, Amanda. It would have taken more than that to render me defenseless."

"You're accustomed to imbibing alcoholic drinks?" Fanny's mouth gaped.

"I've had more than my share, I suppose. Oh, do close your mouth, Fanny. There are far worse things than alcohol. I could tell you about them, but I fear both of you would faint—and how could I possibly explain that to the family?" Sophie pointed toward a launch filled with summer visitors. "I'd guess they're on their way to the party at Hopewell Hall. I do wish your mother would have given permission for us to attend. I'd love to sneak off to that party, but this isn't like being at home. Here, I have your mother watching after my comings and goings."

There was little doubt Sophie was unhappy. She'd been pouting ever since discovering Aunt Victoria had sent regrets to the Browning residence on Farwell Island. Several of William Browning's grandsons were hosting a party at their grandfather's island, and all three of the girls had hoped to attend. Even Fanny enjoyed the occasional gatherings hosted at the home of the man who had spawned his fortune making uniforms for the Union Army during the American Civil War. Hopewell Hall provided a spectacular view from its perch high above the river, and though Fanny didn't care about mingling with the elite, she did enjoy exploring every island she visited and watching the variety of boats and barges that consistently dotted the waterway.

Amanda patted Sophie's folded hands. "There will be parties all summer long, dear Sophie. Mother wanted us all in attendance to welcome your sister. After all, this has been a trying time for Louisa and her children."

Sophie shrugged. "My entire life has been trying."

Fanny giggled.

"Don't you dare laugh at me, Fanny. You have no idea of the difficulties I've been forced to endure."

Fanny leaned forward and peeked around Amanda. "You are so dramatic, dear Cousin. I fear I haven't noted the many tragedies you've suffered. Do tell us of all your horrid life experiences so we may commiserate with you."

Ever melodramatic, Sophie gazed heavenward and exhaled deeply. "How could you possibly fail to notice, Fanny? While my mother was alive, she was always consumed with my brother and sisters. Even when they were gone from home, she didn't have time for me. She was either worried about Dorian being forever lost to her in the Canadian backcountry or worried about my sisters' marriages and the births of her grandchildren. There was never time for me."

"You may be exaggerating just a wee bit," Amanda said.

"And how would you know, Amanda? Your mother is constantly at your beck and call. You don't know what it's like to be ignored by your mother. While Mother was alive, my father spent all his time working for Grandfather and was seldom home. As for me, I don't miss either of them."

"Sophie Broadmoor! How can you say you don't miss your mother?" Amanda clucked her tongue.

"You can't miss what you never had." Sophie's rebuttal dripped with sarcasm.

"That's not true," Fanny declared. "I never knew my mother, but I feel a deep longing in the pit of my stomach at the very thought of her. You were fortunate to have your mother for so many years. One day you'll agree with me. And you should make an effort to spend time with your father, too. If something should happen to him, you'll regret not having made the effort."

Sophie groaned. "Haven't you become the idealistic soul! My father is so consumed with his Home for the Friendless that I could disappear from the face of the earth and months would pass before he even realized I was gone."

"You do have a flare for the dramatic," Amanda said with a chuckle. "And if your father is so uncaring, why does he provide aid to the homeless and why does he make an appearance on the island during the middle of the week? My father seldom arrives until Saturday afternoon and departs on Sunday evening or Monday morning. He's rarely on the island, yet I don't condemn him as heartless."

"I suppose that's because you're a better person than I am. And don't think my father is here because he's interested in my welfare. Do you see that young man he met at the dock only a few minutes ago?"

Fanny and Amanda strained forward and watched their uncle crossing the lawn with a young man they'd never before seen. Fanny cupped her hand over her eyes and squinted. "Who is he? I don't believe I've met him."

"You haven't. He's Paul Medford, father's new protégé and a recent graduate of Bangor Theological Seminary. You'll notice Father has scads of time for Paul. He clings to every word young Mr. Medford utters."

"He works for your father? Doing what?" Amanda asked.

Sophie turned her back on the two men as they continued toward the house. "Father advertised in the newspaper and contacted several divinity schools, stating he planned to hire a man to live at the shelter—someone who had a heart for ministering to the less fortunate and was willing to reside on the grounds with all those *friendless* people he takes in." Sophie wrinkled her nose. "According to Father, Paul is a gift from God, a man who seeks nothing more from life than helping his fellow man. The man is a true bore. He thinks of nothing but God and those wretched people who live at the shelter."

"I think he's quite handsome," Fanny remarked.

"I find him somewhat plain," Amanda observed, "but I'm sure he must be very kind."

"I suppose because I am rather plain, I attempt to find beauty in the simple," Fanny said.

Amanda chuckled. "You are far from plain. With your beautiful skin, those auburn curls, and beautiful brown eyes, you are a beauty."

Fanny didn't argue with her cousin. If the conversation continued, they would think she was begging for compliments, but compared to her cousins, she was very ordinary.

Sophie leaned close to Amanda. "Paul would be perfect for you, Amanda. Just like you, he thinks people should spend all their time serving mankind through charitable works."

Fanny leaned against the tree while her cousins argued about Paul Medford and Amanda's aspirations to perform charitable work. They all three realized the one who would have the final say in Amanda's future would be Uncle Jonas. They also understood that he wouldn't agree to his daughter's seeking a career. He would expect Amanda to wed. He would insist her husband be a man of wealth and position, regardless of Amanda's personal desires or the physical appearance of her intended. Amanda was his only daughter, and Uncle Jonas would not permit her to marry some beggarly fellow who didn't meet his expectations. For years, Amanda had worked alongside her mother performing charity work, and her mother knew of her desire to continue with such endeavors. But her father had also made his desires known: she could perform her charity work as a married woman, just as her mother had done before her.

A passing launch drew close to the water's edge, and several of their friends waved and hollered greetings. "They're likely on their way to Hopewell Hall. I do wish my sister would have chosen some other day for her arrival. You might know that she had to select the day when the Brownings are hosting their party." Sophie pulled a handful of grass and tossed it into the air.

"We'll be attending parties, dances, and picnics all summer long, Sophie. You may as well cheer up. Your continued pouting hurts no one except yourself." Amanda waved to the group as they continued down the river. "And I'd think you'd want to offer a show of support for Louisa. Life can't be easy for her with three little children and so recently a widow, too."

"Louisa should have no difficulty. Her husband left her with a handsome inheritance. She had best keep her purse strings tied or Father will be seeking a large contribution for his Home for the Friendless."

"Sophie! What a terrible thing to say." Amanda frowned at her cousin. "You've become quite disparaging of late, and it doesn't suit you well."

"Say what you will. I know my father. He had Paul arrive today so it would coincide with Louisa's arrival. Oh, what if he's planning some wild matchmaking scheme between the two of them? Now wouldn't *that* make for an interesting summer!"

Fanny couldn't believe Sophie's flippant attitude. "Louisa's husband has been dead for less than a year. Your father would never consider such a thing."

Sophie pulled her hair off her neck and bunched it together atop her head. "You must admit it's a delicious idea. If Amanda has no interest in Paul, I shall mention him as a possibility to Louisa myself."

"You wouldn't! Promise me you'll do no such thing." Fanny reached across Amanda and grasped Sophie's arm. "If you're angry with your father, then talk to him, but don't add to your sister's pain and bereavement with such irresponsible antics."

"Oh, I suppose you're correct. Louisa isn't to blame for our father's behavior."

Fanny gave a sigh of relief. She couldn't believe her cousin would entertain such a foolish idea. Then again, after hearing of Sophie's behavior at the Independence Day party, Fanny knew she shouldn't be surprised. Obviously, the breach between Sophie and her father had widened considerably during the past year. It seemed Sophie hoped to gain her father's attention with her outlandish behavior. Instead, he seemed even more distant and aloof.

"It appears your sister has arrived while we've been discussing her future." Amanda pointed toward the dock. Louisa was holding a child by each hand as the *Little Mac* slowly moved away from the dock.

Sophie shaded her eyes and looked. "I suppose we should go down and see if she needs our help."

When Sophie made no move to get up, Fanny jumped to her feet. She extended her hand and helped Amanda up from the grassy slope. "Come on, Sophie. Let me help you up."

"There's no rush. And where are the servants? Don't they see her down there with her luggage and the children?" Sophie slowly got to her feet. Before heading off with her cousins, she stopped to fold the blankets and stack them beneath the tree.

The wails of the little boys were carried on a rush of wind as they walked alongside their mother. Louisa bent down to pick up one of the boys, and the other immediately ran from her side. The child fell as he reached the graveled path, and the nanny hurried to lend aid to Louisa and the injured child.

"Hurry, Sophie. Louisa needs our help with the children and her baggage," Fanny shouted. A sudden wind whipped at the girls' skirts, and whitecaps crested the breaking waves.

"There's a storm moving in. We'd better get the luggage before it begins to rain."

They hurried toward the dock as another gale of wind swooped down from the sloping path. Slowly but then beginning to gather a trace of speed, the unattended baby carriage rolled down the dock. Fear clawed at Fanny's throat. "Is the baby in there?" She gasped for air. "Did the nanny have the baby in her arms?"

Amanda's blond tresses whipped about her face. She clawed at the hair and held it from her eyes. "I don't think so. *Hurry!*"

Fanny sprinted at full speed with Amanda and Sophie on her heels. A roar of wind muted their urgent screams for help. Fanny squinted. Surely her eyes deceived her. The buggy had picked up speed. Without slowing her pace, Fanny uttered an urgent prayer for the child who might be lying in the buggy. Her shoes clattered and echoed on the dock's wood planks. Her screams continued. If she could only lengthen her stride, she would reach the buggy before it plunged into the water.

She stretched in a mighty leap, but the toe of her shoe caught between the planks as she landed. She hurtled forward, unable to gain her balance. A keening wail escaped her lips, and she could do nothing more than watch the carriage topple into the dark water below.

10

Michael was in the boathouse when he heard the first scream. More screams followed and sent him running from the shelter up the path toward the house, where he saw several people yelling and pointing at the river.

Fanny was lying prone on the dock, her arms stretched toward the end of the structure. He turned and saw what appeared to be a carriage dropping off the end of the pier and into the water. Horrified, he raced to the dock's edge and jumped into the water. The buggy had tipped sideways in the water, and the hazy sun cast an eerie shadow across a pale blue blanket. Michael fought his way through a surging wave and grasped the object. He lifted the bundle into the air and was greeted by a howling cry. Jumping to avoid a wave that threatened to toss him off his feet and the baby into the chest-high water, Michael struggled to maintain his balance while holding the infant. He leaned forward and fought against the current that pummeled and pushed him toward the wood pilings supporting the dock.

"Michael! Can you move this way so I can reach the baby?" With her cousins holding her legs, Fanny lay flat on the dock and stretched her arms over the edge.

Easing his foothold, Michael allowed the current to move him toward the dock. The wind briefly abated and he lifted the baby high into Fanny's hands before ducking beneath the deck and grabbing hold of a wood piling on the other side. He worked his way forward into the shallows and then hefted himself onto the dock. Keeping his wits about him, Michael spotted the buggy, now wedged in a stand of rocks not far from the dock. After retrieving a pole from alongside the pier, he freed the soggy carriage from the rocky crevice.

The wind snatched Mrs. Clermont's flower-bedecked hat and bounced it across the lawn as she raced toward the dock. From the terror reflected in her eyes, it was obvious she'd observed the frightening scene. "Evan! Is he all right?" Her scream pierced the air.

Several family members followed behind carrying blankets while Mrs. Clermont shouted commands and clutched the infant to her chest. She grabbed one of the blankets and wrapped it around the wet child.

Michael sat hunched on the edge of the dock. Mrs. Clermont slowed her pace and stepped to his side. "Thank you for saving my child. Once the baby is cared for and asleep, I shall speak with you."

The staff and family members who had continued to scurry to the dock during the incident now gathered around Mrs. Clermont. While the group walked toward the house as one huddled mass of humanity, Michael was left to consider the woman's final comment. She had thanked him, but did she expect some explanation of what had occurred? If so, he surely couldn't tell her. He'd not observed anything until the carriage careened into the water. Surely she didn't hold him responsible. After all, she *had* thanked him for saving the baby. He forced himself upright. Right now there wasn't time to dwell on the matter.

The storm clouds and rough gales had continued to build with surprising ferocity, and unless the wind turned, the water would soon be rising. Though he longed to change out of his wet clothes, he couldn't spare the time. He must secure the boats.

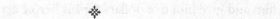

While the nanny rushed off to unpack dry clothing for the infant, Louisa fiercely rubbed his tiny limbs with a soft towel. With each wail, the baby's lower lip quivered, but the bluish purple shade had now vanished from his lips. His rosy complexion had been restored—due either to Louisa's robust toweling or to the fact that his body temperature had returned to normal. Fanny couldn't be certain where to assign credit.

Sophie held her fingers to her ears. "That baby certainly has healthy lungs, doesn't he?"

Louisa glanced up at her sister. "Yes, and his name is Evan— not *that baby*."

"I don't need your criticism, Louisa." Sophie glared at her sister. "If it weren't for the three of us, he'd have drowned in the river."

"I believe it was that young man on the dock who saved Evan, not you."

"But it was our screams . . ."

Fanny tugged on Sophie's sleeve and tipped her head close. "Not now, Sophie. Your sister is quite upset. She's likely blaming herself for leaving the baby unattended."

Dinah Hertzel, the baby's nanny, hurried into the parlor with a fresh diaper and soft gown for little Evan. "You sit down and rest, ma'am. I'll dress the lad." She took in the gathered throng. "Perhaps one of you could fetch a cup of tea for Mrs. Clermont."

One of the servants hurried to the kitchen, and Louisa sat down beside her father. "I believe the young man who saved Evan's life should be rewarded. Once the storm abates, I'm going to visit him at the boathouse. I need to properly thank him and give him five dollars for his heroic act."

Quincy rubbed his hand along his cheek. "I doubt the young man expects any remuneration for his action, but I agree he should receive a reward. I do think it should be ten dollars rather than the five you've proposed."

"I would think the life of a baby would fetch a much higher price," Sophie muttered.

Louisa folded her arms across her waist and glowered at her sister. "If he were an educated man accustomed to receiving large sums of money, I might agree. However, to someone of his class, five or ten dollars is a handsome sum. He'll be pleased with whatever he receives."

William Broadmoor nodded. "I heartily agree. He's young and uneducated. If you give him any more than that, he'll squander it all on a good time."

Victoria Broadmoor tapped her son on the shoulder. "Are you suggesting that educated men don't squander their money on a good time? I believe I recall several educated young men— members of this family, in fact—who have misspent money on many a frivolous activity."

"Based upon the fact that the water was no higher than his chest, his risk was limited, and he's not entitled to any more than ten dollars," Jefferson declared.

"Well, where were you, Jefferson?" Sophie demanded of her cousin. "I didn't see you out there in the water! And the waves were exceedingly strong. He could have been pulled under and the baby along with him."

"George and I were playing a game of billiards in the game room. Besides, we were sufficiently doused on the Fourth of July, if you remember."

"I agree with Jefferson," George said. "I think his risk was minimal, at best, and ten dollars is sufficient."

"Of course you agree. You agree with everything your brother says," Sophie rebutted.

Fanny could barely keep up with the continuing battle. Rather than celebrating Evan's safety, they were entrenched in a silly dispute over money. It was an inconsequential sum to a wealthy family yet still deemed worthy of an argument.

She walked outside, anxious to be away from her family's nonsensical disagreement. The glimmer of sunshine peeking from behind a bank of clouds brought a smile to her lips. The wind had shifted, and the storm appeared to be moving to the south. She was relieved they wouldn't suffer a night of pounding rain and lightning.

From the far end of the lower veranda, she noticed the side door to the boathouse remained ajar. She wandered to the dock, anxious to speak with Michael and thank him for rescuing her youngest relative. After lightly rapping on the door, she peered inside. "Michael? Are you in here?"

"Over here!"

She spotted his mass of dark curls on the far side of the boathouse. "I'm pleased to see the storm has passed."

"Be careful you don't trip and fall on those boards," he called.

She gathered her skirts and picked her way across the expanse. "I wanted to make certain you were all right."

"I'm fine. Once I hoisted the boats out of the water, I was able to get into some dry clothes. How's the baby?"

"He's fine, thanks to you. I can't tell you how much I admire your bravery. You jumped into the water with no thought for your own well-being. Little Evan is alive, thanks to your heroic action."

He shook his head. "You're making far too much of what happened. By hanging over the edge of the dock, you placed yourself in greater danger than I faced in the water. And if you hadn't screamed, I wouldn't have known anything was amiss. Mrs. Clermont has you to thank for saving her child."

"No, Michael. You're the hero. Please don't say otherwise. Not to me or to anyone else in this family. You've performed a brave deed this day, and you shouldn't discount saving a life."

He wrapped his callused hands around the handle of the boat pulley.

Fanny looked up and noted the straps that had been secured around the *DaisyBee*. "You're preparing to lower her back into the water?"

He nodded. "The storm has moved on. No reason to keep her out of the water. Someone may want to take a boat ride later this evening."

"That sounds like a wonderful idea. Was that an invitation?"

"Not unless you have a chaperone. I don't want to lose my job. I'd be forced to leave this island that I love, and I'd miss my mother's cooking, too."

She giggled. "I couldn't bear to be the cause of such horrid consequences."

He turned the pulley handle, and Fanny watched as he lifted the boat high enough to remove the wood planks. He then lowered each one, careful to keep it from falling into the water in the slip below. His muscles rippled as he fought to control each of the heavy timbers. His strength and agility to handle the task on his own amazed her. Through the years, he had developed a system that served him well.

"If you're going to remain down here for a while, you might as well sit down," he shouted over the squeals of the pulley. "I think I better oil this thing. After the launch is back in the water, I'm going to take care of the skiffs and canoes." He held the handle of the pulley with one hand and pointed to the nearby corner. "There's a chair over there. It looks a mess, but it's clean."

Michael's assessment was correct. The chair had seen better days. Layers of white had been applied years ago, but in the dampness of the boathouse, the paint had peeled away to leave a jagged design of wood splotches. Fanny hiked the skirt of her pale green lawn dress and perched her straw bonnet on the chair's curved finial. There was a peace to this place: the hypnotic rhythm of the water lapping against the timbered boat slips, the musty smell of wet wood—she felt as though she could drink in the sights and smells forever. This island offered a sense of security and well-being that she experienced nowhere else. Michael was fortunate to live here. She could only hope to convince Uncle Jonas that this would be the perfect place for her, too.

The boat slowly settled into the water, and she applauded. "Good job."

He leaned forward in a deep bow. "Thank you, dear lady. Your kind words are a pleasurable reward for my difficult labors."

"You are most welcome, sir," she said with a grin. "As for rewards, I do believe Cousin Louisa will be offering you a monetary gift for saving little Evan."

"That's not necessary. In fact, receiving money for meeting the need of another would cause me great discomfort. I don't want or expect to be paid for doing what is right."

He lifted one of the canoes from its place of safety overhead. Fanny rested her elbow on one knee and cupped her chin. Michael's attitude continued to astonish her. Through the years they'd occasionally discussed their faith in God. Like Michael, she had gone to church with her family. They filled several rows each Sunday morning and were frequently lauded for their monetary gifts to the church. But her family didn't live their faith—not as Michael and his parents did.

While her family argued over both important and trivial matters, she'd never witnessed such behavior in Michael's family. Instead of arguing, they always talked and worked together to find a resolution to their problems. His family appeared to find joy in simple pleasures, while her family constantly moved from one obsession to another, always searching for something that would make them happy. Even with a household of servants and the most modern conveniences life could offer, they bickered and argued in a gloomy state of existence. Rather than love and affection, the family money was the glue that held the Broadmoors together. The bribery required to bring them together each summer was evidence enough to support Fanny's bleak assessment. Uncle Jonas didn't hide his obsession, and although Uncle Quincy used a great deal of his money to help the homeless, he'd become obsessed with his mission, placing it above God and family. He willingly offered support to the impoverished while ignoring the needs of his own children, especially Sophie. The Broadmoors gave and spent their money only where it would garner accolades and respect among their peers.

With an involuntary shiver, Fanny understood that money had replaced even the God they self-righteously claimed to serve.

"I miss the days when we were free to wander at will and enjoy ourselves," Fanny said with a sigh. "My favorite memories are of this island—and of you."

Michael looked up, and his expression seemed pained. He quickly refocused on his work. "Nothing ever stays the same."

"I suppose not. I feel that my life has come quite undone—once again. Every time I lose someone, I feel as though a part of me has died, as well."

Michael stopped and came to her. "I'm truly sorry, Fanny. I know how close you were to your grandfather."

"It's not just that." She felt tears form in her eyes and blinked hard. "I never realized just how much the Broadmoor family hates one another, and this island."

"I thought you knew."

"I knew they bickered and that often the summer was spent with one group or another secluded away from everyone else because of some riff. But honestly, no. I didn't realize how much hatred existed among them until I saw them fighting and backstabbing at Grandfather's funeral."

"I'm sorry."

"The reading of the will was even worse. They are so jealous—so worried that someone will get more than they will. They're like a pack of wolves picking over a dead man's bones."

"Greed and money make people do strange things."

"I suppose my desire for a family simply caused me to over-look the truth. I thought everyone was as eager to come here as I. I thought they loved it as much as I did. It's the only place

I've ever been truly happy, despite it being where Papa . . . where he . . . died. I was confident that the others longed for this respite just like I did."

Michael knelt down beside her. "No. Your love of this place is special. Few share your heart in that matter. But I know how you feel. I love it, too. Just as I . . ." He fell silent as if embarrassed and then jumped quickly to his feet. "Fanny, you should go back to the house. You're a grown woman, and it's not seemly for you to be here alone with me."

Fanny looked at him for a moment before rising. "I suppose I shall lose you, as well. Nothing ever stays the same."

Michael watched her walk slowly back toward the house. He longed to go after her and convince her that she was wrong, but his mother's warning rang in his ears. He wasn't ever going to be allowed to court a Broadmoor.

Fanny faded from view as she topped the hill. Michael felt her absence like an intense pain that would not abate.

"You'll never lose me, Fanny" he whispered. "But I know I shall lose you, and that will be my undoing."

11

Saturday, July 10, 1897

Fanny fidgeted in her chair. The evening meal was progressing particularly slowly, either by Aunt Victoria's design or due to some unknown difficulty in the kitchen. The servants didn't appear flustered during their appearances in the dining room, so Fanny eventually concluded the pace had been set by her aunt.

Aunt Victoria delighted in entertaining, especially when the local newspaper could report Edward and Elizabeth Oosterman had accepted her invitation for a private supper party. Mr. and Mrs. Oosterman topped the list of prestigious and influential people who summered in the Thousand Islands. Their attendance at any social gathering of the wealthy ensured success—and newspaper coverage. Fanny wasn't certain who had given the Oostermans their ostentatious designation, but topping the list was assuredly tied to their wealth. Money spoke volumes among the summer people.

Mr. Oosterman sat to Uncle Jonas's right. At the opposite end of the table, Mrs. Oosterman was seated beside Aunt Victoria. With Mrs. Oosterman on one side and Louisa on the other, Fanny had quickly grown bored. Rather than George and Jefferson, she wished Sophie and Amanda had been seated across from her. Instead, her female cousins were at the other end of the table. Thus far the dinner conversation had consisted of wearisome discussions about guest lists, menus, and themes for summer parties.

Mrs. Oosterman suggested a masked ball be considered a possibility for the summer agenda of frivolity. "I would even consider hosting the ball myself. What do you think, Victoria?"

Fanny sighed. She wished the women would discuss something other than parties—she didn't know what, but anything would be more interesting than what they'd been covering. She glanced to her right. "How is Evan faring, Louisa? I haven't seen him since Wednesday. I hope he hasn't developed a cold or the croup since the accident."

"He's well," Louisa whispered.

Mrs. Oosterman choked on a spoonful of clam chowder. "What's this about an accident? You never mentioned any accident to me, Victoria. Was someone injured? I didn't see anything in the newspaper." She cast a disparaging look at her hostess.

Aunt Victoria frowned. "A minor incident. It was really nothing, Elizabeth." A forced smile replaced the frown.

"Nothing?" Fanny exclaimed. "Evan's carriage blew off the pier, and he nearly drowned, and you say it was *nothing*?"

"Whaaat?" Mrs. Oosterman clasped a hand to her chest. "I heard nothing about this tragedy? How is that possible?"

Victoria shook her head. "It isn't a tragedy. The baby is fine. You know the old saying, Elizabeth. 'All's well that ends well.'

Louisa preferred the incident to remain quiet. We'd been very successful—until this evening." The frown returned.

"Dear me, this is shocking. I trust you discharged the child's nanny. I daresay, decent help is impossible to find nowadays. Don't you think?"

Fanny now realized why there had been no mention of the accident. The family was embarrassed someone might discover Louisa had left her child unaccompanied on the dock. Now the incident would be discussed over luncheons, after-dinner drinks, and dinner parties, with each guest adding an additional twist to the story. Though gossiping about other families was commonplace at the Broadmoor dinner table, being the topic of discussion held little appeal. Fanny hadn't intended to stir up a hornet's nest. She would surely receive a rebuke once their guests departed.

Aunt Victoria made a valiant attempt to change the subject, but Mrs. Oosterman wouldn't be deterred. She wanted every detail. With her diamond and ruby necklace draped across her dinner plate like a swinging pendulum, the old dowager leaned forward to gain a better view of Louisa. "I know you must be mortified, dear Louisa, but we all make mistakes. This was simply an accident. Personally, I believe it would be beneficial if others knew of what happened. You might prevent another such tragedy if others learn what occurred."

"I'll give your suggestion some thought, but I was hoping for a quiet summer. I came only to spend time with my family."

"*And* because Grandfather's will required it," Jefferson added with a chuckle.

Mrs. Oosterman perked to attention. "Truly? His will required a summer visit to the island?"

"Ouch!" Jefferson quickly leaned down and rubbed his shin.

"Please forgive my son's rude behavior. He ofttimes forgets indelicate matters are not to be discussed at the dinner table. Teaching him good manners has been a genuine struggle."

The spotlight moved away from Fanny and Louisa and now shone on Jefferson and his remark. Anxious for more details, Mrs. Oosterman immediately pardoned Jefferson's faux pas and pressed on. "Edward and I consider ourselves more than mere summer acquaintances, Victoria. We count you and Jonas among our dearest friends. You're like family to us."

The compliment worked. In hushed tones Aunt Victoria confided in Mrs. Oosterman. The older woman soaked up each detail like a dying plant in need of water. Fanny doubted Mrs. Oosterman's sincerity and thought Aunt Victoria's trust badly placed, but she didn't interfere. In fact, she didn't utter another word throughout the remainder of the meal.

Once they'd completed their lemon cream pie, Jonas pushed away from the table and suggested they all gather on the upper veranda, where the men could enjoy a cigar and a glass of port along with a view of the river and the early evening breeze. He didn't wait for a response before leading the group away from the dining room.

"What was all the whispering at your end of the table?" Jonas asked Mrs. Oosterman as she walked alongside her host. "Edward and I thought you two women might be plotting a huge party or a shopping excursion in Brockville."

"Quite the contrary. Victoria and I were discussing some of the conditions contained in your father's will." She tapped a finger along the side of her elaborately styled hair. "That Hamilton always was one step ahead of the rest of us, wasn't he?"

Fanny remained in the shadows, listening to her uncle's response regarding the distribution of the Broadmoor estate.

"My father didn't always use the best judgment, I fear, but there's nothing we can't live with. We will, of course, abide by Father's wishes and vacation on the island each summer. Though the time away from Rochester interferes with my work schedule from time to time, I do count it one of life's pleasures that I can spend time on the island, especially with fine friends such as you."

Fanny nearly laughed aloud. She knew Uncle Jonas would have done most anything to avoid coming to Broadmoor Island—anything except forfeit a portion of his inheritance. She thought his false bravado annoying and slowly inched her way toward the far end of the veranda. No one would miss her if she slipped away for a walk. Sophie and Amanda had already returned indoors. If the others came looking for her, they would assume she had joined her cousins. Yes, fresh air and exercise would prove a perfect cure for her unkind thoughts of Uncle Jonas.

Choosing the well-worn path that led to the special place she'd shared with her father, Fanny inhaled a deep breath. Her perch provided an excellent view of the beauty these islands provided. At every angle the miniature islands offered a re-splendent picture of God's creation, each island as unique as the people who inhabited it. From verdant fields to wooded shores, from rocky promontories to stately groves or dense thickets, the islets peeked out of the tranquil waters and beckoned her to explore.

She could almost hear her father's voice, smell his cologne. "You've been gone for so long now," she whispered, "and yet it feels like just yesterday."

Glancing at the place where she'd found him, Fanny remembered every detail of that day. He had seemed so peaceful, so content. He had simply gone to sleep. Fanny walked to the place where he'd died and sat down as she had often done in the past. Somehow, sitting here was comforting. She imagined herself on her father's lap, safe and protected.

"Papa, why must things change? Why must people die and leave us sad and alone? Grandfather is gone now, and Uncle Jonas will control my life. He has no heart for me—no love of the things and people I adore."

The wind blew gently, rustling the brush and grass around her. Fanny closed her eyes and tried to let go of her anxious thoughts.

Life would be much simpler if Uncle Jonas would agree to her plan and grant permission for her to remain on the island when the rest of the family departed for their respective homes. She loved Sophie and Amanda, but she wouldn't fit into either of their families. Not that Uncle Quincy would ever make such an offer. He remained far too involved with his good works to provide a proper home for Sophie, much less for his orphaned niece.

She tucked her knees beneath her chin and opened her eyes to watch the sun descend in a glowing display of blazing pink, mottled with hues of orange and lavender. Much too soon the setting sun was swallowed into the distant horizon, and she longed for the ability to request another performance.

"Another beautiful sunset in the glorious Thousand Islands." She recognized Michael's voice and twisted around. "Oh yes. Weren't the pinks especially beautiful this evening? I only wish it could have lasted longer."

In four well-placed giant steps, he was beside her. "You need only wait until tomorrow evening for a return appearance. Who knows? You may see an even finer vision in twenty-four hours." He plopped down and offered a grin. "I'm sorry for being so short with you earlier. I never want to cause you pain."

"You weren't short with me. I was just keenly feeling my losses. I came here to feel some sense of peace again."

He nodded. "I knew I would find you here. Mother said she was cooking for a dinner party tonight. Did you have the good fortune of being excluded?"

Compared to the stuffy social set who attended the round of parties each summer, Michael was a breath of fresh air. He was a constant reliable friend who never changed. Perhaps it was because he grew up on this island with his parents' steady hand in his life; she couldn't be certain. But Michael was never envious or impressed by the wealth and pomposity that invaded the islands each summer.

"I wasn't excluded from the evening meal, but I did manage to sneak away while some of the family gathered on the veranda. I had tired of their party planning and gossip long before I escaped." She pointed toward a fish that broke the water and then splashed back into the river. "Uncle Jonas was complaining that my grandfather hadn't distributed his assets in accordance with my uncle's wishes."

"It was your grandfather's property. I'd say he could do whatever he wanted with it."

"Those are my sentiments, also, but money is the all-important commodity in the Broadmoor family. Uncle Jonas wants the power that he thinks money gives him; Uncle Quincy wants his share in order to perform good works for others, although he consistently forgets his own daughters need his time and attention; many of the others simply want the things the money will buy and the social status they are afforded by virtue of wealth. I dislike their superficial nature."

"Don't become disheartened. You may be overreacting to some of the things they say and do."

Fanny gave him a sidelong glance. "You may be correct. It is truly a gift to know I will always have a roof over my head and a warm meal when I'm hungry. Granted, it may not be the exact roof I want or the food I desire, but wealth does offer a certain security and comfort."

"But our genuine comfort and security should come from the Lord and not from our earthly possessions, don't you think?"

"You're absolutely correct; it's the things that money cannot buy that I love the most." She spread her arms. "This island and the river, for instance. God's creation abounds out here, yet no one in my family can see it. They view this island as an obligation they must endure. How can that be possible?"

"They've never taken time to consider this island a privilege to be savored and enjoyed. Consequently they don't see what you do, Fanny. Perhaps they never will." He stood and offered her his hand. "It's getting dark. I'll walk you back to the house."

She enjoyed the warmth of Michael's hand and wished he hadn't withdrawn it once she'd stepped down from the rocks. "Have you mentioned our earlier conversation to your mother and father?"

His dark eyes shone in the waning light. "About remaining here on the island?"

"Yes. Have they indicated if they would be willing to have me move to the island? I know they may find it difficult to approach Uncle Jonas, but I could pave the way once I know if they'd be willing to speak with him."

Michael pulled a leaf from a tree branch and folded it between his fingers. "I'm sorry, Fanny. I haven't spoken to either of them just yet. I thought it might be best to wait until everyone is more settled." He flipped the leaf to the ground. "It's always hectic during the first few weeks, what with the new routines, added people, and the like."

She was thankful for the evening shadows. Otherwise, he'd surely detect her disappointment. "I understand. Whenever you think best," she said, feigning her best lighthearted tone. "And if they refuse, please tell them I will understand. I don't want my request to cause them discomfort."

"I don't know what their reaction will be, but I believe they'll agree unless your uncle Jonas opposes the idea. In that case I doubt they'd be willing to offer much argument." He directed her away from the path. "This is a shorter route back to the house."

Fanny wasn't interested in locating a shorter direction. If she had her way, she'd remain in Michael's company awhile longer. But what could she say? *Please don't take me back to the house? I prefer to spend my time with you?* She couldn't possibly behave in such a forward manner. Michael had already gone against protocol by coming here to be alone with her. Two or three years earlier it wouldn't have mattered, but now that she was considered a young woman of marriageable age, the rules were different. And so she followed along, the thick grass folding beneath her feet in a soft, silent cushion.

Once they were alone on the veranda, Jonas and Mr. Oosterman settled in chairs overlooking the vast lawn. For well over a half hour, Jonas had attempted to steer their conversation toward financial investments. Each time he thought he'd neared success, Mr. Oosterman changed directions. Jonas hoped to learn a few tips from the wealthy investor, tips that might rescue him from the mistakes he'd already made. However, Mr. Oosterman was more interested in discussing his latest flare-up of gout, an ongoing medical problem that caused him severe pain from time to time.

"The doctor keeps telling me that if I'll give up rich food and alcohol, I'll see great improvement. Now I ask you, Jonas, what good is having money if I can't enjoy a fine meal followed by a good glass of port?"

"I suppose you must evaluate the options and decide for yourself. Are the food and drink important enough to you to make enduring the possible pain worth it?" Jonas shifted in his chair. "Much like deciding upon the proper investment, don't you think?"

"How so?"

"If you're willing to endure a loss, you take greater risks with your investments. Isn't that how you've managed to increase your fortune? By taking risks?"

Mr. Oosterman's barrel chest heaved up and down in time with his laughter. "I pay other people to make those decisions for me. Don't tell anyone, but I've never enjoyed devising plans for multiplying my money. It takes away from the time I have to spend it." Once again, his chest heaved up and down.

Jonas sighed. Either Mr. Oosterman was telling the truth or he played his cards close to his vest. Jonas couldn't decide which. One thing had become obvious: Edward wasn't going to give away any secrets this evening.

Mr. Oosterman reached for the bottle of port sitting on the nearby table and poured himself another glass. Jonas stared across the landscape and then narrowed his eyes. He couldn't quite make out the faces of the man and woman who were approaching the house. Then a shaft of light danced off her hair and he recognized Fanny, but that wasn't Jefferson or George walking with her. He strained to the side; then he recognized the man. *Michael!* Those two were spending far too much time together. Even with the added duties he'd assigned the young man and Fanny's social obligations this evening, the two of them had made time to wander off together. Unacceptable! He would speak to Michael.

Though he had hoped to return to Rochester immediately following Sunday dinner, Jonas knew that the Sunday evening vesper service would provide another opportunity for Michael and Fanny to enjoy each other's company. And he did not dare suggest the family miss the service. They'd think he'd turned heathen. The only time they missed the service at Half Moon Bay was when the weather threatened their safety. He would leave first thing Monday morning.

No one seemed exactly certain how the services had first begun, but Jonas surmised they'd been started years ago when religious camps and revivals operated on the islands. Though the camps had lost popularity, they still maintained a presence on some of the larger islands.

And the boat services had never lost their appeal. Folks would load into their skiffs, canoes, or launches and arrive at the bay each Sunday evening. Preacher Halsted's pulpit was a permanent fixture perched on a hillock near the water's edge. The ladies in their Sunday finery and the gentlemen in their summer suits would sit in boats that were anchored close enough so that the occupants could shake hands with one another. Boats would arrive each Sunday evening and fill the entire bay. Reverend Halsted used a speaking trumpet for important announcements, though he refused to shout his message through the cumbersome horn. Those at a great distance might not hear all of the preacher's words, but they joined to sing God's praises on the preacher's cue.

If necessary, Jonas could have navigated the launch, but questions would have arisen if he dismissed Michael from the chore. So Jonas had remained. He accompanied the entire family to the launch but shook his head when Fanny attempted to board. "Wait until Louisa is situated with the children." With practiced ease, he directed Quincy's daughter and her children to the location near Michael and continued directing the other family members to their seats. Fanny would be sitting between Amanda and his wife. Pleased with the arrangement, he sat down beside his wife and hoped the services would be short this evening. He wanted to speak with Michael upon their return.

Jonas didn't notice exactly when Mr. and Mrs. Oosterman arrived, but their boat was soon wedged beside the Broadmoor launch. Mrs. Oosterman waved and smiled; then she pointed to Louisa and nodded.

Louisa offered a faint smile. "Why is she pointing at me?"

"I'm sure I don't know, my dear. Just smile and wave," her aunt instructed.

There was no time to contemplate Mrs. Oosterman's behavior, for Reverend Halsted had already raised his speaking trumpet to his lips. "Announcements for the week are as follows: Eliza Preston will entertain all young ladies between the ages of fourteen and twenty at her parents' cottage on Tuesday for an afternoon of Bible study, followed by tea and a nature walk."

The preacher continued to read the remainder of the week's activities before turning the speaking trumpet in the direction of the Broadmoor launch. "I am told that we've had nothing short of a miracle occur already this summer. The infant grandson of Quincy Broadmoor was snatched from the very depths of the river and brought back to life by our own Michael Atwell."

"Praise God!" one of the attendees called out from his boat. Jubilation followed from all quarters, and soon one of the men burst forth in a chorus of praise.

The preacher waved toward the *DaisyBee*. "Would one of you like to say a few words?"

Folks were straining in the direction of the Broadmoor launch. Quincy was suffering from a stomach ailment and hadn't accompanied the family to the vesper service. The responsibility to acknowledge God's blessing would fall to Jonas. He stood and cupped his hands around his mouth. "We're all pleased to say that little Evan is doing just fine, and we're glad to have him right here with us." He motioned to Louisa to hold the boy in the air.

"Hallelujah!"

"Praise God!"

"You did a fine thing, Michael."

The shouts surrounded Jonas, and he dropped into his seat and shook his head. "*Right*. Praise God," he muttered. "I had the pleasure of paying the ten-dollar reward."

Thursday, July 15, 1897

Sophie spotted her cousins sitting beneath a distant stand of trees that shaded the water's edge. Without thought to proper etiquette, she hurtled down the sloping hill at breakneck speed. Had Amanda remained in place, Sophie would have plowed her over. Sophie stretched out her arms and headed for one of the large fir trees to break her run. A whoosh of air escaped her lungs as she collided with the ancient conifer.

Fanny jumped to her feet and hurried to her cousin's side. "Are you injured, Sophie?"

She grunted and rubbed her arms. "That didn't go quite as I had intended." She examined the bloody scratches that lined her hands and sat down.

Amanda returned to her previous spot on the blanket and dropped down between the other two girls. "Whatever were you thinking, Sophie? Or were you? Don't you realize you could have seriously injured one of us or yourself? Sometimes I think you give little thought to your behavior! You're no longer five years old, you know."

Sophie wrinkled her nose and deftly extricated a piece of tree bark from her flowing tresses. "I may not be five, but I'm not an old woman, either, Amanda. If I want to have fun, I will. And why did the two of you leave me when you knew I planned to join you?"

Amanda stiffened. "Are you implying that I act like an old woman?"

"Most of the time you act older than your own mother. You're so intent upon acting proper that you're afraid ever to have fun. I know you want to please everyone, Amanda, but you need to please yourself on occasion, too."

"I don't need you to tell me how to behave, Sophie. At least I don't embarrass the family by making a spectacle of myself."

Before Sophie could offer a rejoinder, Fanny clapped her hands together. "Please don't argue. We're supposed to be enjoying our time together." She examined Sophie's hands and then pulled a handkerchief from her pocket. "You were having a private conversation with Paul, and we didn't want to interrupt. That is the only reason we came ahead without you."

"I wish you would have interrupted. Paul Medford has become an albatross around my neck. He seems to view me as a part of his assigned duties."

"How so?" Fanny poured a trickle of water from the jug they'd carried from the house and wet her handkerchief. Thankfully they'd not chosen lemonade to accompany their picnic lunch. She daubed Sophie's hand with the damp hankie.

Sophie took the cloth from Fanny and began wiping dirt from her arms. "He said he came to the island in order to bring Father some reports regarding his charity shelter, but I know that's not true. My father is planning to return to Rochester later in the week, and I'm certain the paper work could have waited until his return."

"What has any of that to do with your belief that you've become an assignment of sorts?"

"If you'd just wait a minute, I'm getting to that part." Sophie frowned at Amanda. "Paul whispered that he needed to speak to me alone about a matter of importance. I joined him outside." She glanced at Fanny. "That's when you two saw me with him. He told me that he had heard some unsettling gossip about me from several sources in Rochester."

Amanda arched her brows. "Unsettling in what way?"

"That my behavior is occasionally viewed as inappropriate for someone of my social standing." She giggled. "As though I have any social standing."

"You *do* have social standing, Sophie. You are a Broadmoor. Your behavior reflects on the entire family." Amanda retrieved a glass from the picnic basket and picked up the water jug. "You act with wild abandon, and the whole family must suffer the consequences. Exactly what has he heard about you?"

Sophie shrugged. "I don't know. I didn't ask him to go into detail, for I truly don't care." She handed Fanny the handkerchief. "Unlike you, Amanda, I don't live my life to please others."

"Perhaps you should give it a try. Paul is obviously attempting to help."

"Help? He thinks I'm immature and take dangerous risks. *He's* the one who needs help. The man is twenty-five years old, yet he talks and acts like an old man. As I said the first time he visited the island, he'd make a perfect match for you, Amanda. You both think there's nothing more important than charity work and meeting the expectations of others." Sophie winked at Fanny. "And you're both averse to having fun."

"I am *not* averse to having fun. It's simply a matter of defining fun. You and I have completely different views."

"That's at least one thing we can agree upon, Amanda." Sophie reached into the basket and removed the tablecloth and napkins. "Are we going to eat our picnic lunch?"

Fanny shook her head. "Why don't we see if Michael will take us to Boar Head Island on the launch? We can eat there and then explore. Besides, we'll be all alone, and that makes it even better. No one will be able to bother us."

"I'm not so fond of being alone, although I'd like to get off of this island. I'd like it better if we'd go to Round Island. We could visit at the New Frontenac Hotel there. There are certain to be more guests arriving by the day."

Amanda gave Sophie a sidelong glance. "If you dislike socializing with prominent families, I don't know why you'd want to visit Round Island or the Frontenac."

Sophie locked her arms across her chest. No matter what she suggested, Amanda would find fault. "I'll defer to Fanny, and we'll have our picnic on Boar Head Island. I can visit the Frontenac this evening. I plan to attend the dance even if the two of you decide to remain at home."

They gathered their blanket and basket and sauntered toward the boathouse. Amanda circled around Fanny and came alongside Sophie. "I'd like to know exactly what rumors are circulating in Rochester, Sophie. How can we dispel such talk if we don't know what's being said?"

"I told Paul I didn't want to hear any of the small-minded tittle-tattle and walked off before he could tell me. I'm certain it has to do with the Independence Day celebration over at Brown Square." She giggled. "I believe I may have been a bit tipsy by the time the evening ended. I was singing with the German musicians. I didn't know the words, but I made up my own. You two should have come along. We had great fun."

Amanda gasped. "I love you dearly, Sophie, but I do wish you'd find some other method to gain your father's attention. In the end, you're hurting yourself more than Uncle Quincy."

They neared the boathouse, and Sophie decided she'd carry the conversation no further. Arguing with Amanda always proved useless. Her cousin would never change her idealistic attitudes, and Sophie didn't plan to change, either—not for Amanda, not for Paul, and certainly not for the sake of the beloved Broad-moor name! She and Amanda stood inside the doorway of the boathouse while Fanny talked to Michael. Strange how animated Fanny became while visiting with him—her smile widened, her eyes sparkled, and her laughter rippled with a delightful lilt that Sophie had never before heard in her younger cousin's voice.

Fanny beamed and waved her cousins forward. "Michael says he's willing to take us over to the island, and he'll come back and pick us up at four o'clock. Does that suit?"

Sophie wrinkled her nose. "Nearly four hours is a long time, don't you think?"

"Boar Head is a large island," Michael said. "You'll find plenty to keep you occupied. If you want to take some fishing poles along, there's a great ledge where you'll be able to sit and fish." He curled his fingers into a fist and pointed his thumb at Fanny. "Your cousin can bait your hooks, and if you catch a fish, she'll be able to help you out with that, too. Fanny's an expert when it comes to fishing."

Sophie saw the way Michael looked at Fanny. Were these two interested in each other? She glanced at Amanda and wondered if her cousin noticed the attraction, but she appeared oblivious.

"I thought I heard voices down here." Theresa O'Malley en-tered through the side door, glanced around, and immediately flashed a pouting smile at Michael. "Are you all going on a picnic?"

Michael shook his head. "I'm merely providing boat service for these ladies. I won't be gone long. If anyone is looking for me, you can tell them I've gone to Boar Head Island."

Theresa tucked her hand beneath his arm. "Oh, may I ride along with you? I've completed my chores, and Mother said I didn't need to return to the house for an hour."

Sophie didn't fail to note the way Theresa gazed into Michael's eyes—and that demure smile. Theresa had set her cap for him!

"I promise I'll be good company on the return trip," Theresa cooed.

"I don't know," Michael mumbled.

Sophie felt pity for the girl. Like Sophie, Theresa was obviously bored to tears on this island. "Oh, do let her ride along, Michael. What difference does it make?"

But one look at Fanny told her that it did make a difference. Fanny's earlier sparkle had been replaced by a brooding stare. So there *was* something between these two. Fanny was jealous of Theresa. And from the possessive hold Theresa maintained on Michael's arm, Theresa was jealous of Fanny. Little Fanny was hiding a secret. Uncle Jonas and Aunt Victoria would not approve! This picnic might turn out to be more interesting than she'd anticipated.

Fanny's eyes met Michael's as he helped her into the boat. She read the apologetic look—at least that's what she wanted to believe. Having Theresa accompany them wasn't his fault. After Sophie's comment, what else could he do? Of course he could have discouraged her from remaining so close to his side throughout the excursion. Fanny peeked from beneath the brim of her straw hat and watched Theresa talking to him. He seemed engrossed in what she was saying. Fanny looked away when Theresa placed a possessive hold on Michael's arm. Perhaps he enjoyed her company. A picture of Michael carrying Theresa out of the woods on the day of her arrival paraded through Fanny's mind, and she turned away. And he'd been unusually distant since Sunday, when they'd gone to vespers. In fact, he'd avoided her on several occasions since then. She could feel tears beginning to form in the corners of her eyes. She'd be unable to explain if someone should notice.

Theresa continued to cling to Michael's arm. By the time they arrived at the island, Fanny was pleased to disembark. Having Theresa along had diminished her pleasure. The three of them waited while Michael unloaded their belongings.

He touched Fanny's sleeve as he handed her the fishing poles. "I'll return at four o'clock." He set a can of worms on a rock near her feet. "I'm sorry," he whispered before returning to the launch.

Fanny remained near the shoreline and watched as the boat churned through the murky water before picking up speed. Theresa's enthusiastic waves continued until they were nearly out of sight.

"I think she's quite taken with Michael, don't you?" Sophie leaned forward and picked up the can of worms.

"It would appear that way." Fanny swallowed hard and pushed back the lump in her throat.

"But I don't think she loves him as much as you do."

Fanny twisted around to face Sophie. She rubbed her fingers along the nape of her neck in an attempt to relieve the dull ache that was working its way up her skull and toward her temples. "I have no idea what you're talking about. Michael and I are friends. You know we've spent many hours together since we were young children. I believe you're permitting your fanciful imagination to run wild."

Amanda giggled. "How could you even say such a thing, Sophie? When Fanny is interested in a young man, she'll be looking for someone of her own social class. Not that Michael isn't a fine man," she quickly added. "But someone of his class could hardly ask my father for Fanny's hand."

Though Fanny did not dare object to Amanda's remarks, she wanted to tell her cousin she was guilty of snobbery in the extreme. Amanda had pledged to spend her future helping the less fortunate, yet she possessed her father's view regarding class and status. Did she not understand her attitude would spill over to those whom she attempted to serve in the future? Her cousins were at opposing ends of the spectrum. Sophie wanted the world to know she had no use for class or society, although she enjoyed the pleasures wealth could buy. On the other hand, Amanda thought social status of import. She viewed the family social status as a way of opening doors to aid charitable causes.

Strange that she could clearly articulate her cousins' beliefs, but when it came to her own convictions, Fanny experienced difficulty. Perhaps because she disliked confrontation, she had never clearly decided what she believed. Fearful of being ridiculed or appearing foolish, she typically kept her thoughts to herself. Only when she talked to Michael did she feel she could freely express herself. From all appearances, Theresa felt entirely comfortable in his presence, also.

Sophie wiggled the can of worms beneath Fanny's nose. "Are we going to fish or explore the island? This is your outing of choice, so you lead the way."

"Let's spread our blanket. We can decide after we've eaten lunch." Without waiting for her cousins' consent, Fanny flipped the blanket into the air and spread it on a well-shaded spot not far from the water's edge.

While Amanda and Fanny unpacked the basket, Sophie reclined on the blanket and eyed each selection. "You could have requested something other than sandwiches, Fanny. Rather boring fare, don't you think?"

"I did the best I could. Mrs. O'Malley and Mrs. Atwell were busy planning the week's menus. I didn't want to interfere, so I prepared our lunch on my own."

"Do tell! Aren't you becoming quite the domesticated young woman! No need for servants to do your bidding? I believe you *would* fit into Michael Atwell's life without much difficulty." Sophie removed several grapes from a large cluster and tossed one into her mouth.

"Make yourself useful and pour our drinks, Sophie." Amanda flashed a sour look across the blanket.

"Oh, all right, but I do wish you'd quit your bossing, Amanda. It's very unbecoming, you know." Sophie placed her hands on the ground and pushed herself up. "Ouch! What was that?" She examined her palm. "Now, look. What with my earlier scratches and now this cut, I'm truly injured. Where's your handkerchief, Fanny?"

While Sophie blotted the cut with the handkerchief, Fanny lifted the corner of the blanket and brushed her fingers over the ground. There! Something sharp protruded through the grass. Probably just a rock, but she yanked the grass and weeds surrounding the object. "Hand me one of those spoons, Amanda."

"You're going to dig in the dirt with the good silver?"

"Forevermore, Amanda, just give me the spoon. It isn't the good silver—I promise." Fanny grabbed the utensil from her cousin's hand; soon she'd excavated the sharp object. After removing the traces of dirt with one of the napkins, she extended her palm. "Look."

Sophie shrugged. "A flat piece of rock. So what?"

"No. It's an Iroquois arrowhead," she said with an air of authority.

"How would you know? I agree with Sophie. It looks like a pointed flat stone."

"No." Fanny shook her head. "Michael had several in his pocket, and he showed them to me. He's been collecting them since he was a little boy. He has some that he has discovered are Iroquois and a few that are Mississauga. Both tribes inhabited the islands years ago." While her cousins helped themselves to the chicken sandwiches, Fanny used her napkin to continue polishing the arrowhead. "This is ever so exciting. I wonder if we can find some others."

Amanda glanced heavenward. "Please, Fanny. Let's not make this some archaeological expedition. You're not another Sir Austen Henry Layard."

"Who's *that*?" Sophie asked before taking another bite of her sandwich.

"He's the famous archaeologist that grandfather met in England a long time ago. He died a few years past. Surely you remember. He discovered the remains of the Assyrian regal monuments and cuneiform inscriptions and concluded they were the visible remains of Nineveh. He wrote a book about his second expedition. Grandfather told us about it several times."

"Isn't Nineveh in the Bible or something?"

"Yes, it's in the Bible, but this is—oh, never mind." Amanda tossed a grape seed toward the water. "You're not even listening."

"Wouldn't it be wonderful to discover some ancient ruin?" Fanny tucked the arrowhead into the pocket of her dress.

Sophie sighed and leaned against the trunk of an ancient white spruce. "It would be more exciting to discover some nice fellows. I'm bored. I haven't met even one new man who strikes my fancy. I'm ready to go home."

"Well, *that's* not going to occur. We're here for the duration of the summer, so you might as well decide to enjoy yourself." Amanda repacked the picnic basket and closed the lid with a decisive thump. "Are we fishing or exploring, Fanny?"

"We'll explore first, and then we'll fish. That way we'll see Michael when he returns."

"And I'll wager you're hoping he'll return without Theresa. Am I right?" Sophie nudged her cousin and giggled.

Fanny pretended she didn't hear.

13

Monday, July 19, 1897

Jonas had planned to catch the early train, but his plans had gone awry when Victoria insisted upon accompanying him to Clayton in order to visit one of her favorite dressmakers. He'd missed the early train, so the first day of the workweek would be a complete loss. She ignored his grumbles and told him it was summertime and he should relax. Women! They didn't understand the complexity of operating a business and acquiring assets. They did, however, possess the ability to spend money without difficulty.

During their short boat ride from the island, Victoria regaled him with details of the fabric and the dress she was having fashioned for one of their upcoming parties. When he thought a response was expected, he offered no more than a grunt or a nod. The two of them had been married long enough that she should realize he cared not a whit about chiffon and muslin or whether a dress was pleated, tucked, or puffed. He reminded himself that a woman's brain could be easily occupied with matters of little import, whereas a man's mind required the meaty issues of life.

He offered his hand to Victoria and assisted her onto the boat dock that bordered the Clayton train tracks. She tucked her hand beneath his arm. They appeared the perfect couple.

When they'd safely traversed the tracks and reached the platform, Victoria pecked Jonas on the cheek. "I do wish you'd make an effort to return on Thursday evening rather than Friday. The family could enjoy a nice long weekend together. Promise you'll do your best."

Jonas touched the brim of his hat. "I'll try, but with my late departure today, I doubt I can return before Friday. You do remember that I may have guests with me."

She stopped midstep. "Guests?"

A train whistle wailed in the distance, and Jonas glanced down the tracks. "I told you that I plan to use my free time each evening deciding upon eligible suitors for Amanda and Fanny. I told you I'd be bringing the young men to visit at the island."

"But I didn't think you meant so soon. I wanted to discuss the matter further, Jonas. I've already told you that I'm opposed to this matchmaking idea. I want the girls to marry for love, not because they've been forced into an arranged marriage."

He craned his neck and peered down the tracks. Why didn't the train arrive? He was tired of explaining the same thing over and over to his wife. Why couldn't women merely accept that their husbands knew what was best!

"As I've already told you, it is much too risky to allow them to make such weighty decisions. Besides, it's time the girls accepted a few of the responsibilities that accompany the wealth they've enjoyed all these years. Marrying well is expected, and young women can't be trusted to make wise choices."

A breeze played at the hem of Victoria's pale blue muslin gown. "And I say they are intelligent young ladies who should have a say in choosing a husband."

Jonas sighed. "Why do you argue with me? We didn't marry for love. Surely our marriage is proof enough that love can grow."

"Speak for yourself, Jonas Broadmoor." With a stomp of her leather slipper, she turned and strode off without a backward glance.

"Don't forget to alert the staff there will be additional guests arriving for the weekend," he called.

His wife didn't acknowledge him, but Jonas knew she'd heard the reminder. In time he'd win Victoria over to his way of thinking. If necessary, he'd tell her Fanny's interest in Michael was proof enough that the girl couldn't be trusted to marry a man of worth. Even if Victoria didn't come around to his idea, she would accept his decision. She had no choice.

Once settled on the train, Jonas searched his mind for potential candidates, primarily for Fanny. He would concentrate on her first. Finding the proper man for Fanny was urgent. There were plenty of young men who would prove acceptable for his own daughter. But the man for Fanny must be very carefully selected. He'd need a man of social position. Yet the proper candidate must be willing to adhere to Jonas's commands. Someone with an eye toward attaining the wealth and power associated with the Broadmoor name, a man who would not otherwise be considered.

Suddenly he was struck by a thought of brilliance. This would not be so difficult after all! Many powerful families in New York had suffered through the depression and still remained in a state of economic instability. Others would never recover. For the present, they all maintained their social standing within the ranks of New York society. Fanny's group of suitors would be the sons of such men! Any of them had much to gain by marrying young Frances Jane Broadmoor and would be easily managed.

Indeed, he would speak to his lawyer as soon as possible. Mortimer would surely know of some suitable young men—and if he didn't, his younger son, John, would prove helpful. Still unmarried, John Fillmore enjoyed the social life; he was certain to know any such eligible men. Of course Jonas wouldn't confide in John. He'd rely upon Mortimer to extract the information from his son. While Jonas trusted both the lawyer and his older son, Vincent, implicitly, he thought John exceedingly lazy. Somewhat akin to his own sons Jefferson and George.

"Must be this generation," Jonas muttered hours later as he stepped down from the train. Weary from his journey, he departed the station and signaled for a cab. There would be little accomplished at this late hour. He'd go directly to the house. First thing tomorrow, he'd set his plan in motion.

Jonas signaled Mortimer toward his table at the Revere Hotel. Over a lunch of thick open-faced beef sandwiches and strong coffee, the lawyer placed his stamp of approval upon Jonas's plan and agreed to provide a list of candidates posthaste, even a name or two by the end of the day. Then the men departed for their respective offices.

Jonas paced in front of his wide office window that offered a view of Main Street and inhaled a deep breath. His office clock chimed five but still no word from Mortimer. Neither anger nor irritation would serve him well. He wanted to schedule private meetings with each of the men tomorrow. If Mortimer didn't furnish names, Jonas would be delayed.

While still contemplating his departure for home, the telephone rang. "Jonas! I'm glad to find you still in the office." Mortimer's voice crackled through the line. "I have some names for you if you'd like to jot them down."

Though Jonas still didn't like telephones, it was at times such as these that he appreciated the contraptions. He knew telephone usage would continue, but Jonas had little respect for the telephone company. He'd been unimpressed when the company had imposed continuing increases that had eventually compelled the subscribers to form a users' strike that had continued for two full years. Not until the Rochester Common Council had ordered the telephone company to remove its unused poles from the streets of Rochester was a compromise finally reached and telephone usage resumed.

The company immediately expanded to the more affluent neighborhoods of Rochester and even began to offer reliable long-distance service. Much to his wife's dismay, Jonas refused to have the jangling piece of equipment in his home. But work was another matter. One must keep pace with the competition and be accessible. He'd learned that lesson long ago.

"Just the names and nothing more. I don't like discussing private concerns on the telephone," Jonas said.

Mortimer grunted his agreement and offered four names. "I'm not so sure about that last one. John recommended him, but don't set up an appointment with him until you hear from me tomorrow."

"Three provide a sufficient beginning. You're certain these men meet our criteria?" He recognized only one of the names.

"Two of them are from New York City but are currently in Rochester seeking new opportunities. I know their fathers. I can stop by the house this evening if you'd like further information before contacting them."

Jonas hesitated. "I don't even know *where* to contact them."

Mortimer laughed. "One is staying at the Regent Hotel, and the other has a room at the Exeter."

Jonas heard a click on the telephone line and hesitated. "I'd prefer discussing this in person." Someone had picked up another phone and was listening to their conversation. Annoying contraption! "On second thought, why don't you come over around eight o'clock and have a brandy. We can speak privately."

"Good enough."

Jonas continued to hold the receiver to his ear. Two clicks followed Mortimer's farewell. Someone *had* been listening. Little wonder he seldom used a telephone. He'd learned early in life that people were nosy and enjoyed gossip. His wife and daughter were prime examples. They constantly discussed every tidbit that came their way, while men tucked away useful bits of information and discarded the remainder as nonsensical prattle.

Donning his hat, Jonas departed for home. There was much to accomplish this evening. The moment he entered the house, he instructed the housekeeper to serve his dinner in the library, a practice he often employed when the family was away. Tonight, the solitude would permit him time to consider his plan in broader detail.

After a brief time upstairs to refresh himself, Jonas returned to the library and set to work. He had made little progress when the maid entered with his tray. Nodding, he signaled her to place the tray near the doors leading into the garden. Jonas didn't particularly enjoy gardens or flowers, but he appreciated what the flower industry had done for Rochester. Visitors were continually amazed at the city's resilience and adaptation to change. Both his grandfather and father had realized the need to follow that same example.

For a time, the numerous flour mills in the area earned Rochester the nickname Flour City, but the flour industry eventually moved west to accommodate the wheat farmers, and Rochester lost its prominence in flour production. The city had already become acclaimed, however, for its beautiful flowers and the production and shipping of flower seeds. The city's nickname switched from Flour City to Flower City, and the Broadmoor family purchased an interest in the flower industry. Thereafter, Hamilton and Jonas invested large portions of the family wealth in the Eastman Dry Plate and Film Company and Bausch and Lomb, two other local businesses. Thus far, the investments had proven themselves valuable, and Jonas remained certain he would reap huge financial rewards for years to come. At least those investments had proven sound. If only they would produce enough profit to cover the mess his failures had caused.

After wiping his mouth, Jonas pushed his tray to the side, returned to his desk, and awaited Mortimer's arrival. As expected, his trusted attorney arrived precisely on time. Their discussion led to drafting an outline for a speech Jonas would give to each of the young men. They'd briefly considered bringing them all together for a dinner meeting but soon decided upon individual appointments. In a private meeting Jonas would be better able to evaluate the pliability of each man and determine if an invitation to the island should be extended. Groundwork would be clearly established with each man at the initial meeting. Together, Jonas and Mortimer drafted a letter including an appointed time to meet with Jonas on Thursday. The men agreed an hour would be allocated for each candidate. When Mortimer departed at eleven o'clock, Jonas was confident he would find the perfect husband for Fanny.

On Thursday morning Jonas arose early and stepped onto his bedroom balcony. Like an emperor inspecting his kingdom, he surveyed the perfectly manicured gardens below. Jonas performed the daily ritual except during foul weather. And Rochester had its share of foul weather. Not as dire as Buffalo. But what city's weather could compare to that of Buffalo—or wanted to, for that matter. He inhaled a vigorous breath of fresh air and promptly returned indoors.

Giving special attention to his attire, he chose a pinstripe suit with matching vest. The suit had been delivered by his tailor only three weeks earlier. These were young men who should recognize quality and detail at every quarter, and Jonas wouldn't disappoint them. After his usual breakfast of coddled eggs and fresh biscuits, he stepped into his carriage. As was his custom, Jonas entered his office at precisely eight o'clock and was greeted by Mr. Fryer, his office clerk for the past fifteen years.

By now Mr. Fryer knew Jonas's preferences, and few words were necessary between them. A fresh pitcher of water and glasses had been placed on the table, the mail had been opened and arranged in order of importance, and a neatly written list of the day's appointments rested atop the mail. Behind the closed door, Jonas perused his mail and silently practiced the speech he would give to each of the young men.

At exactly nine o'clock, a knock sounded on his door. "Yes?"

"Mr. Frank Colgan to see you, sir."

"Please show him in."

Jonas stood behind his desk and extended his hand to the young man who followed Mr. Fryer into the office. "Jonas Broadmoor," he said while evaluating the strength of Mr. Colgan's grasp.

"Frank Colgan. Pleased to make your acquaintance, Mr. Broadmoor. I hear good things about you."

"Do you?" Jonas signaled for the man to sit. "Such as?"

Colgan's eyes widened. "Excuse me?"

"You said you hear good things about me. I wondered exactly what you've been told."

The young man stammered, "That you're an influential member of the community, and ah—"

"A free bit of advice for you, Mr. Colgan: I don't appreciate hollow flattery."

Mr. Colgan's complexion paled. "I do apologize."

"Accepted. Now, let's move on. I'm sure you're wondering exactly why I've asked you to come to my office. I'll come right to the point."

Jonas explained his plan to find the perfect husband for his niece: a man willing to follow direction and refrain from gossip, an intelligent man of good social standing, a man willing to live a life of ease with his niece, a man willing to grant Jonas permission to continue handling his niece's inheritance. "Does my proposal interest you, Mr. Colgan?"

Frank squirmed in his chair. "Is she quite homely or disfigured? Is that the reason for this arrangement, Mr. Broadmoor?"

Jonas laughed. "On the contrary, she is a lovely girl, but I suppose there are those who might consider her somewhat plain. A bit strong-willed perhaps but well educated, a fine figure, and capable of running a household."

"In that case, when shall we be wed?"

"Not so fast. If you agree to all of the terms, you will be one of several young men who will vie for my niece's affections. You see, this arrangement between us is to be kept secret. Once Fanny makes her choice—whether she chooses you or not—you will be paid a handsome sum . . . if and only if you play by all of the rules I've set forth. In the event you mention this arrangement to *anyone,* I will deny any knowledge of having met with you, and you will receive nothing from me." Jonas leaned across his desk. "And should you betray me, you will face great difficulty being accepted in proper social circles or securing meaningful employment."

Frank rubbed his jaw. "And you're making this proposal to all of the men who will meet your niece?"

"I didn't say that, Mr. Colgan. You may be the only person to whom I make this offer. On the other hand, I may have this conversation with all of the men who court my niece. You won't know. But if another suitor should mention he has spoken to me, it would behoove you to report his conduct to me. That man will be removed as a possibility." Jonas leaned back in his chair. "Well? What say you, Mr. Colgan? Are you interested in competing for a life of luxury?"

"It appears I have nothing to lose. Even if your niece chooses someone else, I'll be paid a handsome sum."

"Exactly right."

This young man would make a perfect candidate. If he didn't think he had anything to lose by participating in this venture, Frank Colgan would be easily manipulated. Jonas extended an invitation for a weekend visit to Broadmoor Island, and Mr. Colgan readily accepted.

Jonas closed his office door and walked to the window. He removed his pocket watch and checked the time: exactly one hour had passed from the time Frank had entered his office until Jonas watched him hail a cab. Tucking the watch into his pocket, he returned to his desk. One interview completed and three to go. If the remainder of the appointments went as smoothly as this one, he would be most pleased.

14

Fanny pulled a brush through Amanda's thick blond hair. Amanda's golden mane fanned across her shoulders like a luxurious cape. Though Fanny tried her best not to envy her cousins, she couldn't help but compare her own bushy auburn curls to Sophie's shining tresses or Amanda's flawless locks. Fanny pinned a loop of her cousin's blond hair into place.

"I don't like the way you placed that curl." Sprawled across the bed in a most unladylike position, Sophie pointed to the side of Amanda's head. "It should be lower, over on the side."

Initially Fanny followed Sophie's instruction but then moved the curl back to its previous position. "You're wrong. It looks better here."

Sophie flopped onto her side and rested her chin in her palm. "Hairstyles have changed, Fanny." She watched a moment longer and then jumped up from the bed. "Let me do it."

Fanny willingly relinquished the brush and walked to the bedroom window. From her vantage point, she could see Michael leaning over the skiff pulling a string of fish from inside the boat. A successful day of fishing! She wished she could have been with him.

"What do you see down there?" Sophie asked.

Fanny didn't want to turn away from the window for fear Michael would disappear. "Nothing."

"You're far too intrigued for there to be nothing down there." Fanny didn't hear Sophie approach. "I see! It's Michael you're watching. Whether you want to admit it to us or not, I know you have feelings for him."

"You're right, Sophie. I am fond of him." Why should she continue to deny what she'd known was true since seeing Michael carry Theresa out of the woods the day they had arrived? Besides, Sophie would hound her until she made an admission.

"I knew it!" Sophie danced around Fanny, wielding the hairbrush overhead. "You see, Amanda? I told you, but you said I was wrong. You should never doubt me in matters of the heart. I'm always right."

Amanda frowned. "Remember what I told you the other day, Fanny. You're a Broadmoor. Father will never permit such an arrangement. Think what Grand-mère would say if she were alive. You know she would be disappointed at the very idea."

"I don't think so. She and Grandfather loved and respected the Atwells. I think she would have approved."

Amanda joined her cousins at the window. "You're dreaming, Fanny. They may have respected the Atwells, but they wouldn't have blessed your marriage to Michael."

"I said I was fond of him. It's the two of you who are discussing marriage." Fanny folded her arms across her waist and wished she could escape this conversation. Her cousins had ruined her earlier pleasure over seeing Michael.

"Well, once Fanny reaches her majority, she can marry whomever she chooses," Sophie said, toying with the brush. "She will be quite wealthy, after all, and no one will be able to tell her what to do."

"Money won't keep people from telling a woman what to do," Amanda replied. "Especially when it comes to matrimony. No, if anything, Fanny will have it much harder now. She will be scrutinized and watched at every turn."

"Do you truly suppose so?" Fanny asked.

Amanda nodded. "No one, especially my father, is going to allow you to take such an important matter into your own hands."

"All the more reason Fanny should take charge now," Sophie said firmly. "Honestly, you'd think you two were chained to Uncle Jonas's arm. He cannot be everywhere at one time. You should think long and hard about what you want out of life and make it happen for yourselves, rather than wait for someone else to dictate it."

"But wisely choosing a mate is the most important thing in the world," Amanda said. "Especially when you are a part of a more privileged class of people. The wealthy make so many decisions that affect the lives of the poor."

"There you go again worrying about the poor," Sophie said in a tone that clearly betrayed her exasperation. "You are such a ninny sometimes."

Amanda retrieved the hairbrush from Sophie and returned to the dressing table. "We'd best finish our hair if we're going to be dressed by the time Father arrives from Rochester. Mother said he might be bringing some additional guests for the weekend, and she appeared none too pleased."

"Oh? Who? I do hope it's none of Uncle Jonas's business associates. We'll be forced to remain at home all evening. They'll expect us to join them for a game of whist or charades. I was in hopes we could go to the hotel in Clayton. There's a dance tonight." Sophie's dark eyes sparkled, and she winked at Fanny. "Maybe Michael would agree to take us in the skiff."

Fanny smiled, but in truth she was still caught up in Amanda's comments. "I don't know. Let's wait and see."

The three girls were on the upper veranda when they spotted the launch nearing the dock. Amanda cupped her hand over her eyes and squinted. There were additional passengers in the boat. "I can't see well enough to determine who Father has brought with him."

Sophie leaned over the railing and continued to watch until the boat neared the pier. "I can't see one woman among the passengers." She glanced over her shoulder. "Strange, don't you think?"

"I just hope he hasn't brought old Mr. Snodgrass with him. I don't think I could bear an entire weekend of his attention," Fanny said.

"Perhaps Uncle Jonas is thinking Mr. Snodgrass would be a good match for you, Fanny." Sophie doubled over in a gale of laughter.

Fanny shook her head emphatically. "I would run away first!"

"I don't think you need worry. Unless my eyes deceive me, the men with Uncle Jonas are all young and quite good-looking."

"I recognize only a few of those men," Amanda said.

"Let's go downstairs and meet the rest. For once Uncle Jonas was thinking about someone other than himself when he chose guests to visit the island," Sophie said as she pushed away from the railing and hurried indoors. "We may not need to go to Clayton after all."

Amanda reached out to stop Fanny as she followed after her cousin. "Wait. I want to say something."

Fanny turned in surprise. "What?"

Amanda frowned, then seemed to recompose her feelings. "I didn't mean to upset you earlier. It's just that I've overheard my father and mother talk on so many occasions about the responsibility of seeing me properly wed. I know how my father feels about such matters, and I know that the fact you've inherited your father's share of Grandfather's estate will create problems for you that you may not have expected."

"But why? I don't see how that should change anything."

"I know. But mark my words, it will. With Father being put in charge as your guardian, he will endeavor to do whatever is necessary to safeguard your fortune and his reputation. The idea of you with Michael is something he would never consent to. I know without a doubt he would do whatever was necessary to keep you apart."

"Does he not care at all about true love?" Fanny asked in disbelief. "Wouldn't he want you, or even me, for that matter, to be happy?"

Amanda sighed and looped her arm through Fanny's. "Father will want whatever benefits him the most, unfortunately. Just guard your heart. Otherwise, I fear the results will not be to your liking."

Jonas didn't fail to note the covetous looks of several of the young men as the launch approached Broadmoor Island. He enjoyed seeing a good plan come to fruition, and if this first step was any gauge, he and Mortimer had developed an excellent strategy. Careful to make a mental note of those who appeared most impressed with their surroundings, he sauntered toward the house with his entourage. Together with the candidates he'd interviewed, Jonas had invited three bachelors from Rochester who were acquainted with his wife and family.

That idea had been one of Mortimer's suggestions. *"The ladies of your household may question why you've brought all these strangers and become suspicious. You must also take a few eligible men with whom they're acquainted."* Using all the resources at his disposal, Mortimer had suggested several, and three of them were willing to travel to the island with him that weekend. There had been insufficient time to properly interview the final choices, but Jonas would remain vigilant throughout the weekend. If Fanny demonstrated an interest in one of the added candidates, Jonas would take the proper steps to meet with the young man next week.

Jonas hadn't felt so alive in a long time. He enjoyed nothing more than a good challenge. "I do hope all of you are going to enjoy your weekend here at Broadmoor Castle."

His delight increased twofold when the three girls stepped into view and the men murmured words of approval. A good sign. He waved the girls forward but was disappointed when it was Sophie who immediately broke away from the other two and rushed forward while Amanda and Fanny waited at a distance.

His pleasure diminished when he caught sight of his wife. She rounded the edge of the porch with a determined step and a firm set to her jaw. The moment he drew near, Jonas forced a broad smile. "I am so pleased to be back on the island," he said before kissing her cheek.

Victoria backed away from his grasp and surveyed the bevy of young men. "I suppose you should make introductions, Jonas. I don't believe I've met several of these young men."

Forcing an air of joviality, he waved the men forward. "I know how you young ladies prefer a variety of escorts and thought I should assist in that regard." As though showcasing a new product, he extended his arm with a flourish and introduced each of the men.

"Could you assist us by adding a few young ladies to the mix next weekend?" Jefferson hollered from the veranda.

Jonas ignored his son's remark. He didn't want to be forced into a more detailed explanation regarding the visitors. At the moment, he was counting on his wife's impeccable manners and etiquette to help him survive the evening. Once they were alone, he'd be the object of her wrath. Until then, he knew she would play the perfect hostess. All of these young men would believe she was delighted they had accompanied him to the island.

While Jonas was making the introductions, he'd been doing his best to gauge Fanny's reaction. *Indifference.* Not a spark of interest in even one of the men. In fact, if Jonas hadn't grasped her hand, she would have disappeared.

Before leading Victoria into the house, Jonas insisted the young people engage in a game of croquet. "I'll hear no excuses. I expect every one of you to participate." He glanced at his younger niece and called from the front porch, "Frank, you make certain Fanny doesn't make an escape. She likes to wander off into the woods."

Frank smiled at Fanny. "I'll be pleased to keep her company, Mr. Broadmoor."

Victoria yanked on his sleeve. "What are you doing, Jonas?"

"Offering opportunities, my dear. Shall we go inside?" He didn't await a response, but the hurried click of her heels on the stone porch revealed both her submission and her anger.

The moment Victoria cleared the threshold, she yanked on his arm. "I told you I wanted to discuss this matter further, Jonas. I had hoped that just this once you might abide by my wishes."

"This isn't the time or the place, Victoria. There are tasks to accomplish before the evening meal. I have already decided upon a seating arrangement." He removed a paper from his jacket pocket. "This is a list of names and a diagram. You'll need to prepare the name cards."

Victoria quickly perused the page. "I see that you plan to position Fanny between Frank Colgan and Benjamin Wolgast. And you've seated Fred Portman and Daniel Irwin across from her. I believe she'd prefer to have Amanda or Sophie nearby, and both of them are at the other end of the table." Victoria picked up a pencil and quickly sketched a different arrangement. "Besides, you know how I feel about having the seating arranged man, woman, man, woman, and so forth."

Before she had time to complete her idea, Jonas withdrew the pencil from her hand. "We will use my diagram, Victoria. This is not open to discussion despite your traditional seating arrangement. There is nothing wrong with having several men or women seated side by side. Please advise Mrs. O'Malley to make room assignments for the young men. I trust you had already instructed Mrs. Atwell we would be entertaining dinner guests this evening."

"I told her the possibility existed, but I certainly didn't expect you to arrive with *seven* young men. We can only hope that she prepared enough extra."

Jonas shrugged. "Mrs. Atwell is accustomed to cooking for large groups. She'll adjust. Incidentally, when is Mrs. Oosterman hosting her masked ball? Is that next Saturday evening?"

"Yes. Why do you ask?"

"I'll likely want you to secure invitations for at least some of the young men I've brought with me this weekend. I'm certain Mrs. Oosterman won't object to the addition of eligible young bachelors at the party."

"Such a request goes against every rule of proper etiquette, Jonas. I'll not ask her to enlarge her guest list on my account—especially at this late date."

"Then you may do so on *my* account." He patted her shoulder. "Place the blame on me, but do not fail to secure the invitations. I'll give you the names before I depart on Sunday evening."

Victoria stormed from the room without another word.

Fanny had endured the game of croquet, but her spirits plummeted when she entered the dining room and noted the seating arrangement. Aunt Victoria had placed her near the head of the table, where she would be surrounded by Uncle Jonas and several of his unexpected guests. Glancing over her shoulder, she picked up her name card and switched places with Sophie before slipping out of the room. No one but Aunt Victoria would be the wiser, and her gregarious cousin would doubtless be delighted to entertain the young men.

"There you are, Fanny. We were beginning to wonder what had happened to you." Her uncle beckoned her forward with a broad smile.

Fanny wondered if he'd had an extra glass of port, for he was behaving in a far friendlier manner than normal. Unless issuing a command, Uncle Jonas barely spoke to her. She longed to join Amanda on the other side of the veranda, but she dared not ignore her uncle's order.

"I understand you and Frank were declared winners of the croquet game."

The blond-haired man she'd been paired with for the game of croquet flanked Uncle Jonas on his right. Mr. Colgan had been friendly enough—in fact, more friendly than she preferred, but she'd rather talk to Amanda or Sophie. "The win is due to Mr. Colgan's ability. He appears to have quite a knack for the game."

"Don't sell yourself short, Fanny. I've challenged the others to a rematch and have already insisted that you'll remain my partner."

"I don't know, I—"

"That sounds like a splendid idea. I believe you're sitting next to each other at dinner. The two of you can discuss your strategy then." Uncle Jonas winked at Frank. "Unless Benjamin succeeds in occupying Fanny's attention. If memory serves me correctly, he's going to occupy the chair to Fanny's left."

Fanny gulped. How did Uncle Jonas know the seating arrangement? Had he already been in the dining room? For that matter, Fanny wondered if all of the other guests had been in the dining room before she came downstairs. What if everyone discovered what she had done with the place cards?

"I don't believe so, Uncle Jonas. Aunt Victoria knows I always request a chair near Amanda or Sophie." She pointed to the lake. "Do you fish, Mr. Colgan?" Perhaps if she changed the topic, Uncle Jonas would forget the seating arrangement.

Frank shook his head. "Do *you* fish, Miss Broadmoor?"

From his grin, Fanny knew her answer would surprise. "Indeed I do, Mr. Colgan. Fishing is one of my favorite pastimes."

"Then I hope you'll agree to take me fishing during my visit this weekend, Miss Broadmoor. I would be delighted to have you act as my instructor."

Now what? Her plan to change the conversation from the seating arrangement had turned into an afternoon of fishing with Mr. Colgan. She didn't have time to object before Uncle Jonas was offering to have Mrs. Atwell pack a picnic lunch for their proposed outing.

"I suggest you take a canoe and row over to one of the far islands, where the fishermen usually meet with great success," Uncle Jonas proposed. "Early morning is best. Why don't the two of you plan on going out tomorrow? I'll see to the arrangements for the canoe. No need for you to go down to the boathouse, Fanny. I'll have Michael tie one of the canoes to the small dock, since it's closer to the house and will be more convenient."

The family seldom used the small dock. It had been constructed years ago, before completion of the new boathouse. Her grandfather had considered having it dismantled, but Grand-mère had objected, citing its proximity to the house. Grandfather had bowed to her wishes, though Fanny didn't recall Grand-mère ever using the small dock.

"No need adding to Michael's workload, Uncle Jonas. Surely Mr. Colgan doesn't consider a walk to the boathouse taxing." If luck was with her, Fanny would have a few minutes alone with Michael. She'd make certain of it!

"That's why I pay the staff, Fanny dear. You need not worry about Michael Atwell's workload. The canoe will await you and Frank at the small dock in the morning."

The maid announced supper before Fanny could offer further argument. Not that she could change her uncle's mind. From the set of his jaw, he appeared resolute, and her thoughts had already returned to the exchanged place cards. Following Aunt Victoria's usual custom, the guests circled the table searching for their names. When Fanny stopped at the chair next to Amanda, she didn't fail to note her aunt's surprise.

Uncle Jonas signaled his wife. "I'm not certain we're all in the proper seats, are we? After all, Amanda and Fanny are seated next to each other."

"I do believe we all know how to read, Jonas. I daresay, the name cards are clearly printed with each guest's name." Aunt Victoria offered an apologetic smile to the group. "Would you please check your name card to ensure you're at the proper chair?" Murmurs and nods followed the request. When no one made a move, their hostess shook her head. "I'm sorry, Jonas. It appears that you're mistaken. After all, there is nothing wrong with having two young women seated side by side."

15

Saturday, July 24, 1897

Late the next morning Fanny spotted Amanda sitting beneath a stand of white spruce not far from the little dock and waved from the canoe. She was pleased to be returning home. Fishing with Frank had been an exercise in futility. Though she'd done her best to teach him the proper technique for baiting his hook, he'd been as inept as a young child. He'd bloodied his fingers not once but on three separate occasions. And all had been in vain, for he'd accomplished nothing other than to feed his worms to the fish.

And he wouldn't be quiet! She had explained that fishing was a silent sport, but Frank had ignored her requests to cease his incessant talking. When she finally confronted him, he actually admitted fishing didn't interest him in the least. The fishing trip had been a ploy to gain her full attention—at least that's what he'd said. And that was when Fanny decided they would immediately return to Broadmoor Island.

Frank had argued they should remain until after their picnic lunch, but Fanny refused. Seeing Amanda confirmed her decision. Perhaps the two of them could take the picnic lunch Mrs. Atwell had packed and retreat to the far side of the island by themselves for the remainder of the afternoon. The thought prompted her to hurry Frank in his attempt to guide the canoe alongside the dock. She didn't fault him for his clumsiness, for he'd had little experience paddling a canoe. However, her irritation continued to mount when he steadfastly failed to follow her instructions.

Fanny glanced over her shoulder and pointed at the paddle. "Turn the paddle in the other direction or we'll head back into the current, Frank."

She hoped he would listen, for this outing had gone on long enough and she had no desire to have to paddle back upstream.

"I think I can use my—" The canoe lurched back and forth.

"Sit down, Frank! You're going to cause us to—"

Before she could complete her sentence, Fanny was immersed in the St. Lawrence River. She flapped her arms and sputtered, her gown and petticoats quickly soaking up water like a parched flower bed. Her new straw hat bobbed toward shore, and remnants of Mrs. Atwell's carefully packed sandwiches were already providing sustenance for a hungry duck. She need not worry about Frank, for he had remained with the now overturned canoe and was trying his best to climb atop it. Using his arms and legs for support, he wrapped himself around the canoe like a bear clinging to a tree trunk, only to fall back into the water again and again.

After two wide arcing strokes, Fanny forced her torso down and into a standing position. Fighting against the weight of her drenched clothing, she pushed through the water with determined strides and maneuvered toward the dock.

Amanda stood grinning at the water's edge. "We have a bathtub, Fanny. You need not bathe in the river."

Fanny held out a hand for her cousin to help her onto dry land. "If you weren't wearing that lovely gown, I'd be tempted to pull you in here with me."

The two of them giggled, and Amanda glanced toward Frank, who continued to cling to the canoe, even though he couldn't seem to climb atop. The river's motion was gently bringing him toward the dock and shallower water.

"When are you going to tell him he can touch bottom?"

"I thought I'd wait a few minutes longer." She turned toward the dock and shaded her eyes. "Can you swim, Frank?"

"No! Would you send someone to help? I don't have strength enough to lift my weight onto the canoe. If I turn loose, I'm going to go under."

"I'd attempt to save you myself, but I believe I'd pull us both under, what with all this water weighing down my dress. Amanda can swim, but I don't want her to ruin her new dress. You do understand, of course."

"Yes, of course!" he hollered. "Send one of the other men or the fellow over at the boathouse."

His hands were beginning to slip, and Fanny could see him fighting to gain control. She tipped her head toward Amanda. "Oh, I don't suppose I should torture him much longer, should I?"

"I suppose not. He does look rather frightened—and you do need to get out of those wet clothes."

The two girls headed toward the path. When they'd neared the house, Fanny turned around and cupped her hands to her mouth. "Frank! You can touch bottom if you'll put your feet down."

The two girls watched for a moment, but Frank continued to clutch the canoe as it bobbed against the dock. Amanda shook her head. "He doesn't follow instructions very well, does he?"

"That, my dear cousin, is exactly why we ended up in the river! When he grows weary enough, he'll discover I've told him the truth." Fanny opened the door for her cousin. "Shall we go inside?"

Jonas couldn't believe his eyes—or his ears, for that matter. Considering the number of guests visiting for the weekend, the house had seemed unusually quiet, and he had walked outdoors expecting to see the young people engaged in a game of croquet. Instead, he was greeted by a call for help and immediately ran toward the river.

There, beside the dock, he caught sight of young Frank Colgan clinging to one of the Broadmoor canoes. "Let go and stand down, Frank. The water is less than six foot."

"I can't swim," Frank shouted.

Jonas wiped the beads of perspiration from his forehead and attempted to restrain his irritation. "You don't *need* to swim! You can walk. Put your feet down!" He could see the hesitation as Frank finally dropped his legs and then loosened his hold.

"I *can* touch the bottom." Relief flooded the young man's voice, although he continued to remain close to the dock's edge while wading out of the river.

"What happened? And where is my niece?" Jonas took several backward steps as Frank stepped onto dry ground and then shook like a wet retriever.

"Oh, sorry, sir. I didn't mean to get you wet." He slicked his hair back with one hand. "Fanny and Amanda are inside."

"Then would you care to explain what you're doing pretending to be drowning?"

Frank's eyes opened wide and he trembled. "I wasn't pretending, Mr. Broadmoor. I truly believed I was going to die."

How cruel of the girls to walk off and leave a man to think he might die. The very thought! "Are you telling me that my niece and daughter were aware of your dilemma and didn't advise you there was no need for concern?"

"Fanny told me, but I was afraid to let loose. What if she hadn't been telling the truth?"

Jonas massaged his forehead. Clearly this young man was foolish enough to serve the purpose for which he had been brought here, yet if he wouldn't follow a simple direction that could save his own life, Jonas wondered if Frank would prove a wise choice. Without prompting, the young man would likely forget to come in out of the rain. Jonas wanted a man he could control, but he didn't want a dolt. Maybe Benjamin or Fred would prove a superior selection.

Jonas sent for Michael to retrieve the canoe and then directed Frank upstairs to change into a dry suit. After dealing with Frank, Jonas needed to solidify his plan. Just when he had thought his strategy was moving forward with ease, Frank had dashed his hopes.

He returned to the veranda and a short time later heard Amanda and Fanny giggling. "You girls come out here immediately."

"Yes, Father?"

He ignored his daughter and beckoned to Fanny. "I discovered Frank in the river a short time ago." He wagged his head back and forth. "He's upstairs changing clothes. I suggest you go and join our other guests."

Fanny arched her brows and glanced toward the lawn. "I have no idea where your guests have gone, Uncle Jonas. Besides, Amanda and I are going to enjoy a late lunch at the far end of the island. If we can convince Mrs. Atwell to supply us with a few sandwiches, that is. Our picnic basket is at the bottom of the river."

Fanny grasped Amanda's hand and the two girls marched inside. The fishing excursion with Frank had been a misstep, but Jonas would not permit one mistake to foil his plan. He couldn't permit the entire afternoon to pass by without the remaining prospective grooms vying for Fanny's attentions.

He'd nearly given up hope when the two girls returned with their picnic basket a short time later.

Then, as if in answer to his plight, Jonas heard the sounds of excited chatter and laughter. "The others are returning, and it would be rude if you two ran off by yourselves—a breach of etiquette."

"They weren't expecting me to return until this afternoon— remember? I'm supposed to be fishing with Frank."

The note of triumph in Fanny's voice struck a nerve, and Jonas strengthened his resolve. With a flap of his hand, he signaled the girls to sit down and walked to the far end of the veranda. He would not be manipulated by a seventeen-year-old female. Fanny Broadmoor would *not* ruin his plans for her future inheritance.

The sight that greeted him at the far end of the lawn had a more disquieting effect on him. Sophie paraded toward the house, surrounded by the entourage. They swarmed around her like bees seeking their queen. What were those young men thinking? They'd obviously forgotten the reason he'd brought them here. Jonas waited until Benjamin looked in his direction and motioned the group to hurry along.

Jonas detected the pout on Sophie's lips. Quincy needed to gain control of his daughter before she acquired a tawdry reputation. Jonas had recently heard remarks about her behavior, and he made a mental note to speak with his brother. Though he cared little about Sophie, Jonas didn't want any scandal tarnishing the family name.

"Where have you been?" Jonas clenched his jaw.

Sophie flicked an errant strand of hair over her shoulder. "Jefferson, George, and I have been giving our visitors a tour of the island. We're famished and returned for some lunch and a game of croquet."

"Good. I'm certain you'll want Fanny to join you. She returned from her fishing excursion earlier than expected."

The young men offered their hearty agreement while Sophie continued to pout. But as long as Jonas achieved the desired result, he cared little whether he pleased or angered Sophie. He escorted the group around the veranda while hoping Fanny hadn't decided to disappear in his absence. The girl was proving more headstrong than he'd suspected and certainly more difficult to handle than his own daughter. Both Sophie and Fanny had lacked proper rearing. Had they received appropriate instruction early on, they would have adopted the compliant nature of a true lady. But all of that would now change—at least for Fanny. His strong hand would be directing her behavior and her future.

One by one, Jonas pulled aside Daniel, Fred, and Benjamin for a private discussion and a reminder that Fanny should be the object of their affection. Only Benjamin argued.

He tugged on his stiff shirt collar and fidgeted like a schoolboy. "I like Sophie a lot, Mr. Broadmoor. And Fanny doesn't appear to be interested in having me around. If it's okay with you, I'd rather take my chances at winning Sophie's heart."

"This has nothing to do with love or winning a young woman's heart, Benjamin. Have you so quickly forgotten this is about money—a large inheritance?"

Benjamin winked. "But Sophie is a Broadmoor. One day she'll inherit, too."

The young man's sly grin took Jonas by surprise. Benjamin was plotting to have his cake and eat it, too! Perhaps this young fellow wouldn't prove as tractable as Jonas had thought. "Don't expect Sophie to come into a large sum of money. Her father will pour his inheritance into his Home for the Friendless. Even if there should be some small remainder, Sophie has four siblings who would share in such funds. You would reap little financial gain from such a marriage, and even that would not occur for years." Jonas squeezed Benjamin's shoulder. "This is your decision, but I expect you to remember our agreement." The boy's shoulder quivered beneath his grasp, and Jonas smiled. Benjamin had understood his warning.

Jonas ordered Amanda to the kitchen with instructions for Mrs. Atwell to prepare a picnic lunch large enough to feed all of their guests. But when Fanny attempted to join Amanda on her errand, Jonas blocked her path. "Amanda doesn't need your assistance, Fanny; she knows her way to the kitchen. You can help Daniel gather the mallets and balls for the croquet game. He doesn't know where they're located."

Daniel hastened to Fanny's side. "I'd be most pleased to have your assistance."

"I'll help, too," Benjamin said. "We can set up the wickets now and begin our game as soon as we've eaten our lunch."

Soon all of the young men were following Fanny's bidding as she directed placement of the wickets—all except George and Jefferson, who were lounging on the lower veranda, watching in amusement.

Sophie paced in front of them until George begged her to sit down. "I realize you're angry because you've lost your admirers to Fanny, but do take heart. She's not at all interested in any of them. Watch her! She's merely tolerating their attention. And the men are out there because Father insisted. To ignore his request would have been rude. Bide your time, Cousin. They'll soon be fawning over you again."

Amanda rounded the corner, and both of her brothers jumped to their feet. "I do hope you've come to announce lunch. We're starving," George said.

"I'm afraid not, though you may as well help yourself to the lunch Mrs. Atwell packed for Fanny and me. It's over near the front door. Don't eat it all, or you'll ruin your appetite."

Jefferson laughed. "Don't worry. I doubt your dainty sandwiches will be sufficient to ruin my dinner."

Amanda dropped onto one of the chairs. "They appear to be having a gay time."

Sophie glanced over her shoulder and then joined her cousin. "They all are quite nice and very attentive. At least they were until your father turned their attention toward Fanny."

"In truth, I thought Father had decided upon those young men as possible suitors for me. Silly, but I actually believed he'd been thinking of me while he was in Rochester last week. He'd recently mentioned finding a young man who would prove a perfect match." Amanda rested her chin in her palm. "Not that I desire a husband anytime in the near future, but my father is seemingly more interested in Fanny's future than that of his own daughter."

TRACIE PETERSON ❖ JUDITH MILLER

"And that surprises you?" Sophie groaned. "In case you haven't noticed, none of the Broadmoor men have ever taken an interest in their daughters—unless it offered some advantage."

"I suppose that's true enough," Amanda agreed. Her father had never doted upon her. In fact, he'd shown her very little attention throughout the years. It was one reason she'd been stirred to seek fulfillment in charity work rather than a marriage to someone who would likely treat her as impersonally as had her father throughout the years. "Why, then, do I feel betrayed that this group of men wasn't invited for my benefit? I knew Father would concern himself with finding Fanny a proper husband. He is, after all, her guardian."

"Not only that, she's become exceedingly wealthy," Sophie added.

"Still, I thought he would give her time. She is only seventeen, and I'm nineteen."

"But you're completely dependent upon your father's money and therefore the situation is not quite so urgent. Uncle Jonas is your father, but he's devoted his time and thought to Fanny and her future rather than yours." Sophie turned her gaze back toward the group of men knocking the croquet balls across the lawn. "I believe your father has chosen one of those fellows as Fanny's husband. I think he's going to force her into an arranged marriage. Something I would rail against. You should count yourself fortunate."

"What makes you think that's what he's doing? Grandfather just died. Surely Father would not expect Fanny to consider matrimony just yet."

"Do open your eyes, dear girl. He sent her out with Frank this morning, and now that she's returned, he's busy arranging for her to spend time with the others. Maybe he hasn't selected the exact one yet, but I'd guess he's trying to choose a favorite.

If you watch closely, you'll see that he keeps maneuvering several of the men toward her."

Amanda sighed. "You may be right. I had mentioned that very possibility to Fanny but hadn't expected it this soon. I know Father will worry about undesirables trying to woo her now that she has a fortune. Still, none of us will have the final say in the person we wed. The women in our family are expected to marry a person of their own social standing."

"Did I hear the two of you discussing the possibility of prospective husbands?" Both girls swiveled toward the sound of Beatrice's voice, and she laughed. "It appears I surprised both of you."

Sophie glared at her sister. "You were eavesdropping—not a particularly admirable behavior."

"And you would certainly know about admirable behavior, dear Sophie. Have you decided to marry one of those fops Uncle Jonas brought with him for the weekend, Amanda?"

"Quite the contrary. Sophie thinks my father has brought them as possible suitors for Fanny. I haven't decided if that's the case, but she may be correct."

"I don't care whether she finds a suitable husband or not. I still can't believe Grandfather left a third of his estate to that little snippet. It's completely unfair! And she has no brother or sisters—no one with whom she'll have to share." Beatrice's lips drooped more than usual.

"Would you like all of us to apologize for being born, Beatrice?" Sophie asked. "Your greed is even more unbecoming than your eavesdropping."

Beatrice wagged her finger. "One day you'll care. Then it will be too late."

Sophie chuckled. "Too late? I have no control over how the family money is divided, and neither do you. More to the point,

I don't care if Fanny receives a greater share of the estate. Just as your future was decided by the men in this family, mine will also be determined by their whims." Sophie smoothed the bodice of her gown as Fanny and the men sauntered toward the lower veranda. "For now, dear Beatrice, I intend to assert my own will and have more fun than proper society permits."

16

Saturday, July 31, 1897

Fanny buttoned Sophie's dress and then bade her cousin turn around. "I do fear your father won't be pleased with the gown you've chosen."

"My father won't even notice. He seldom is aware of me, even when I'm in the same room." The topaz necklace that circled Sophie's neck sparkled in the soft light. "Beatrice will swoon when she sees I've pirated our mother's necklace and brought it along." Sadness shone in her eyes as she touched a finger to the jewels. "I always thought Mother looked beautiful when she wore this necklace."

"And so do you," Fanny said. "She would be pleased that you've chosen to wear her necklace."

Sophie brightened. "In any case, I doubt Father will attend this evening. He dislikes parties and dancing. He'd much rather be in Rochester working alongside Paul than out here on the island with his family." She shrugged. "But then, I'd rather be in Rochester, too."

Fanny arranged a lace insert in the décolletage of her emerald green gown. "I thought you were excited about the ball."

"I am, but the ball lasts for only one night." With a giggle, Sophie leaned forward and attempted to remove the insert from Fanny's dress. "You're old enough to wear your gown without an insert."

Fanny swooped to one side and warded off Sophie's maneuver. "Perhaps, but I prefer to use it. And remember, you're the one who says we should be free to make our own choices. I didn't attempt to force you to add an insert to your dress, did I?"

"You're correct. I'll permit you to make your own choice, but I truly believe it's Aunt Victoria's decision rather than your own," Sophie replied. "And speaking of Aunt Victoria, where has she secreted Amanda? I haven't seen her since we came upstairs to prepare for the party."

"I imagine she's in her rooms. I think she wants to surprise us with her dress. Aunt Victoria had it designed especially for the ball. Show me your mask," Fanny requested.

Sophie held a half-mask of shimmering gold to her eyes. In an effort to further camouflage the wearer's identity, filmy lace and feathers had been attached to the edges of the mask. Yet anyone who'd ever met Sophie would identify her behind the mask. With or without a mask, her beauty shone like the sparkling gems in her necklace.

While Sophie had expressed excitement when Uncle Jonas returned with several of the young men who had visited the previous weekend, Fanny cared little. None of them had captivated her interest, though she was surprised when Sophie pointed out the fact that Frank Colgan wasn't among the returning men.

"I thought him rather good looking," Sophie remarked as they exited the bedroom.

"Perhaps, but not very bright. If his arms would have provided him with the necessary strength, he'd likely still be in the water hanging on to the canoe." Fanny looped arms with her cousin, and the two of them descended the stairs.

The young men had departed for the Oosterman mansion fifteen minutes earlier. Once Michael had delivered them, he would return for the ladies. At Mrs. Oosterman's request, Aunt Victoria insisted every effort be made to keep the guests' identities secret until the unmasking at midnight. While Sophie preened in front of the hallway mirror, Fanny stepped onto the upper veranda. A full moon shone overhead, and Fanny strained forward, unsure if the distant lights were stars glistening on the black water or the flickering oil lamps of the *DaisyBee*. Her heart tripped as she caught sight of the tangerine glow from beneath the boiler and heard the distinct hissing of the engine.

Not much longer before she would see Michael. He'd been uncharacteristically absent from the boathouse every time she'd gone to see him during the week. Even Mrs. Atwell hadn't seemed forthcoming when Fanny had inquired about Michael's whereabouts. She merely shrugged and mumbled that she hadn't seen him and then excused herself to complete chores somewhere else in the house. It was as if both mother and son were attempting to avoid her, yet she couldn't imagine why. She could recall nothing she'd done to offend either of them.

Fanny was still on the veranda when the rest of the Broadmoor women arrived downstairs. With Aunt Victoria taking the lead, they all walked the short distance to the boathouse, where Michael awaited them. One by one he assisted each of the ladies into the boat. Finally it was Fanny's turn. Seizing the opportunity, she gave his hand a squeeze, but her spirits wilted when he ignored the affectionate gesture. She claimed one of the few remaining seats, all of them located at a distance from Michael. There would be no opportunity to speak to him during the boat ride.

Aunt Victoria remained in charge of the group, issuing instructions throughout the journey. They were to keep their masks in place at all times, they were to make every attempt to disguise themselves from their dance partners, and they weren't to withhold their dance cards from any gentleman in deference to another. Her aunt cast a stern look at Sophie when she issued that particular directive. "All female guests are to enter by the side door, and we will gather in the parlor. Mrs. Oosterman has arranged for each of us to be individually escorted into the ballroom." Aunt Victoria appeared delighted by the idea. "Her method will aid in keeping our identities secret. Each of the male guests will be assigned an identifying number that will be used to sign your dance cards."

Sophie poked Fanny in the side. "Why is Aunt Victoria so anxious to please Mrs. Oosterman?"

"Uncle Jonas has instructed Aunt Victoria to cultivate a friendship with Mrs. Oosterman. Their wealth supposedly exceeds our family's fortune. At least that's what Amanda told me," Fanny whispered. "Sounds like something Uncle Jonas would say. Money is always at the top of his list."

"Money and control," Sophie murmured. "Did you hear Beatrice upbraid me before we left the house this evening? The minute she spotted Mother's necklace, she lit into me. Had it not been for Aunt Victoria's intervention, I believe Beatrice would have ripped it from around my throat."

"You should have told her you were wearing it with your father's permission."

Sophie's even white teeth shone beneath the boat's lantern light. "Oh, but I'm not. He doesn't even know I removed it from the safe." She chuckled as Michael steered the boat alongside the Oosterman's dock.

Servants awaited them on the dock, holding brightly lit brass lanterns. The Broadmoor ladies were escorted to the parlor with a formality befitting royalty. Though Fanny considered the decorum overdone in the extreme, Aunt Victoria and Beatrice extolled the pomp and ceremony.

Sophie nodded toward her sister. "Beatrice *is* full of herself this evening, isn't she? Did you see her fawning over Mrs. Oosterman? Who would ever think we were blood sisters? After being around my family, I'm more and more convinced that I must be adopted."

Fanny laughed at her cousin's remark, but before she could respond, Sophie was the next to be whisked away. Fanny was one of the final guests to be escorted into the ballroom. Not that she minded. Less time in the ballroom meant fewer hours tolerating the fanfare and grand gestures that pervaded these gatherings—and less time socializing with the masked male guests. Though the women invested much more time in their costumes and masks, the men were always more difficult to recognize. They all tended to wear their black formal wear, disguise their voices, and wear simple black masks. One or two of the rotund or bald male guests could be easily discerned, but in recent years the men had begun the practice of donning old-fashioned powdered wigs to disguise themselves. Fanny noted most had employed the practice this evening.

She spied the shimmering golden hue of Sophie's gown. A group of male guests surrounded her cousin, all of them vying to scribble their assigned numbers on her dance card. Fanny backed toward a narrow cove alongside the doors leading to the wide veranda. If all went well, she could fade into her surroundings and then escape outdoors once the dancing began.

Unfortunately, her aunt had stationed herself with a clear view of all the exits while she talked to Uncle Jonas. The two of them ceased their conversation and glanced around the room.

Her aunt spotted her and signaled Uncle Jonas. Fanny watched in dismay as her uncle grasped a young man by the arm and directed him toward her. She wanted to run, but her limbs wouldn't budge. She remained paralyzed as the man approached and bade her good evening.

When she didn't respond, he grinned. "Is it that you don't want me to recognize your voice, or has the cat got your tongue?" He grasped her dance card between his thumb and forefinger. "It appears that I'll have the privilege of being the first to sign your card. Perhaps I should fill every dance with my number. Would that displease you?"

"I don't believe that's permissible." She stared into his eyes, hoping to gain some clue. "I have no idea who you are. Rendering any further opinion in regard to my displeasure is, therefore, impossible."

He signed his number on several lines before returning her card. "Since you appear to desire a man who plays by the rules, I'll abide by your instruction." He tipped his head a bit closer. "I've signed your card for four dances. I hope you won't believe me overly presumptuous when I tell you that I secured both the first and last dances of the evening as well as the two that precede the short interludes prior to dining. With any good fortune, perhaps I'll discover our hostess has seated us side by side for at least one of the evening's repasts."

"Since you have no idea who I am, you may soon discover you've made an ill-conceived decision." Fanny glanced over the man's shoulder and noted that her uncle continued to keep her in his line of vision. "Unless someone has already revealed my identity."

"Now why would you think such a thing?"

His words rang false to her, and she knew this must be one of Uncle Jonas's weekend visitors. It truly didn't matter which one, for she had no interest in any of these men. "You'd best locate some other dance partners before the music begins. Otherwise you'll be required to join the old men discussing politics in the den."

"Or join you on the veranda for a cup of punch."

The man had effectively blocked her into the alcove from which she longed to escape—but escape she must. If not, she'd be forced to spend the entire evening in his company. "I do believe that gentleman on the far side of the room beckoned to you," she said.

When he stepped aside in order to gain a better view, Fanny edged free. "If you'll excuse me, I must speak to someone in private." Before he could object, she hurried away to the ladies' parlor for a brief reprieve. How she disliked these parties!

By Sophie's standards, the evening had thus far proved a success. She'd been one of the first to make an entrance into the ballroom and *the* first to be surrounded by a host of men. Just what she preferred. One man in particular intrigued her. Though he'd been among the first to surround her, he hadn't immediately fought to place his number on her dance card. Not until she'd coyly pressed the card into his hand did he succumb and poise a pencil above the lines.

She grasped his hand with her lace-gloved fingers. "Not there. Write your name on the line that precedes the supper repast. We'll have additional time to visit." With a flick of her hand, her lace fan spread open and she brushed it beneath his chin. "You would like to visit with me, wouldn't you?"

He nodded his head. "Until then."

His hasty departure surprised her. Unlike the other men, who couldn't seem to get enough of her, this one seemed distant and aloof. She spotted her uncle Jonas across the room visiting with a circle of friends and excused herself from the gathered men. Though she would have preferred to speak to her father, she'd not yet located him among the crowd.

She waited while the men completed their boring discussion. She half-listened to their talk of rumors circulating in the English newspapers that Japan would go to war with the United States if the Senate ratified a treaty to annex the Hawaiian Islands. Why did men enjoy discussing war? she wondered. Whether the debate was about Cuba or Japan, they seemed to revel in it. If there wasn't a current conflict to discuss, they thrashed out the possibilities of all imminent prospects.

When the men dispersed a short time later, Sophie tapped her uncle Jonas on the arm. Confusion registered in his expression, and she finally said, "It's me, Sophie."

His jaw tightened. "I can see that it's you. I recognize the jewelry. Does your father know you're wearing that necklace? That is a family heirloom that belonged to my mother."

Sophie ignored the question. "And it was a wedding gift to my mother from Grand-mère. Have you seen my father?"

"He's not here. I believe he sent a note to your aunt saying he had urgent business in Rochester. Quite frankly, I believe he simply wanted an excuse to avoid tonight's party. I can't imagine any matter of urgency in regard to a homeless shelter."

"Perhaps there was a fire and a sudden influx of starving children arrived, Uncle Jonas. Would you consider *that* an emergency?" She shook her head. "Probably not, for those children wouldn't be of any use to your financial empire, would they?"

"You had best withhold your caustic remarks, young lady. If I recall, you hold no greater fondness for that homeless shelter than the rest of the family." His lips tightened into a frown.

She offered an apology, but not because she was sorry. She wanted information about that mysterious man, and her father wasn't available to help. Uncle Jonas was her only remaining choice. "I wonder if you know that young man standing to the left of the double doors leading to the dining hall."

Her uncle took a step forward and peered. "No, I don't believe I do. It's difficult to be certain at this distance and with these ridiculous wigs and masks, but he's no one I easily recognize. He's not one of the men who arrived with me. And I don't recall seeing him when the men gathered prior to the party. As I said, though, it's nearly impossible to be sure." His scowl returned. "Is his behavior boorish? If so, I'll seek Mr. Oosterman's assistance and have him thrown out on his ear."

Sophie placed her hand on his arm. "No, nothing like that. In fact, quite the opposite. He was most genteel."

Her uncle's frown disappeared and he offered an affirmative growl. "You let me know if you have trouble with any of these young fellows."

Sophie stifled a giggle as she hurried off. Jonas would be aghast to know the number of fellows she'd been able to handle without any assistance over the past several years.

During the next hour Sophie charmed her dance partners while keeping a lookout for the stranger who had captured her interest. He had remained near the doors until moments ago, when she noticed him seeking out a dance partner. She was surprised to see him circle the floor with Fanny. Perhaps he *was* a friend of the family.

She rushed to Fanny's side the moment the young man escorted her back to the edge of the floor. Sophie's next dance partner approached, but she waved him away and grasped Fanny's hand. "Who was that fellow you were dancing with?"

Fanny shrugged. "I don't know. We didn't talk much."

"Tell me everything he said," Sophie persisted. "I'm attempting to discover who he is, but even Uncle Jonas doesn't know."

"I fear I'll be little help. Our exchange was no more than polite conversation regarding weather and the like. Oh, he did mention he had recently moved to Rochester."

"You see? You discovered more than you thought. Did he say why or exactly when he moved?"

"I didn't inquire, but your dance partner awaits you."

"Very well, but if you think of anything else, be certain to inform me after this dance."

Sophie couldn't believe her cousin had shared an entire dance with the dashing young man and hadn't gained further information. Of course, he'd not been particularly forthcoming when she talked with him, either. Once they were together on the dance floor, she'd discover who he was. She wished the time would pass more quickly and his number would be the next on her card.

Several of her dance partners remarked upon her detached demeanor, but Sophie offered no apology. They had merely filled the time until this moment arrived. Her partner escorted her to the edge of the dance floor, and she waited for the stranger to approach. Unlike the other men, he didn't hurry to claim her. She wondered if he had forgotten he had claimed this dance.

Not until the musicians took up their instruments did he casually stroll along the edge of the dance floor and stop in front of her. He offered his hand. "I believe I have this dance?"

Sophie offered a comely smile. "The music's already begun. I thought perhaps you'd forgotten." She had expected him to tell her that he could never forget a dance with someone so lovely. Instead, he silently led her onto the dance floor without apology or compliment. "You've piqued my curiosity. While

I've been able to identify most of the men in this room, you remain a mystery. Have we ever met?"

He grasped her waist and they joined the dancing couples on the floor. "My dear lady, you're in disguise, yet you believe I know who you are. You assume too much. Tell me, are you summering in the islands, or have you come here only for this party?"

"I make my home in Rochester, but my family has summered in the Thousand Islands for many years." She tipped her head back and gazed into his eyes. "Now you must tell me something about yourself."

"Why?" he asked, expertly guiding her across the floor between two other couples.

"Because I told you something about myself. That's only fair."

"Fair? Is that what you expect? Everything in life to be fair?"

"I do, but generally I'm disappointed," she admitted.

"It's good you've come to that realization. There's little equality this side of heaven. The rich continue to amass wealth while the poor remain hungry."

She detected pain in his gentle laugh and wondered if he had experienced the hunger of which he spoke. Surely not, for the people invited to these parties had been reared in wealth. Who *was* this man?

"You bewilder me, kind sir. I can place neither your voice nor the dark brooding eyes behind your mask. Yet somewhere deep inside, I believe I know you. Will you give me no hint at all?"

"Tell me of your dreams, miss. How do you plan to spend the remainder of your life? How will you bring joy to the lives of others?"

The music stopped; they stood facing one another. She tapped her folded fan lightly against his chest. "Your questions are intriguing. Most men ask how they can make *me* happy."

"Do they? And is that because most men believe you're unhappy or because they realize you'll permit their attentions only if they attempt to meet your every expectation?"

Her jaw dropped at the unexpected question. The two of them remained face-to-face, but Sophie found herself at a loss for words.

Mr. Oosterman signaled for quiet while his wife stepped forward. The men and women were instructed to form separate lines. Their hostess patiently waited until two distinct rows had been created. She then explained that each man's number had been written on a small piece of paper, folded, and placed in Mr. Oosterman's top hat. She stepped in front of the first woman, dipped her veined hand into the top hat, and read a number. The diamonds that decorated her fingers sparkled in the dim lights as she waved the man forward. One by one, each man was randomly assigned to escort the next woman in line to dinner.

Sophie held her breath when Mrs. Oosterman stood before her. The mysterious man's number had not yet been drawn. She longed to hear his number. Instead, the number belonged to her cousin Jefferson. Even with their masks in place, she could recognize both George and Jefferson from across the room. He hurried to her side when Mrs. Oosterman called his number.

"Aren't you the lucky one?" he whispered.

"Oh, do stop, Jefferson. It's me—Sophie. Don't you recognize your own cousin?"

His shoulders sagged. "With all of these ladies here, why'd I have to get stuck with one of my own relatives?"

"*Stuck?*" Sophie jabbed him with her elbow. "You could have been partnered with old Mrs. Beauchamp. Think about shouting into her ear trumpet for the next ninety minutes. Cousin or not, that thought alone should make you happy to be paired with me."

Jefferson mumbled his apology, but Sophie had already returned her attention to the mystery man. His number must now be at the very bottom of the hat, for Mrs. Oosterman was nearing the end of the line and his number still hadn't been picked. She tilted her head toward Jefferson. "Who's the third man from the left? Do you know him?"

Her cousin glanced down the line at the few remaining men. "No, I don't believe I've ever seen him before. I've talked to nearly all of the men this evening, but I don't even recall seeing him when the men gathered in the ballroom before any of the women arrived. Despite the masks, I can pick out nearly every man in this room—except him."

Jefferson's intrigue nearly matched her own, and both of them gasped when Mrs. Oosterman finally called the stranger's number. *Fanny!* He'd been paired with their younger cousin. Fanny wouldn't extract any information from her dinner partner. In fact, she'd likely remain silent throughout the meal.

Sophie tapped her fan on Jefferson's arm. "We must do something. I want to know who he is."

Jefferson's eyes gleamed from behind his black mask. "I'll help, but you must promise to tell me if you discover his identity."

Sophie clutched his arm. "Oh yes. I promise. Do you have a plan?"

He chuckled and patted her hand. "You'll see. Wait here."

The paired guests had already begun the slow march into the dining room when the stranger suddenly stepped into line beside Sophie. "I hope you won't object to a change in partners."

Sophie didn't know how Jefferson had managed this, but she would be forever in his debt. Throughout the meal she teased and cajoled the masked stranger, all to no avail. When dinner had ended and she'd made no progress, Sophie expressed her dismay. "What must I do to discover who you are?"

He pondered the question for several moments. "Walk with me before the dancing resumes, and perhaps then I will tell you."

She didn't hesitate—not even for a moment. Before Mrs. Oosterman had completed her instructions for the remainder of the evening, Sophie was tugging on the stranger's arm. After she took a possessive hold on his arm, they strolled outside toward the Oostermans' huge pier and boathouse.

Moonlight and starlight commingled to adorn the dark water with bright dancing prisms and beckoned them onward. When they reached the end of the pier, Sophie released his arm. "You've still not even given me a clue." She tightened her lips into a tiny pout to entice him.

He laughed and softly grasped her shoulders. For a moment, she thought he might lean down and kiss her. She hoped he would. Instead, he gently turned her toward the water. "You may turn around when I tell you."

She remained still and looked down at the water, her excitement mounting with each shallow breath.

"You may turn around."

Ever so slowly, she made the half-turn. Shock, anger, frustration—her emotions mounted inside her like a bubbling volcano and then exploded with one unwitting backward step. *"Paul!"*

Paul Medford's name was all that Sophie screamed before falling into the water. The skirt of her golden gown floated up to surround her like a misplaced halo.

17

Sophie's shrill scream echoed in the stillness.

At Jefferson's insistence, Fanny had walked outdoors following the evening meal. Not that she disliked being away from the hubbub of the mingling guests, but she hadn't particularly desired company. She much preferred being alone with her thoughts. Besides, Jefferson had appeared more interested in following after Sophie than enjoying a stroll through the lighted gardens. And though the possibility of seeing Michael near the Oostermans' boathouse had appealed to her, Fanny knew she'd dare not visit with him in Jefferson's presence.

The two of them raced toward the pier. Fanny's shoes slid on the grassy slope, and a mental picture of her body sprawled on the lawn in some ungainly position with her skirts arranged in an unladylike fashion flashed before her. She grasped Jefferson's arm in a death grip. His objection served no purpose, for she tightened her grip even more.

"What do you think has happened?" she panted. The moon outlined a huddle of men—likely the skippers of the guests' boats. Several appeared to be holding poles.

"Looks like someone's in the water. Let's hope it's not Sophie." The cadence of Jefferson's reply synchronized with their pounding feet.

Fanny was certain her cousin had screamed the name Paul, but she couldn't imagine why. The only Paul any of them knew was Paul Medford, Uncle Quincy's assistant, and he hadn't even been invited to the party. And why would he be? Fanny considered Paul quite nice, but Mrs. Oosterman wouldn't consider someone such as Paul an acceptable addition to her guest list.

One of the launches equipped with a small searchlight aimed a beacon toward the pier, and Fanny gasped at the sight. Two burly men had hauled a drenched and wilted Sophie from the river. Her sopping gown was ruined, her beautifully coiffed hair hung in dripping ringlets, her mask was tipped sideways atop her head, and greenish-brown weeds poked between the topaz stones of her mother's cherished necklace. She continued to clutch her beaded reticule in one hand while she gestured to Fanny with the other.

Fanny gasped in surprise when her cousin's knees buckled under the weight of the gown. Sophie had angled herself forward but lost her balance and tipped in the opposite direction. Without a moment's hesitation, Paul grasped her by the arm and managed to hold her upright. Had he faltered, Sophie would have been underwater for the second time in one evening.

"Don't you touch me!" She slapped Paul's hand from her arm, and both Fanny and Jefferson hurried to her side.

"What's he done to you?" Jefferson asked.

Sophie glared at her cousin. "What does it *look* like, Jefferson?"

Jefferson's jaw sagged. "He pushed you into the river? Why, I . . ." He balled his fists and positioned himself in a fighting stance near the end of the pier.

"Oh, forevermore, Jefferson, do put your arms down. Next they'll be fishing you out of the river," Sophie exclaimed.

"I didn't push her into the river. She accidentally stepped backward and fell in." Paul glowered at Jefferson. "I can't believe you'd think I'd do such a thing."

Michael stepped forward and offered two blankets he'd retrieved from the *DaisyBee*. "Wrap these around her. Do you want me to bring the boat around and take you back to Broadmoor Island?"

Fanny draped one of the blankets around her cousin's shoulders and nodded. "You must get out of these clothes, Sophie."

She pulled the blanket tighter and turned around to thank Fanny but instead her jaw dropped in horror. Word had obviously spread, and a group of guests was hurrying toward the pier. "Hurry! Get me into the boat before they all come down here and see me looking like this." She grabbed Fanny's hand. "Please say you'll come with me."

"Yes, of course." Fanny motioned toward the crowd. "Head them off, Jefferson. Tell them the excitement is over and all is well."

Jefferson headed off to do her bidding. Once Michael had departed to retrieve the launch, Paul approached. "I'm terribly sorry, Sophie. I didn't intend to startle you, and the last thing I wanted was to have you fall in the water." He took a step closer. "You do believe me, don't you?"

Sophie clenched her jaw. "I believe you're a fraud, Paul Medford. What are you doing here, anyway? You say you disdain the ways of the wealthy, yet you mingle with us when you can hide behind a mask. What are you doing here, and how did you obtain an invitation to permit your entry?"

"Your father gave me his and suggested I use it."

"My father? But why?"

"He knew I wouldn't be recognized. He suggested I speak with some of the guests about the possibility of donating to the shelter." Paul shrugged. "I told him it was a bad idea, but he persisted. Eventually I yielded to his request—and here I am."

"Yes, here you are," Sophie said. "And I thought you were someone special."

Fanny poked her cousin in the side. "Sophie!"

Paul smiled. "It's quite all right, Fanny. I know I'm someone special. Perhaps not in your eyes, Sophie, but in God's eyes, I'm extremely special—and so are you." He glanced toward the approaching boat. "I believe that would be your ride."

Michael held out his hand to assist them into the boat and then waved at Paul. "Do you want a ride over to Broadmoor with us?"

"No, but thanks for the offer."

"You shouldn't be offering him a ride," Sophie hissed. "It's his fault I'm soaking wet!"

Michael eased the boat away from the pier and headed out into the water. "I thought you said it was an accident."

After a good deal of prodding, Fanny managed to elicit the truth from her cousin. Though Jefferson hadn't betrayed Sophie's confidence, his explanation of why he needed to change dinner partners had never been fully explained until now. "You truly shouldn't involve others in your deceit, Sophie."

"Well, it's not as though I've tainted him. Jefferson is far more cunning than you can imagine, dear Fanny. He was pleased to act as my accomplice. I still can't believe it was Paul beneath that mask."

Michael steered the boat alongside the pier near the boathouse. "The water is too shallow or I'd take you over to the little pier, where you'd be closer to the house."

"This is fine. I'm going into the boathouse to remove my gown and petticoats. I can wrap the blanket around me. You can take Fanny back to the party. I'll be fine."

"Oh, but I don't want to go back."

Sophie shook her head. "You must. Uncle Jonas will be angry if you don't return," she said and headed to the boathouse.

Fanny's heart pounded an erratic beat. The boat ride would permit her time alone with Michael, but one look at his face was enough to reveal he didn't relish the idea. Nevertheless, she didn't want to anger her uncle.

Careful to keep his distance, Michael set about his duties without a word, pushing the craft away from the pier. Fanny got up and moved to his side.

"You should sit down. If we hit rough water, you might lose your footing. I don't want you to fall."

She folded her arms across the waist of her taffeta gown. "What is wrong with you, Michael? What have I done that you're treating me like a complete stranger? I've been to the boathouse every day this week, and the minute I come near, you mysteriously vanish."

"I don't know what you're talking about. I've been busy all week. Your uncle has assigned me some additional chores. Unlike you, I must work in order to earn my keep and live on Broadmoor Island."

Fanny reeled at his response. What had happened to her friend—the man she believed cared for her, the man she thought she loved. Silence hung between them like a thick early morning fog. She longed for the words that would touch his heart but doubted her ability to melt his frosty demeanor. He stood with his shoulders squared and his jaw taut until they reached the Oostermans' pier.

He stepped out of the boat and then offered his hand. She grasped hold, and when he attempted to withdraw, she refused to turn loose. "Tell me what I've done, Michael. I truly have no idea why you're angry."

He wiped a tear from her cheek with the pad of his thumb. "I'm sorry, Fanny. I don't want to hurt you, but these feelings . . . we can't . . ."

She closed the gap between them. "Please, Michael. You're my best friend. Please don't do this."

"Victoria! Take Fanny back to the house." Uncle Jonas's voice boomed through the evening silence. He took a menacing step toward Michael. "And you!" He pointed his index finger beneath Michael's nose. "Over here. We need to have another talk."

Fanny pulled against her aunt's grasp. She didn't want to go back to the Oosterman party. She wanted to remain and hear what Uncle Jonas said to Michael. Why was he so angry?

"Didn't Jefferson explain what happened? I returned to Broadmoor Island with Sophie—she asked me to ride along with her, but then she insisted I return to the party. Why is Uncle Jonas angry with Michael? He was merely performing his duties."

"Come along, Fanny. You'll only make matters worse if you don't do as your uncle asked."

"You mean commanded," Fanny muttered. She glanced over her shoulder. Uncle Jonas and Michael stood toe to toe. There was little doubt Michael was receiving a stern lecture.

Her aunt ignored the remark. Once they'd reached the decorative stone wall that circled the Oosterman mansion, the older woman slowed her pace. "You'll be pleased to know that Mrs. Oosterman has changed her plans for the unmasking. Rather than waiting until the end of the evening, we played a delightful little game in which we removed our masks. I am so sorry you missed it, but I'm sure Amanda will give you all the details."

Fanny wasn't certain why that information should please her, except that she wouldn't be required to wear a mask for the remainder of the evening. Unlike Sophie, she hadn't cared who was behind the masks.

"I believe your uncle Jonas told me there are a number of gentlemen inquiring about your whereabouts. Is your dance card full?"

Fanny wanted to fib, but she shook her head. "No. There are some empty spaces."

"Let me see." Her aunt stood watch while Fanny opened her lozenge-shaped reticule and retrieved the card. "Oh, dear me!" She clutched a hand to her bodice. "You've hardly any dance partners at all." Victoria turned the card over and slowly wagged her head. "This is very sad."

"It's fine. I don't enjoy dancing."

"You were intentionally avoiding dance partners?"

"I wasn't hiding, but I didn't flirt, either. You know I dislike these parties, Aunt Victoria. I prefer exploring the island or fishing with—" She stopped short of uttering Michael's name and waved toward the mansion. "I don't like all of this."

The older woman patted her lace-gloved hand atop Fanny's arm. "You must adapt, Fanny. I understand you enjoy outdoor activities, but if you are to find the proper man to love and marry, you must attend the functions where you will meet him."

The two continued toward the sweeping veranda. Music drifted through the open ballroom doors. Fanny dared not tell her aunt she'd already located the man she wanted to marry, for neither her aunt nor any other member of the Broadmoor family would consider Michael proper—not for Frances Jane Broadmoor.

Jonas couldn't sleep. When he could take no more of the tossing and turning, he rolled out of bed and shoved his arms into his dressing gown. Though it wasn't yet six o'clock, the sun was already breaking the horizon in a blaze of bright tangerine and gold. He opened the French doors that led from the bedroom and stepped onto the covered balcony. Lapping water and twittering birds were the only sounds that greeted him. Peaceful. Perhaps that's why his parents had loved this place. It provided the peace and quiet that eluded them in the city.

He leaned on the pink granite ledge that surrounded the balcony and knew it wasn't the tranquil setting that had drawn them to this island each summer. Quite the contrary. It had been his mother's incessant desire to create a family circle for Fanny that had been the motivation for the family gatherings at Broadmoor Island. Fanny! Always Fanny. And it had been Fanny who had caused his sleeplessness last night.

Thus far she'd shown no interest in any of the young men he'd brought to the island. Even with the promised incentive of a future of wealth, none of the men had been able to capture her interest. Young men nowadays certainly didn't have the ambition required to succeed. Look at his youngest sons! As far as Jonas was concerned, the two of them lacked enough enthusiasm to perform a decent day's work and enough intelligence to make a sound decision.

His thoughts were interrupted by the sound of a woman's soft lilting laughter, and he stepped along the balcony until he reached the south end. Theresa O'Malley had followed Michael out of the rear of the house. She was fawning over him like a woman in love. Jonas rubbed the dark stubble that lined his jaw and considered the young woman. If he handled the matter properly, perhaps Theresa would prove helpful.

Jonas waited until midafternoon, when few family members and guests remained on the island. His wife had announced plans during the noonday meal to travel to Round Island for the annual picnic hosted at the Frontenac Hotel. Jonas thought the family could find sufficient entertainment on their own island, but Victoria had insisted. And he'd relented, as long as he didn't have to accompany them and endure the mindless conversation of weekend guests visiting the hotel or the endless games of badminton and croquet that had become favorite summer pastimes of his family.

He pushed away from the desk in the mansion's cherry-paneled library and made his way down several hallways to the rear of the house.

Mrs. Atwell looked up from her piecrust and stopped midroll. "Is there something wrong, Mr. Broadmoor?"

Jonas understood the concern he detected in her questioning expression. His visits to the kitchen were rare, and entering Mrs. Atwell's domain naturally gave rise to apprehension. He glanced about the kitchen. Theresa was nowhere in sight. "I thought you might have a pitcher of lemonade." He touched a finger to his throat. "I'm feeling a bit parched."

Mrs. Atwell wiped her hands on her apron. "I can bring a tray to the library or the veranda if you'd like."

"I don't want to interrupt your work. Where's Mrs. O'Malley's daughter? Perhaps she could bring the tray."

"She should return in a few minutes. She was helping her mother press linens, but I don't mind stopping to prepare a cool drink for you."

He waved her back to the worktable. "I wouldn't think of it. Just have Theresa bring it to the veranda when she returns. There's no hurry." He didn't wait for the older woman to object before leaving. He knew his servants well enough to realize Mrs. Atwell would prepare the tray, and if Theresa hadn't returned to the kitchen in short order, Mrs. Atwell would go and find her. He'd made his wishes known; he expected them to be met.

He stopped in the library long enough to retrieve a book from the shelf. He didn't want to read, merely present the appearance of a man relaxing with a book and anxious for a glass of lemonade. He chose a chair near the distant railing, where he could see if anyone approached.

Though he'd already checked his watch three times, only twenty minutes passed before Theresa approached with a pitcher of lemonade, a tall glass, and a small plate of dainty cookies.

She placed the tray on the glass-topped wicker table. "Would you like me to pour your lemonade, Mr. Broadmoor?"

"Yes. Then please sit down," he said, indicating the chair directly beside him. The fact that Theresa's hand shook when she lifted the pitcher didn't surprise Jonas. In varying degrees, he had an unsettling effect upon all of the Broadmoor servants. It was a fact that pleased him. He waited in silence until she poured his drink. He took a sip and nodded his approval.

"Is there something else I can fetch for you, sir?"

"No. However, I was wondering if you would be interested in making a bit of extra money."

She gasped and touched her hand to her heart. "I am not *that* kind of girl, Mr. Broadmoor."

"Of course you're not, Theresa, but I think you're a young lady who would be willing to help me play a trick on someone." He watched her and could see she was weighing the possibilities. "Would you like to hear more?"

She inched forward on her chair. "Yes."

"First, you must promise that our little talk be kept a secret. If you should tell anyone, it could mean that both you and your mother would find yourselves unemployed. Do I make myself clear?"

She gave him a somber nod.

"I want you to devise a plan by which Fanny will see you and Michael sharing an intimate moment—a kiss or embrace, whatever you prefer."

Theresa bent forward and rested her arms across her thighs. "You want Fanny to think Michael and I are in love with each other?"

"Something like that. Are you interested?"

She rubbed her hands together and giggled. "This sounds as though it could prove to be a great deal of fun! And I believe I am just the person to help you—if the price is right."

Jonas frowned. Moments ago, the girl's hand had been shaking while she poured his lemonade, and now she was going to attempt to haggle over her price. She had best not get greedy or he'd have her off the island by nightfall and her mother along with her!

"Why don't you tell me what price you believe is right, Theresa." He waited, pleased when she appeared baffled. Exactly what Jonas had hoped for.

"Fifty cents?" Her voice quivered.

He nodded. The silly girl would have gotten much more had she kept her mouth shut. He'd been prepared to give her a dollar. "We have a bargain. Now, off with you to the kitchen before your mother or Mrs. Atwell comes looking for you. And remember, not a word of this to anyone, Theresa."

18

Monday, August 2, 1897

Mortimer Fillmore looked old. Had there been a mirror close at hand, Jonas would have checked his own appearance. Mortimer was only a few years older than Jonas, but the man appeared ancient. A light breeze drifted from off the water, and wisps of white hair splayed about the lawyer's head like arthritic fingers. He relied upon a hand-carved walking stick to aid in his climb up the sloping grass embankment from the boathouse. The sight of his decrepit lawyer was enough to make Jonas consider his own mortality.

Mortimer had ascended half the distance to the house when Jonas spotted the man's older son and partner, Vincent, hurrying after his father. He pointed to his arm and the older man leaned heavily upon his son. Jonas doubted whether his own sons would ever show him such compassion or concern.

He stood and waved to the two men. "Welcome! I'm pleased you were willing to come out here and keep me company for an afternoon."

Mortimer's chest heaved, and he gasped for air as he dropped into the wicker settee on the lower veranda. "I need to rest a few minutes." He signaled for his son to sit down while he continued inhaling great gulps of air.

Vincent offered Jonas an apologetic look. "I attempted to convince him he didn't need to come out here. He's been ill this past week. I told him you would understand and that I could relay any information to him later today, but he insisted."

"Quit talking about me as though I'm still in Rochester, Vincent." Mortimer glanced at Jonas. "The doctor says it's my lungs, but what do doctors know? They take my money, but their guess usually isn't any better than my own."

Jonas laughed and agreed, but there was little doubt Mortimer was suffering from some debilitating illness. "I won't ask you to make any further trips to the island until you're feeling better, Mortimer. You need to get well, my friend." He patted the older lawyer's shoulder. "Why don't we go into the library, where you'll be more comfortable, and I'll have one of the servants bring some refreshments. Are you hungry?"

The men followed him into the library. When they'd finished their refreshments and Theresa had cleared away the trays, Jonas closed the doors. "Let me tell you why I've brought you here." Both men came to attention, the younger of the two pulling out a pencil and paper, poised to jot down notes. Jonas appreciated Vincent's attention to detail, but he shook his head. "Don't make notations, Vincent. I don't want this conversation committed to writing."

Vincent immediately returned the paper and pencil to his leather case. "I didn't want to forget anything you might want completed upon our return to Rochester."

"Quite all right, Vincent, but you won't forget today's conversation, for I've brought you here to gain your ideas rather than assign any specific tasks." Jonas leaned back into the thick padding of his leather chair and explained that the family had left for a trip to Brockville.

"Off to spend your money shopping for new gowns and baubles, I suppose," Mortimer said.

"And to visit a few of the familiar sights they used to visit when my mother was alive. She instilled a love of the town in most of them. I didn't object, for I wanted to meet privately with you, and I had promised Victoria I would spend at least one entire week on the island." He chuckled. "She was unhappy with me when she discovered I'd chosen the week they would be in Brockville. I believe she may return early, just because I'm here."

"Women! Who can figure them out?" Mortimer coughed and wheezed, finally taking a drink of water before settling back in his chair. "What kind of ideas do you want to discuss, Jonas?"

"I continue to feel an enormous sense of discomfort concerning my niece's inheritance. I've developed a plan whereby I'll be able to appropriate a portion of her money by simply falsifying paper work to show poor investments. However, it's the bulk of her estate that concerns me. Although I'm attempting to find her a malleable husband who will give me authority over the money, Fanny has been less than cooperative. Thus far she's shown no interest whatsoever in any of the young men I've brought here."

Mortimer offered his son a sideways glance. "Too bad Vincent is married. Otherwise, this could be easily remedied. I'm sure he'd be able to sweep the girl off her feet."

Vincent tugged at his collar and glowered at his father. "No need to discuss *that* idea any further."

"Then let's discuss some ideas of how I can gain control of her funds once she reaches legal age. She's an obstinate girl. There's no way of knowing if I'll convince her to marry." Jonas lifted the lid of his humidor. "Cigar?"

Mortimer reached toward the desk, only to have Vincent grasp his hand. "No cigars, Father."

Jonas removed one of the fat cigars and lovingly passed it beneath his nose. He inhaled the scent and offered an appreciative sigh.

Vincent massaged his forehead. "More important, you need to consider what would happen to all of that money if Fanny should attain legal age and remain unmarried. Who would ultimately receive her estate? Is she intelligent enough to seek legal advice and prepare a will once she's attained the age of majority? Depending upon her social mores, she could elect to bequeath her estate to a church or a charitable group."

Mortimer inched forward in his chair and pointed at Jonas. "That's not so farfetched, considering the fact that Quincy has nearly bankrupted himself with his Home for the Friendless. Fanny might decide to leave her money to such an institution. They tell me this sort of thing runs in families."

Mouth agape, Vincent stared at his father. "Don't be ridiculous, Father. We're talking about bequeathing money to a charity, not some mental disease."

"Nearly the same thing, don't you agree, Jonas?" Mortimer cackled.

"In most cases. Of course there are rare occasions when money to the proper charity can yield great benefit. However, this would not be one of those instances. My brother has squandered far too much of the Broadmoor fortune."

Mortimer rubbed his arthritic hands together. "Let's hope you have more control over that girl than you do over your brother. He's a disgrace, Jonas."

Vincent momentarily buried his face in his hands. "I'm beginning to think you're suffering from a lack of oxygen to your brain, Father. Your insults are uncalled for. What has come over you?"

Mortimer shrugged. "Merely speaking the truth and attempting to help Jonas with a plan. What do you propose?"

Vincent rubbed his forehead again. "It's truly a conundrum. I could prepare a will for her, but she's not of legal age to sign such a document—it wouldn't be binding in the court."

Jonas perked to attention. "But it would show clear intent that Fanny had planned for the estate to come to me, and you or your father could obtain the services of one of those *friendly* judges. That process might lead to an agreeable outcome."

Mortimer frowned. "I suppose it could work, but we'll probably all be dead before the girl—you had best continue working toward arranging a proper marriage partner."

Jonas nodded slowly. "You're absolutely correct, Mortimer."

Mortimer thumped his cane on the floor. "Well, of course I am."

"Please, Father, Jonas and I need to discuss the idea of a will in further detail. If Fanny should predecease you, do you think your brother or other family members would protest the document and attempt to have the document set aside, based upon Fanny's tender years?"

Jonas considered the matter for several minutes. He knew there would be a hue and cry if he were to receive the share allocated to Fanny. Most of the family coveted her money as much as he did. Money had set the relatives against each other for years. Jonas found it rather entertaining. "What if the will provides a clause in which Fanny acknowledges her tender years? It could further state that she fully understands the terms, and it is her desire to name me as her sole heir. Perhaps a judge would then be willing to overrule any protests."

Vincent jumped up from his chair and paced in front of the windows. "Yes, I like that idea. And we could have a clause specifically stating that even though the document has been drawn and signed while in her tender years, she desires for it to remain her final declaration until set aside in writing."

"Yes! I believe we're on to something. How soon could you have the document delivered to me?"

Vincent glanced at his father. Mortimer had nodded off. "I want to be certain nothing is overlooked. Would next weekend suffice?"

"Yes, but have it delivered by a courier. With the family here, another visit might give rise to questions."

"Tell me, Jonas, how will you persuade her to sign the document? If she's as bright as you indicate, won't she insist upon reading the contents?"

"I'll be giving that matter thought. In the interim we need to consider every possible method to have the girl disinherited. Then my father's bequest to her could be easily set aside. Surely we can think of something."

Vincent shook his head. "I don't see how she could possibly be disinherited, Jonas."

Mortimer jerked to attention. "Nothing's impossible where money's involved. Right, Jonas?"

"You are entirely correct, Mortimer."

Theresa descended the stairs, her feet striking each step with a heavy thud. Since reaching her agreement with Jonas Broadmoor, she had done her utmost to capture Michael's interest. She'd been to the boathouse more times than she cared to think about, and she'd attempted to use her feminine wiles on each occasion. Although Michael had answered her questions and was cordial during her visits, he always shied away from her advances.

The previous day she'd even attempted to lure him away from his work under the guise of a fishing expedition. After packing what she considered a delightful picnic lunch and securing her mother's permission to be gone for the afternoon, Theresa had gone to the boathouse filled with anticipation. With Fanny and the other women away for their shopping excursion in Canada, she'd decided the time alone would give her an opportunity to begin her seduction. But Michael had steadfastly refused. His excuses were as numerous as legs on a centipede.

After an hour of cajoling, she'd finally dumped the contents of the picnic basket into the water. Seeing their lunch enter the murky water had been the only thing that had evoked any emotion from the man. He'd been aghast to see the traces of crusty chicken sandwiches floating on the water, but he hadn't even noticed that he'd wounded her feelings. She'd never faced such difficulty luring a man. His constant refusals were taking their toll on her ego. If she was going to succeed with Michael, she needed help—a desperate thought.

Theresa plodded down the hallway toward the kitchen. Her mother would be going over the day's schedule with Mrs. Atwell and would expect to see her. The voices of the two women drifted into the hallway, and Theresa quickened her step. The older women might offer some insight, especially Michael's mother.

Entering the kitchen, she forced a bright smile. "Good morning," she said in her cheeriest voice.

A hint of suspicion immediately shone in her mother's eyes. "Is that *my* daughter? Cheerful so early in the morning?"

Theresa frowned. "I'm usually cheerful in the morning."

Her mother laughed, shook her head, and immediately returned to her discussion with Mrs. Atwell. Theresa quietly listened while the two women prepared a lengthy shopping list for the following week.

Mrs. Atwell ran the tip of her pencil down the list and gave an affirmative nod. "I believe we've thought of everything. I'll give Michael our list and send him to Clayton tomorrow morning."

Theresa stepped closer and reviewed the menus the two ladies had prepared for the following week. "Which one of these meals is Michael's favorite?"

Mrs. Atwell appeared confused. "None of them. Michael prefers the more common fare I've been serving this week while the family's been in Brockville. Thus far, Mr. Jonas hasn't voiced an objection," she said with a grin. "I think Mr. Jonas prefers butter-browned fresh fish and fried potatoes more than the fancy dishes we serve when the missus is in the house."

"And what about dessert? Does Michael prefer your pies or one of your lovely cakes?"

Mrs. Atwell dipped out a cup of flour and sifted it into a crock. "Why all this interest in what Michael enjoys for his meals? Are you planning on assuming my kitchen duties?" She pointed toward the crock. "If so, you can begin by mixing up the dough for this evening's dinner rolls."

Theresa laughed. "I don't think you want me making the rolls, Mrs. Atwell. They'd likely come out of the oven as flat as pancakes."

"Then why the interest in what Michael likes to eat?"

Theresa plunged forward. "Well, don't tell him I said so, but I think your son is most interesting." She pressed her fingers to her dark tresses. "Although most men tell me I'm quite pretty and seemingly enjoy my company, Michael completely ignores me. I don't know what I've done that has caused him to behave in such a standoffish manner."

The older woman brushed the flour from her hands. "Michael's behavior has nothing to do with you or your fine looks, Theresa. Michael has eyes for only one woman. And after all these years, I doubt he'll be tempted by the sway of your hips or a fashionable hairstyle."

Theresa's mother clucked her tongue. "You had better encourage him to keep on looking, Maggie. We both know he's never going to have that one."

Mrs. Atwell finished mixing the dough and plopped it onto the wooden worktable. She plunged her fingers into the heavy dough. "What's a mother to do? He's a grown man, and he knows she's out of his reach, but it doesn't change his feelings."

Theresa turned and exited through the kitchen door leading to the back lawn. Let the two women argue about Michael. They weren't going to offer any help to her predicament. She circled the house, her thoughts a jumble of confusion. If she failed Mr. Broadmoor, he'd likely fire her. Worse yet, he might discharge her mother, too.

"Theresa!"

Mr. Broadmoor stood on the upper veranda with his arms folded across his chest. He pointed toward the ground. "Meet me on the lower veranda."

Theresa sighed. Mr. Broadmoor was going to expect a report on her progress. No doubt he'd find her excuses unacceptable. Perspiration dampened her palms. Theresa swiped her hands down her skirt and prepared to be chastised. She forced a smile as Mr. Broadmoor stepped onto the porch. His white shirt appeared nearly as stiff as the set of his shoulders.

He didn't waste time with idle chitchat. "How are matters progressing between you and Michael?"

She remained standing, though Mr. Broadmoor had settled into one of the cushioned wicker chairs. "Not as smoothly as I had hoped—though it's not from my lack of trying," she hastened to add. The older man remained attentive while she proceeded through the litany of difficulties she'd experienced. She was certain he was unhappy with her. He rubbed his jaw and stared into the distance.

When she could no longer bear the silence, Theresa sat down beside him. "I even spoke to his mother and inquired how I might win his affections."

Jonas arched his brows. "And?"

"Mrs. Atwell said he had eyes for only one woman, and she didn't think I'd be successful."

"Hmm. So even his mother realizes he's smitten with my niece." Jonas studied the vessel slowly moving downriver. The steamer whistled two short blasts, and Captain Visegar waved his hat high in the air. The aging captain conducted fifty-mile cruises through the islands twice a day in his *New Island Wanderer*. Visitors came armed with the captain's brochure that described the different islands, the beautiful mansions, and résumés of the various owners. "I have an idea that Michael won't be able to refuse."

Theresa leaned forward, anxious for details. Her excitement mounted as Mr. Broadmoor described the harbor lights cruise that was conducted every Saturday night. "Perhaps you've heard some of the family or guests mention it?"

"I haven't, but it sounds like great fun. However, I doubt Michael would invite me."

"I'll take care of that. My wife and I will host all of our guests on the tour this Saturday night. I'll purchase tickets for you and Michael. I'll tell him that I mistakenly purchased the incorrect number of tickets and ask that he act as your escort, since this is your first summer on the island and you've not been on the tour."

"What a wonderful plan."

"Indeed. And I'll expect you to make good use of your time on the cruise. Make Fanny believe that Michael is romantically interested in you." He leaned forward in his chair. "May I count on you to do your very best?"

She gave an enthusiastic nod. "Trust me. You won't be disappointed, Mr. Broadmoor."

19

Saturday, August 7, 1897

Fanny slumped in her chair. "I don't want to be included in the searchlight excursion this evening. I truly cannot believe your father purchased tickets and expects all of us to attend." She rested her chin in her palm. "The entire outing is unlike him. He detests socializing with anyone other than his equals and discourages the rest of us from doing so, too."

Amanda giggled. "With the entire family and all of our guests, he's likely assumed there will be no space for any other passengers."

Sophie wrinkled her nose. "I hope that isn't true. I want to mingle with some other people—we've been with family all week long. I think I'll send Michael to Castle Rest and have him deliver an invitation to Georgie and Sanger Pullman. They're always enjoyable company."

Amanda turned from her dressing table. "You'd best not send out any invitations without Father's approval."

Sophie had already retrieved a piece of writing paper from Amanda's desk and didn't hesitate while dipping her cousin's pen into the bottle of ink. "I'm not sending an invitation. I'm merely telling them we'll be on the steamer and they should join us if they have no other plans for the evening." The minute she'd completed the note, Sophie jumped up from the writing desk.

"I'll go with you. I've a need of fresh air," Fanny said.

Sophie playfully grasped her cousin's arm. "Would you feel the need for fresh air if I wasn't going to search for Michael Atwell?"

Fanny ignored the question. Sophie already knew the answer. Though they invited Amanda to join them, she declined. The two cousins hastened toward the boathouse, their laughter drifting overhead on the warm afternoon breeze. The clatter of their shoes on the wooden dock surrounding the boathouse eliminated any element of surprise. Michael was watching the door when they entered.

He continued to sand one of the small skiffs. "What can I do for you ladies?"

Sophie held out the envelope. "I was hoping you'd have time to deliver this note to Castle Rest within the hour. Is that possible?"

Michael stroked his palm along the black walnut gunwale of the skiff. "So long as Mr. Broadmoor has no objection." He stepped closer and retrieved the envelope.

"If Uncle Jonas should ask, I'll tell him you made the delivery at Sophie's instruction," Fanny replied.

He nodded. "Good day then, ladies." Michael tucked the envelope into his pocket and picked up the sandpaper.

Sophie stared at him when he didn't budge. "When are you going to depart?"

Michael shrugged. "In a half hour or so. It doesn't take long to get to Pullman Island."

She waved toward Michael's pocket. "That's a note asking the Pullman brothers to join us for the spotlight tour of the islands this evening. The sooner it's delivered, the better."

The sandpaper dropped from Michael's hand and fluttered to the floor. "You're going on the cruise, too?"

"What do you mean, *too*? Are you going?" Sophie shot a grin in Fanny's direction. "As much as you're around boats, I wouldn't think you'd be interested in a cruise on someone else's vessel."

Fanny pinched her cousin. If Michael was going to be on the boat, that changed everything. The idea of a late-evening cruise now held appeal, and she didn't want Sophie to influence Michael otherwise.

"He's taking *me* on the cruise, aren't you, Michael?" Theresa sashayed to Michael's side and grasped his arm in a possessive hold.

Fanny wilted at the sight.

Michael wrenched free of Theresa's grasp. "I'll deliver your note immediately."

Theresa hurried behind him. "Oh, may I go with you? I've completed my chores and—"

"No. Against the rules," he curtly replied before jumping into the launch. "Am I to wait for a reply or merely leave this with one of the servants, Miss Sophie?"

She pondered for a moment. "No need to wait for a reply, but ask that it be immediately delivered to either Sanger or Georgie."

Michael touched two fingers to the brim of his cap and saluted. Had Sophie not yanked on her sleeve, Fanny would have remained to watch his departure. Truth be told, she would have waited until he returned. She couldn't believe he had invited Theresa to accompany him on a cruise that was touted as the islands' most romantic tour. Yet he hadn't denied the assertion. And her pride wouldn't permit her to question Theresa.

Fanny plodded back toward the house with Sophie at her side. "Can you believe Michael asked her? I think it was probably the other way around. Theresa purchased the tickets and asked him. Or his mother's forcing him to go as a favor. She and Mrs. O'Malley are friends. I'd wager that's what happened." She tipped her head to the side and arched her brows. "Don't you think, Sophie? I mean Michael absolutely wouldn't have taken it upon himself to do such a thing. I don't believe it—not for a minute!"

Sophie stopped in her tracks. "Do you want me to answer, or have you already sufficiently answered the question for yourself?"

"I'm not certain. I want you to respond but only if you say what I want to hear."

Sophie giggled. "At least you're honest. I think Theresa played a large part in arranging the evening with Michael, but you must remember that Michael is a grown man. He has the ability to say no—and he obviously didn't." She grabbed Fanny's hand and continued up the hill. "You need to make him jealous. Michael needs to see that you can attract other men. Perhaps we should ask Sanger or Georgie to help us with our plan. One of them would be willing to play the part of an amorous admirer. That would be great fun."

"No. I don't want to involve anyone else. The twins would ask questions, and soon everyone would know of my feelings for Michael."

"Then simply act interested in one of those young men in Uncle Jonas's entourage. Problem resolved."

Fanny didn't agree, but she didn't argue with her cousin. Unlike Sophie, she had never learned the finer points of flirting. What's more, she had no desire to cultivate her cousin's womanly wiles.

Fanny's excuses failed. Uncle Jonas had turned a deaf ear to her every attempt. She'd even resorted to going behind his back and seeking her aunt's permission to remain at home, but that too had proved futile. In the end there had been no escape. Along with their weekend guests and other members of the household, Fanny donned her finery and boarded the *DaisyBee* for their ride to Clayton. They were packed into the launch like sardines in a can, with Fanny squeezed between Daniel Irwin and Benjamin Wolgast. Theresa had positioned herself as close to Michael as humanly possible—or so it seemed to Fanny. At least they wouldn't be sandwiched together in close quarters once they boarded the *Wanderer*. Hopefully she could escape Daniel and Benjamin as well as their tiresome anecdotes.

"Which one have you chosen?" Sophie whispered as they disembarked in Clayton.

"Neither," Fanny hissed.

Sophie grabbed her by the hand and pulled her away from the crowd. "If you're going to gain Michael's attention, you must do as I say. I'll be required to sic Georgie or Sanger on you if you don't choose someone and begin to flirt."

"Don't you dare, Sophie!"

Sophie cast a triumphant look over her shoulder. "Then do as I say, Cousin."

Fanny surveyed the men and then noticed that Michael and Theresa had distanced themselves from the Broadmoors and their guests. Obviously they were uncomfortable. She experienced a twinge of pity and then shoved the feeling aside. Michael should have known better. Did he care so much for Theresa that he would subject himself to this awkward and humiliating situation? Perhaps he did. The thought was sobering.

"Come along now. We don't want to detain the captain or the other passengers." Uncle Jonas stood at the edge of the pier while waving them forward.

As predicted, her uncle had assumed there wouldn't be space on the *Wanderer* for anyone other than his guests. He'd been wrong—and he was unhappy. Her uncle had attempted to persuade the captain to send the additional passengers over to ride on the *St. Lawrence*. Citing the fact that angry customers made for bad publicity, the captain hadn't yielded to Uncle Jonas. The captain was bright enough to understand that a rare excursion by Jonas Broadmoor and his family didn't hold enough sway to offset the possibility of a bad reputation among the hordes of vacationers who arrived daily and didn't hesitate to spend their hard-earned cash for an outing on his boat.

Her uncle did his best to arrange their seating in a segregated manner, waving Jefferson, George, and both of the Pullman twins toward the rear of the boat when they attempted to mingle with the tourists. Unexpectedly, he directed Michael and Theresa toward the rear of the boat, also.

With a smug smile, Theresa squeezed onto the seat and forced Fanny closer to Daniel, who immediately assumed she was seeking his attention. When he fumbled for her hand Fanny yanked away and accidentally elbowed Theresa in the ribs. Theresa yelped in pain while Aunt Victoria shook her head and clucked her tongue. "Please don't cause us any embarrassment, Fanny."

Fanny glared at Daniel. "Keep your hands to yourself and there won't be any further problems."

Daniel grinned and casually draped his arm across the back of the seat. "That should give you a little more room." He tipped his head closer and winked. "You need not be coy with me. I can always tell when a lady is captivated by my charm."

"Can you? Then I'm certain you realize I find you a total boor," she whispered before turning her attention to her aunt. "Did you tell Uncle Jonas we visited Mrs. Comstock while we were in Brockville, Aunt Victoria?"

"Thank you for the reminder, Fanny," she said and then addressed Jonas. "Mrs. Comstock mentioned that her husband wants to visit with you in the near future regarding some investments."

Jonas rubbed his hands together. "I'd wager he's concerned about George Fulford infringing on his patent medicine business. Did you invite them to come to the island for a visit?"

Victoria nodded. "I did. She was going to check with her husband, but they may visit in late August if their schedule permits."

The boat continued slowly downriver while the captain pointed out the colored gaslights that lit numerous islands, including their own. When Theresa and Michael moved from their seat toward the rail, Fanny edged away from Daniel. He immediately closed the gap.

"What other news was circulating in Brockville? Was there much talk of the gold strike in the Yukon?"

At the mention of the gold strike, the young men's excitement escalated. Daniel finally shook his head in disgust. "Only a fool would waste his time running off in search of gold. The men return broken and destitute."

"You'd best not make such a comment in front of our father," Sanger told him. "It's Colorado gold that helped him on his way."

Daniel laughed. "You'll not fool me with that story. It was his luxurious railroad cars that made the Pullman money—not gold."

"Sanger's speaking the truth," Georgie said. "Of course not all of those men were as fortunate as our father, but for those who were . . ." His voice trailed off on the breeze. "I'm just glad I don't have to concern myself with making money. There's far too much time and energy involved in the process, and I wouldn't want to rob my father of the pleasure. Besides, I much prefer the spending process, don't you, Sanger?"

Fanny noted Michael's obvious interest as he leaned forward to listen to the conversation. Gold—and lots of it, one of the fellows reported. Ready for any man willing to head north. Fanny experienced a sense of satisfaction when Theresa's attempt to lure Michael into a conversation failed. Like the rest of the men, he was far more interested in the Yukon gold than the colorful island lights or the moonlight dancing on the water.

Fanny yanked the thick-bristled brush through her unmanageable curls. "Did you see how Theresa behaved this evening? She draped herself across Michael like a wool shawl on a cold night!"

Amanda giggled. "I do think that's an exaggeration, dear girl. And I don't believe I saw Michael object to her attentions."

Sophie slipped into her nainsook nightgown and tied the pale blue ribbons. "I'm not so sure. He attempted to withdraw from her several times, but she followed after him like a puppy dog longing for affection. Do you think she loves him?"

"How could she love him? She barely knows him," Fanny protested.

"No need to take your anger out on me," Sophie said.

Amanda unpinned her hair and let it fall around her shoulders. "I thought you had released all your anger when you poked Theresa in the side. I heard her complaining to Michael when we returned home. He had to nearly lift her off the *DaisyBee*."

Fanny slapped the hairbrush onto her dressing table. "Oh, pshaw! She wasn't hurt in the least. Can't you see that she's nothing more than a flirt and a fraud? She wasn't injured, and she doesn't truly care for Michael. He's simply a diversion, another conquest."

"Sounds as though you're describing Sophie," Amanda said with a grin.

Sophie tapped her finger to her chin. "Hmm. I suppose it does." She immediately brightened. "If she's truly like me, then she doesn't care about Michael and you need not worry yourself, Fanny. I think you should confront Michael and ask him if he has feelings for Theresa. The two of you have been friends for years. If he's half the man you profess, he shouldn't object to giving you an honest answer."

Amanda immediately warned against Sophie's suggestion. Such a confrontation would be foolhardy, she advised. So by the time Fanny departed for her own bedroom, her thoughts were a jumble and she'd arrived at only one conclusion: she wanted Michael for herself.

Fanny's sleep was fraught with dreams of Theresa and Michael. Theresa in a beautiful wedding gown while Mrs. Atwell held a wedding cake high in the air for inspection; Theresa's name inscribed on the cake in large black letters; a happy Michael retrieving a wedding ring from his pocket to show her and then turning to place it on Theresa's finger. At the sound of wedding bells, Fanny awakened with a start. Her forehead was damp with perspiration, and the ringing bell that had awakened her was a boat on the river. The wedding had been a dream—or a nightmare.

Fanny's decision was clear when she descended the stairs. The rest of the family hadn't yet come down for breakfast. Michael would be at the boathouse, and Theresa would be helping with breakfast preparations. Fanny and Michael could talk without fear of interruption—if he didn't find another excuse to avoid her.

The river cooled the August breeze, and Fanny longed to be out in the skiff fishing with Michael. He'd refused her every request, citing his increased duties, yet he seemed to have time for Theresa. Her decisiveness waned as she opened the boathouse door. What if he said he loved Theresa? What would she do?

Michael turned as she opened the door. Surprise shone in his eyes, but he didn't move. She hurried toward him, anxious to close the distance that separated them. "We need to talk, Michael." He glanced over his shoulder toward the rear exit, and she touched his arm. "Please don't make excuses and run off. I thought you cared for me, that you were my friend. Yet every time I come near, you flee. What have I done?" When he didn't answer, she forced herself to ask the question that burned in her heart. "Is it Theresa? Do you love her?"

"What?" He grasped her shoulders and looked into her eyes. "How could you ever think such a thing? I love you!" He shook his head. "Forgive me. I shouldn't have said that."

She touched her palm to his cheek. "I love you, too. If it is true, why should your words remain unspoken?"

"Because it only deepens my pain. We live in different worlds, Fanny. You know that as well as I do. Your uncle will never grant me permission to marry you."

"And that's why you've been avoiding me?"

He nodded toward the door. "Let's take a walk."

Together they strolled up the slope and then turned and walked toward a wooded area offering a magnificent view of the river. Her heart had soared at Michael's declaration of love. Surely they could devise some reasonable method and overcome her uncle's objections.

Michael held her hand while she sat down on one of the outcroppings that overlooked the river. He dropped down beside her and stared across the water. "Life seems so simple when we're out here alone, doesn't it?"

"But it can be, Michael. Once I'm of legal age, Uncle Jonas can't prohibit our marriage. We need only wait until then."

"You underestimate his power. He knows we care for each other—why do you think he's been forcing me to spend time with Theresa?"

Her jaw went slack. "So that's why you've been unwilling to go fishing or spend time with me. And all along I thought—"

"That you'd done something to anger me?" He shook his head. "You've done nothing. But your uncle insists I mustn't spend time with you. I'm required to follow his orders, Fanny. If I disobey his wishes, it could be disastrous—not only for me, but for my parents, also. I've been praying for a solution, but I'm not certain whether what has recently come to mind is actually God's answer or if I'm grasping at straws." A branch crackled and Michael jumped to his feet.

Fanny giggled and pointed to a squirrel that skittered toward them and up a nearby tree. "It's only a squirrel."

"We had better return. You'll be missed if you don't appear at the breakfast table."

He grasped her hand firmly and tugged her to her feet. Her heel caught in the hem of her skirt, and she lurched forward against Michael's chest. He gathered her in his arms and held her close. She gazed up into his eyes. He lowered his head and their lips lightly touched.

Thick grass muffled the sound of approaching footsteps.

"What is the meaning of this!" Her uncle's words reverberated through the early morning calm like a roaring clap of thunder.

20

"I object!"

"*You* object? You have no voice in this matter." Jonas paced the library. Only hours ago he'd caught his niece in the arms of a servant. "I am your legal guardian. You will sit down and listen." Jonas turned and glared at Michael. "I thought I had made myself perfectly clear. This situation that you've created must come to a halt." He clenched his jaw. "Must I discharge your entire family in order to make you believe that I will not tolerate your behavior?"

"That's not fair, Uncle Jonas," Fanny challenged. "They've done nothing wrong. Are you so cruel that you would make others pay for something they didn't have any say in?"

"I told you to listen," Jonas said, glaring at his niece. "Unless you want to find yourself relieved of any future freedoms, I would suggest you obey me."

"Please. I beg you," Michael appealed. "My parents would be devastated if they were forced off the island. This is their home—and mine, too. They would be heartbroken."

"If you're truly concerned about your parents, why have you continued to disregard my orders?" Jonas drummed his fingers on his desk. "Well?"

"I've made every attempt, sir. What you saw this morning was innocent. Fanny tripped and I caught her in my arms." He wiped his palm across his forehead. "The kiss and the words of endearment weren't planned. And I did tell her we could never entertain thoughts of a future together."

"You tell her you can't have a future together and then you kiss her? What does that ungentlemanly behavior tell her—or me, for that matter?"

"What I wanted her to know is that I truly love her, but you do not consider me a possible suitor or marriage partner."

Jonas chortled. "And do you consider yourself worthy of my niece, Michael?"

He shook his head. "Even if I had as much wealth as you, I would not consider myself worthy of someone so sweet and kind."

"Oh, do stop with your gibberish. Love isn't what's important. Social standing and wealth must always be the first consideration when choosing a husband for any of the Broadmoor girls." Jonas tucked his thumb into the pocket of his vest. "With the money that Fanny will inherit, I feel an even greater responsibility to protect her future with the proper man."

"And am I have to have no say on this subject?" Fanny asked.

Jonas saw the fire in her eyes. He thought to answer angrily but calmed himself and drew a couple of deep breaths. He needed to find a way to win Fanny's cooperation—or at least her understanding.

"Fanny, long ago your father told me that he only wanted the very best for you. He felt you deserved to be well cared for and provided for. You were the reason he gave up his own home and moved in with our parents. You were the most important person in his life, and he wanted you safe."

"I believe he also wanted me loved," Fanny protested.

"Absolutely. And who better to love you than family. He always told me that if anything happened to him, he would want me to step in and be a father to you. Of course when he did pass on, your grandmother wanted to direct your schooling and such. I decided not to protest because it helped her through her grief over losing your father. Now there is no one else to challenge—now I can fulfill my promise to your father."

"If you care about me," Fanny said, meeting his gaze, "you'll understand that I love Michael. It doesn't matter to me that he's not rich."

"But in time it will, Fanny. In time you will resent that he cannot provide for you in this manner and style."

"If I were wealthy, would you consider me a proper choice for Fanny?"

Jonas leaned back in his chair and studied Michael. The boy had courage and didn't easily back down. He was a hard worker and a talented boatswain. But a suitable match for a Broadmoor? He knew his answer would hold little sway, since Michael would never accumulate any wealth.

"I would give you consideration," he said.

"No. I would like your word as a gentleman that if I become wealthy, you will grant me permission to marry Fanny."

Jonas frowned. "How do you propose to make this money? If you have no plan, I see no reason to continue this discussion."

"The Yukon."

"The Yukon?" Fanny questioned, her eyes wide in surprise.

"You want to go off in search of gold?" Jonas asked doubt-fully. "It takes money to purchase the necessities to enter into such a venture."

"I have money saved that I'm willing to use."

Jonas could see the young man's excitement mounting as he continued to talk about his plan to travel north. Though the idea hadn't previously occurred to him, having Michael leave for the Yukon would be ideal. With him out of the way, Fanny would soon be more easily managed. And once Michael was in the Yukon, who could say if they'd ever see him again. After all, his nephew Dorian had taken off for Canada three years ago, and other than one letter shortly after his departure, they'd heard nothing from him.

If and when Michael returned to the Thousand Islands, Fanny would be married to a man of Jonas's choosing, and her money would be controlled by her uncle. Indeed, Michael's idea of a trek into the Yukon held promise. Jonas furrowed his brow, as though contemplating the matter. He didn't want to appear overly excited by the proposal. "Have you discussed this with your parents? I'm certain they'd object to your plan. Your father has come to rely on you a great deal."

"My parents would point out the possible pitfalls of such a decision, but they wouldn't stop me from doing what I believe is an answer to prayer."

"Prayer? You think God wants you to go into the goldfields, Michael?" Jonas chuckled.

"I prayed for you to grant me permission to marry Fanny. You've done that."

Jonas held up his hand. "Not exactly. Here is my agreement. You go to the Yukon and search for gold. I will even agree to loan you enough money to purchase the necessary supplies for your venture. However, Fanny must agree to accept the invitations of other gentlemen during your absence. She is young and has experienced very little of life. She believes she loves you, but she is very young. I don't want her to make a mistake."

"But I don't want to see other men. I'm willing to wait until Michael returns," Fanny argued. "I know I won't change my mind."

Jonas tented his fingers beneath his chin. "You are too young to know anything with certainty. If you won't agree to my terms . . ."

"Please, Fanny. It's the only way," Michael whispered.

She searched his face, a slight frown wrinkling her brow. "If you're truly certain you want me to agree."

He nodded.

"I'll agree." She fingered the pearl button at her neckline. "But the invitations you accept on my behalf shall not outnumber those you accept for Amanda." She settled back in her chair. "I believe that's a fair agreement."

Jonas slapped his hands on the desk. "I'm setting the terms of the agreement—not you. Amanda's future is not under discussion."

"Perhaps not, but won't it appear strange and hurtful if I'm living in your home and you are more involved in my future than that of your own daughter?" She leaned forward as if to press home her point.

Though he was loath to admit it, Fanny was likely correct. Victoria had already expressed her displeasure over arranged marriages. If he was going to maintain control of Fanny's future, he must show the same care regarding his own daughter. Otherwise, there would be far too many of Victoria's incessant questions and bothersome discussions.

"Since Amanda is older than you, I'm certain you won't be surprised to hear that I am planning a full social calendar when the family returns to Rochester." He folded his hands across his midsection. Fanny may have thought she'd outwitted him, but he'd bargained with some of the most powerful men in the country. This girl had no idea what lay in store for her.

Michael edged forward on his chair. "If there's nothing further, Mr. Broadmoor, I believe we have reached a final agreement."

"One more thing, Michael. I don't know when you plan to depart for the Yukon, but the clandestine meetings at the boathouse and out in the woods must cease immediately. I don't want Fanny's reputation ruined."

"Nor do I, Mr. Broadmoor. I can assure you that I would never take advantage of—"

Jonas waved his hand. "I, too, was a young man, Michael. Most young men intend to conduct themselves in an honorable manner with young ladies, but—well, we need not say any more regarding this topic, especially when a woman is present in the room."

Anger clouded Fanny's eyes. "You are insinuating that we . . . that Michael and I . . . that . . ."

"Exactly. You say you are in love and have asked that I believe you. I know passions run deep when young people are in love. Consequently, I must insist the two of you adhere to my decision."

Michael's agreement was enough to please Jonas. With a final admonition for them to heed his restrictions, he dismissed them.

Fanny tugged on Michael's sleeve once they stepped outside. "We need to talk." She pointed to the far end of the veranda.

"You heard your uncle. We're not supposed to be alone. Do you want him to withdraw his agreement so soon, Fanny?"

"We are standing in full view of anyone who might pass by the open windows or walk outdoors. I hardly see how he could object." Fanny ignored his protest. Keeping an ear attuned for the sound of his footfalls, she strolled toward the cluster of wicker chairs.

She nodded toward one of the chairs, but Michael remained standing. "Please, Fanny."

"I do wish you would have mentioned your thoughts about the Yukon to me prior to striking an agreement with Uncle Jonas." When she reached for his hand, he took a backward step. "I don't believe that your going off in search of gold is the answer to our dilemma. And who can even guess the dangers you'll encounter or how long you'll be gone."

He squatted down and leaned against the stone rail that circled the porch. "We'll have to trust God to keep me safe. I truly believe this is our answer. I'll write to you every chance I get."

Fanny's gaze settled on his scuffed work boots. "We both know letters will be scarce. And what about the mail service in a place such as the Yukon?"

"In the end, I believe our gain will be worth the sacrifice. Not the money, but the fact that I will have received your uncle's blessing. I don't want to come between you and your family or make any decisions that either of us will later regret." Michael bowed his head until he looked into her eyes. "I do love you, so don't you fall in love with one of those dandies that come knocking on your uncle's door."

She attempted a smile, but a tear trickled down her cheek. "I don't want to spend time with any man but you. How soon will you plan to leave?"

"Please don't cry." He wiped away her tear with his thumb. "I should head out as soon as possible. If arrangements can be made, probably within a week."

She gasped. "So soon? I thought you would at least wait until the family departed at the end of summer."

He shook his head. "The sooner I leave, the sooner I'll return. My father can look after the boats and pick up supplies in Clayton for the few remaining weeks your family will be here. And if I can't spend time with you on the island, there's no need for me to stick around, is there?"

She didn't want to offer an affirmative answer, for she had already contrived a plan to have Sophie help her arrange secret meetings with Michael. Yet she wondered if he would agree. He seemed determined to abide by his agreement with her uncle.

"You would never leave without telling me good-bye, would you?" She met his gaze and saw the love in his eyes. He didn't need to say a word. His answer was as clear as the blue sky overhead.

"Fanny!" Her uncle stood in the doorway, his face as red as the tip on his cigar.

With a fleeting good-bye to Michael, she hastened toward the front entrance. Let him bluster—they hadn't broken their agreement. "You shouldn't be smoking that smelly cigar, Uncle. I doubt that it's good for your health."

"What's bad for my health is a niece who doesn't do as she's told." He stubbed out the cigar and followed her into the house. "Breakfast is waiting. You'll be delighted to hear my announcement."

She doubted that she'd be delighted. Her uncle sounded far too pleased with himself. Most of the family and their guests had already gathered around the breakfast table by the time

Uncle Jonas took his place at the head of the table. They'd hardly begun their fruit compote when he signaled and asked for quiet.

"I've an announcement that I believe you'll all find most pleasant." All eyes turned in his direction. "The Thousand Island Club will be hosting the annual polo matches in two weeks. And I know that you ladies will be anxious to show off your latest fashions. I have made arrangements for all of us to attend."

Aunt Victoria frowned. The weekend of the polo matches had always been a weekend free of guests. "It's difficult managing during that weekend, Jonas. There are so many activities, and we must be coming and going at different times. I truly don't know . . ."

He glanced around the table with a look of expectancy. "Our guests won't expect you to look after their every need. We have a houseful of servants who can assist them if you're busy, my dear."

Sophie forked a piece of melon. "I agree with Uncle Jonas. The more the merrier. I'm sure these fellows can find their way to the kitchen or ring for a servant if need be."

The young men nodded their heads and murmured their agreement. "Very kind of you to include us, Mr. Broadmoor," Daniel said. "I look forward to additional time with your family." He glanced across the table at Fanny and winked.

She curled her lip and turned away. What a rude man! Did he believe she would think his bold behavior endearing?

"May I request your permission to escort Fanny to the polo matches and ball, Mr. Broadmoor?" Daniel inquired.

Fanny smiled demurely. "I'm sorry, but I've already accepted another invitation, Daniel."

Her uncle glowered. "Without my permission? I think not."

"You object to Sanger Pullman?" She tipped her head to the side and waited for his response.

Sophie giggled. "I'm sure Mr. Pullman wouldn't be pleased to hear that you find one of his sons an unacceptable suitor."

"I never said any such thing, Sophie, and don't you consider repeating such a comment. I was merely surprised by Fanny's announcement. Naturally, I have no objection. However, in the future, I would appreciate it if you would speak to me *before* making any arrangements, Fanny."

Fanny politely agreed. She didn't participate in the remainder of the breakfast conversation, for her thoughts were awhirl. Plans had to be made and expedited as soon as possible. She signaled for Sophie and Amanda to meet her outside the minute they'd finished breakfast. Fanny led her cousins across the front lawn to a spot that afforded a clear view of anyone who might approach.

"Sit down over here by this tree." Fanny glanced over her shoulder to make certain none of the young men had followed. "I am in dire need of your help."

Sophie straightened the delicate edging on the sleeve of her dress. "There's no doubt about that!"

Fanny ignored the remark and hastily explained Michael was departing for the Yukon and that he'd made an agreement with Amanda's father. "Please promise you'll not tell anyone about this. Not even your mother, Amanda."

"I promise, but I find all of this most unsettling. I don't understand why my father believes he must be so involved with your future. I understand he's your legal guardian, but he's taking those duties more to heart than parenting his own children."

"No need to become so dramatic, Amanda. You should be thankful it's Fanny he wants to control. Remember, you're the one who keeps telling us you're intent upon discovering your true calling in life rather than merely finding a man and exchanging marriage vows."

"I never meant that I didn't want to wed some day, and Father should care about the plans for my future, too."

Sophie snapped open her fan with a flick of her wrist. "Oh, do enjoy your freedom, you silly goose."

The men had been gathered on the porch but were now strolling toward them. Fanny grasped Sophie's hand. "I need you to speak with Sanger about the polo matches and the ball. Ask him if he'll act as my escort."

Sophie chortled. "You treacherous girl! I wondered when Sanger had invited you."

"You mean—" Amanda gasped.

"That's exactly what she means, Amanda." Sophie snapped her fan together. "I truly didn't think you had a devious bone in your body, Fanny, but it appears that Uncle Jonas's desire to control your life has turned you from the straight and narrow."

Fanny ignored the remark. "Will you help me?"

"Of course I will. I'll have Michael deliver a note this very morning."

Amanda tied a ribbon around her hair and walked to the window. "Here comes Sophie, and she has an envelope in her hand. Do you think she's already received word back from Sanger?"

Fanny joined her cousin near the window. "Let's hope so. This has been a most worrisome day. If your father discovers my misdeed, he'll force me to accept Daniel's offer. And that's an invitation I find most distasteful."

Waving the envelope overhead, Sophie rushed into the room and dropped onto the side of the bed. "Bad news, I fear."

Fanny stepped forward. "What do you mean?"

"Martha Benson has already accepted Sanger's invitation to the polo matches and dance."

21

Saturday, August 14, 1897

Amanda and Sophie stood on the veranda and watched as the *Little Mac* docked and two men disembarked and trudged up the path toward the house. Sophie shaded her eyes. With a scowl, she turned away and folded her arms across her waist. "Oh, forevermore! I do wish Father wouldn't bring Paul with him every time he makes an appearance on the island."

"Paul seems very nice, except when his surprises cause you to fall into the river." Amanda giggled.

"I don't find your comment humorous. And if you think he's so nice, you may entertain him during his visit. I grow weary of his chiding comments." Sophie ran down the path and greeted her father with a kiss on the cheek.

Except for a curt greeting, Sophie appeared to ignore Paul until they arrived at the veranda. With a mischievous grin, she pulled Amanda forward and then turned her attention to Paul. "Amanda tells me she would like to visit with you about her interest in charity work. If you're very nice, I'm certain she'd be glad to offer you a glass of lemonade, wouldn't you, Amanda?"

Amanda glared at her cousin. She didn't want to participate in this silly charade, but she wouldn't be rude or embarrass Paul. "Yes, of course. I'd be delighted to fetch a pitcher of lemonade."

Paul hurried behind her and opened the door. "May I help?"

"You young people shouldn't be interested in spending your day indoors. It's much too pretty a day," her mother said as she walked down the front stairway. Light spilled through the door and Victoria squinted. "Ah, Paul. I didn't realize you were here. May I assume Quincy has finally arrived?"

"Yes, Mrs. Broadmoor. We were detained in Rochester. Problems arose that needed immediate attention."

Mrs. Broadmoor instructed one of the servants to bring lemonade to the veranda as she grasped Paul's arm. "Do come outdoors and tell us all about what's been happening." With a quick look around the porch, she turned to Paul. "And where is Quincy? Has he gone off in search of Jonas? I'd think he would want to spend some time visiting with Sophie."

"He spoke with Sophie upon our arrival, but I believe she hurried off to play croquet with some of the gentlemen who are visiting." Paul's gaze drifted toward the sounds of boisterous laughter beyond the house. "Mr. Broadmoor had a matter of great import to discuss with your husband."

"Regarding your delayed arrival? We expected Quincy to arrive Friday evening and here it is Saturday afternoon." Mrs. Broadmoor motioned the approaching servant to place the lemonade on a nearby table. "Why don't you pour us each a glass, Amanda?"

"I know he disliked the delay, Mrs. Broadmoor. There was a fire in a tenement building that left many with nothing but the clothes on their backs. A number came to us seeking food and shelter. We couldn't turn them away in their hour of need." Paul shook his head. "We don't have adequate space for them all, but they have nowhere to go. Some of the churches are collecting clothes and donating what they can to help defray our additional expenses, but the budget of the Home for the Friendless is already stretched beyond its limits."

Victoria wiped the beads of condensation from her lemonade glass with a linen napkin. "Dear me, this is unfortunate. The timing couldn't be worse, what with so many of us out of the city for the summer."

"Financial donations have been limited for that very reason. We have willing hands, but we need funds with which to purchase food and help these people reestablish a place to live."

"No doubt you are in dire need of the organizational skills of the Ladies' League. I do wish I could offer assistance, but we won't be returning to Rochester until early September." Victoria set her glass on the table. "That's not so far off. Could you make do until then?"

"What about me, Mother?" Amanda chimed in. "I could return with Uncle Quincy and help. You know I desire to devote my energies to charitable work. This would permit me a grand opportunity to test my skills."

"Oh dear, Amanda. Neither your father nor I would agree to such an idea. I am surprised you would even suggest such an arrangement."

"There are servants at the house. I wouldn't be alone. Perhaps some of those homeless people could come and stay at Broadmoor Mansion or at our house until they . . ."

Victoria paled and shook her head. "*That* is not even a possibility. While we are called to help the less fortunate, sound and rational judgment is necessary. The fact that you would even make such a foolhardy suggestion demonstrates your inexperience."

Amanda frowned. "If we have an empty house, servants, and food, why is my suggestion inappropriate?"

"I greatly appreciate your offer to help," Paul interjected, "but I must agree with your mother. Though I commend your charitable spirit, an unescorted return to Rochester would be highly inappropriate."

Amanda rested her arm on the chair. "I can't go into the mission field unless I am married, and I am in need of an escort if I'm to be of assistance in the city. How am I ever to fulfill my desire to make a difference in the world?"

"Forgive me for being so bold, but I am surprised you're not making marriage plans, Miss Broadmoor. I'm certain you have no lack of eligible suitors."

Amanda tapped her fan in her palm. "I do plan to wed and have children one day. But before that time arrives, I want to explore other possibilities. It would appear, however, that society will not permit me to do so without my good name being ruined."

Paul laughed. "I believe you can discover a way to help others while still meeting the proper rules of society. I'm certain the Ladies' League would be pleased to add your name to their membership roster and assign you a myriad of duties upon your return to Rochester."

Victoria took a sip of her lemonade. "But that is neither here nor there at this moment. I'm curious about Quincy's discussion with my husband. If it is financial aid he is seeking, I doubt Quincy will meet with much success."

"I have prayed your husband will look upon the plight of these people with sympathy and be anxious to share his resources," Paul said.

"You obviously have much to learn about my father, Paul." Amanda pointed her fan at Sophie and the group of young men. "Shall we join the others in their croquet game?"

He had gained Mr. Broadmoor's permission to bid Fanny good-bye, yet Michael knew his time with her would be brief. Along with Paul Medford and Messrs. Jonas and Quincy Broadmoor, Michael would board the Monday morning train to Rochester. Following his employer's instructions, Michael arrived on the veranda at precisely six-thirty. Mrs. Broadmoor escorted Fanny outdoors to meet him for their final farewell.

The older woman bade him good morning and then strolled to the far end of the veranda, where she could keep watch over them. Michael had hoped for a few minutes alone, but Mr. Broadmoor obviously wanted to ensure the opposite.

Fanny grasped his rough hands between her own. "I wasn't told until last evening that you were leaving this morning. I've been awake all night."

Dark circles rimmed her deep brown eyes. Her sorrow reflected his own, though he forced himself to smile. "I slept little myself. Please don't be sad, Fanny. I know this is what I am supposed to do. Your uncle's agreement to loan me the money for my necessary supplies is truly a blessing. If all goes well, I'll still have time to get to the Yukon before winter sets in. Then I can work all winter and spring and return before summer's end next year. You'll have had little time to miss me."

"I already miss you, Michael. I've missed you since the moment you made your decision to leave." She squeezed his hand.

"You must remember that even though my uncle will force me to accept these silly invitations and attend social functions, my heart and my thoughts are only for you."

"And mine are only for you and our future together. You'll write to me once I've sent word, won't you?"

"You know I will."

Her lips quivered, and pushing aside all thoughts of propriety, he pulled her into an embrace. "Please don't be sad, my love. One day soon we'll be able to build a wonderful future together. I promise you."

She tipped her head back and looked into his eyes. "And if you don't strike gold? What then, Michael? Will you give me your word you won't let that stand in the way of our future together? I must know that when you return, we will be married—even if it requires disobeying my uncle's wishes."

He looked up and saw Mrs. Broadmoor's disapproving signal. He released his hold and nodded. "You have my word. Rich or poor, upon my return we will be married if you haven't changed your mind."

"I won't change my mind, Michael. I would marry you this minute if only my uncle would agree. By the time you return, I shall be old enough to marry without his permission."

A loose strand of hair flew into her eyes in the early morning breeze, and Michael's heart ached with the thought of leaving her behind. Now that they had declared their love for each other, it seemed unfair to be parted, yet this was the only way. "You must keep me constantly in your prayers, dear Fanny, and I will do the same." Before Mrs. Broadmoor could object, he pulled her into his arms and softly kissed her lips. "I love you with all my heart, and I shall return to you at the earliest opportunity."

Mrs. Broadmoor's heels clicked on the veranda as she hurried toward them. "Michael! Your behavior is completely inappropriate." She grasped Fanny's arm. "As is yours, young lady. What would your uncle say if he walked out here and saw the two of you embracing?" She creased her forehead in an angry frown. "He would be outraged. And not merely at the two of you. I would receive my comeuppance for failing to chaperone properly."

"Don't be overly harsh, Aunt Victoria. Surely you can understand our feelings. You were young and in love at one time, weren't you?"

With a faraway look, she said, "I was once young, Fanny. Now come along. I hear your uncle. We'll walk down to the dock and you may wave good-bye."

Jonas rubbed his forehead and contemplated the happenings of the last few days. None of it good. He'd angered Quincy with a refusal to assist the latest batch of homeless victims with a monetary contribution. After returning to Rochester, he had lined Michael's pockets with sufficient funds for his travel and supplies. He had bade him farewell and offered hollow wishes for success. Until last evening, Jonas suspected the young man couldn't possibly meet with success. Now he wasn't so certain.

After spending several hours at his gentlemen's club and hearing reports of the vast amount of gold already brought out of the Yukon, his concerns had begun to mount. Like many others, Jonas had read newspaper accounts and listened to what he considered exaggerated stories, but now those reports had been verified. At an early morning meeting with his banker, William Snodgrass, Jonas had heard more of the same: *"Biggest strike ever to be discovered—gold just lying around for the taking."*

He thought he'd sent Michael off on a fool's errand, but now it seemed he was the one who would be made the fool. In all likelihood the young man would return in short order with a burgeoning bank account and firm plans to wed Fanny. Although Vincent Fillmore had delivered the will, Jonas had not yet developed a plan to secure Fanny's signature. He massaged his temples as the pain behind his eyes continued to mount. Never before had he experienced such difficulty in formulating a plan. And never before had the stakes been so high. There was little doubt Fanny would continue to balk at any talk of marriage. Disinheritance seemed the only avenue he'd not thoroughly explored.

Jonas removed a sheet of paper from his desk drawer and wrote Fanny's name and birth date across the top of the page. Along with her parents' names, he listed every detail of her life—at least all of those he could recall. None of it was of any assistance. He shoved the paper into his desk and removed a packet of headache powders.

Without a defined plan to secure Fanny's fortune, returning to the island and a weekend of polo matches, balls, and firework displays caused the unbearable throbbing in his head to worsen. He poured a glass of water. He would think of something—he always did.

22

Saturday, August 21, 1897
Broadmoor Island

Mr. Atwell stood on the pier and welcomed the family members and guests as they stepped aboard the *DaisyBee*. Daniel had attempted to position himself near Fanny, but she had immediately surrounded herself with Louisa's children. The sight of the baby in her arms had obviously been enough to stave off his advances, for he'd stepped to the other side of the launch. She'd not yet decided how she would keep him at bay once they arrived at their destination. There was little doubt her uncle would be keeping a close watch on her. Once he discovered Sanger in the company of another woman, she would likely be expected to answer difficult questions.

"Any ideas yet?" Sophie inched forward and whispered into Fanny's ear.

She shook her head. "No, but I'm certain something will come to me once we arrive."

Sophie giggled. "If it doesn't, you can be sure Daniel will step in to act as your escort. He's been watching your every move even more closely than Uncle Jonas has."

Their approach to Wellesley Island was slowed by the numerous vessels arriving for the day's festivities, but once they docked and disembarked, Sophie grasped Fanny's hand. "Come along and stay close to me. I spotted Sanger and Georgie. I'll see if we can join them. That way, Uncle Jonas may not notice you're actually unaccompanied." She glanced over her shoulder and motioned to Amanda, who hastened to come alongside them. "Has your father paired you with a beau for the day?"

"In his concern over Fanny's escort, he didn't worry over me," Amanda told them. "Several of those fellows he brings with him each weekend asked to accompany me, but I declined. For the life of me, I cannot understand why it is considered such a necessity to have an escort to all social functions."

"Because we're supposed to be looking for a husband." Sophie chuckled. "Just look at the three of us. I'm having far too much fun to settle upon one man; Fanny doesn't want anyone but Michael; and you, dear Amanda, would rather care for the needy than find the proper husband. We certainly don't fit into the mold of proper young ladies."

Sophie waved and called out to Sanger and Georgie.

"Sophie! That's most unladylike," Amanda chided.

"I care little, so long as I gain Sanger's attention. If we stay close to the Pullmans throughout the afternoon, your father won't realize Fanny is without an escort. At least that's my hope."

The ladies paraded across the grounds, anxious to flaunt their fashionable gowns and parasols. Though the gowns they would wear to this evening's ball would be more elaborate, wearing lovely dresses, hats, and parasols to the polo matches had become a ritual not to be outdone by any other. While the men admired the horseflesh that had been transported to the island by barges earlier in the day, the women assessed the gowns worn by their social counterparts.

When the first half of the match ended, the spectators flooded onto the field in a sea of dark suits and beautifully colored gowns and parasols for the stomping of the divots, which was the only enjoyable portion of the polo match as far as Fanny and her cousins were concerned. In her venture onto the field, Fanny didn't consider Sanger's whereabouts. She had stomped several clumps of dirt into the ground when she suddenly came face-to-face with her uncle.

He grasped her elbow and nodded toward Sanger Pullman. "Would you care to explain why Sanger is with that young lady instead of with you? If I didn't know better, I would guess he was her escort rather than yours."

"Martha Benson?" Fanny balled her hands into tight fists and squeezed until her fingernails were cutting into the palms of her hands. "The Benson family is visiting with the Pullmans for the weekend. It seems Mrs. Pullman had arranged for Sanger to escort Martha without his knowledge. He was most apologetic, but since neither of us wanted to cause Martha unnecessary embarrassment, we agreed simply to make do. The arrangement is working out nicely, but I do thank you for your concern, Uncle."

Her uncle stared across the grassy expanse toward Sanger and Martha for a moment. "Your arrangement will prove impossible at this evening's ball. Sanger can hardly act as an escort for two young ladies. Whom would he choose for the grand march? I'll speak with him and then have Daniel join your group."

Fanny clenched her jaw. "No need. I wouldn't want to run the risk of Martha overhearing your conversation. You may send Daniel to join me if it pleases you."

"It pleases me very much."

The memory of her uncle's smug smile lingered in Fanny's mind long after he had walked away. While continuing to stomp on divots, Fanny strolled off in the opposite direction. She didn't plan to stand there and wait for Daniel Irwin to join her.

Fanny looped arms with Sophie and, using the toe of her shoe, pushed a clod of dirt into a hole on the playing field. "I'm sorry that our plan has failed." She tromped the lump with the heel of her shoe.

Sophie quickly stepped back. "I'm glad my foot wasn't beneath your heel, Fanny. I'd be injured for life. Tell me what has happened to cause a change of plans."

Fanny lowered her voice to a whisper and quickly explained. When she looked up, Daniel was loping across the field toward her. She sighed. "After my earlier refusal, I had hoped he would decline Uncle Jonas's suggestion."

"You never know what could happen between now and the ball. Perhaps a word or two in the proper ear and Daniel will lose interest in you." Sophie tapped her index finger to her pursed lips. "I may have an idea that will annoy our dear uncle and free you from Daniel."

Jonas had watched Daniel and Fanny in earnest for the remainder of the polo match. Although Daniel had been welcomed into the group of young people, Fanny had seldom been near his side. Not once had he succeeded in separating her from the crowd. Jonas had had a long chat with the young man when they returned home to prepare for the ball, and he now hoped he'd made his point. At least the group of young people would be required to break into couples for the dances.

He coached Daniel before they departed for the ball and hoped the young man would heed his advice. Although the men he'd brought to the island were malleable enough, none seemed particularly skilled as suitors. Or perhaps they were unaccustomed to such a headstrong girl as Fanny.

Jonas's spirits flagged when they boarded the *DaisyBee* and Fanny immediately managed to separate herself from Daniel. Instead of attempting to reestablish his position, Daniel stood near the rail, obviously content to watch the passing scenery.

Jonas grasped Daniel's arm. "You need to sit beside Fanny or bring her over here to stand beside you."

Daniel glanced over his shoulder. "There's no space near her, and I doubt she wants to stand."

Jonas glowered. The young man had no resolve. Perhaps Fred Portman would have been a better choice for Fanny. First the difficulties with Frank, and now Daniel appeared to have little pluck. If Daniel didn't step up and take command, Jonas would soon cross him from the list of possible candidates.

When the boat docked at Round Island, Jonas barred Fanny's escape. "You don't want to appear uncultured, Fanny. You need to wait for Daniel to assist you off the boat and escort you."

"I'm perfectly capable of walking without assistance, and I'm sure no one cares if I enter the lobby of the hotel without an escort."

Jonas touched her arm and shook his head. "Please remember our agreement, Fanny. I don't think you want to cause me problems so early on, do you? I believe Michael would prefer to hear that you are behaving in a cooperative manner and honoring the terms of our agreement." She clearly abhorred his interference, but he cared little.

Jonas waved Daniel forward. "I trust you will have no further problems this evening," he whispered.

Although Jonas hadn't been thrilled with the news, the Broadmoor women had been delighted that Charles Emery's New Frontenac Hotel had been selected as the site for this year's ball. The hotel had been remodeled and enlarged by Emery seven years earlier and now stood seven stories tall and boasted over four hundred rooms, each with its own electricity and bath. Many of the guests who attended the polo matches took rooms for the entire week preceding the games and would remain at the hotel until the festivities concluded.

Jonas viewed the size of the edifice as a detriment to keeping an eye on Fanny and Daniel. The girl would likely seize every opportunity to distance herself from her suitor. And there were ample places where she could conceal herself in a structure of this magnitude.

Colored lights shone upon the path, and banners and flags welcomed the guests. Those who weren't attending the ball sat on the huge porch and watched the beautifully gowned women and the accompanying men in their formal attire as they ascended the steps to enter the center hallway. The pleasant sounds of a string quartet welcomed the guests, although dancing would not begin until after the grand march. Until then, Jonas hoped Daniel would keep Fanny at his side. He had wanted to help keep the girl in line, but his wife was intent upon greeting every person in the room—to discover who was wearing the most elaborate gown, he surmised.

Fortunately, their delay at the dock permitted Victoria only time enough to speak to a small number of the guests. The full orchestra soon took to the stage, and Charles Emery stepped forward and announced that the couples should prepare for the grand march.

Jonas craned his neck and finally spotted Fanny and Daniel. They were among the same group that had formed together earlier in the day. He did wish Daniel would force her out of that crowd. At this rate the man would never make any progress winning Fanny's affections.

Arm in arm the couples slowly began the promenade. When Jonas and Victoria reached the front of the line, they stopped and faced the next couple moving down the row. The number of couples was daunting, and the promenade would likely take longer than he wished. He took a modicum of comfort from the realization that the misery of his counterparts equaled his own.

His smile disappeared when he looked down the line and saw Martha Benson clinging to Daniel's arm. What was he doing with Martha? The fool was grinning like a Cheshire cat. Directly behind them, Fanny walked alongside Sanger Pullman. She beamed at her uncle as she walked past him. Well, he would see to her the minute the promenade ended.

"A word with you, Jonas."

Jonas sucked in a deep breath and turned to greet George and Hattie Pullman. "Good evening. Good to see both of you."

"Hattie had some concerns about the young man who escorted Martha Benson during the promenade," Mr. Pullman stated. "I assured her there was no need for concern. Sanger told me the young man was your guest, and I knew he would be of reputable character and position if you welcomed him into your home." He chuckled. "I'm right, aren't I, Jonas?"

Jonas cleared his throat. "He's a nice enough fellow . . ."

When her husband faltered in his response, Victoria added the words Hattie Pullman wanted to hear. "Rest assured that he is a fine young man or my husband wouldn't consider him a possible suitor for any of the unmarried Broadmoor girls."

Hattie nodded. "I didn't want to insult you in any manner, but Emily Benson and I are dear friends, and I assured her I would confirm the young man's credentials. We don't want our daughters selecting young men who can't keep them in the manner to which they've been accustomed. Don't you agree, Victoria?"

"To a degree, though I think love can overcome many obstacles."

Jonas laughed. "If you ever had to do without money, I believe you'd soon change your mind, my dear."

George slapped Jonas on the shoulder and agreed with his assessment before leading his wife off to assuage Mrs. Benson's fears. Fanny's ploy to disobey him could cause more problems than even Jonas could handle.

He must develop another plan.

23

Wednesday, August 25, 1897
Rochester, New York

With his eyes closed, Jonas leaned back in his chair, determined to arrive at a solution that did not require Fanny's cooperation. He'd accomplished nothing of substance since returning from the island. The weekend had been a complete disaster, and though he had originally planned to remain until Thursday, he departed Tuesday morning. He needed the solace of his office in order to arrive at some logical solution.

What to do? What to do? The question flashed through his mind the next morning like a beacon in a lighthouse. He opened his eyes and pulled a sheet of paper from his desk drawer. He stared at what he'd written. Notes regarding Fanny, along with a few comments about Winifred and his brother—nothing that seemed to help. Jonas had never liked Winifred. She'd been a poor choice for his brother. He'd married beneath himself. She was nothing more than a companion to a very wealthy friend of his mother's. A companion! Nothing more. And when

275

she died in childbirth, Langley professed he could never love another. Had it not been for Winifred, Langley would still be alive. *Love!* His brother had taken his own life because he thought he couldn't live without that woman. *Nonsense!* And it appeared their daughter was going to follow in their footsteps. Just like her parents, Fanny was determined to marry for love. Winifred had demonstrated the havoc a poor bloodline could wreak in a family.

His brother's brief marriage had caused a myriad of difficulties. Jonas rubbed his cheek and attempted to remember exactly when they had wed. Victoria would remember, but he had no penchant for tracking such dates. He did recall Fanny's birth had been premature. That's right! His mother had been angered over the gossip that followed Winifred's death. There had been whispered remarks that she had been pregnant prior to the wedding. His mother had countered the remarks, but rumors had persisted that perhaps this had been God's punishment upon the young couple.

Langley had cared little what anyone said. Throughout the weeks and months following Winifred's death, he could be found sitting beside her grave or with the infant. Jonas had been certain his brother would blame Fanny for Winifred's death, but Langley had proved him wrong and loved Fanny. However, the child had never been enough to counter the depth of his grief.

Now Jonas wondered if those rumors and Fanny's premature birth could work to his advantage. He smiled and folded the sheet of paper. If he could prove Fanny wasn't Langley's child, his problem would be solved. He would no longer need to worry about brokering a marriage and the possibility of a husband who might later turn obstinate, for Fanny wouldn't be entitled to share in the Broadmoor estate. He rubbed his hands together and pushed up from his chair. Suddenly he was hungry.

There was a spring to Jonas's step when he entered his men's club for lunch. He greeted his fellow businessmen with an affable smile and cheerful hello. Both the conversation and companionship during the noonday meal bolstered his spirits. It wasn't until he was preparing to depart that he spotted Harold Morrison at a distant table. The man had defaulted on his loan and had been avoiding Jonas.

Though not prone to loaning money, when Morrison had first approached him, Jonas had considered the loan to be a sound investment opportunity. Harold had promised a six-percent return on the money and prompt monthly payments. And although Jonas should have checked in to Harold's assets more carefully, he'd thought there was little risk. The man had inherited his father's burgeoning lumber business in Syracuse ten years prior and had planned to expand into Rochester and Buffalo.

The expansion had caused Morrison to become overextended, and he sought a large yet short-term loan. Jonas hadn't asked to see his books or required any verification from Harold's banker to ensure the man's assets were secure. Pity that hadn't been the case, and his failings were just one more issue that was slowly eroding Jonas's financial security.

Recently Jonas had heard rumors that Harold could be found at the gaming tables at all hours. "Rather early in the day for whiskey, isn't it?"

Harold started and turned. "Jonas! I've been meaning to stop by your office and speak with you."

"Good! Let's walk over there right now."

Morrison glanced at the clock. "I have another meeting in a few minutes."

"It will have to be delayed. I've been waiting three months for your payments. You haven't responded to my correspondence or my calls. I don't want to make a scene here in the club, Harold."

With a look of resignation, Morrison pushed away from the table. "I suppose I can spare you a few minutes."

They were silent during the brief walk to Jonas's office. There was no need for small talk. Money would solve their problem, not idle chatter. And from all appearances, Jonas doubted he would receive any money from Harold—at least not anytime soon.

Once inside his office, Jonas pointed to a chair. "Sit down." Jonas walked to the other side of his desk and dropped into his chair. He leaned back and fixed his eyes on the nervous man across the broad desk. "When you needed money, I couldn't keep you away from my office door. Now that your payments are due, I can't locate you. Explain yourself, Harold. You owe me at least that much."

Harold stared at the floor. "I've come upon hard times. I can't make the payments. I'm sure you've heard the rumors."

"Look at me!" He waited until Harold met his gaze. "I want to know *why* you can't make the payments and what you're going to do about it. Repayment of my money has nothing do with rumors. You had no difficulty articulating your wishes when you approached me for the loan. Tell me exactly what has placed you in this precarious situation."

"I didn't lie to you, Jonas. I wanted to expand the business, but I had already amassed gambling debts when I borrowed from you. I used part of your money to pay off those debts and thought I could win back that amount with what I had left."

"So my money was never invested in your business? Is that what you're telling me?"

"If you'd loan me a few thousand, I could make it all back."

"You're pathetic, Harold. To knowingly jeopardize a business that has been in your family for years is abhorrent. I would think your father is rolling over in his grave."

"I know." Harold raked his fingers through his thinning hair. "I would do anything to extract myself from this situation, Jonas. Anything! I will be completely ruined if I can't find someone to help me."

"I would say your options are limited. No banker will lend you funds to pay off gaming debts, especially when you've already mortgaged your business beyond its worth. And me? Well, I'd be a fool to do such a thing, wouldn't I? If those men you owe gambling debts don't do you harm, I can have you thrown in jail for nonpayment of your liability to me."

Harold slumped and buried his face in his hands. "Is there no help for me then? No way you can see your way clear to assist me?"

"You say you'll do anything?"

Harold looked up. The man's eyes shone with expectancy. Jonas had hooked him with far greater ease than he could reel in a muskellunge from the St. Lawrence Seaway. Fortunately for Jonas, Harold didn't have the fighting spirit of large game fish.

"Yes, anything. I can't bear to bring any further shame upon my poor wife. If I can dispel the rumors and pay off my outstanding debts, my wife will be able to maintain her place in proper society. I owe her that much."

Jonas didn't hide his contempt for the man. "You owe *me* much more. If I have your word that you will do exactly what I tell you, I am willing to wipe the slate clean. I will return your note marked paid in full. In addition, I'll give you a sum that should pay off your gambling debts. You will remain away from the gaming tables until our business is complete—no drinking, either. You'll need a clear head if you're to work for me."

"Whatever you say, Jonas."

The man would be like putty in his hands for the moment, but Jonas wondered if he would be so compliant once he learned what was expected of him. "I want you to visit our family on Broadmoor Island this weekend."

"Oh, my wife will be delight—"

"Hear me out. This won't be a social visit. You may recall that my brother Langley died a number of years ago. The two of you would be the same age."

Harold nodded his head. "I met him at social functions on several occasions. Nice fellow, as I recall."

"My brother's wife, Winifred, died in childbirth. Their only child, Fanny, was under the care of my parents after Langley died. With my father's recent death, Fanny has become my ward. As my brother's only heir, Fanny will inherit a full share of the Broadmoor estate when she reaches her majority." Jonas leaned across his desk. "Needless to say, I do not want that to occur."

Harold nodded again. "She'd have no idea how to handle such wealth."

"Exactly. But the girl is headstrong, and I know she won't take my counsel. Consequently, I see no other way to protect my father's holdings than to take control of her share."

"Good. Good. You can invest it for her, and when she's older and wiser, you can turn it over to her."

Jonas didn't comment on the man's assessment. "The only way I can gain Fanny's share is to have her disinherited."

"But how can you do that?"

"Oh, *I* won't. Having Fanny disinherited is how *you* will repay your debt to me. Sit back and listen while I explain."

Jonas savored his good fortune for a moment. "When you visit us at Broadmoor Island, it will be for the purpose of identifying yourself as Fanny's father."

Harold's jaw went slack. "What? But I—"

"I know you've been married less than ten years, Harold. You were a single man back when Fanny was born. I'm certain your wife realized that you had *befriended* a few women before you married."

"But you would cause this young woman to think her mother had been . . . well, less than virtuous. I doubt that's something you want to do. Investing her estate and keeping her future financially intact doesn't seem worth the pain she'll suffer." He rubbed his forehead. "And what are my wife and I to do with her? Would she come and live with us? Would you rip her from the only family she's ever known? This is more than I can even fathom."

The man was a greater fool than Jonas had imagined, for he truly believed Jonas was merely attempting to protect Fanny's estate. "I didn't ask or expect you to understand. Only I know the depth of Fanny's future needs. She is a young woman accustomed to wealth. Her inheritance must be protected. As for her living arrangements, once we've established you are her father, I can generously step forward and suggest she remain under my roof."

"This is all so difficult to comprehend. How will I be able to prove any of this, and how can I answer any of her questions? I know *nothing* of her mother."

"Relax, Harold. We have the remainder of the week, and you will learn all that you must know. As for proof that you are Fanny's father, we will need nothing more than a letter from Winifred telling you of her plight but that she has accepted

Langley's marriage proposal." Jonas drummed his fingers atop his desk. "I will take care of those details."

"I don't know, Jonas. This isn't at all what I expected."

"What *did* you expect, Harold? That I would erase your debt and require only some simple task of you?" Jonas shook his head. "You have asked much of me. I expect the same in return. Well? Have we reached an agreement?"

Harold nodded, but his enthusiasm had disappeared.

"I want you here in my office at nine o'clock in the morning. I will develop your entire story this afternoon, commit it to paper for you to study here in my office, and gather some photographs that will assist you in your endeavor."

Harold grasped the chair's armrests and pushed himself up. "Nine o'clock. I'll be here." The words lacked any fervor.

"I expected a bit of enthusiasm—and your thanks. I've saved you from ruination, yet you look as though you've lost your last friend."

"I'm afraid I've suffered a much greater loss. My dignity." He departed without another word.

Jonas smiled. He had no pity for men like Harold Morrison: they were weak and easy prey for the powerful. They deserved to fail. Survival of the fittest prevailed—among both man and beast.

24

Friday, August 27, 1897
Broadmoor Island

Preparations for the first family picnic and treasure hunt were in full swing by Friday afternoon. In a surprising announcement, Uncle Jonas had suggested the family develop a new tradition that could become an annual event. Though the family had been surprised by his uncharacteristic interest in family and fun, they all contributed ideas and had finally agreed upon the picnic and treasure hunt as a tradition that all of the family members could enjoy.

Fanny, Sophie, and Amanda had requested permission to take charge of the treasure hunt. Throughout the week they had developed two separate hunts—one for the older children and adults and one for the younger children. The three of them had agreed they would assist the small children so that their parents could enjoy the festivities. They had scoured the island, seeking easy locations to hide their clues and treasure for the children and more difficult sites for the adult set.

"All that's left is to hide the clues first thing in the morning," Amanda said.

"I see no reason to wait. Why not go ahead and be done with it today? There's not a cloud in sight, Amanda. You worry far too much," Sophie chided.

Fanny folded the handwritten notes. "It's not merely the weather that's worrying Amanda. If we hide the clues ahead of time, the older children are sure to sneak off and find them. They'll ruin the fun for the others. I agree with Amanda. We should wait."

Sophie frowned. "The two of you fret overmuch. We need not tell any of them."

"We dare not do it. One of them would track us. Have you not noticed that they've been watching us the entire morning?"

"I'll merely explain that they will be ruining their own fun if they choose to do so," Sophie rebutted.

Amanda shook her head. "And does that stop you from sneaking about and discovering your Christmas gifts each year, Sophie?"

"No, but it does ruin the excitement on Christmas morning. I can explain how disappointed I've been each year."

"And how will you explain that you still continue the practice?" Fanny strengthened her resolve. "We must wait until tomorrow morning. If you don't want to get out of bed, then Amanda and I will hide the notes."

"Better yet, we could hide them tonight after everyone has gone to bed. I'm certain I could locate a few fellows who would like to help us." Sophie's eyes sparkled with excitement. "What do you say? We could have great fun."

Fanny and Amanda both rejected the idea with an emphatic *no.*

"The two of you are less fun than two old spinsters."

Amanda giggled. "I'm not old, but there are those who already consider me a spinster."

"Apparently not your father, for he spends far more time worrying about Fanny's gentleman callers than yours." Sophie gathered up the clues and tucked them inside a bag.

"Earlier this summer, it truly bothered me when Father seemed intent upon finding the proper husband for Fanny. However, the truth is I don't want a husband right now—perhaps ever. So there was no reason for my jealousy. Besides, Fanny and I have talked. She has never desired Father's matchmaking efforts." Amanda stood and walked toward the doors leading to the veranda. "Now that we've completed our task, we should join the others in a game of lawn tennis."

Sophie wrinkled her nose.

"Or the three of us could go fishing," Fanny suggested.

"Lawn tennis it is," Sophie said. "I truly do not know how you can enjoy fishing. If you aren't out in one of the canoes or a skiff, you're sitting on the dock with your fishing pole. Honestly, Fanny, you should live on this island."

"I couldn't agree more. It's Uncle Jonas who disapproves. I could have great fun out here in the middle of winter."

Sophie grinned. "Yes, I know. You'd be carving a hole in the ice so you could continue with your fishing."

"Or joining the locals for sleighing or the annual ice races. I don't think I'd be bored for a minute. Of course I'd miss the two of you, but you could come visit me."

They all three knew their discussion was nothing more than idle chatter. Fanny would never be permitted to remain on Broadmoor Island. She would be expected to continue to see the parade of men her uncle marched through the front doors—but only until Michael returned. That was the thought that warmed her heart.

As Sophie predicted, the morning dawned bright and clear. The three young women were up and out of the house before the others arose. With the clues in hand, they followed their preplanned course, and soon all of the papers were hidden. A treasure box filled with candy was hidden for the young children, while the treasure chest for the adults contained a note entitling the winner to either a new fishing pole, which had been Fanny's idea, or a small piece of jewelry from Crossman's Jewelers, Sophie's suggestion.

"If we hurry, we may be able to return for another hour of sleep," Sophie said as they rounded the corner of the house on their return. But her hope proved incorrect. The excitement of the upcoming day had been enough for the children to arise far earlier than usual.

"This is as wearisome as Christmas Day," Beatrice's husband, Andrew, lamented as he chased after his young son. "The children thought they were going on the treasure hunt before breakfast."

Amanda laughed. "Anticipation is half the fun."

"Not for the parents," Andrew growled. He scooped his son up into his arms and headed toward the dining room.

As the breakfast hour wore on, they agreed the meal had been an effort in futility, at least as far as the younger children were concerned. None of them wanted to eat. All were excited for the day of fun and festivities to begin, especially when Uncle Jonas announced he'd arranged for a huge fireworks display after dark. By ten o'clock the children were gathered on the front lawn awaiting the adults with growing anticipation.

Uncle Jonas stood on the top step of the veranda with the family gathered around. "You must listen closely to your instructions, and there will be no pushing, shoving, or cheating." With a flourishing gesture, he motioned Amanda, Fanny, and

Sophie to the veranda. "You may now give your instructions for the treasure hunt."

The girls took their place at his side while Amanda explained the rules. With a clear view of the waterway, Fanny shaded her eyes and watched as the *Little Mac* approached and docked. A man stepped off of the boat, and she glanced at her uncle. "We're about to begin. Were you expecting additional guests?"

He shook his head. "No, but we can wait a few minutes more."

The children were running around the lawn playing tag, and their parents unsuccessfully attempted to maintain control. The rest of the family murmured and guessed who the visitor might be.

Aunt Victoria soon approached her uncle. "Who in the world is that? Did you invite a business associate without advising me?"

"No. But I believe I recognize him. I think it may be Harold Morrison. What in the world is *he* doing here?"

Her aunt arched her brows. "How would *I* know? He's certainly not here to see me."

"No offense intended, Victoria. I didn't mean to insinuate he was here to see you."

The man removed his hat and waved it overhead. Her uncle nodded. "That's Harold Morrison, all right. Haven't seen him in ages."

"He owns the lumberyards over in Syracuse," Andrew said.

"You know him?" Jonas asked.

"No. I heard he was going to expand his business into Rochester six or nine months ago, but I've heard nothing more. Maybe it was Buffalo. I can't remember."

Fanny remained on the porch with her cousins as Uncle Jonas stepped forward and greeted Mr. Morrison. He was a kind-appearing man with thinning dark hair and a rather long angular face. Not handsome but not unattractive, Fanny guessed him to be a few years younger than Uncle Jonas. Keeping a downward gaze, he nervously pressed the brim of his hat between his fingers while he spoke to her uncle.

"Mr. Morrison would like to speak to you, Fanny. Of course a private conversation would be completely inappropriate. I've told him I must be present if he wishes to speak to you."

Fanny narrowed her eyes and stared at the stranger. "I have no idea why you want to speak to me, Mr. Morrison, but if we are to have a conversation, I prefer that my Aunt Victoria act as my chaperone."

Jonas nodded. "We can both—"

"I'm certain one chaperone is more than sufficient, Uncle Jonas. You must take charge of the day's festivities. The children are anxious to begin the treasure hunt. I'll remain behind, and when Mr. Morrison has spoken to me, we will join the family."

Uncle Jonas's complexion flushed deep red, and Fanny knew it wasn't from the heat. Her choice had angered him, for Uncle Jonas disliked confident women. Not that Fanny was feeling self-assured. In truth, she was frightened to hear what this stranger had to say.

Her uncle shook his head. "If it's a matter of business he wishes to discuss . . ."

Aunt Victoria waved aside the comment. "Why would a stranger wish to discuss business with a mere girl?"

He tipped his head closer. "Because she will soon inherit a great deal of money?"

Aunt Victoria lowered her parasol. "Fanny hasn't come of age, so her money is not yet an issue. I'm certain Mr. Morrison doesn't have anything to say that I can't handle. And if he does, he'll need to speak with you after the treasure hunt or make an appointment to call on you at your office next week." She grasped Fanny's hand. "Come along, dear."

"Why don't we all wait for Fanny? The children can play a game of croquet," Amanda suggested. "Fanny worked very hard on the clues, and I don't want her to miss the fun."

Mr. Morrison removed a handkerchief from his pocket and wiped his forehead. "I've obviously come at a bad time for all of you." He glanced at Fanny. "I don't want to ruin your festivities, but I fear I'll lose courage if I don't speak to you today."

"If it will help, you may tell me right this moment. There's nothing you can't say in front of my family."

The children had scattered, but the adults had fixed their attention upon Harold Morrison. A daunting group, to be sure. Fanny stepped closer and offered an encouraging smile. She couldn't help but take pity on him.

He bowed his head and mumbled something she couldn't quite make out, all the while pressing his hat brim between his fingers.

She couldn't be certain what he'd said, and she leaned to one side in an effort to make eye contact. "I'm sorry. I don't believe I heard you correctly. Could you speak up, sir?"

Mr. Morrison straightened his shoulders and looked at her. There was a sorrowful look in his eyes. "You are my daughter, Frances. My name is Harold Morrison, and I am your father."

Her legs felt weak and shaky, and she grasped the railing. She didn't want to faint. Questions flooded her mind, yet the words stuck in her throat. Mouth agape, she stared at him as though he had two heads. Aunt Victoria held her around the waist, and Jefferson hurried forward with one of the wicker chairs from the far end of the veranda.

Fanny dropped into the cushioned seat and cleared her throat. "I believe I must have misunderstood you, Mr. Morrison." She looked into his eyes. "I thought you said you are my father." She watched him nod his head in agreement. "That's impossible, sir. As you can see, I am surrounded by my true family. I am the daughter of Winifred and Langley Broadmoor."

Mr. Morrison glanced over his shoulder. The entire family had drawn near, eager to hear every word that passed between the two of them. Even the children had returned to their parents' sides and grown quiet.

Mr. Morrison turned back to face her. "Perhaps we should go indoors with your aunt and speak privately." He touched his fingers to his jacket pocket. "I have a letter from your mother."

Victoria glowered. "And I have a number of questions for you, Mr. Morrison." She leaned forward and grasped Fanny's hand. "Come along, dear, and we shall see this matter settled."

"I can't believe this stranger would declare such a thing, Aunt Victoria," Fanny whispered. "Must we truly discuss this any further?"

"I think it best we hear him out and put the subject to rest." She patted Fanny's hand. "Mr. Morrison's assertion is momentous. I believe it's probably best that your uncles come inside with us."

Her aunt was likely correct. Fanny's thoughts were no more than an incoherent muddle. She would need clearheaded people to guide her through this maze. The five of them entered the parlor. Uncle Quincy and Uncle Jonas stood at either end of the fireplace, while Mr. Morrison sat down opposite Fanny and her aunt. Instead of heading off for the treasure hunt, the remainder of the family had gathered on the front porch, where the open windows provided access to the ongoing discussion.

Fanny inhaled a deep breath. "Well, Mr. Morrison. I believe you mentioned a letter?"

Mr. Morrison withdrew the missive from his pocket. "Please understand that I hold the memory of your deceased mother in deepest respect."

Her uncle Jonas cleared his throat. "I imagine she's more interested in seeing that letter than hearing of your respect for her mother."

"Yes, of course." Mr. Morrison blushed, and the letter trembled in his fingers. "Years ago your mother and I were friends—more than friends. We had a short-lived but passionate romance. She was a fine woman, and I don't wish to disparage her in any way, Miss Broadmoor."

"Oh, do get on with it, man," Jonas commanded.

"I loved your mother. I believe she loved me. It was through that love that you were conceived."

A chorus of gasps fluttered through the open windows, and Fanny captured a fleeting glimpse of her cousins. Like her, they appeared stunned into silence. Fanny extended her hand and took the letter. She withdrew the missive from the envelope and slowly read the words.

"Anyone could have written this letter, Mr. Morrison. I have a birth certificate and baptismal record that list my parents—my real parents."

"May I?" Her aunt nodded toward the missive. Fanny handed her the paper and watched her aunt scan the contents. "As well as I can recall, this does resemble your mother's script, and the dates and personal information appear correct."

Harold withdrew a photograph from his pocket. "This is a picture she gave to me."

Fanny had seen a similar picture of her mother wearing the same dress—in a photo album at her grandparents' house. She stared at this stranger who claimed to be her father. Her stomach churned, and she feared she might expel its contents. She swallowed hard and shook her head.

"Why, after all these years, have you come forward? This makes no sense."

He massaged his forehead. "I could no longer live this lie. I've developed a weak heart over the past year, and I couldn't bear the thought of going to my grave without speaking the truth. Whether you choose to believe me or not, I knew I must make an effort to do the right thing."

"Still, I don't know what good purpose you think is served by bringing me this message. Did you never speak to my mother again? And what of my father? Did he know?"

Mr. Morrison folded his hands and rested them on his knees. "Your mother and I did not see each other again. As you read in her letter, she requested that I never contact her, and I honored her wish. I thought it best for all of you. But now, with Winifred and Langley deceased and my poor health—I thought you deserved to hear the truth."

"I believe you cared more about clearing your own conscience before you met the Almighty, Mr. Morrison." Her aunt pointed at the man's chest. "You gave little thought to the damage your careless actions would cause this young woman."

"That's not true, Mrs. Broadmoor. I want nothing but the very best for Frances. It was for that reason I never interfered in her life until now. I stand to gain nothing by divulging the truth, and surely one more person to love her is not a bad thing."

Jonas stepped away from the fireplace. "We all need time to digest this information, Mr. Morrison. May I suggest the New Frontenac Hotel on Round Island if you wish accommodations for the remainder of the weekend?"

Mr. Morrison stood. "If you care to discuss the matter further—any of you, I will remain at the hotel until the first of the week." He smiled at Fanny. "I am very pleased to have made your acquaintance. You are a lovely young lady."

25

The remainder of the day was chaotic: a mixture of pitying stares, curious children, and unanswered questions.

When nightfall arrived, Fanny was pleased for the cover of darkness that could hide her tears. There had been little time to think on her situation, but now that the family had picnicked, searched for treasure, and watched the fireworks, there would be ample time. She watched as children were herded off toward the house and wondered if she'd ever again spend a summer on this island. A tear trickled down her cheek, and she brushed it away.

"*There* you are! Sophie and I have been looking everywhere. Why are you off by yourself?" Amanda asked as she settled on the grass beside her.

"I'm attempting to sift through what has happened to me. One minute I was surrounded by a huge family of people I love, and the next minute I was told that none of you are even related to me." She pulled her handkerchief from her pocket. "Can you even begin to imagine how that must feel? I've been set adrift. To think that the two of you are not my cousins is impossible."

Amanda enveloped her in a warm embrace. "That letter doesn't change our love for you. We shall always be the dearest of cousins. Do you think that after all these years of love and friendship, Sophie and I could simply walk away from you?"

Sophie plopped down beside them. "Personally, I'm quite hurt that you would even consider such a thing, Fanny." She giggled. "After all, it takes both of you to keep me on the right path."

"And even then we fail," Amanda remarked. "You know we'll never allow anything to come between us and ruin our friendship, don't you?"

"I know you'll try your best. But our lives are bound to change. I just don't know how much, and I'm frightened."

"Then maybe you need to face your fears head on and find out." Sophie pointed toward the boathouse. "The three of us could have Mr. Atwell take us over to the hotel and you could talk to Mr. Morrison. It's not too late. Sitting here in the dark and worrying isn't going to resolve anything. We need to take some positive action."

"I'm not certain that's the correct manner to handle this. I think you should wait until morning when you've had a night of rest and can think more clearly," Amanda said.

"Don't be silly, Amanda. She's not going to sleep when her thoughts are stirring like a paddle churning cream."

"That's what I love about you two. You couldn't be further apart in how you think."

"And you're our balance, Fanny. You always bring us back and center our thoughts." Amanda squeezed her shoulder.

"However, this time I'm correct. I don't think we should do anything until morning."

"I'm not sure I agree with you, Amanda. Come morning, the entire family will be offering their ideas of what I should do. Sophie's correct: I need to gather more information from Mr. Morrison." She stood and smiled down at them. "Either of you want to come along?"

Jonas puffed on his cigar. "The family seemed to enjoy the day of festivities, don't you think?"

Quincy nodded. "Had it not been for Mr. Morrison's unexpected news, the day would have been a grand event. His visit certainly put a damper on things."

Jonas flicked the ash from his cigar. "True, but the family seemed to recover by afternoon's end. They were in high spirits during the fireworks display. And I don't believe the treasure hunt could have been any more fun for the youngsters."

"I'm having difficulty digesting the truth of what Morrison revealed. It's difficult to believe that Winifred would have gone to her grave with such a secret. She and Langley were such a devoted couple."

"Who knows? She may have told him. If you'll recall, our brother wasn't prone to confiding in either one of us. He adored Fanny. Even if he knew, he wouldn't have wanted to cause the girl embarrassment—losing her good name and social position."

Quincy frowned. "I hadn't thought of that issue. Indeed, she will suffer if people no longer consider her a Broadmoor. Fanny's name will be crossed off every dowager's social directory, and her situation will become the latest item of gossip at their parties."

"Sad but true. To be accepted, it takes both name and money."

"Hmm. And what about the money?" Quincy asked. "What does all of this mean in regard to Father's estate? It would seem that Fanny will be excluded from receiving Langley's one-third portion, does it not?"

"I hadn't even thought about the inheritance issue." The lie crossed his lips with ease. "I'll check into the matter with Mortimer or Vincent after we return to Rochester. I'm certain they can offer sagacious advice on how we must proceed. The girl is already suffering dearly."

"Oh, of course, of course," Quincy agreed. "I wasn't suggesting we immediately inform her of the dismal future that may await her. Sad that she may be solely reliant upon Mr. Morrison for her well-being."

Jonas snuffed out his cigar and nodded. "Very sad, indeed."

"Then again, the two of us could offer her aid. She has, after all, been reared as a member of this family her entire life. If you thought it best, I believe I could see my way clear to help her when I receive my inheritance." Quincy leaned forward and rested his arms across his thighs. "It would be the charitable thing to do. Of course I couldn't let my children know. Other than Sophie, they would be livid—especially since I plan to invest most of the money in the Home for the Friendless."

Jonas shook his head. "*That* is not an investment. You will never see any return on your money, so quit referring to it as such. As for continuing to financially support the girl, I'm not so sure. There might be legal ramifications involved with that idea. We had best rely upon Mortimer and Vincent. We wouldn't want to act in haste and then be required to withdraw our offer. Such behavior would only cause the girl further distress. If they approve, then we will discuss the matter further."

"Very thoughtful, Jonas. I wouldn't want to cause her any additional anguish. I'm certain both Father and Mother would have wanted us to do something to help. They did, after all, consider her more a daughter than a grandchild."

Quincy had taken the conversation into another realm, one that Jonas didn't want to explore with his brother. He had merely wanted to draw Quincy's attention to the fact that Fanny would no longer inherit. Now his brother wanted to support the girl. If he didn't turn the conversation, Quincy would likely suggest they simply forget Harold Morrison's arrival and give her one-third of the estate.

"You are most thoughtful, but let's remember that Fanny has already received more direct monetary aid from Mother and Father than any of our children. And remember that Father was a strong believer in the Broadmoor bloodline."

"True enough." Quincy pressed his hands on his thighs and stood. "I believe I'll retire to my room. I have some paper work that needs my attention before going to bed. I'll rely upon you to speak with the lawyers and settle these troubling issues."

"Rest assured that I will take care of everything." Jonas smiled and bid his brother good-night.

Mortimer Fillmore would be surprised to hear how easily Jonas's plan had come together. There might be a few legal issues to overcome, but that's why Jonas retained a wily lawyer. Mortimer and Vincent should easily prevail in any possible legal battles. He walked to the edge of the veranda and inhaled the clear evening air. This had been an excellent day. He would sleep well tonight.

Michael's father didn't question the girls. It wasn't proper for an employee to question family members regarding their decisions. But Fanny had seen the question in his eyes when she asked him to take her to Round Island. He'd appeared even more concerned when he saw Sophie was to be her companion. Amanda had declined, although before Sophie and Fanny departed, she agreed to conceal their whereabouts if someone should discover they weren't in their rooms.

"Just say that Fanny convinced me to go night fishing with her," Sophie had instructed.

Fanny didn't know if anyone would believe that lie. Sophie wouldn't even go fishing during the daylight hours. They could only hope no one would realize they'd left the island.

"What if he's already gone to bed for the night?" Fanny whispered as the boat slid across the dark water. A knot the size of a grapefruit had taken up residence in her stomach. One part of her wanted to ask Mr. Morrison questions, but the other part wanted to hurry back to Broadmoor Island, rush upstairs to her room, and bury her head beneath the covers. Perhaps she would awaken and discover this had all been a nightmare.

"Don't borrow trouble, Fanny. He's staying at the liveliest hotel on the islands. You'll probably find him sitting on the veranda with a glass of port and a cigar, considering all that has occurred today."

Mr. Atwell docked the boat a short time later and assisted them onto the pier. "Shall I wait for you ladies?"

Fanny blinked. "Yes, of course. We should return within an hour." She waited until they were out of hearing distance. "Why did he ask if he should wait, Sophie? Do you sometimes spend the night over here?"

"On one or two occasions I stayed with the parents of friends from school who were staying at the hotel." Sophie made no apology for her behavior. She seldom judged others and didn't seem to care what others thought of her. There evidently was nothing that frightened Sophie.

They walked side by side toward the bright lights of the hotel. "What if this had happened to you, Sophie? How would you feel?"

"I don't know. I would feel betrayed, naturally, but at least Uncle Jonas won't be able to tell you what to do in the future." She grinned. "Then again, Mr. Morrison may be even worse."

Fanny shuddered. She hadn't considered that Mr. Morrison might be a cruel or unkind man. He had seemed quite nice when they talked earlier in the day. But anyone could appear gentle and kind for short periods. Perhaps she could remain with the family until her birthday; then she'd have her inheritance and could move out on her own. Or could she? Nothing had been said about whether she would be entitled to the money her grandfather had bequeathed to her. But he wasn't really her grandfather anymore, so what would that mean now?

No need asking Sophie, for she wouldn't know, either. If her talk with Mr. Morrison went well, perhaps she would ask him. Uncle Jonas had mentioned Mr. Morrison was a businessman. Surely he would have some idea how such matters were settled.

"There he is!" Sophie elbowed Fanny and then pointed toward the open-air seating. "Over in the courtyard with the woman in the rose and beige gown."

Mr. Morrison had spotted them. He briefly spoke to the woman and then rose from his chair. Sophie tapped her foot as music began to play in the other room. She edged toward the entertaining sounds. "I'll be in there when you're ready to go home." Fanny wanted to grab her hand and beg her to remain, but Sophie no doubt sensed the conversation with Mr. Morrison should be private.

The woman didn't turn around. Was she Mrs. Morrison? He hadn't revealed if he had a wife or children. *Children.* She might have sisters and brothers she had never met. The thought was both exciting and disagreeable. What if they disliked her? And what of his wife? What did she think of all of this—if that was, indeed, his wife. She would inquire.

"Frances. This is a surprise. I had hoped for time alone in a neutral setting where we might speak freely, but I hadn't expected you this evening." He looked through the archway at the huge clock in the lobby. "I'm surprised you are out so late."

His look was filled with concern, but he didn't chastise her imprudent behavior.

"Shall we sit over here where it is a bit less noisy?"

She evaluated his every feature and nuance, searching for something recognizable, some connection to herself. But nothing about this man's appearance was familiar—not the tilt of his head, the curve of his lips, or the slant of his eyes. And though his mannerisms were those of a sophisticated, well-educated gentleman, they were dissimilar to a Broadmoor's. She hadn't arrived with high expectations, but she had hoped to discover some connection to this man who claimed to be her father.

They sat side by side. Father and daughter. Perfect strangers. The thought overwhelmed her. She grasped the arm of the settee. This would seem no more than an illusion if she didn't hold on to something tangible.

"The woman you were sitting with when I arrived—is she your wife?"

"Yes. I thought it would be better if the two of us became better acquainted before you meet her. She is a forgiving woman. Although I don't deserve her kindness, she came along to offer me moral support." He folded his hands in his lap. "You may be surprised to hear that this has been very difficult for me also." His smile was gentle. "Nothing in comparison to your experience, of course."

"Has she always known? Your wife, I mean. Did you tell her about my mother and you before the two of you married?"

"No. We've had this discussion only recently." He stared at the floor. "She knew nothing of your existence." He looked up at her. "I hope it doesn't hurt you to hear me say that. I fear I've already caused you a great deal of pain."

"I believe the act of clearing one's conscience can be a very selfish act. While it helps the offender, it often inflicts pain on others. I have a married friend back in Rochester. After a year of marriage her husband made admissions regarding his missteps outside their marriage vows. He felt cleansed and ready to begin anew, but his confession cut her to the depth of her soul. I doubt whether she'll ever recover."

"So you think it would have been better if he continued to live a lie and had never told her?"

Fanny shrugged. "Who am I to say? I do know that his confession didn't help their marriage. My friend is most unhappy. If her husband had asked for God's forgiveness, changed his ways, and lived with his secrets, I believe their marriage could have survived. Right now, I'm not certain what will happen. It's most unfortunate that his struggle with conscience didn't occur until after he had stepped outside of his marriage vows."

"From what you've said, I can only assume you wish I hadn't cleansed my conscience."

"What purpose does all of this serve, Mr. Morrison? Your revelation has injured your wife, besmirched my mother's name, and I've not yet counted all the consequences I will endure. Was revealing your secret so important at this late date?"

His eyes revealed the pain she'd inflicted with her words. She hadn't meant to hurt him, but she wasn't going to tell him she was pleased to have him waltz into her life and turn it upside down after seventeen years.

"My plan was ill-conceived. I truly regret having come forward—I shouldn't have even considered such an idea. The damage I've caused you is irreparable, and I do apologize."

She reached forward and touched his hand. "I didn't mean to wound you, Mr. Morrison. Please . . . tell me about yourself. Do you have children? I mean other than . . ." She couldn't complete the sentence. This man could not so easily supplant her father or his memory.

"No. Unfortunately my wife and I have no children. We had always hoped to have a child. My wife would have been an excellent mother. Why don't you tell me about your life, Frances?"

"Fanny. No one uses my formal name—except in school, where the teachers always insist upon using my given name."

"Then if you have no objection, I shall address you as Fanny, also. You had a happy childhood?"

"Oh yes." Since Mr. Morrison had inquired, Fanny didn't hesitate to tell him of the close bond she'd shared with her father—their love of fishing and nature and the many hours they'd spent together on Broadmoor Island and in the gardens at Rochester. She spoke of her beloved grandparents and the affection they'd showered upon her throughout the years. Mr. Morrison listened intently when she told him about her love for flower gardening and her special lilacs.

"My wife is an avid gardener, too," he said. "I'm certain she would enjoy showing you her flowers someday."

His offer was gentle, but Fanny didn't want to see anyone else's flowers. She wanted to return home and enjoy the Broadmoor gardens. "What can you tell me about my mother, Mr. Morrison? My father found it painful to speak about her, and my grandparents discouraged such questions. Consequently I know little of my mother."

"Like you, she was very attractive, gentle spoken, and attempted to please others. She found it difficult to refuse my advances, for she disliked quarrels and arguments. I knew that and used it to my advantage. What occurred was totally my fault. I would never want you to think less of your mother. She was a truly wonderful woman."

Like everyone else in her life, Mr. Morrison seemed reticent to reveal many details. Perhaps after all these years, he'd forgotten. "How long did you know my mother before she married?"

"Less than a year. She was wise to select your father over me. He loved her and provided well for both of you."

"He was devastated by her death. It has always been difficult to think that my birth was the cause of her death. As a child, I wondered if my father would have preferred it the other way."

"I'm sure you brought him much joy."

She may have provided him with occasional joy, but Fanny wondered if her father might still be alive if she had died at birth. No need to dwell on the thought. She couldn't have changed it then, and she couldn't change it now. Life-and-death matters were beyond her control. At present the clock was ticking, and she needed to find out what Mr. Morrison expected from her and if he'd given thought to the future—specifically, to her future.

Throughout the remainder of their visit and almost against her will, Fanny discovered herself drawn to Mr. Morrison. His gentle character and honesty remained prevalent throughout their discussion. He didn't shy away from her questions, though she wished he remembered more of the past. But after seventeen years of attempting to forget his past, she couldn't expect him to recall the minute details.

They parted with an agreement that Mr. Morrison would return to Syracuse and give Fanny and the Broadmoors time to consider her future. Mr. Morrison didn't want to dictate Fanny's choices, but he did offer her a home in Syracuse with him and his wife. He explained that he owned a large lumberyard in Syracuse and his attempts to expand the business had caused him to fall upon hard times. Fanny would be required to adjust to a meager lifestyle if she moved to Syracuse. She thought that somewhat surprising, since the Morrisons had rented accommodations at the New Frontenac Hotel.

Not that she begrudged them the fine accommodations, but it seemed a man of limited means would choose a small hotel or a boardinghouse in Clayton or Alexandria Bay. Then again, perhaps he believed it was the least he could do for his wife, considering the pain he'd caused. Who could know what Mr. Morrison had been thinking. Fanny could barely manage to keep her own thoughts in order.

Mr. Atwell was patiently waiting when the two girls returned a short time later. As the boat cut through the water and headed toward Broadmoor Island, Fanny stared down into the water. Sophie had recognized her need for silent comfort and hadn't assailed her with questions. If only Michael were here with her now. If only he'd waited just a brief time longer before departing for the Yukon. If only Mr. Morrison hadn't made an appearance. *If, if, if.*

Hopeful the morning light would provide some clarity on decisions that must be made, Fanny thanked Mr. Atwell for delivering them safely home. He grasped her hand and assisted her onto the dock. "If you need to talk, we're here, Fanny."

Had the Broadmoors already spread word among the staff? She had wanted to tell Michael's parents herself. "I'd like that. I'll come and talk with both of you tomorrow."

She also wanted to be the one who would write and tell Michael of the changes in her life. But until she received word from him, she had no idea where to write. And he'd already warned her that mail could pose a problem once winter set in—and winter arrived early in the Yukon. Fanny hoped a letter would arrive before that time. She wondered how he was dealing with the changes in his life, for the thought of moving just to Syracuse was nearly more than she could bear. She could only pray the family would want her to return with them to Rochester.

26

Wednesday, September 1, 1897

Fanny hurried downstairs to the kitchen. This would be her last opportunity to have a few minutes alone with Michael's mother before returning to Rochester. Her uncle had refused Fanny's request to remain on the island with Mr. and Mrs. Atwell. Until everything was settled and a final determination made in regard to her future, he declared she would live with his family in Rochester. He didn't say how long that might take, but Aunt Victoria had assured Fanny there was no need for concern. Fanny wasn't so certain. Uncle Jonas had never offered such encouragement. Rather, he frowned whenever Aunt Victoria claimed nothing would change.

A frayed cotton apron covered Mrs. Atwell's dress. She looked up from the mound of bread dough and greeted Fanny with a broad smile. "You'll write to me the minute they've decided what's to happen, won't you? I don't want to send my letters to the house in Rochester and discover you've moved to Syracuse."

She wiped her hands on the corner of her apron. "This is all going to work out according to God's plan, my dear. You must keep your spirits high and not lose faith in the Almighty."

"I'll do my best, and I'll write to you every week. Maybe more often. I do wish I knew what was going to happen. I've never before been so uncertain about where I belong."

"You belong to God, child, and that's what you must keep at the forefront of your mind. Mr. Broadmoor and Mr. Morrison may shift you around from pillar to post, but your Father in heaven has you in the palm of His hand." She wrapped Fanny in a warm embrace. "Fretting will serve no purpose. When you feel insecure, talk to Him. And search your Bible for verses that will sustain you."

For as long as Fanny had known Mrs. Atwell, the woman had been offering living proof of her faith in God. Trust in Him came so naturally to the older woman that it always found a place in their conversations. Now, however, it was more important than ever, and Fanny cherished the advice. "I'll try, but I won't deny that I'm frightened."

Mrs. Atwell kissed Fanny's cheek. "I know you are, but you're going to be just fine. Before you know it, you and Michael will be married, and you'll look back on this day and wonder why you ever worried."

"I wish I would have discovered this before he left. If I'm not a Broadmoor, there is nothing to stand in the way of our marrying. Uncle Jonas would have no reason to protest."

"But your father might," Mrs. Atwell replied. "I wouldn't borrow trouble, child. I'm positive you've nothing to worry about. The entire matter will soon be behind you."

Fanny didn't argue, but she wasn't convinced Mrs. Atwell was correct. Somehow she feared the forthcoming days would be the most difficult she would ever face. She must believe God would be at her side. Otherwise, she would be completely on her own.

Forcing a brave smile, she said, "I wish we could remain until the weekend, but everyone else wants to return to Rochester for the Labor Day parade."

"I'm sure you'll have a good time if you just give yourself permission to forget your worries." Mrs. Atwell squeezed Fanny's shoulder. "I do wish I could visit longer, but I'm running behind schedule with breakfast. Mr. Jonas will be acting like a wildcat with a sore paw if he misses the train because the family didn't have their morning meal on time."

After a final peck on the cheek, Fanny hurried back upstairs. The entire family would depart for Rochester today, but most of the servants would remain behind to pack their belongings and help Mrs. Atwell clean and then close the main portion of the house before taking their leave. They likely enjoyed being alone in the house without members of the family ordering them around. She could picture the servants laughing and joking while they cleaned and covered the furnishings, washed the windows and removed the screens. Once the family had left, did they pretend they were the masters of the house? Did they eat their evening meal at the formal dining table with the good silver or sit on the veranda sipping lemonade? She wondered if Mrs. O'Malley would permit such behavior.

Fanny placed a few remaining items in her valise and carried it downstairs to the veranda. She wandered off toward the boathouse. In summers past she and Michael had spent much of their time fishing for bass and pike and enjoying a shore dinner over an open fire. She could picture him squatted down with a large skillet, browning slabs of buttered bread or frying perfectly browned potatoes to accompany their catch of the day. Her heart ached at the remembrance, and she hurried back to the house for one last look. What if she never again could return to this place she so loved?

Although they'd had more than sufficient time, Uncle Jonas had hurried the family onto the *DaisyBee*. Once they'd arrived in Clayton, he'd marched up and down the platform, watching with obvious anticipation for the arrival of the train. They were then herded into the Pullman car that had been rented for the family's journey. Her uncle Jonas dropped into his seat beside Aunt Victoria as though he'd performed a hard day's labor.

"Much more pleasant traveling by myself," he muttered.

"Excuse me?" Aunt Victoria rose to attention in apparent offense.

"Trying to maintain a proper head count of the family is enough to cause a headache. My comment was not meant as a reflection upon you, my dear. I am always pleased to have you with me."

"Do you think she believes him?" Sophie whispered to Fanny and giggled.

"I doubt it, but at least she put him on notice that she'll not tolerate such comments. Aunt Victoria is about the only one who can put him in his place."

"What are you two whispering about?" Amanda asked. She moved from her seat across the aisle and joined them.

"Just commenting that your father had better watch his step or he'll be sleeping in the guest room tonight," Sophie replied.

"Sophie Broadmoor! I can't believe you said that. Where my father sleeps isn't a proper topic of discussion for young ladies." One by one Amanda tugged on the fingers of her gloves. "You should be thankful Mother didn't hear you."

"That much is certainly true." Mischief danced in Sophie's eyes. "She'd likely swoon at the mention of sleeping with your father, don't you think?"

All three girls glanced across the aisle and were met by Victoria's questioning gaze. "Is something amiss?"

"No, Mother, nothing at all," Amanda replied.

"I've been thinking that since you did so well in finishing school, you might enjoy a year or two of higher education while Michael is away, Fanny. There's no telling how long he may be in the Yukon, and education is never wasted. What do you think? Does the idea hold appeal?"

Jonas cleared his throat. "Higher education is expensive, my dear. You're forgetting that until we unravel Fanny's situation with the lawyers, we don't know if Fanny will have the finances available to attend school."

Victoria clasped a hand to the frilly collar of her blouse. "Jonas! We can't wait around for lawyers and judges. They are prone to dragging things on for insufferable periods of time. I made application for Fanny at several schools before we departed for Broadmoor Island. If we've received an affirmative response, and if Fanny wants to attend, I'm quite sure you can afford to pay the fees."

"I don't believe this is a discussion we should be having at the moment."

Fanny didn't miss the warning in her uncle's eyes. The look successfully quelled any further discussion of her future but didn't dampen Sophie's spirited disposition.

"What about new gowns for the Labor Day festivities, Uncle Jonas? Do you think there's enough in the coffers to purchase a new gown or two?" She pursed her lips and shook her head. "Then again, such an expenditure might cause the Broadmoor fortune to teeter on the brink of financial disaster."

Her uncle leaned forward and glared across the aisle. "Your father needs to have a conversation with you about your impudent behavior, Sophie. You are a disrespectful young lady. Your lack of regard for your elders is most unbecoming. It seems my brother should be concentrating his efforts on your manners rather than worrying over the homeless and poverty stricken."

"Perhaps it is a good thing my father continues to maintain the charity. If you continue in your efforts to cast Fanny aside, she may need a place to live."

It wasn't difficult to assess the impact of Sophie's comment. Aunt Victoria paled, Uncle Jonas's complexion turned the shade of a boiled beet, Amanda remained bug-eyed, and Fanny's stomach roiled. She gave thanks that she hadn't eaten any breakfast. The grain of truth in Sophie's remark had been sufficient to create a stark reaction. If nothing else, Sophie had become an expert at causing a stir.

Beatrice leaned over the back of the train seat. "She has a father she can go and live with, Sophie." Cruelty shone in her eyes. "I heard Grayson tell Andrew that Mr. Morrison is an extremely poor businessman who may lose the family business if he doesn't cease his—"

"That's entirely enough, Beatrice." Her uncle pointed toward the rear of the car. "I believe I hear one of your youngsters calling you."

Beatrice remained firmly planted and glared at her uncle. "You agreed heartily enough that she shouldn't inherit a full third of Grandfather's estate. I don't know why you think it improper for me to discuss the topic now."

Her aunt Victoria scooted to the edge of her seat. "Your behavior nearly matches that of your sister, Beatrice. This is neither the time nor the place for your comments. If your mother were alive, she'd be quite disappointed. Your greedy attitude is most unbecoming."

"*My* greedy attitude? There isn't a person in this family who doesn't long for the power and influence associated with wealth. Your children can well afford to appear pious and appalled by the mention of receiving a fair share of Grandfather's inheritance." Beatrice's lips tightened into an unattractive snarl. "They know you will protect their position and they will be cared for. Our father, however, is more interested in giving his money to the homeless. He doesn't consider the fact that his philanthropy will likely force a life of destitution upon his own family."

Jonas appeared to regain his composure. "You are off on a tangent that makes little sense, Beatrice. What happens to Fanny's inheritance will have no impact upon what your father chooses to do with his share of the estate. That is something best discussed with him in private." With a dismissive wave, Jonas snapped open his newspaper.

"You can't hide behind your newspaper forever, Uncle Jonas. This matter will be settled, and I see no difference whether it's on a railcar or in the parlor of your East Avenue mansion." Beatrice turned and tromped back down the aisle.

Sophie grinned. "Beatrice is in rare form today, don't you think?"

"You'd think Andrew would attempt to control her," Amanda whispered.

"She'd snap his head off if he tried. He ignores her because it makes his life easier. No different from the way my father ignores me. Neither one of us is able to gain the attention of the men in our lives."

Fanny rested against the seat and closed her eyes. She had hoped to enjoy the journey home with her cousins. Instead, her joy had been replaced by a feeling of gloom and foreboding.

Even if she remained in Rochester, her life would never be the same. Obviously Beatrice and the like-minded society dowagers of East Avenue would make certain of that. Though she could easily live without the fancy dresses and parties, there was much of her old life Fanny would sorely miss.

Jonas studied the paper work. During a visit to Broadmoor Island by Mr. and Mrs. William Comstock, Jonas had agreed to further invest in Comstock's patent medicine company. He didn't mention, however, that he was in the process of planning an even larger investment in George Fulford's expanding patent medicine company. For that, Jonas planned to use a large portion of the money his father had bequeathed to Fanny. If by some fluke the court found her entitled to receive a share of the estate, he could allege he'd merely been acting as guardian of her estate. If the investment turned sour, he would make every attempt to force that portion of the estate upon his brother Quincy. Of course, should it prove to be as sound an investment as Fulford projected, Jonas would claim it as his own. Either way, he would protect himself—or his lawyers would.

He placed the papers on Mortimer's desk and picked up a pen. "You're recommending I move forward, are you not?"

"Indeed. As a matter of fact, I'm investing some of my own money in Fulford's Pink Pills for Pale People. Business has soared, and I think we'll see a fine return."

Jonas nodded and scribbled his signature on the designated line. He returned the pen to its holder and pushed the paper across the desk. "Now, let's discuss my niece and the demise of her bequest from my father."

Mortimer rubbed his arthritic hands together and shuffled to the office door. "We had better have Vincent join us for this conversation. As you're well aware, my days of standing in a courtroom have come to an end. With my supervision and assistance, Vincent will be in charge of any conflict arising from the estate."

Moments later Vincent entered the room with his pencil and notebook. No clerk would be included in these meetings. Jonas wanted to be certain no one else knew what was discussed among the three of them. "No memos or notes, Vincent. I want nothing committed to paper regarding our meetings." He leaned forward and arched his brows. "Do I make myself clear?"

"Very clear, Mr. Broadmoor." He placed the paper and pencil on his father's desk. "Why don't you tell us what has transpired since we last met."

Without need of further encouragement, Jonas launched into the details. Mortimer appeared mesmerized by the tale, but there was little doubt Vincent was much less than enthusiastic. "This is, quite frankly, beyond anything I'd bargained for, Mr. Broadmoor. Although preparation of Miss Broadmoor's will was improper, I was relieved when you told me you'd been unable to gain her signature. As for this latest scheme, I am at a loss." Vincent sighed. "Do you realize both the legal and moral implications of what you've done? You are denying this girl more than her inheritance: you are denying her the memory of a father she loved, and you've besmirched the reputation of her mother."

Mortimer thumped his cane on the floor. "Do you realize how much money is in the balance? You had best throw off that cloak of self-righteousness and change your attitude."

Vincent's nervous laughter didn't offer the level of accord Jonas expected.

"Since when is your law firm worried about ethics and morality?" Jonas demanded as he stood and turned to face Mortimer. "Should I be seeking another lawyer to handle my business?"

"Of course not, Jonas." The old lawyer motioned toward the chair. "Sit down. We're going to get this resolved to your satisfaction." He pinned his son with an angry glare. "Aren't we, Vincent."

"Yes, but I do believe we should make every attempt to cause the least harm possible to the girl."

Jonas groaned. "I don't believe this is going to work, Mortimer."

Mortimer poked Vincent with the tip of his cane. "You listen to me, young man. This *is* going to work, and *you* are going to make it work. Do I make myself clear?"

Jonas clearly understood the veiled threat. So did Vincent, for he quickly offered his assistance. "If you're planning to send the girl to visit Mr. Morrison in Syracuse, I'm willing to accompany her in order to observe what transpires."

"No need. I plan to have her visit for an extended period of time. How long do you think it will take before we can have the court declare she's not a blood relative and is not entitled to any share of the estate?"

Vincent picked up the pencil and nervously tapped it atop the desk. "I surmise that none of the family will protest the process. Still, there are statutes we must follow, and the court's docket must be considered, too. I would guess six to nine months until all is said and done. Of course, if the girl hires counsel to represent her in the proceedings, it could take much longer."

Jonas jumped up from his chair. "Six to nine months is far too long!" He paced back and forth like a caged animal. "She doesn't have money to hire a lawyer."

"But Mr. Morrison may be able to find a counselor who would handle the case on a contingency basis. And if Morrison can prove he isn't Fanny's father and that his assertion was made under duress . . ."

The comment brought Jonas's pacing to a halt. "You think a lawyer might be willing to risk such a thing?"

"I can't say with absolute authority, but an argument could certainly be made that your father may have known of Fanny's parentage. Who's to say? Her attorney might find a witness who would testify your father knew Langley wasn't Fanny's father."

Had this man gone completely daft? "The three of us realize that isn't possible, since Langley *was* her father. Are you forgetting this plan is based upon a lie of my own making?"

"No. But you're obviously forgetting there could be others willing to perjure themselves for a price. In somewhat the same manner as you've convinced Mr. Morrison to succumb to your scheme, a wily lawyer could hire a witness. One who would testify your father was aware of the truth regarding Fanny's lineage."

This was becoming more complicated by the minute. He had hired lawyers to achieve his desired goals, not to speak of failure. Working with Mortimer had been much less difficult when he'd been in practice by himself. However, with Mortimer's failing health, Jonas couldn't depend solely upon the old lawyer. Had he realized Vincent possessed so many scruples, he would have taken his legal business elsewhere.

"And you're concerned we might not be able to convince Mr. Morrison that he should dissuade Fanny from seeking legal counsel?" Jonas asked.

Vincent shrugged. "I don't know your niece or Mr. Morrison. If the girl is not easily swayed, I have no doubt she could find someone to assist her. The contingency fee would be quite handsome—certainly worthy of a hard-fought battle, don't you think?"

"Any other obstacles you'd like to throw in the pathway to our success?"

"If you're truly interested."

Now what? Was there no end to this man's desire to fail? "I prefer men who possess a positive attitude, Vincent. Is failure your objective?"

"Not at all. My objective is always to win. That's why I always consider the flaws in a case before I step into the courtroom. I want to be prepared."

"I'm pleased at least to hear you want to succeed," Jonas muttered.

Vincent once again began tapping his pencil. "Let's remember that Mr. Morrison has a long history as a gambler. After thought and consideration, he may view this entire matter as a gamble."

Jonas leaned forward. "How so? If he wants to free himself of debt, he must do my bidding."

"Not necessarily. Once he and Miss Broadmoor develop more of a relationship, he may decide that the two of them could strike a deal. One that would be of greater financial benefit to him. What if he tells your niece the truth and the two of them enter into an agreement that once she receives her inheritance, she will pay off his debt and perhaps even give him additional funds? Even if she pays him no more than you've offered, he's freed himself from the criminal act of perjury. In addition, he can assuage any feelings of guilt with thoughts that he hasn't permanently injured the girl's future or reputation. Of course the same couldn't be said for you if that should occur."

With an unexpected rush, the warmth of the afternoon over-powered Jonas and beads of perspiration lined his brow. He withdrew a fine linen handkerchief from his pocket and swiped it across his forehead. Was Harold Morrison cunning enough to create and carry out such a plan? He recalled Morrison's distaste when he'd heard the particulars. Surely the man wouldn't go to such lengths when Jonas had already offered him a simple method to extricate himself from his financial difficulties.

Jonas studied Vincent for a moment. He couldn't decide if the young lawyer was truly attempting to help him or if he was hoping to create an avenue of disentanglement for himself. Either way, he had presented Jonas with food for thought. He should have talked to the lawyers before arranging Fanny's visit with the Morrisons in Syracuse.

27

Stephen's Passage, Alaska

"Headin' for gold, eh?" an older man asked Michael.

Standing on the deck of the steamer *Newport*, Michael nodded and gave the man his hand. "That I am. Michael Atwell's the name."

The man exchanged a shake and smiled. "The name's Zebulon Stanley, but you can call me Zeb."

"Glad to meet you, Zeb." Michael looked out at the passing collection of islands. "This sure reminds me of home." Although it was the first week of September, the air had a chilled promise of colder days to come.

"Where you from?"

"The Thousand Islands. Are you familiar with the area?"

"Can't say that I am." The older man scratched his beard and shrugged. "No, I can't say that I've ever heard of such a place."

"It's in the St. Lawrence River between New York and Ontario. There are thousands of little islands similar to these. But instead of being barren of homes, many of our islands have huge castlelike estates. The very wealthy own them and usually spend their summers in leisure there."

"Oh, so you're already very wealthy?"

Michael laughed. "Not me. Not my parents, either. We worked as island staff for the Broadmoor family. I'm quite handy with boats."

"Do say. So what brought you up this way?"

"Well, of course the gold rush," Michael admitted. "Sounds like it's quite the adventure."

"Oh, it is, quite the adventure," Zeb repeated. "'Course I was up here awhile before gold was discovered, so it's less so for me."

Michael noted the man's unkempt appearance. He was, as Michael's mother might have noted, rather scruffy around the collar. Still, he was a companionable enough soul, and Michael figured he might well learn something about the frozen north.

"So you're already familiar with the Yukon?"

"I am. Been up here nearly five years now. I'm what they call an old sourdough."

"What's it like? I've heard all sorts of stories."

"Most of 'em are probably true. 'Cept for maybe the ones about picking up gold nuggets the size of babies' heads."

"What about how the gold is just lying there waiting to be picked up?"

The man laughed. "Well, the gold is there, that much is true. But it's hardly lying around. You have to work for it."

"I don't know anything about gold mining. What kind of thing is required? Do you go digging into the ground like you do for coal?"

"Seems all mining is about digging. The only problem with the Klondike is that the ground is frozen most all of the time. We have to light fires to warm up the dirt and melt the frozen ground.

Then we dig that up and sluice it, using water from the creek or river," Zeb replied. "It's quite the process. You put the dirt in these rocker boxes and go to work. The goal is to wash away the dirt and rocks. The gold sinks 'cause it's heavier. Of course some folks don't want that kind of setup. They prefer panning for gold."

"How is that done?"

"You take a round pan and basically do the same thing as the sluicing but on a much smaller scale." He pretended to hold a pan. "You put it in the creek and get some soil from the bed. Then you rinse it like this." He made a motion as if shaking a pan gently back and forth. "You keep rinsing it with the water until the debris is gone and the gold sinks to the bottom."

"And you can do this in any river or creek?"

"Not all of them have anything to offer. And there are claims that have to be filed with the authorities. A lot of the good ones have already been taken."

"Do you have a claim?"

The man nodded. "Me and my brother Sherman have a small one. He's up there right now keepin' it safe from intruders."

"Did you come down to get supplies?"

"Yeah. The winters are mighty long up north. Dark, too. We figure to work through as best we can, but we need equipment." Zeb looked around. "You come north with someone?"

"No," Michael told him. "My employer did loan me the money, but I'm traveling on my own."

"So you have a grubstake," Zeb said. "That's good. Too many folks try to come north without supplies, and they die. The wilderness ain't that forgiving."

Michael nodded. "I know that well enough."

"I doubt most of these folks do," Zeb said, tipping his head toward the throngs of passengers. "They haven't got any idea what's in store for them. They don't know about anything but the glory stories of gold." He looked at Michael. "What about the gold caused you to leave your home?"

Michael leaned back against the railing. "A beautiful young woman."

Zeb grinned. "A woman? Like I said, me and my brother have been up there for a long while. I don't recall a woman being a part of the deal."

"My employer has a niece, and . . . well, we're in love. We want to marry, but he doesn't believe me worthy. We struck a bargain that I'd come north and make my fortune, and then he would allow us to marry."

Zeb rubbed his chin thoughtfully. "And if you don't make your fortune?"

"I can't even begin to think that way," Michael replied. "Fanny means everything to me. If we can't be together . . . nothing would be the same."

"I had me a gal once," Zeb began. "She was a pretty little thing. Sweet and gentle, and boy, could that girl cook."

"What happened?"

"She passed on. We'd been married about six years when she died in childbirth. Baby died, too."

"I'm sorry. Fanny's mother died in childbirth," Michael offered, but he wasn't really sure why.

"It was only the good Lord that kept me from following them both into the grave," Zeb admitted. "That and Sherman. Neither one would leave me for even a minute for fear of what I'd do to myself."

Michael could imagine how he might feel if Fanny died. Would he want to go on living? The thought caused him a moment of panic. What if she died while he was gone? What if she took sick and needed him?

"Are you a God-fearin' man?" Zeb asked.

"Most certainly." Michael smiled. "I learned Bible stories at my mother's knee. My father's, too, for that matter. Working with the boats and transporting the wealthy back and forth on the river gave me a lot of time to pray and to listen."

Zeb nodded. "I knew there was something about you. Just felt like when I saw you that I ought to come and talk with you. I have an idea if you want to hear it."

"Sure. What do you have in mind?"

The steamer blew its whistle, and only then did Michael notice that they were heading in toward land. "Is this Skagway?"

"No. Juneau. It's a fair-sized settlement—another gold camp. I heard it said that prices are actually cheaper here than in Seattle. Once the stampede was on, everybody in Seattle tripled their prices. I was fortunate. I secured my stock when I first got into town, before the word got out."

"So you came down with the *Portland* and *Excelsior*?" Michael asked, knowing those two ships had changed the lives of many across the nation.

"I did. Me and a million dollars worth of gold."

Michael's jaw dropped. "You found a million dollars in gold?"

"No. I found plenty, but not that much. No. The whole ship carried some sixty passengers out of the north, and together we had over a million in gold."

"I can't even imagine what that would look like." Michael strained to see the small settlement of Juneau from the ship.

"Well, maybe you will once you work the claims for a while. That's what my idea is. Why don't you come work for Sherman and me? We'll see to it that you get a fair cut. You won't have to worry about filing your own claim, and we're already set up and working. Most of these folks won't see gold until next summer, but we'll be working through the winter."

"Do you think I could make myself a fortune by this time next year?"

"I do. Our claim is a good one."

Michael suddenly grew suspicious. "Why would you do this for me?"

Zeb laughed. "It might sound strange, but you remind me of myself, and Sherman and I can use the extra hand. We're not young anymore. You have your supplies, so it's not like we'd be hard off having you there. And what might sound even crazier still, I think God put us together for a purpose. That seems as likely a reason as any I can think of."

Michael grinned. "God does work in mysterious ways. But what about Sherman?"

"He'll be glad for the help. We talked about hiring on someone. We even talked about a third man coming in as a partner. You're younger and in better shape than either of us, so I know we'll get a fair amount of work out of you. Say, why don't we talk about it over some grub. I know a little place here in Juneau where we can get a decent meal. The ship will be here for hours, so we have plenty of time."

"Sounds good," Michael said, returning his gaze to the town. The mountains rose up behind the settlement, displaying white crowns of snow. Michael had to admit the beauty was startling. Everything seemed so massive—so impressive. If only Fanny were here to share it.

They were delayed leaving Juneau due to a storm, but when they finally arrived in Skagway, Michael felt a new sense of direction. He and Zeb had struck a good friendship as well as a solid agreement. Michael would work for the Stanley brothers through the winter and net twenty percent of what he found.

Of course Sherman would first have to agree to the arrangement, but Zeb felt confident his brother would be willing to part with ten percent of his share in order to accumulate that much more gold. And based on what Zeb had told him they'd made from last year's work, Michael stood to make thousands of dollars. The thought pleased him immensely.

"Well, we're here," Zeb said, slapping Michael on the back. "Now the hard work begins. You'll have to face the Chilkoot."

"Is that the mountain pass you were telling me about?"

He nodded. "There are two ways north from Skagway. One goes straight up from the town. It's a vicious trail, though. I prefer the route out of Dyea. It's a little town to the west of here. It's too shallow to take a steamer in to dock, so we dock here and then hire a boat to take our supplies over. There's a lot of Tlingits looking to make a few dollars."

"Klinkets?" Michael questioned. "What's that?"

"Local natives. They're good folks. Peaceable types unless you cheat them."

"Sounds reasonable. I tend to be the same way myself," Michael said with a grin.

Zeb leaned closer. "We're not going to hole up in Skagway tonight. We'll get a boat to take us right over to Dyea. Most folks will stay here. They don't know what they're doing. We'll get on over and hire us some help. You did say you had some cash to your name, didn't you?"

"Some. Not a whole lot."

"Given the fact that you'll be making upwards to a hundred trips up and down that mountain without help, you'll be happy to pay some of the natives to pack the goods for you."

"You mean there are no wagons to take the stuff? No boats?" Michael realized he knew just about as little as the rest of the newcomers.

Zeb shook his head. "It's hard terrain. Not at all kind. Like I said, this is a most unforgiving land. If you have any doubt about that, you'd best put it aside now. You'll be walking most of the way. Boat ride comes after you get up and over the Chilkoot Trail."

"And we have to carry everything?"

"Afraid so. Some of it can be hauled a ways by horse or mule. Not a whole lot of 'em available, though. You can sometimes pull a load. The Tlingits can make some great sledges, but they only work until you get to the pass itself."

"I see. Well, I suppose there's nothing to be done about it," Michael said, squaring his shoulders. "I'll have to trust you on this one."

Zeb met his gaze and smiled. "Nah. Don't go putting your trust in me. The good Lord is the only one who deserves that. It's not going to be easy, but with a little hard work and a whole lot of prayer, I'll get you to the gold fields ahead of this stampede. And the sooner we get there, the sooner you can get back to your little gal."

Michael looked at the daunting mountain peaks already topped with snow. He couldn't imagine how a man could ever manage such an arduous feat. The terrain looked jagged and severe. Zeb's words about the land being unforgiving were gradually beginning to make sense.

I can do this, Michael told himself. *For Fanny and for our future, I can endure whatever I must.* He gazed heavenward, past the craggy peaks and snow. *I can do all things through Christ which stengtheneth me.* The verse from Philippians had never seemed so comforting as it did at this moment, for Michael was sure there was no possible hope that his own strength could see him through the challenges to come.

28

Wednesday, September 8, 1897
Syracuse, New York

In a crisp tone the conductor announced the upcoming stop before continuing on to the next railcar. Fanny's heart beat in quick step when the train lurched and hissed to a halt a few minutes later. *Syracuse.* She'd been filled with a mixture of anticipation and dread ever since bidding Amanda, Sophie, and Aunt Victoria farewell at the Rochester train station. In truth, she'd been suffering from a bout of nerves since Uncle Jonas announced she would make the journey.

Her fingers trembled as she pulled on a pair of lightweight summer gloves. She told herself this could be no worse than listening to the murmurs when she attended a social function with her cousins or hearing the rumors passed on by *thoughtful* acquaintances who always began their sentences with the same verbiage: *"I thought you'd like to know what I heard."* Their proclamation was immediately followed by a ghastly report of her mother's illicit behavior or a mean-spirited comment regarding

Fanny's parentage. And they always smiled and offered pitying looks while they delivered the painful tidbit. Fanny didn't know which was worse: hearing the comments or knowing that the messenger took pleasure in the delivery.

Hat in hand, Mr. Morrison stood near the terminal doorway. Fanny spotted him the minute she stepped off the train. He waved his hat, and when he stepped forward to greet her, she surveyed the area. He seemed to be alone. Mrs. Morrison had apparently chosen to remain at home; Fanny hoped the woman's failure to come wasn't an indication that she would be unwelcome in their home. Mr. Morrison's letter of invitation to come for an extended visit had spoken of his wife's desire to meet Fanny. She wondered if he'd spoken the truth.

His gaze traveled to the small valise in her hand. "You have other baggage, I assume?"

"Yes, my trunks were loaded into the baggage car." She looked over her shoulder. Two burly men were unloading them and placing them at the far end of the platform. She'd not had the luxury of a Pullman car on this excursion. If all she'd heard about Mr. Morrison was true, she doubted whether she'd ever have such a luxury again.

She waited while Mr. Morrison made arrangements for her trunks to be placed in an old horse-drawn wagon. She had expected a carriage, but she supposed a wagon would prove reliable, and there'd be no need to pay extra for the delivery of her trunks. Mr. Morrison assisted her up onto the wagon but offered no apology or explanation for their transportation. With a click of his tongue and a snap of the reins, the horses stepped out.

When they'd traversed only a short distance, Mr. Morrison said, "My wife would have come to meet you, but she wanted to have a fine meal prepared for your arrival. She decided a good meal after your journey was more important than waiting at the train station." He gave her a sidelong glance. "I hope you agree, for she would never intentionally offend anyone."

A breeze that carried the scent of approaching fall weather rippled through the air and tugged the first of summer's dying leaves from nearby trees. A desire to be at home, where she could help the gardener prune the bushes and prepare the gardens for winter, created a dull ache in Fanny's bones. The ache deepened when she considered the truth: she had no place to claim as her home.

Since Grandfather's death, Fanny could no longer consider Broadmoor Mansion home. Uncle Jonas had moved her under his roof, but neither he nor Fanny considered his house to be her home, either. Like the leaves that fluttered along the street, she had been discarded and set adrift.

Now she would be immersed in a situation for which she felt ill prepared. Then again, she didn't think any amount of education or training would have prepared her to live in the same house with a long-lost father and his wife of many years. She realized dignity and grace would be required, but days filled with forced smiles and uncomfortable conversation held little appeal.

The conveyance made a final turn, and Mr. Morrison pulled back on the reins. The wagon came to rest in front of a modest white frame house with a pleasant enough yard and large front porch. Lilac bushes had been planted to advantage, and Fanny imagined a spring breeze carrying their sweet scent through open windows to perfume the interior. Mr. Morrison jumped down from the wagon and circled around to assist her.

A thin woman with chestnut brown hair stepped onto the porch and shaded her eyes. Although she waved, her right hand remained affixed to the handle of the front door. She conveyed an anxiety that matched Fanny's own. Fanny understood, for she would have taken flight if there had been someplace for her to run.

Mr. Morrison held on to her hand and gently drew her forward. "Come along and I'll introduce you to my wife. I can return for your baggage after you're settled inside."

Settled? Fanny doubted she would ever again feel settled until Michael returned to claim her as his bride. She didn't withdraw from Mr. Morrison's grasp. Without the strength emanating from his hand, she would surely sink to the ground in an embarrassing heap.

With a sweeping gesture, he motioned his wife forward. "My dear, let me introduce you to Miss Frances Jane Broadmoor." He gently squeezed Fanny's hand. "However, she tells me she prefers to be addressed as Fanny."

Mrs. Morrison released the door handle. "I'm pleased to meet you, Fanny. And you may call me Ruth—or Mrs. Morrison—whichever you decide is more comfortable."

"For now, Mrs. Morrison seems appropriate."

The older woman opened the door and ushered Fanny inside. "If you wish to reconsider your choice at any time, please don't feel the need to request permission."

Once they'd been introduced, the woman's earlier trepidation appeared to melt away. She asked her husband to retrieve Fanny's trunks and proceeded, with neither apology nor embarrassment, to point out the few amenities their home offered, explaining that they'd fallen upon hard times.

"Many people suffered greater losses through the depression, and we've had a few setbacks along the way. But even if we're never restored to our previous financial status, I still consider myself fortunate." Mrs. Morrison glanced toward the street, where Mr. Morrison was removing Fanny's trunks from the wagon bed. "I've been blessed with a wonderful husband, we've never gone hungry, and we have a roof over our heads. God has been faithful to answer my prayers."

Perhaps Mrs. Morrison didn't know that, rather than the economic downturn, her husband's gambling was rumored to be the cause of their financial woes. Fanny doubted whether the woman's praises for her husband would ring forth with such conviction if she'd heard those tales. Then again, Fanny couldn't be certain the gossip was true. Who could believe her cousin Beatrice? True or false, Beatrice repeated every morsel of tittle-tattle with great delight. And Mr. Morrison did seem a nice enough man.

"I do hope you'll find your room comfortable. I know you're accustomed to much finer accommodations. Harold said I shouldn't worry. He said you knew you wouldn't be coming to a huge mansion with servants and the like." She tucked a strand of hair behind her ear. "Come along and I'll show you to your room."

Fanny couldn't help but notice the faded print and worn cuffs of Mrs. Morrison's gown. Although she'd clearly done her best to control the fraying cuffs with a thread and fine stitches, the dress had surely seen better days. Once again, Fanny wondered how a couple with such meager means had afforded a stay at the New Frontenac Hotel. Mrs. Morrison didn't appear the type who would squander money on such an extravagance. When they became better acquainted, Fanny would broach the subject.

The room was very small, and Fanny doubted her clothes would fit into the wardrobe, but she didn't mention her concerns. Instead, she simply accepted Mrs. Morrison's invitation to unpack her belongings. "I'll join you downstairs once I've finished."

"Supper should be ready by then. I do hope you don't mind simple fare. There was a time when Harold and I—" She stopped short. "I'll be serving chicken this evening, and I hope you'll find it to your liking."

"I'm certain it will be most enjoyable. Thank you."

Fanny unlatched her trunk and shook out her dresses. She'd hang her best gowns, and the others could remain in her trunk until she discovered an alternative. The bedroom offered a view of the backyard. She surveyed Mrs. Morrison's garden from the window. Though the spring and summer blooms had disappeared, the older woman clearly enjoyed flowers. Mr. Morrison had spoken the truth: if nothing else, she and Mrs. Morrison had gardening in common.

Supper had been preceded by a prayer, offered by Mrs. Morrison at her husband's request. An odd occurrence as far as Fanny was concerned. She was accustomed to the men in the family performing the ritual. Apparently Mr. Morrison had detected Fanny's surprise, for he had quietly remarked his wife's prayers were more likely to reach the ears of the Almighty than his own unworthy utterances. Fanny didn't comment because until then she'd never given thought to God having a preference of whom He heard from. Perhaps He did. If so, she thought Mr. Morrison's assessment was incorrect. The world considered women's thoughts of little value. Wouldn't God then prefer to hear from men? She would write that question in her diary tonight so she could ask . . . Whom would she ask? Mrs. Atwell! Michael's mother frequently spoke of her faith in God. She could pen Mrs. Atwell a letter this evening and ask. Moreover, she wanted to advise the older woman of her change in address.

Fanny insisted upon clearing the table and drying the dishes. It seemed strange to work in the kitchen yet not uncomfortable. Mrs. Morrison chatted while she washed the dishes and asked Fanny simple questions about her childhood. "Did Harold drive you past the house where we lived before moving here?"

"He didn't mention it if he did. Is it on the way from the train station?"

She dipped a saucer into a pan of rinse water and handed it to Fanny. "It would depend on the route he took. Our old house had belonged to Harold's parents. Originally it was constructed by his grandparents after they became wealthy. The lumberyard was a thriving business for many years."

"I heard it mentioned that he had planned to expand his business to Rochester and Buffalo."

Mrs. Morrison arched her perfectly shaped brows. "Truly? Harold never mentioned expanding the business in my presence."

"Then perhaps I misunderstood." Fanny couldn't remember who had spoken of the expansion. It may have been her uncle Jonas; then again, it could have been Beatrice's gossip. She wished she hadn't remembered the information or at least had kept it to herself. Mrs. Morrison appeared alarmed.

"When did you hear talk of this proposed expansion, Fanny?" Mrs. Morrison stared into the soapy pot and continued to scrub.

"I don't recall. In all likelihood I overheard some of my uncle's business associates and completely misunderstood." She shrugged her shoulders. "Who knows? They may have been discussing the Bancroft Lumberyard."

Mrs. Morrison frowned. "But that closed two years ago."

Fanny wanted to kick herself. She should have remembered it had closed! Lydia Bancroft's father had died unexpectedly, and when Lydia's brother refused to return to Rochester and take over the business, Mrs. Bancroft had sold off the existing stock and closed the doors. Mrs. Bancroft later sold the building, and against Lydia's protests, the two of them had moved to New York City.

"Then perhaps it wasn't even a lumberyard they were speaking of, Mrs. Morrison. I can't be certain." Fanny nodded toward the backyard. "I see you enjoy gardening. I'm fond of flowers myself."

Thankfully Mrs. Morrison was more interested in discussing her annuals and perennials, so no further mention was made of her husband's business plans. When the conversation lulled, Fanny spoke of her childhood and the lilac bush she'd planted after her father's death. She hesitated and looked at Mrs. Morrison from beneath hooded eyelids. "I know what that letter says, but I don't think I'll ever be able to think of another man as my father."

Mrs. Morrison wiped her wet hands on the corner of her apron. "I don't believe either of us would ever expect you to do so, Fanny. From what you've told me, Mr. Broadmoor was a fine father, and you must revere his memory."

Fanny hung the dish towel to dry. "How long have you known about me?"

"Not long. My husband told me only a few days before we went to the Thousand Islands." She stared into the distance. "Those islands are the most beautiful place I've ever visited. I should like to return there one day—under more pleasant circumstances." Her comment seemed to jar her back to the present. "Not that anything about you is unpleasant . . . I didn't mean to imply . . ."

"I know, Mrs. Morrison. You need not apologize. I know this must be very difficult for you, also."

The older woman sank onto one of the wooden chairs. "Yes. It was such a surprise, you know, after all these years." She reached for Fanny's hand. "I always wanted a child, but we were never able . . ." She inhaled a ragged breath. "Knowing that you are Harold's child is a good thing. I am not saddened by the news, merely surprised that he never told me. I thought I knew everything about Harold." At the sound of Mr. Morrison's footsteps, she released Fanny's hand. "We should join my husband before he thinks we've deserted him."

While they sat on the front porch making small talk, Fanny wondered how the Morrisons would explain her to their friends and neighbors. "Am I to be introduced as a visiting relative or friend of the family? I don't want to say or do anything that would cause either of you embarrassment."

Mr. Morrison gestured for his wife to answer.

"What is your preference, Fanny? We are happy to concede to your wishes."

"If we say I'm a relative visiting from Rochester, they will expect further explanation and wonder why they've never before seen me in your home, don't you agree?"

"Why don't we say you are a relative who has come to visit for the very first time? We need not say anything further unless questioned." Mrs. Morrison offered a kind smile. "Our friends don't delve into our private affairs, and acquaintances have no right to do so. If the need arises, I believe I can discourage further questions." Mrs. Morrison's response reflected a quiet conviction that dispelled Fanny's concerns. Should questions arise, she would direct them to the older woman.

Mr. Morrison knocked the bowl of his pipe against the porch rail. "How were you received in Rochester after your return from Broadmoor Island?"

Fanny watched the charred tobacco flutter to the ground below. "It was more difficult than I anticipated."

He tamped fresh tobacco into the pipe. "The social set was ready to discard you like last year's fashions, I suppose?"

"They continued to invite me to the parties, but I was not treated in the same manner. In fact, I doubt they would have invited me at all had I not been residing under my uncle Jonas's roof. Until the matter is settled in court, they'll simply continue to twitter and gossip. If the judge declares I'm not a Broadmoor, I doubt I'll see any of them again—except for Sophie and Amanda." She glanced at Mrs. Morrison. "They're two of my cousins, and we're as close as sisters. They would never abandon me."

"I'm sure they wouldn't. And they are always welcome in our home." Mrs. Morrison reached for her mending basket and then decided against the idea. "I believe it's soon going to be too dark to accomplish any sewing out here on the porch."

A red glow shone from the bowl of Mr. Morrison's pipe, and Fanny studied his profile as a curl of smoke wafted above his head. He was a fine-looking man, but she could see no resemblance. Blood or not, she much more closely resembled the Broadmoors.

29

Tuesday, September 14, 1897
Rochester, New York

Jonas stared heavenward. Why must he listen to yet another of Victoria's verbal onslaughts? His wife questioned the validity of Mr. Morrison's claim of fatherhood as well as Jonas's decision to send the girl for a lengthy visit. And since Fanny's departure, there'd been no escaping her scolding arguments.

"Are you listening to me, Jonas? You cannot hide behind a newspaper." Victoria flicked the paper with her fingers. "In addition, I might point out that your behavior is beyond rude. I am attempting to have a discussion with you, and you're behaving like a child."

Jonas sighed and refolded the paper. A man couldn't even enjoy an evening of quiet in his own home. There was no escape. His wife wanted to have yet another *discussion*. Either he'd participate or Victoria would continue to carp at him for the remainder of the night.

"We've already gone over all of this, Victoria. Must we do this every evening? I grow weary of rehashing the same thing over and over."

"How can we be rehashing something we've never discussed? I talk, you ignore me, and we go to bed. There has been no discussion, only avoidance. I don't believe Mr. Morrison is Fanny's father, and I want to bring her back home."

"On the other hand, I believe Mr. Morrison *is* her father, and I agreed she could remain in their home." He reached for his newspaper, but Victoria slapped her hand atop his.

"Not so quick, Jonas. I want to know why you, a man who constantly questions everything, would so easily accept a letter supposedly written by Winifred years ago as substantial proof. We can't be certain that letter is authentic. I fear you are doing Fanny a grave injustice." She sat down in the chair opposite and clung to his hand, as though he might attempt an escape. "Even if Mr. Morrison is Fanny's father, I believe Langley would have known before he married Winifred. Langley and Winifred were devoted to each other, and he remained devoted to Fanny after Winifred's death. I simply cannot accept this."

"Have you considered that the question of Fanny's parentage is what drove him to take his own life?"

"Jonas!" Victoria withdrew her hand. "What an awful thing to say—and it makes no sense. If he was burdened by the child's lineage, he would have refused her at birth—immediately after Winifred's death."

"Since he didn't do that, I can only assume Winifred didn't tell him. Let us remember the child was born when they had been married only eight months."

"She was premature, Jonas. She was so tiny that she nearly died. Many babies are born early—do you not remember Amanda's birth?"

Jonas shook his head. "But she wasn't our first child. If she *had* been . . ."

"You would have accused *me* of impropriety?" Anger flared in his wife's eyes.

"This conversation has nothing to do with us, Victoria. Let's get back to the topic at hand. Winifred's letter is substantiation enough for any court, and it's enough for me."

"How do you know what the court will require? And who can truly verify that Winifred wrote that letter? Even if she did write it, who can attest that Langley and your parents didn't know?"

Jonas massaged his temples. "My father would have told me."

"*Pshaw!* Your father adored Langley. If asked, he would have protected Langley's secret. His will was drawn with specificity, and I believe he wanted Fanny to have Langley's share of his inheritance. Even if all of this is true, Langley and your parents considered Fanny a member of this family."

"With all due respect, my dear, you're forgetting that Mr. Morrison is the one who stepped forward to claim Fanny as his child. We'll let the court decide."

Victoria folded her hands. "The court can decide whatever it wants, but Fanny is still a member of this family. Mr. and Mrs. Morrison should let Fanny decide where she wants to live, and no matter what any judge rules, you and Quincy should see that Fanny receives her inheritance."

Jonas gulped and choked until Victoria finally clapped him on the back. Give the inheritance to Fanny? Had Victoria taken leave of her senses? He attempted to clear his throat as tears rolled down his cheeks.

His wife offered a fleeting look of concern. "Are you all right?"

He nodded. "Yes," he croaked. "I totally disagree with your thinking. For all concerned, it's best we follow the dictates of the court. We both know that there are members of the family who would strenuously object to your plan, particularly in regard to the inheritance."

"And you are one of those family members, aren't you, Jonas? You said as much at the reading of the will, before any of this business with Mr. Morrison came to light. Do the right thing, Jonas. If you'll pray about your decision, I believe you'll change your mind."

Jonas squirmed under his wife's watchful scrutiny. She'd changed her tactics. She had departed from her earlier theory of a bogus letter and was now attempting to sway him with religious conviction. It seemed there was no end to what she would attempt in order to win her argument. However, there was too much at stake for him to relent now.

"I'll consider what you've said, but don't expect me to change my mind."

"At a minimum, I want Fanny back under our roof. I'll not see this family abandon her."

"We have not abandoned her. She is no more a Broadmoor than a stranger walking down the street. She is likely quite happy with her new family."

"Father! I cannot believe what you said." Amanda stared wide-eyed at her father as she walked into the room. "Fanny is my dear cousin and best friend. How can you cast her aside and speak of her as a stranger? Are you so heartless? Is it because you want her money?" Amanda curled her lip in disgust.

"Her money? It is not hers, Amanda. She is not a Broadmoor. This is a private conversation between your mother and me. And you'd do well to remember that you enjoy the pleasure of new gowns and jewelry—all the fine things money can buy."

"I'll give up my jewelry and fine gowns if you'll permit Fanny to return home to live with us." Amanda sat down beside her mother. "Please say you'll agree, Father."

Jonas shook his head. "It isn't my decision. Mr. Morrison has the final say in where Fanny will live. For the present, he has chosen to have her in his home." Jonas rose from his chair. "I'm not going to discuss this any further."

He'd not satisfied the wishes of his wife or daughter, of that he was certain. However, he had to escape or he'd soon be ensnared by the two of them. Handling Victoria's questions was difficult enough, but when she worked in tandem with Amanda, he knew flight was the only answer. A visit to his men's club would provide a needed respite.

With his mind set upon peace and quiet for the remainder of the evening, Jonas stepped down from his carriage and approached the front steps of the men's club—a place where he could enjoy a good cigar, read his paper, and visit with fellow businessmen about the latest fluctuations in the business world, or at least in Rochester.

He started as a man approached from the shadows. "I hoped I might find you here. I didn't want to come to your house."

"Morrison! What are you doing in Rochester?" Jonas looked about, half expecting to see Fanny somewhere nearby.

"I'm by myself. We need to talk."

"Not here," Jonas said. There had been enough rumor-mongering since Fanny's departure. He didn't want to fuel the gossip by appearing inside the club with Harold Morrison at his side. They needed to be on their way. One of the members could arrive or depart at any moment. The thought caused his palms to perspire. "We can go to my office." After giving the driver instructions, Jonas and Harold climbed into the carriage.

"I wanted to tell you . . ."

Jonas held up his hand to stave off the conversation. "Not until we are inside my office."

"Who is going to hear? The carriage driver? You don't trust your own driver?" he whispered.

"I trust very few people, and my hired help aren't counted among that small number."

Save for the creaking of the carriage and the sound of the horses' hooves clopping down the macadam street, the remainder of the carriage ride was made in silence, which allowed Jonas time to gather his thoughts. Seeing Harold Morrison had been far from his mind when he'd arrived at the club. Pieces of his conversation with Mortimer Fillmore came to mind, and he wondered if Fanny and Mr. Morrison had already been scheming. Had Morrison arrived with a plan to bilk him out of more money? The thought alone made him edgy.

"After you," Jonas said when the carriage came to a halt in front of his office building. Stepping down from the carriage, he instructed the driver to wait in front of the building. "We shouldn't be long. I'll want to return to the men's club."

Jonas led the way, unlocking doors and turning on lights until they were inside his office. Harold didn't wait for an invitation to sit. "I want to discuss Fanny's future with you."

"I do wish you would have sent word that you wanted to speak to me. I prefer my business appointments during office hours. And I prefer they be scheduled in advance."

Harold leaned back in the chair. "I consider Fanny's welfare more of a family concern than a business matter. One that shouldn't require an appointment."

"If you've come here thinking I'm going to up the ante, you're sadly mistaken, Harold."

"On the contrary. I've come here because I believe what we are doing is completely unconscionable. Fanny is a sweet young lady who deserves much better. I have come here hoping you will be of the same mind and we may come to a gentleman's agreement."

Jonas grunted. "When did *you* develop a conscience?"

"After observing the pain the two of us have caused that young girl. You with your greed and me looking for an easy way out of the mess I've created with my gambling."

"I have no problem seeing you in jail for nonpayment of your debt. I think before we jump to any rash conclusions about the handling of this matter, we need to explore all of the ramifications, as well as the possibilities." Jonas leaned across his desk. "Remember, your wife will be left to her own devices if you are in jail. Can she support herself?" Jonas didn't wait for an answer. "Go home, Harold. You'll hear from me by the end of the week."

Fortunately Harold didn't argue. The driver delivered Jonas to his men's club. After bidding Morrison good-bye, Jonas issued his driver instructions to deliver Harold to the train station. He added whispered instructions to his driver to remain at the station to see that Harold boarded the ten-o'clock train to Syracuse. The last thing Jonas desired was another surprise visit from Harold Morrison.

30

Thursday, September 16, 1897
Syracuse, New York

Fanny wiped her hands on an old towel and leaned back on her haunches. She'd spent the morning planting tulip bulbs that would add early color to Mrs. Morrison's flower garden come spring. In spite of all the changes forced upon her, Fanny was thankful for the kindness of Mr. and Mrs. Morrison and for this flower garden. Mrs. Morrison had given her free rein to garden in both the front yard and the back. Working in the dirt provided a connection between her former life in Rochester and the present, although she remained uncertain what this new life held in store for her. She patted the dirt that covered the bulbs. The cold earth would hold them snug until spring, when they would force their green sprouts through the hardened ground and eventually bloom into a low-lying canopy of yellow, red, pink, and white.

And what of herself come spring? she wondered. Would she remain dormant through the winter months and burst forth with a life of promise, or would she be one of the bulbs that didn't have the strength to survive the harsh winter? Maybe her life would resemble those occasional blooms that made the effort to push through the ground but failed to ever bloom. That's how she felt right now—as though she'd never have the energy to bloom again.

A tear trickled down her cheek and surprised her. She swiped it away with her sleeve, annoyed that she'd permitted her feelings to erupt into tears. The back door slammed, and she glanced over her shoulder.

Mrs. Morrison waved a letter overhead. "Mail for you, Fanny."

The sadness disappeared, and her heart pounded in quick time. *Michael! Please let it be from Michael,* she silently prayed while pushing up from the ground. If she knew that he was safe and that he continued to keep her in his thoughts, she could withstand the changes that swirled around her. She ran to Mrs. Morrison's side. One glance at the flourishing script on the envelope was enough to send her spirits plummeting back to the depths of despair.

Mrs. Morrison smiled as she handed her the missive. "Mr. Morrison and I received one, too."

Fanny opened the seal and removed the piece of thick stationery. An invitation. She perused the printed words and shoved it back into the envelope. A ball would be held at the home of Jonas and Victoria Broadmoor on the second of October, and she was cordially invited to attend. She nearly laughed at the paradox. For seventeen years she'd been a Broadmoor; she still carried the name. But now she received an engraved invitation, as if she were any other social acquaintance. Not even an additional word of greeting. The gesture stung.

"We'll need to send our acceptance or regrets," Mrs. Morrison said.

Fanny heard the question in her statement. "I would enjoy seeing my cousins, but I will leave the decision to you and Mr. Morrison. There is, of course, expense involved if we should attend."

Mrs. Morrison glanced at the frayed sleeve of her gown. "I have nothing appropriate to wear to a formal ball, but you could go."

Surely the Morrisons had attended formal functions in the past—before they had fallen on such difficult circumstances. Though they'd never attained the same social standing as the Broadmoors, they would have been invited to balls and parties in Syracuse. "Perhaps we could update one of your old gowns?"

A faint smile traced Mrs. Morrison's lips. "I was fortunate enough to sell all of my gowns when we were in desperate need of money. The funds helped for a short time."

Fanny thought they were still in desperate need of money, but she refrained from saying so. Since her arrival, Mrs. Morrison had been nothing but kind. Such a comment would sting. "What about the dresses you wore when you and Mr. Morrison were in the Islands earlier this summer?"

"My last two. I sold them so we would have the funds—" She stopped short. "We needed the money. Let's wait and see what my husband has to say about the invitation."

Fanny wondered if the funds had been used to furnish her bedroom or cover the expenses of the additional food she consumed each day. The thought saddened her. She returned to her gardening. She pushed the small spade into the ground and turned the dirt. If the Morrisons wanted to attend, she would find a way to pay their expenses.

Mr. Morrison mentioned the cost of train tickets during the evening meal but added he would find some method to cover the expense if the two ladies wished to be present at the ball. The thought of a reunion with Amanda and Sophie outweighed Fanny's trepidation at having to face the local gossips. Mr. Morrison hadn't mentioned the cost of a hotel room, although he surely realized they'd not be able to return to Syracuse after the ball. Though Fanny was sure she would be welcome to stay with Amanda, there was still the cost of a room for the Morrisons.

She penned a letter to Amanda setting forth her concerns. There was little doubt Uncle Jonas would be of no assistance, but perhaps Aunt Victoria would help with a solution. Fanny would post the letter and the two acceptance cards the following day. There had been no further mention of attire for the ball, but Fanny had come upon the perfect solution.

On Friday morning, after Mr. Morrison departed the house, she located his wife in the parlor working on her embroidery. "I have an idea for your gown. To wear to the ball," she quickly added.

Mrs. Morrison looked up from her sewing. "Then you are much more innovative than I, for although I gave the matter great thought last night, I've been unable to reach an appropriate solution. I shouldn't have agreed to attend."

"On the contrary, I should have thought of my solution earlier. You and I are approximately the same height, although you are considerably thinner. There is no reason we cannot alter one of my gowns to fit you. There is sufficient time, and you are adept with a needle." Fanny's enthusiasm mounted. "My rose-colored gown would be the perfect shade for you." She grasped Mrs. Morrison's hand. "Come upstairs and let's take a look at what would be best."

Mrs. Morrison didn't budge. "I wouldn't consider such an idea. Your gown would be ruined." She patted Fanny's hand. "And you have no idea if and when you will ever have sufficient funds to purchase new dresses. You must take good care of what you have in your wardrobe."

"I will not accept your refusal. I insist. Otherwise I will be forced to remain here in Syracuse, for I won't attend the ball without the two of you. I know you wouldn't want me to miss this opportunity for a visit with my cousins. I've longed to see them again." Fanny hoped her added comment would be enough to sway the woman.

For a brief time Mrs. Morrison appeared lost in her own thoughts, but finally she gave an affirmative nod. "I won't be responsible for spoiling your chance to visit Rochester. I know it is important." She tucked her sewing into the basket and held Fanny's hand. "Let's go upstairs and look at your gowns."

Fanny had been correct. The rose color was perfect against Mrs. Morrison's pale complexion. It added color to her cheeks, and though the dress hung on her, she now appeared years younger. With the gown turned inside out, Fanny pinned the sides to conform with Mrs. Morrison's form.

Mrs. Morrison removed the dress, careful not to stick herself with the pins. "If we leave the extra fabric in the seam allowance, I can remove the stitching once we return home. After the gown is pressed, no one will suspect it was ever altered."

Fanny giggled as she held the bunched up fabric in her hand. "If you leave this inside the dress, you'll look as though you have some sort of deformity. You must trim away the extra fabric. Otherwise the dress will fit improperly. I insist." Fanny waved toward her wardrobe. "As you can see, I have plenty of others, and there are more in my trunks. In fact, I didn't bring all of my clothing because I didn't know how long I would be staying here."

"If you insist, then I shall do as you've asked. You are a very kind young lady, Fanny, and I'm thankful you've come into my life." She gathered up the dress and hung it across her arm. "I only wish all of this hadn't caused you so much pain."

Fanny wished the same. Beside the fact that she'd been yanked from her home and from every person she'd ever considered family, she'd said good-bye to Michael. If she had received this news of her parentage before Michael's departure for the Yukon, there would have been no reason for him to leave. Jonas Broadmoor would have had no reason to object to the marriage of Harold Morrison's daughter to his boatswain on Broadmoor Island.

And though they'd not yet received any final determination from the court, Fanny was convinced she would be disinherited. Uncle Jonas would make certain she was stripped of both the family name and her inheritance. Likely that would please many of the greedy family members who had objected to the bequest. But she refused to dwell on the thought. If she continued to reflect upon such matters, she would become as bitter and unkind as Sophie's sister Beatrice.

Late the next week a reply arrived from Amanda. The letter contained sufficient funds to cover the cost of train travel and hotel expenses for the Morrisons, along with an invitation for Fanny to stay at the Broadmoor home for the duration of her visit. Amanda had secured the funds from her mother, and from the tenor of the letter, it seemed Aunt Victoria was eager for Fanny's visit. She doubted Uncle Jonas would be nearly as pleased. In fact, Fanny wondered if he knew they would be in attendance. Surely her aunt hadn't extended their invitations without his knowledge. Then again, when Aunt Victoria set her mind to something, she didn't worry about Uncle Jonas or the possible consequences.

Mrs. Morrison had been feverishly working on her dress, and when Fanny presented her with the funds for the train tickets and hotel accommodations, her eyes welled with tears. "I truly do not think I should be taking this money from you. I'm not certain my husband would approve. Especially for something as frivolous as attending a ball."

"I believe it will prove to be money well spent. Mr. Morrison agreed we could attend. Please tell him it is my desire to have the money spent to cover the costs. I only hope we will all have an enjoyable evening."

Fanny didn't mention her cousin had sent the money; thankfully, Mrs. Morrison didn't inquire. Mrs. Morrison probably thought the Broadmoors had given her substantial funds before her departure. The older woman tended to believe others possessed her same thoughtful nature. Fanny wished that were true.

The weekend of the ball approached more rapidly than Fanny had expected. Mrs. Morrison had completed the alterations on her gown two days ago. Once pressed, the dress looked as though it had been custom made for the older woman. Mrs. Morrison had added a layer of fine ecru lace to the sleeves and neckline, the final touches that gave the gown a fresh appearance. Fanny doubted that even her cousins would recognize it. However, they were certain to recall the one that she would wear.

The thought evoked a remembrance of Sophie's complaints throughout the past years—her cousin's anger when her father hadn't purchased her a new gown for a special party. Fanny wondered if Uncle Quincy had succumbed to Sophie's desire this time and if Fanny would be the only one wearing an old frock. She pushed aside the idea. In the future she wouldn't have need of such finery.

When Michael returned, they would use his gold to purchase their own island and build a home. One for his parents, too, if they should so desire—she hoped they would. And though she might find use for one or two gowns for annual parties held at the New Frontenac, she wouldn't be distraught if she couldn't attend. Parties held little appeal. It was Michael and the possibility of living on the islands that filled Fanny with joy.

She had sent a note to Amanda advising they would arrive on the three o'clock train. When the train pulled into the station, she hoped it would be her cousin or Aunt Victoria waiting to greet her and not Uncle Jonas. "Please not Uncle Jonas," she murmured.

Mrs. Morrison stopped in the middle of the aisle. "What, dear? I couldn't hear you over the train's noise."

"Nothing important," she said.

As she stepped off the train, Fanny surveyed the waiting crowd for some sign of her cousin or aunt. Moments later she heard Amanda's voice calling to her and caught sight of her parasol waving in the air. "Over here, Fanny!"

When Amanda finally reached her side, her hat was askew and she was out of breath.

"I am so sorry I'm late. I thought I had more than enough time, but the street was blocked with fire equipment." She gazed heavenward. "Of all days, there has to be a fire today."

"Dear me, I do hope nobody was injured." Mrs. Morrison clasped a hand to her bodice.

Amanda's cheeks tinged pink. "My remark was rather insensitive, wasn't it?"

"Yes, but we'll forgive you. Did your mother or father come along?"

"Mother sends her regrets. She wanted be here, but she's overseeing preparations at the house. You know Mother: she believes everything will fall apart if she isn't there to supervise."

Once Mr. Morrison gathered their luggage and joined them, the driver delivered Mr. and Mrs. Morrison to the hotel. Fanny bid them good-bye and said she would await their arrival at the ball. She squeezed Mrs. Morrison's hand. "I don't want the two of you to feel alone or out of place when you arrive."

"That's very kind of you, Fanny. We'll look forward to seeing you tomorrow evening. I hope you girls have a lovely visit."

Once the carriage lurched forward, Amanda leaned closer. "Has it been absolutely terrible for you, Fanny?"

"They are very nice people, but I could never think of Mr. Morrison as my father. I am fond of his wife, though."

Throughout the remainder of their carriage ride, Amanda pressed for additional details. Fanny answered her questions honestly, but she didn't elaborate. Somehow she felt a need to protect the privacy of the Morrisons. They'd suffered enough embarrassment. There was no need for every detail of their lives to be scrutinized and dissected by Rochester's social set.

"Do tell me more about what you've been doing. You mentioned several young men in your latest letter to me. It seems your father has redirected his matchmaking efforts. I can honestly say that I don't miss that aspect of my life." Fanny giggled. "I hope he hasn't decided upon any of those young men who were at the island this summer. They were a miserable lot. Not one of them would make you happy."

"No. He's found several others, but I've told him that I've made up my mind to remain single for the time being. He doesn't believe me, but he'll soon learn that I'm serious about a career." She tipped her head close. "I've decided I want to begin college and then attend medical school."

Fanny didn't say so, but she knew Uncle Jonas would never agree to Amanda's plan. And if Uncle Jonas didn't agree, he would simply refuse to pay. *Money.* As far as Uncle Jonas was concerned, money was the answer to everything.

31

Saturday, October 2, 1897

The guests had come dressed in their finery, the women wearing the latest fashions they'd purchased in Europe or creations their dressmakers in New York City or Rochester had stitched to exacting measurements. The array of colors and fabrics decorated the rooms like a bouquet of spring flowers. The women in those gowns, however, weren't nearly as sweet as the scent of fragrant blooms. Fanny couldn't help but hear the murmurs of women hiding their lips behind opened fans while they ridiculed or envied the guests clustered in yet another group. Some things never changed. She didn't miss the petty gossip fueled by insecurity and jealousy. At every social gathering the women took inventory of one another, each one always fearful she'd be found lacking.

Fanny kept a vigilant watch on the front door, and the moment she saw Mr. and Mrs. Morrison approach, she hurried across the foyer. They were every bit as elegant as any of the other guests. Indeed, Fanny thought Mrs. Morrison outshone most of the women in attendance. A deep flush colored her cheeks, probably from nerves, but it added to the older woman's natural beauty. Although Mr. Morrison's cutaway wasn't new, it was stylish. Together they made a striking couple.

"I'm so glad you're here. I was becoming concerned."

Mrs. Morrison handed her wrap to the servant. When her husband stepped away to hand his hat to the butler, she whispered, "Mr. Morrison isn't feeling well. I wanted to remain at the hotel, but he insisted we couldn't disappoint you."

He did appear pale. This party was taking more of a toll on the couple than Fanny had anticipated. They should have remained in Syracuse. Other than permitting Uncle Jonas an opportunity to publicly display that she was no longer a member of the Broadmoor family, this final social appearance served no purpose. She hadn't given the matter sufficient thought before sending their acceptance.

Fanny touched Mr. Morrison's arm. "I'm so sorry you're feeling unwell. There's no reason to remain. I can have a carriage take you back to the hotel, and we can depart first thing in the morning."

"I'll not hear of it. We've come to attend a ball, and that's what we're going to do. My wife looks beautiful, as do you, Fanny. We are going to hold our heads up and act like we belong, even if we don't."

The butler edged around them, and with Fanny clasping Mr. Morrison's right arm and Mrs. Morrison clutching his left, they were announced to the staring throng of guests. "Mr. and Mrs. Harold Morrison and Miss Frances . . ." The butler stopped. He'd known Fanny since she was a tiny girl and appeared confused. He cleared his throat. "And Miss Frances Broadmoor."

Murmurs filled the vast flower-scented room. The butler hurried away, obviously uncertain if he'd properly announced the threesome. If Uncle Jonas had wanted Fanny introduced as a Morrison, he should have told the servant. And though her uncle seemed anxious to erase her name from the family tree, the court had not yet rendered a decision.

Since her arrival the day before, Jonas had done his best to avoid her. He'd excused himself immediately after the evening meal, citing work that needed his attention before morning. Not that Fanny had expected him to welcome her back into the fold, but she had hoped to hear the latest news regarding the court proceedings. When she had asked at supper, her uncle told her that in polite society such topics were not discussed at the dinner table. His gibe that she'd forgotten proper etiquette in such a short time had nearly caused her to come undone. She'd wanted to lash out and tell him that although the Morrisons might not have money, they had far more refinement than he'd shown since her return. But she'd remained silent. She was, after all, a guest in his home.

The three of them entered the room and clustered in a far corner. Fanny was determined to remain close at hand and keep any of the nosy dowagers at bay. She doubted whether Mrs. Morrison could hold her own against them—especially if they approached in twos or threes.

"Would you like something to drink, Mr. Morrison? A glass of punch or water? Do you think that might help?"

"I think the only thing that would help get me through this would be a stiff shot of whiskey and a determination to match." He offered a faint smile. "I already have the determination, but

I don't think it would be wise to request the whiskey." His lack of color was disconcerting.

Mrs. Morrison remained close by his side. "He's having chest pains again. With rest, they usually subside within a few hours."

Fanny looked up in time to see her aunt swooping across the room, her gown flowing behind her in a sea of green silk. She descended upon them, her bejeweled neckline shimmering in the pale light cast by the crystal chandelier. "Mr. and Mrs. Morrison, I am so pleased you could join us this evening. I have truly enjoyed having Fanny back with us. I hope you'll permit her to remain a few extra days to visit with all of the family."

The stiffness in Mrs. Morrison's shoulders relaxed. "Whatever Fanny desires will be agreeable with us."

Her aunt took a step closer to Fanny, but her focus remained fixed upon Mrs. Morrison. "Your gown is quite lovely." Victoria turned toward Fanny. "I seem to remember you owned a gown of that same shade." She stared a moment longer. "Or perhaps it was a shade or two lighter. Do you recall the one I'm thinking of?"

Fanny nodded. "I remember. Rather plain. Unlike Mrs. Morrison's dress, mine lacked embellishment."

"You're absolutely correct. I never did think the dressmaker did that gown justice. In any case, I do hope you're all ready to partake of a fine meal." She tipped her head as though confiding a deep secret. "We have an utterly marvelous group of musicians for the dancing that will follow."

Mrs. Morrison responded politely. At the mention of food, Mr. Morrison's pale complexion turned slightly gray, and Fanny wondered if he'd be able to remain for the entire evening. Fortunately they were soon ushered into the dining room, where they were seated side by side. Fanny was pleasantly surprised to see Amanda and Sophie draw near.

Sophie winked as she led Amanda to the chairs directly opposite Fanny and Mrs. Morrison. She picked up the name card and smiled. "You see? I told you we were seated near Fanny."

Fanny giggled. "Up to your old tricks, Sophie?"

"Of course. Until people cease their attempts to seat me next to some of their stodgy old guests, I'll move my place card and sit where I please."

Amanda nudged her cousin. "That is completely improper behavior, Sophie."

"In that case I suppose I could return yours from where it came. You'll be seated beside your father's old banker, Mr. Snodgrass." Sophie grinned across the table. "Fanny can tell you how much fun you'll have."

Fanny's curls bobbed. "And he'll expect to remain your escort and dance partner for the remainder of the evening. You do remember my embarrassment, I assume?"

Amanda turned contrite at the mention of Mr. Snodgrass. "I suppose it doesn't matter. There are enough guests that Mother won't remember where we're supposed to be seated."

"You're truly the fortunate one, Fanny," Sophie said. "Even though you have no money, you're no longer under Uncle Jonas's thumb."

Mrs. Morrison unfolded her napkin and placed it across her lap. "I believe Fanny misses all of you very much. She's such a well-mannered young lady that I doubt she ever had difficulty following her uncle's rules."

Fanny shot an annoyed look at Sophie. Once in a while Sophie needed to think before she said whatever popped into her mind. At least she seemed to realize she had caused Mr. and Mrs. Morrison discomfort with her offhand remark and said little throughout the meal. As their apricot pudding was served, Fanny inquired how Paul Medford was adjusting to his career at the Home for the Friendless.

"I don't know how he has sufficient time to perform his duties. He's too busy attempting to intervene in my life." Sophie dipped her spoon into her creamy dessert. "He says Father is preoccupied and doesn't realize I need supervision. What do you think of that, Mrs. Morrison?"

Mrs. Morrison sipped her coffee. "Perhaps your father has granted this young man permission to act as a surrogate parent during his absences."

"Ha!" Sophie pointed her spoon in Paul's direction. "Do you see that young man sitting beside Amanda's mother?"

"Yes."

"That's Paul Medford. He's not that much older than me, so I don't think he's capable of acting as a parent, surrogate or otherwise."

Mrs. Morrison leaned to see around her husband. "Rather a nice-looking young man. Have you considered that he may be romantically interested and that's why he's attempting to look after your best interests?"

Sophie jerked to attention. "*Paul*? Interested in *me*? I think *not*! We're as different as day and night. Never in a thousand years would I be interested in someone like Paul."

"Opposites can sometimes be a good thing. You each bring different strengths to the marriage," Mrs. Morrison said.

"That might be true for some people, but Paul and I can't move beyond our disagreements." Sophie looked down toward the other end of the table. "And I don't see why everyone says he is nice appearing. I find him rather plain."

Mr. Morrison laughed. "If he were the most handsome man in the room, I believe you'd find him unappealing, for he represents authority. And I would surmise that is something you dislike."

"You're correct. I detest authority. However, I control my life—not Paul Medford. I merely want him to take heed of that fact."

The sound of the musicians tuning their instruments signaled the end of the meal, and soon the guests were all gathered in the ballroom adjacent to the dining room on the third floor. No one seemed to think of the hardship these parties placed on the staff. Truth be told, it wasn't until Fanny saw the work Mrs. Atwell performed at Broadmoor Island that she'd realized the life of a servant was far removed from those they served. When she and Michael were married, they would be more cognizant of such inequities.

Sophie pulled on Fanny's hand. "Come along. Let's see if there are some eligible men looking for dance partners."

Fanny withdrew her hand. "I promised my first dance to Mr. Morrison. I'll join you later."

Sophie nodded. "I'm spending the night here at the house with you and Amanda, so we shall have plenty of time to discuss the men tonight."

Fanny watched Sophie weave through the crowd with grace and agility. No doubt she was making her way toward a cluster of young men at the south end of the hall. Fanny stifled a giggle when she saw Paul following after her. He'd likely attempt to curtail her fun.

The musicians struck their first chords, and Fanny insisted Mr. and Mrs. Morrison dance the first dance of the evening together. "I promise to wait and dance the next waltz with you, Mr. Morrison." She watched as they took to the floor. They made a lovely couple, and there was little doubt of their devotion to each other. Still, Fanny saw no resemblance between herself and the man who was circling the floor with his gentle wife. Sad that they'd never had any children of their own. She thought they would have been excellent parents. Given the opportunity, she thought Michael would be a wonderful father. She hoped one day she could give him a child.

"Daydreaming?"

Fanny turned at the sound of her uncle's voice. "Thinking how sad it is that I didn't discover my lineage before Michael departed for the Yukon. We could have been married and . . ." She hesitated.

"And *what*, Fanny? Live on Broadmoor Island as a servant? Your lineage aside, if Michael is the man you choose to marry, I've done you a service. If he returns a wealthy man, you'll have a life of ease and prosperity rather than a life of menial work. Either way, you should thank me."

Fanny clenched her jaw. "You equate happiness with money, yet you don't appear particularly happy or content. If you'll excuse me, I've promised this dance." She turned and walked toward Mr. Morrison.

He proved to be an excellent dancer as he led her around the floor. "You don't need to remain much longer. You've made an appearance. Uncle Jonas can assert he's a generous and proper gentleman who has deigned to entertain us in his home."

Mr. Morrison took a backward step and pivoted to the left. "You deserve so much more than I can ever give you, Fanny. I can no longer pretend—"

He gasped and clutched at his chest. His color turned sallow, and he stared at her with surprise in his eyes. Slowly he dropped to the dance floor, still clinging to her by one hand. Fanny quickly kneeled down beside him, her gown spread around them like a protective shield. The couples ceased their dancing and gathered around as the strains of music faded in uneven increments. Mrs. Morrison hurriedly broke through the crowd and called for a doctor.

"It's too late, my dear," he said. Ignoring his whispered protests, Mrs. Morrison pillowed his head on her lap.

"Fanny." Mr. Morrison grasped Fanny's hand, and she scooted closer. "I'm sorry for the pain I've caused. I have deceived you. That letter wasn't genuine, and I am not your father. I never met your mother. I'm sure . . ." He gasped for a breath of air.

"Someone get a doctor!" Mrs. Morrison called out.

Murmurs filled the room, and Jonas stepped closer. "This is preposterous. He must be delirious."

A number of the guests collectively shushed Jonas while others glared in his direction. Mr. Snodgrass thumped his cane. "When a man's dying, he speaks the truth, Jonas!"

Mr. Morrison's eyes rolled back in his head for a moment; then he regained strength. "I'm certain your mother was a fine woman. Your parents are Winifred and Langley Broadmoor. I wasn't even in the United States during that time. That fact can be verified." He glanced up at his wife. "In my lockbox there's information to prove what I say."

Fanny stroked his face. "Mr. Morrison, please."

His eyelids fluttered. "You are a lovely girl . . . I wish you could have been my daughter. I didn't do this to hurt you. Please believe my sorrow when I tell you it was simply about the money. I couldn't . . ." His voice faded and Fanny bent low, but his final mutterings remained unintelligible.

With one final breath, he was gone. Mrs. Morrison was softly whispering, but Fanny didn't know if she was praying or attempting to talk to her husband. She glanced upward and saw Paul Medford approach.

He bent down. "Let me help you to your feet."

Fanny grasped his hand and attempted to rise to her feet, but the room swirled around her like a whirlpool sucking her into a dark abyss. Somewhere in the distance she heard her uncle Jonas's voice. She detected urgency in his question, but her lips wouldn't move. She was unable to tell him she hadn't heard Mr. Morrison's final utterance.

32

A cool breeze whispered through the bedroom window, and Fanny heard the murmur of voices. Using what strength she could muster, she opened her eyes.

"You're awake! Finally." Sophie lifted the cool towel from her head. "Aunt Victoria wanted to using smelling salts, but I objected." She grinned. "You can thank me later. I know how you detest the burning sensation."

"Where is . . ."

Amanda moved to the edge of her bed. "There's no one here but Sophie and me. We told Mother we were quite capable of looking after you. With all the commotion, it didn't take long to convince her. She wanted to be certain her party wasn't completely ruined."

"Can't you imagine what the society page is going to say come Monday morning? I can hardly wait to read it: *Man drops dead after dining at the home of Jonas and Victoria Broadmoor.* It's just too delightful." Sophie clasped a hand to her mouth. "Oh, I don't mean it's delightful that Mr. Morrison died, of course. That was horrid. But what kind of man was he, to pretend he was your father?"

Amanda grasped Fanny's hand. "*Enough*, Sophie! Fanny's had a severe trauma this evening, and you're jabbering like a magpie."

Fanny's eyelids fluttered. "Mrs. Morrison? Is she here?"

"Oh no. She left when they took the body—I mean her husband to the . . . well, you know . . . the mortuary. At least I assume that's where they took him. I did hear her say he's to be buried in Syracuse." Sophie hesitated for a moment. "Maybe he's already on the train . . . well, not riding as a passenger, of course, but in the baggage car or something."

"Do stop, Sophie. You're making matters worse by the minute," Amanda scolded.

"How can it be any worse? The man is dead. And deservedly so, I might add. He took advantage of our dear Fanny. I can't imagine what would come over someone to do such a thing." Sophie cupped her chin in one hand. "Do you suppose his wife forged that letter for him? And I thought she was such a nice lady." She wagged a finger back and forth. "So did you, Fanny, and I thought you were an excellent judge of character."

Using her elbows for leverage, Fanny scooted up and propped herself against the pillows. "Mrs. Morrison *is* a wonderful lady, and I think she believed the story, too. Didn't you hear Mr. Morrison tell her there was proof? If she was a part of the hoax, he wouldn't have explained it to her. Like me, I believe she was completely surprised by his confession, and I do want to see her again."

Ever the voice of reason, Amanda recommended Fanny rest now and make her decision regarding Mrs. Morrison in the morning.

"I'm not ill, Amanda. I merely fainted. Come morning, Mrs. Morrison may be gone. I'm certain she'll attempt to leave on the earliest possible train." Fanny glanced at the clock. "You don't think she had time to catch the final train tonight, do you?"

Sophie shook her head. "No. By the time she returned to the hotel for her belongings, the train would have already departed. She'll be required to remain in Rochester tonight."

"Then I shall go and see her this very moment." Before Amanda could protest, Fanny sat up and slid her feet into her shoes. "Please don't be angry, Amanda. If you're overly concerned, one of you can go with me while the other stays here to keep watch. We don't want anyone to discover I've left the house."

"I want to go with you," Sophie squealed.

"Do keep your voice down or someone will hear." Amanda frowned. "I don't like this plan in the least, but if you're determined, I'll remain and keep watch. You can go down the back stairway and through the kitchen. The servants won't question you. I'll do my best to keep your secret, but if Mother comes upstairs to check on you while you're gone . . ." With a beseeching look, she turned her palms upward.

"If your mother comes looking, I don't expect you to lie," Fanny said.

"Tell her I forced Fanny outside for fresh air. That won't be a lie. Just watch as I push her out of here." The three of them giggled while Sophie propelled Fanny out the door and down the hallway.

Once they exited the house, Sophie took charge. Fanny had to admit that her cousin's experience with such escapades was now proving invaluable. Rather than asking one of the Broadmoor drivers to bring a carriage around, they strolled down the driveway, where Sophie hailed a passing cab. "Much less chance of word traveling back to Uncle Jonas as to where we've been," she said.

As long as she had an opportunity to speak with Mrs. Morrison before her departure, Fanny cared little what her uncle might think. However, she appreciated her cousin's concern. They rode in silence until the driver brought the carriage to a stop in front of the hotel.

"Do you want me to wait in the foyer or go up with you?" Sophie asked after instructing the driver to wait for them.

"Sitting in the hotel foyer without benefit of an escort is highly improper," Fanny replied.

Sophie giggled. "You're beginning to sound like Amanda. Let's ask for her room number."

The clerk appeared doubtful he should give them the desired information. Sophie furrowed her brow and leaned forward until they were nearly nose to nose. "If you have ever heard the name *Broadmoor*, my good sir, I suggest you tell me the room number posthaste."

Strangely, the man didn't ask if they were related to the Broadmoors or if they could produce any form of identification before directing them to room 342. Sophie's knack for achieving success astounded Fanny.

"I believe the Broadmoor name frightened him out of his wits. I wonder if he's had a confrontation with Uncle Jonas in the past," Sophie said with a grin.

With her fingers trembling, Fanny formed her hand into a tight fist, knocked on the door, and waited. "Maybe she's asleep."

Sophie shook her head. "I doubt she'll sleep a wink after all that's happened tonight. Knock again."

She lifted her hand again but stopped midair when she heard footsteps. The door opened, and Mrs. Morrison stood in the doorway, pale as a ghost. Fanny opened her mouth to speak, but the words stuck in her throat like a wad of cotton.

Mrs. Morrison grasped her by the hand. "Do come in. I'm very pleased to see you, Fanny."

The night's events appeared to have shriveled Mrs. Morrison's already thin body. She peered at them with eyes that had shrunken into their sockets, and her head bobbled as though she hadn't the strength to hold it upright. Fanny held on to the woman for fear she might collapse before reaching the chairs across the room. Thankfully Sophie remained at a distance and allowed them a modicum of privacy.

"You didn't know, either, did you?" she asked the older woman once they were seated.

"No. I should have questioned him more, but my husband had changed in the final years of our marriage. He remained kind to me, but I knew the financial losses had been extremely painful to bear. He hid many things from me. Men place their value on being able to provide," she said with a faint smile. "I am very sorry for what you've endured. I have spent the last hour attempting to make sense of why my husband would do such a thing, but I have no answer for you.

"If your relatives desire the proof he spoke of, I will make it available to them. I know my husband was genuinely fond of you, Fanny, as am I. Any woman would be proud to claim you as her daughter." A tear rolled down her cheek and dropped onto the gown. She stared at the dark splotch. "I'll send the dress back to you."

"I've no need for the dress, but I would like you to write to me in the future. I will always consider you a dear friend."

The guests had finally departed, and now only the family remained. But the evening had been insufferable. Jonas had expected their guests to immediately leave after Harold's death, but he should have known better. With their curiosity piqued, they had stayed, eager to discuss every detail of the night's ghastly event. Jonas slammed the door to his library and fell into his leather chair. All of his plotting had been for naught. He slammed his fist on his desk and cursed Harold Morrison.

Although most in attendance at tonight's ball had heard of Harold Morrison's initial claim of paternity, Jonas had planned to make an announcement during the evening—unbeknownst to his wife, of course. Victoria would never have approved of such a thing, especially during a party. However, Jonas had viewed the ball as the perfect setting. All of the elite would be in attendance for the formal announcement that Fanny was not a Broadmoor. The men would immediately realize what a financial boon this would be for Jonas, and his status would rise among his peers. Now all of that had been ruined by Harold Morrison's untimely death, and Jonas was once again faced with the dilemma of Fanny's inheritance.

"Here you are!" Quincy strode into the room.

"Have you heard of knocking before entering a room?" Jonas barked.

"My, but you're in a foul mood. I realize the evening was marred by Morrison's death, but I didn't expect to find you in such bad humor." Quincy sat down opposite his brother. "That scoundrel Morrison certainly had you fooled. I daresay I'm surprised, Jonas. You're usually the first one to question the credentials of every one of your business associates, yet this man and his spurious claim slipped by you with surprising ease. How so?"

"What do you mean, how so? If you've something on your mind, speak up, Quincy. I'll not play silly games with you. It's been a long evening."

Quincy rested his forearms on his thighs and stared across the desk at his brother. "We all trusted that you'd checked into this man and his claims. None of us inquired—at least I didn't. For that I blame myself. It never occurred to me that you would be careless."

Jonas jumped to his feet and rested his palms atop the desk. "Careless? Are you implying that I intentionally accepted this man's claims without proper investigation?"

"That's exactly what I'm saying. If you'd properly checked in to the matter, we would have known his claim was false and Fanny would have been saved from this horrid experience." Quincy waved his brother toward his chair. "Sit down, Jonas. I don't believe you meant harm to the girl. I know you're a busy man with many obligations to handle. I blame myself as much as you. In the future, however, we're going to both need to keep a close watch on the girl's affairs and on those who seek to befriend her."

Jonas exhaled a long breath. He needed to remain calm. "I appreciate your concern, Quincy. You're correct. In the future I'll be keeping a close watch. But there's no reason for you to concern yourself with Fanny. I am her legal guardian, and I know you have a myriad of duties requiring your attention at the poorhouse."

"Home for the Friendless, Jonas. It's not the poorhouse."

Jonas snorted. "Same thing, different name. Except your Home for the Friendless has the advantage of Broadmoor money paying the expenses."

"*My* portion of the Broadmoor money. I ask nothing of you, Jonas, and we are digressing from the topic at hand. I believe we must remain vigilant where Fanny is concerned."

"You may rest assured that I will see to doing exactly what is best," Jonas said as he ushered his brother to the door.

Jonas returned to the solitude of his library. He couldn't permit defeat to take hold of him. There must be resolution to this latest dilemma. How could one young girl pose such a problem in his life? He sat in the chair and rested his forehead in his palm, massaging his temples with his fingers and thumb.

Somehow, returning to his earlier plan seemed a form of defeat. But if he was going to succeed in controlling Fanny's inheritance, he must do so. Like it or not he would resume his original plan to find a husband for the girl—a man who could be easily manipulated. In the meantime he must remain vigilant. The girl had likely become even more independent during her stay with the Morrisons.

33

Monday, October 4, 1897

Jonas had planned to depart for work much earlier in the day. His headache of Saturday night had plagued him throughout the day on Sunday. When the persistent pain continued on Monday morning, he downed his headache powders with a glass of water and returned to bed. Though not completely gone, the pain had subsided, and he'd tired of Victoria popping in and out of the room to check on him every fifteen minutes.

After descending the broad staircase, he picked up the mail that had been stacked on the hallway table and then called for his carriage to be brought around. Jonas riffled through the unusually thick stack but stopped when his fingers came to rest on a letter addressed to Fanny. He tossed the remaining mail onto the table and hurried into his library. His head pounded with a blinding ferocity as he shoved the door closed behind him.

He hurried to his chair and slit open the envelope. He shuffled through the pages until he reached the end, where Michael had neatly written his address. He was in a place called Dyea, Alaska. He returned to the first page of the letter and shook his head as he continued to read the details of Michael's journey in search of gold. Between the paragraphs that spoke of his undying love for Fanny was an optimism that frightened Jonas. There was, of course, no way to know if the young man's accounts were puffery or fact. If what he wrote was true, Michael was doing well and held high expectations for his gold mining. He spoke of teaming up with a man who already had a successful claim near Dawson City. The man assured Michael he could make thousands of dollars by the end of next summer.

"Next summer!" How could it be possible? That young man just seemed to be lucky no matter where he went. The thought only furthered Jonas's frustration. Given Michael Atwell's seeming good fortune, he'd probably find some incredible supply of ore and make hundreds of thousands of dollars.

"I need to remain calm. After all, I must see Fanny married to a man of my choosing before March, when she turns eighteen. After that it will be too late. The property laws in this state will negate any control I might desire to exert," he muttered.

He looked at the letter again. Obviously he couldn't allow Fanny to see it. The last few lines of the letter gave him an idea.

I will soon be bound for Dawson and doubt I will have an opportunity to write again until spring. The mail is difficult to deliver during the winter and questionable at best. So please do not despair if you hear nothing from me until summer.

He smiled. Summer would be too late. Fanny would hear nothing from Michael and believe he had stopped caring about her.

Jonas quickly tucked the letter into his desk drawer and stood. His head throbbed with intensity, but he couldn't yield to the pain. This letter from Michael strengthened his resolve to move quickly. He simply had to force Fanny into a marriage before the young man's return.

He shouldn't have come to the office. He'd accomplished nothing, and the throbbing in his head had grown worse by the minute. Like a possessed man, he paced back and forth in an attempt to find some solution—anything that would gain him access to Fanny's inheritance. Well, not truly Fanny's, he told himself. The money rightfully belonged to him. And to Quincy, he begrudgingly admitted. Of course his brother would squander the additional funds on that homeless charity. It would be truly grand if he could come up with an idea to exclude both Fanny and Quincy, but that seemed impossible.

His clerk tapped on the door and entered the office. "I know you said you didn't want to be disturbed, but Mr. Fillmore is here to see you."

"Vincent or Mortimer?" he growled.

"Mortimer. He said it was important."

Jonas waved for the clerk to send Mortimer into his office. Word had traveled quickly. Neither Vincent nor Mortimer had been at the ball on Saturday night, having sent regrets due to a previous engagement, but there was little doubt Mortimer had heard of Harold Morrison's death.

"Jonas! I got back into the city late last night, and this morning I heard—"

"I'm sure you did. There is such pleasure in being the first to pass along a bit of sensational gossip."

Mortimer sat down and massaged his swollen knuckles. "You have anything to do with his death, Jonas?"

"Of course not. Morrison was my means to the girl's inheritance."

Mortimer grunted. "We'll need to withdraw our motion requesting Fanny be excluded as a beneficiary under your father's will. This puts you back where you started, I suppose. What are your plans?"

"I haven't come up with a solution, but I know I must maintain control of Fanny."

"Or at least her money," Mortimer cackled.

"Instead of your gibes, I need a solution."

"What about those young fellows you had courting her this summer? Any way you could fan the flames of love with an added bonus to one of them?"

Jonas shook his head. "Daniel Irwin stopped by last week. He's in dire need of financial assistance. I told him I didn't have anything available. In addition, forcing Fanny to accept his company would likely prove impossible. I'm at a loss."

Mortimer thumped his cane. "Don't be foolish! This is easily enough solved. Find some way where she is required to be in Irwin's company. And tell that young man he had best prove his ability to pour on the charm, for Fanny will not be easily won. I feel certain you'll be able to convince him with promises of the fortune that awaits him once they are wed." The lawyer withdrew his pocket watch and pushed himself upright. "I must take my leave, Jonas. I promised my wife a month in Europe, and I'm off to make arrangements." He pointed his cane at

Jonas. "It's more of a gift to me. A month without listening to her ongoing complaints."

"That's it, Mortimer! Europe! I'll send Fanny, Amanda, and Sophie on a grand tour. Victoria can act as their chaperone. Father had planned on Fanny taking a tour, so the idea won't cause undue suspicion. A stroke of genius. Thank you, my friend."

"Ride along with me and tell me how this is going to solve your problem. I see some deficiencies in the plan."

Jonas grabbed his hat and accompanied the older man outside. He helped Mortimer into the carriage and sat down opposite him. "You're likely wondering how I'm going to marry off Fanny if she's in Europe. Am I right?"

"Exactly."

"I'm going to send Daniel Irwin along. Four women traveling without benefit of a male escort wouldn't be a wise idea. My wife would have far too much difficulty maintaining control over three young women without occasional assistance." His headache had disappeared. He called to the driver to stop the carriage. "I'm going to go and meet with Daniel this very minute. If he agrees to my plan, I'll have this matter settled by day's end."

Uncle Jonas seemed utterly giddy when he returned home later that day. Fanny watched as he joined them in the music room, an uncustomary smile beaming on his face.

"Quincy, I didn't realize you would be here, but I'm glad," he started. "I have a great notion to share."

"I'm sure we can hardly wait," Sophie muttered under her breath. She stepped away from the piano, where Amanda had been entertaining them with a few selections before supper.

"What are you about now, Jonas?" Victoria questioned. "Haven't we had enough surprises for one year? I suppose you'd better sit down and explain, but first let Amanda finish the last movement."

Uncle Jonas remained standing. Fanny knew he didn't have the patience to wait until Amanda completed her piece.

"Never mind the last movement. I have some exciting news. A gift for all of you." He glanced at his daughter. "If you don't mind the interruption."

Amanda turned away from the keyboard and shook her head. "We would be delighted to hear your news, Father."

"I've made arrangements for you three girls and your mother to take a grand tour of Europe. Together—all four of you. You'll depart two weeks from today."

Fanny was stunned. Amanda and Sophie immediately began to object to the idea, while Victoria appeared baffled. Only Uncle Quincy seemed in tune with the proposal.

"Jonas, that must have cost a pretty penny," Quincy declared.

"The cost is irrelevant. It's a gift," he replied. "After all, this family has suffered a great deal because of Mr. Morrison's attempt to steal Fanny's wealth."

Fanny frowned, but it was her aunt who spoke. "Jonas, I cannot possibly just up and leave Rochester. You should have consulted me."

"Truly, Father." Amanda got up from the piano. "I just did a grand tour in the spring. I've no desire to go on another."

"Neither do I," Sophie threw in.

Fanny nodded and folded her hands. "I cannot go, nor will I."

"Ladies, ladies!" Quincy interjected. "You're most ungrateful. Jonas has gone to the trouble and expense of planning a lovely tour for you, and all of you act as though you're being sentenced to a terrible punishment. Where is your spirit of thankfulness?"

The three girls glared at him. Sophie pointed a finger at her father. "I will not go on a grand tour. I have no desire to leave Rochester, nor do Fanny and Amanda."

Aunt Victoria waved for quiet. "Even if I could be readied in time, I'm uncertain I can properly chaperone three young ladies at one time, Jonas. They are all young and beautiful. Their ability to sightsee and attend parties would be limited by my inability to oversee so many activities. I tire of such things after a short time. Besides, Amanda and I have already made her tour. It would be unfair to all concerned."

"I have already thought of that aspect, my dear. Concerns for your safety as well as that of the girls is always foremost in my mind. I wouldn't want you to make the journey without a male escort."

Aunt Victoria relaxed her shoulders. "Oh! If you're planning to join us, then I think this is a splendid idea."

Uncle Jonas smiled. "Then it's settled. I know you don't have the usual amount of time to prepare for the journey, but I'll provide a large allowance so that you may purchase dresses and fabric during the trip."

"I cannot go," Fanny said, standing suddenly. "I will not leave. Michael might return and I want to be here when he does."

Uncle Jonas seemed to consider her words for a moment. "Wait here. I nearly forgot." He dashed from the room and returned only moments later waving a letter in the air. "This arrived earlier for you."

"A letter? From Michael?" Fanny rushed to her uncle and took the note. "Why did you open this? Why didn't you tell me?" She wanted to cry for joy. He had written. He had finally written.

"I accidentally opened it. I thought perhaps it was the correspondence of someone else. I am sorry for not paying closer attention. But as you can see in the letter, Michael has no intention of returning before next summer. You have more than ample time to go on the grand tour. Why, he can't even hope to get you additional letters, as the post is so irregular from that part of the world."

Fanny scanned the letter. It was all true. Michael had written it just as Uncle Jonas said. She supposed there really was no reason not to cooperate. But something in her still rebelled. She didn't want to go abroad. She would much rather return to Broadmoor Island.

"I believe you're going to have an excellent time on board the ship, as well as visiting Paris, Brussels, and Rome," Uncle Jonas began again. "This is the opportunity of a lifetime, and Amanda, we will see to it that you enjoy some new sights along the way."

Amanda folded her arms around her waist. "It seems the adults in our lives never tire of arranging our lives. We are weary of being forced always to yield to what others decide is best for us." She jutted her chin forward. "I know I haven't mentioned this before, but I've applied to begin my college courses and plan to attend medical school. I have no desire to return to Europe."

"Sophie and I don't want to go, either," Fanny said. "I was looking forward to a peaceful time here in Rochester. However, if you must send me somewhere, send me back to Broadmoor Island."

"The plans are made. I will not change them. You are going, and that's all there is to it."

"That's what *you* think," the three of them replied in unison.

Fanny cradled the letter to her chest and left the gathering to let them argue about the trip. She felt a renewed hope in just touching the letter that Michael had penned. Next summer seemed years away, but in truth, she knew it wasn't that long to wait.

"I'll be eighteen by then," she murmured, glancing at the letter once again. She smiled and knew that before Michael returned, she would read this one letter over and over again.

If there was one thing that the events of the summer and the last few weeks had proved to her, it was that nothing mattered as much as the love she held for Michael. She didn't care if they had to live in a tent and grow their own food. She didn't care if society scorned her and rejected her completely. The trials she'd already endured proved to her that she could survive anything—that she was strong.

"Well, I am a Broadmoor, after all," she said with a smile.

Acknowledgments

Special thanks to:

DUDLEY AND KATHY DANIELSON
Clayton, New York

JOHN SUMMERS
Chief Curator, *The Antique Boat Museum*
Clayton, New York